Great Stories Remembered II

FOCUS ON THE FAMILY
presents

Great Stories Remembered II

compiled and edited by Joe L. Wheeler

Tyndale House Publishers, Wheaton, Illinois

GREAT STORIES REMEMBERED II

Library of Congress Cataloging-in-Publication Data
Focus on the Family presents great stories remembered II / compiled and edited by Joe L. Wheeler.
       p.   cm.
   ISBN 1-56179-634-4
   1. Family—United States—Fiction. 2. Domestic fiction, American. I. Wheeler, Joe L., 1936– .
PS648.F27F64   1998
813'.0108355—dc21

      98-27651
      CIP

A Focus on the Family book published by Tyndale House Publishers, Wheaton, Illinois.

Woodcut illustrations from the library of Joe L. Wheeler.

The author is represented by the literary agency of Alive Communications, 1465 Kelly Johnson Blvd., Suite 320, Colorado Springs, CO 80920.

Editor: Michele A. Kendall
Cover Illustration: Clint Hansen
Cover Design: Bradley Lind

Printed in the United States of America

98 99 00 01 02 03 04/10 9 8 7 6 5 4 3 2 1

Table of Contents

Introduction

The Power of Stories
Joseph Leininger Wheeler

Our Creator programmed us to love stories. Anything with a plot to it, we assimilate and make our own. Throughout history, the greatest communicators invariably used stories to get their points across. Storytellers in every culture are held up as heroes. Why do we still read Homer thousands of years later? Because he told stories. Why do some of us prefer to read about David rather than his son Solomon, the wisest man who ever lived? Most likely because David's life is one long sequence of fascinating stories, and Solomon's is not. In our own history, why do so many Americans feel closer to Lincoln than to Washington? Probably because, although both men served as President of the United States, Lincoln, with his storytelling and homespun humor, seems more approachable, like a dear uncle. The greatest storyteller of all, of course, was Jesus. His main vehicle for communicating truth was parables. Clearly, He knew that we learn almost nothing from abstractions and almost everything from stories.

"Daddy, Tell Me a Story"

As I look back through the years during which our children were growing up, the five-word request that came more often than any other was "Daddy, tell me a story." I'd guess the same is true with other families as well.

It seems so simple: A child makes such a request to Father or Mother, and a story is read or told. But the truth is far more complex—and sad. Many of today's parents will give their children almost anything they ask for . . . except time, except themselves. Today the average father communicates with each of his children 44 seconds a day, yet in the average American household, the television set is on for more than seven hours a day (Wheeler, *Remote Controlled* [Hagerstown, Md.: Review and Herald Publishing, Inc., 1993]). The imbalance is staggering. When we realize how pathetically few are the days and nights during which we parents can make a difference in our children's lives, it is truly sobering.

By turning off the TV and making ourselves available to our children, we will be able to affect not only their physical lives but also their eternal lives. Of course, sacrifices will have to be made. Every hour we once surrendered to the media, we will now have to fill with something else—something that will deepen each child's root system in the direction of God and love for all His children and creatures, something that will make each child kinder, more caring, and more determined to serve others rather than self.

The supremely important goal, however, is to make ourselves available to our children during their crucial growing-up years.

Becoming Our Stories

It is said that those we admire most we end up mirroring. In fact, it is safe to say, "Show me your mentors, and I'll show you yourself in future years." Stories can have a similar impact on us. Unconsciously, we mirror the traits of the story characters we dwell on most. They become such integral parts

of our psyches that we would no more wish to live at variance with what they stand for than we'd wish to disappoint a living mentor. Hence the importance of choosing the right role models.

Daniel Taylor, in his book *The Healing Power of Stories* (New York: Doubleday, 1966), says this about stories: "You *are* your stories. You are the product of all the stories you have heard and lived—and of many that you have never heard. They have shaped how you see yourself, the world, and your place in it. . . . Knowing and embracing healthy stories are crucial to living rightly and well."

Great stories refuse to leave us alone. In fact, they can border on the obnoxious: hounding us until we finally make certain behavioral changes. The power of stories is that they represent neutral ground. I may have very different spiritual beliefs from a next-door neighbor, but through stories, I can reach out, and he can reach out, and we can meet. The greatest stories carry their own freight without overt moralizing. It is long past time for us to capitalize on this in our relationships with others.

So I urge you, when your child—or *any* child—makes that life-changing request, "Tell me a story," *tell it!*

This Second Collection

When the first collection of *Great Stories Remembered* was released in the fall of 1996, it received Family Television's highest honor: the Seal of Quality

Award. Far more significant to us, however, has been our readers' continued written responses. Over and over again, you have told us how much the stories mean to you in your daily walk, and how you want to make sure the series continues. In order to guarantee that that happens, many of you have sent in your favorite stories—and from your packets have come some of the stories appearing in this new collection.

For this second collection, we brought back three authors included in the first volume: Grace Richmond ("Their Word of Honor"), Mabel McKee ("Beautiful Living"), and Annie Hamilton Donnell ("The Boy on the Running Board"). We are also introducing authors we feel confident you will love as much as we do: authors such as Arthur Milward, Fulton Oursler, Josephine DeFord Terrill, Pearl Buck, Arthur Gordon, Ida Alexander, Temple Bailey, Frederic Loomis, Margaret Sangster, and Grace Livingston Hill—certainly a stellar storyteller cast if there ever was one!

A number of you expressed appreciation for our seasonal organizational format, so we are retaining that feature, making it easy to find stories for specific holiday use. And apparently, even more of you love the woodcut illustrations, so we are including more of them this time.

As mentioned, it is always a joy to hear from you. If you have any reactions or comments, positive or negative; or if you have stories you would like us to consider for future collections, please send them—along with authorship, earliest publication date, and place—to:

Joe L. Wheeler, Ph.D.
c/o Focus on the Family
Colorado Springs, CO 80920

Winter to Spring

"Revolutions"

Ida Alexander

Precious began it, and all the family followed. But, of them all, poor Mother had the toughest time. She had never realized how difficult "revolutions" were.

It was Precious who first began it. Precious had a way of beginning things, though she was not yet seven. She sat so quietly in her corner that all the family noticed it.

"What's the matter, Precious?" queried Father after a little.

"Nothin'."

"But what are you thinking of, sitting there so quietly by yourself?"

"I'm makin' revolutions," answered Precious.

"Revolutions!" echoed Father.

"New Year revolutions," explained Precious with dignity.

"Oh ho! I see. Let us hear them, Precious."

3

"Mine's not to be bad anymore; not to cry when Elis'beth combs my hair; not to say, 'Shut up!' when the milkman says it's red."

"Good for you!" praised Sidney. "There's no sense in taking offense because folks mention your red hair, dear child."

" 'Tain't red any more'n yours. And your nose turns up—you got freckles—"

The good "revolutions" of Precious were flying before the wind of words. The voice of Mother interposed.

"Your hair isn't red, Precious—exactly. But your face will be, if you let Sidney annoy you. Don't pay any attention to him. He might do better to make some 'revolutions' himself, instead of teasing you into breaking yours."

"That's so," put in Father. "Better try it, Sidney my boy. There's some room for improvement, don't you think?"

"Lots," agreed Sidney cheerfully. "Trouble is, I don't know where to begin."

"You might start by not teasing Precious," suggested Helen.

"So I might—a 'revolution' indeed. What's yours?"

"I won't primp so much as last year. And I'll help Mother more."

"That's my girl!" praised Father. "Your 'revolutions' do you credit."

"We've all got 'revolutions' except Mamma and Papa," Precious reminded them, climbing onto Father's knee.

"Do you think we need them?"

Precious nestled closer. "You might stop scratchin' my face with your beard," she suggested. "It hurts."

"So I might. And I might stop some other things, too. How would it be, Precious, if I got up early Sunday mornings, instead of keeping everyone waiting for church?"

"W-h-y," stammered Precious, "what about our storytime?"

"We'll have to have that early, for I'm going to get up before the roosters crow. I'm not going to have 'revolutions' going on in my own family without having a hand in them."

"Everyone has 'revolutioned' now except Mother," Sidney remarked. "Mother, what's yours? Aren't you going to join in?"

Mrs. Lindsay looked up and then down again, without speaking. Her "revolution" had preceded all the others, even though she had not mentioned it. She did not mention it now.

"Am I in such need of 'revolutions'?" she asked.

"Are you? I guess not! We wouldn't change you for the world," cried Sidney.

"Not the teeniest bit," added Helen.

"Not by a jot or tittle," avowed Father. "Mother is all right just as she is. She suits me."

"Suits all of us, doesn't she, Precious?" said Sidney.

And Precious, nodding in her father's arms, did not dispute the family verdict.

But Mrs. Lindsay disputed it herself. She thought of it as she tucked the covers around Precious and kissed her good-night. She thought of it as she locked the windows and doors and put out old Tabby, the cat. She thought of it as she made a hot lemonade for Father, who showed symptoms of a severe cold.

"I'm a whited sepulcher or something," she reproached herself, "to let them praise me like that and never say a word. I ought to have spoken right out. I know my besetting sin well enough. I've got a temper. I'm too impetuous. I should have acknowledged it immediately."

Before sleep came, she joined the "revolutionists" boldly. "I'll hold my temper in check," she resolved. "I will! I will!"

The resolution guarded her lips the next morning when Sidney turned a cup of cocoa over the best filet table cover. She started to speak, then stopped.

A Happy New Year.

Ring out the Old

Ring in the New

"I'm a duffer," acknowledged Sidney. "Mother, I'm terribly sorry."

"Don't worry," she replied. "I'll get the spot out, and no harm done."

"Send it to the laundry," advised Sidney, "and I'll pay for it out of my pocket money."

There was a general laugh at that, for Sidney's pocket money burned a hole in his pocket and vanished the day that he received it, though he proffered it whenever money was needed or wanted.

When the children were off to school and the house was in order, Mrs. Lindsay examined the beautiful filet cloth. The spot was not the only wrong thing. In some way or another, a jagged tear marred it also. It extended to one of the corners. Mending it would be quite an undertaking. But it might as well be done today and not delayed for a more convenient time.

She went about the work with swift, capable fingers. But before it was entirely finished, it was time to prepare luncheon. All except Father came home to that.

After luncheon, she began again. But it was long before it was mended to her satisfaction. More than once she sighed for Elisabeth, her faithful helper, who was away on a three weeks' holiday that she had long deserved.

Visitors interrupted more than once. But at last, night put an end to the trying day.

"I kep' my 'revolutions' all day," announced Precious triumphantly. "I kep' 'em an' I kep' 'em."

"Good girl," praised the father. "I'll have mine put to the test when Sunday comes. Luckily, mine are for once a week, instead of every day."

Mine are for every hour of the day, thought the mother as Sidney pushed away his plate, with the apologetic and flattering explanation that he didn't like "warmed-over" food.

"I'll wash the dishes, Mother," volunteered Helen. "It must have been a hard day."

Mrs. Lindsay smiled a relieved, weary little smile. Before Helen began, however, a group of girlfriends arrived. She squeezed her mother's hand as she went to greet them.

"I'm so sorry," she whispered. "Leave the dishes till they're gone, and I'll do them."

Mrs. Lindsay shook her head. The dishes, she felt, were the last straw. But a heavier one awaited her.

"Mother," said Helen, following her out to the kitchen, "can we dig up any sort of refreshments? It's so cold, and the girls kind of—hinted."

A quick refusal trembled on the mother's lips. Then the words of Precious returned to her: "I kep' 'em an' I kep' 'em."

"I'll see what I can do, dear," she promised.

Later on she carried in hot chocolate, sandwiches, and cake.

"It's a shame for you to have bothered," the girls cried. "We wouldn't have let you if we had known Elisabeth was away. You must miss her dreadfully."

Mrs. Lindsay did miss Elisabeth. So many things came up where a helping hand was needed. Helen, in spite of her "revolutions," had little time to spare, as the school course was hard.

Mrs. Lindsay struggled on alone. She did it with as good grace as possible, though she often was tempted to rebel.

"Only one more week, and Elisabeth will be here to see to things," she cheered herself. "Surely I can hold out for another week."

The week began badly. The woman who came weekly to do the washing disappointed her.

"I'll do it myself," she resolved. "I'm sick and tired of the way she does it, anyway."

All morning she toiled over the unaccustomed work. The washing was a heavy one. She had not made much impression on it when noontime arrived. She prepared a hurried meal.

When it was over she attacked the washing again, without stopping to wash the dishes. She was tired, and her head ached.

As she hung out the clothes, the telephone rang. She hurried in.

"Hello!" said Father's voice. "That you, Mother? Set a place for old Thurston tonight, will you, like a good girl? He's here for only one night, and I've asked him home with me. Have something extra nice, will you?"

It was lucky for Father, at the other end of the line, that the news struck her speechless for a moment. Before she had recovered, he had excused himself and was beyond her reach.

She sank weakly into a chair. "This is too much!" she cried. "Nobody could stand it. Albert Thurston, of all people! A man used to everything. I can't get ready for him, and I won't. Father can take him to a hotel. I *won't* have anything but a picked-up meal tonight."

But even while she protested, she was planning the dinner in her mind.

She put the washing things out of sight and began on the disorderly kitchen. Her eyes were heavy; the blinding headache continued. But her trained mind and hands obeyed her. There would be little danger of mortification for the father, or of dissatisfaction for the fastidious guest.

Helen, hurrying home from school, was greeted by savory odors.

"Father has company coming," her mother explained. "You'll have to help a little, dear, if you don't mind. I'm depending on you for the salad and salad dressing. Can you spare the time?"

"I'll have to," Helen replied. "I've several long history topics to memorize, but I can do that after he's gone. And I'll get the other lessons in the morning."

Mother and daughter worked swiftly and efficiently. Everything was in readiness when Father and guest arrived. And the bright house beamed a welcome.

Mr. Thurston, man of the world, never guessed what his smiling hostess had suffered in getting ready for him. He enjoyed himself and appreciated the delicious home-cooking.

"Don't forget to invite me the next time I'm in town," he charged Mrs. Lindsay laughingly upon leaving.

"I'll invite you right now," she told him. "Don't forget to come."

The cordially given invitation gave no sign of the relief she felt at his early departure. She sank into a chair when they were alone, her hands over her eyes.

"Poor Mother!" said Mr. Lindsay. "You have one of your old headaches, haven't you?"

"Yes, it has ached all day."

"Well, rest now. Helen and I will do the dishes."

"No, Helen has her homework to do."

"Then I'll do them alone. You can lie on the couch while I work. I wish Sidney had waited."

"He had promised Sam Barrow to come over. He said he wouldn't be long. Sam wanted to see him about something in particular. I had to send him to Mrs. Barrow on an errand, anyway."

It was a relief to her to lie down in the cool dining room and close her weary eyes. But suddenly she opened them to their fullest extent. Something had fallen and broken. Only the finest china had been used for the dinner.

Mrs. Lindsay started to her feet, her head throbbing violently.

Mr. Lindsay came into view with a crestfallen air. He held his hands behind him. His mild eyes looked alarmed. His whole attitude expressed guilt and contrition.

"I—I hoped you'd dropped off and wouldn't hear," he said. "It slipped. I couldn't help it."

"It! What?" Mrs. Lindsay's voice hinted of other words to come.

"Your—your—cake plate. That one of Grandma Pelton's—the one she said there was no other like it in America."

With a herculean effort, Mrs. Lindsay choked back the words that would have relieved her. She turned her face to the wall. "Never mind," she told him. "You couldn't help it, Father."

But Mr. Lindsay's face did not express relief as he turned away. Rather, the lines of worry deepened. He tiptoed back and forth, casting many an anxious glance at the couch.

It was late when the banging of the front door announced the return of Sidney. He came in, all excitement. Mr. Lindsay raised a warning hand. But the mother had heard and sat up.

"Oh Mother!" Sidney began. "Such luck! You never heard the like. Sam is going up north—he's off now—I saw him off. And what do you think? He's left his tame snake and all his polliwogs to me! And I'm to feed the fish in his aquarium and look out for his billy goat, and—"

"Softly, softly, son," chided Mr. Lindsay. "Mother doesn't like snakes and bugs, you know."

"Oh, there's no harm in this fellow. Anybody'd like him. He's a regular pet. I've got him in my pocket."

Mrs. Lindsay rose to her feet. "Sidney Lindsay, take that snake right back where you got it! I won't have it in the house overnight. And what about the material I sent to Mrs. Barrow? Did you ask her to cut it out for me? She promised she would. I want to start on it tomorrow. Where's my material?"

Sidney shifted from foot to foot. "The material?" he echoed stupidly.

"Yes; that voile for your sister's dress."

"Oh, say, Mother, wait a minute and I'll tell you. You see—that material—"

"No, I don't see it."

Sidney seemed to find difficulty in going on. His mother prodded him with her eyes.

"Well, we were by the fire. And—a—spark flew out. We never noticed. And it got—it—got—ablaze—"

"My voile! That fine piece of embroidered voile!"

He nodded miserably. "I—we—it was an accident. My pocket money'll—"

Suddenly, the Mrs. Lindsay of the old year triumphed over the Mrs. Lindsay of the new. Sidney stood abashed before the torrent of words. But the words ceased, and she turned, sobbing, to Mr. Lindsay.

"O-h-h!" she cried. "My 'revolutions'! I've broken them, broken them, broken them!"

Precious slipped a cool hand into her mother's. "Never mind," she cheered her. "I breaked mine today. We could make 'em again."

"That's the way to talk!" said Mr. Lindsay. "Begin all over again. As for the 'revolutions,' I'm mighty glad Mother 'breaked' hers. For when I smashed the plate and she didn't say anything, I made up my mind we'd have the doctor up to take a look at her. I thought she might be sickening of a fever. A fever would be a lot more serious than 'revolutions.'"

"And not so easily broken," smiled Mrs. Lindsay through her tears.

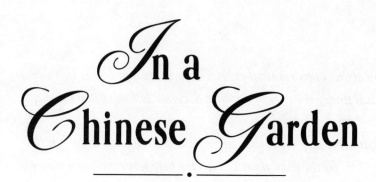

In a Chinese Garden

Frederic Loomis

Because of a simple act of kindness, a woman in a Chinese garden half a world away wrote the busy obstetrician a letter. Because of that letter, not only the doctor's life, but millions of others', were changed.

I have told many times the story of a certain letter, which I received years ago, because the impression it made on me was very deep; and I have never told it, on ships in distant seas or by quiet firesides nearer home, without a reflective, thoughtful response from those around me. The letter:

Peking, China

Dear Doctor,
   Please don't be too surprised in getting a letter from me. I am signing only my first name. My surname is the same as yours.

You won't even remember me. Two years ago I was in your hospital under the care of another doctor. I lost my baby the day it was born.

That same day my doctor came in to see me, and as he left he said, "Oh, by the way, there is a doctor here with the same name as yours who noticed your name on the board and asked me about you. He said he would like to come in to see you, because you might be a relative. I told him you had lost your baby and I didn't think you would want to see anybody, but it was all right with me."

And then in a little while you came in. You put your hand on my arm and sat down for a moment beside my bed. You didn't say much of anything, but your eyes and your voice were kind, and pretty soon I felt better. As you sat there, I noticed that you looked tired and that the lines in your face were very deep. I never saw you again, but the nurses told me you were in the hospital practically night and day.

This afternoon I was a guest in a beautiful Chinese home here in Peking. The garden was enclosed by a high wall, and on one side, surrounded by twining red and white flowers, was a brass plate about two feet long. I asked someone to translate the Chinese characters for me. They said:

Enjoy Yourself
It Is Later Than You Think

I began to think about it for myself. I had not wanted another baby because I was still grieving for the one I lost. But I decided at that moment that I should not wait any longer. Perhaps it may be later than I think, too.

And then, because I was thinking of my baby, I thought of you

and the tired lines in your face and the moment of sympathy you gave me when I so needed it. I don't know how old you are, but I am quite sure you are old enough to be my father; and I know that those few minutes you spent with me meant little or nothing to you, of course—but they meant a great deal to a woman who was desperately unhappy.

So I am presumptuous enough to think that in turn I can do

something for you, too. Perhaps for you it is later than you think.
Please forgive me, but when your work is over, on the day you
get my letter, please sit down very quietly, all by yourself, and
think about it.

Marguerite

Usually, I sleep very well when I am not disturbed by the telephone, but that night I woke a dozen times, seeing the brass plate in the Chinese wall. I called myself a silly old fool for being disturbed by a letter from a woman I couldn't even remember and dismissed the thing from my mind; but before I knew it, I found myself saying again to myself, "Well, maybe it *is* later than you think. Why don't you do something about it?"

I went to my office the next morning and told them I was going away for three months.

It is a wholesome experience for any man who thinks he is important in his own organization to step out for a few months. The first time I went away on a long trip, some years before this letter came, I felt sure that everything would go to pieces. When I returned, I found there were just as many patients as when I left, every one had recovered just as fast or faster, and most of my patients did not even know I had been away. It is humiliating to find how quickly and competently one's place is filled, but it is a very good lesson.

I telephoned Shorty, a retired colonel who was perhaps my closest friend, and asked him to come to my office. On his arrival I told him that I wanted him to go home and pack a grip [suitcase] and come on down to South America with me. He replied that he would like to, but that he had so much to attend to in the next few months that it was out of the question to be away even for a week.

I read him the letter. He shook his head. "I can't go," he said. "Of course I'd like to, but for weeks now I've been waiting to close a deal. I'm sorry, old man, but maybe sometime—sometime—" His words came more slowly. "What was that thing again that woman said? 'It is later than you think'? Well—"

He sat quietly for a moment. Neither of us spoke. I could almost see the balance swaying as he weighed the apparent demands of the present against the relatively few years each of us still had to live, exactly as I had the night before.

At last he spoke. "I waited weeks for those people to make up their minds. I am not going to wait any longer. They can wait for me now. When would you like to go?"

We went to South America. We spent day after day at sea on a comfortable freighter, feeling our burdens slip off with the miles and our tired bodies being made over by the winds that swept across the Pacific from China. In the course of time, we found ourselves in one of the great cities of South America. By good fortune, we were entertained by one of the prominent men of the country, a man who had built enormous steel plants and whose industries were growing rapidly.

During the visit, Shorty asked our host if he played golf. He replied: "Señor, I play a little; I would like to play more. My wife is on a vacation in the United States with our children. I would like to join her. I have beautiful horses here that I would love to ride. I can do none of these things because I am too busy. I am 55 years old, and in five years more I shall stop. It is true I said the same thing five years ago, but I did not know how much we would be growing. We are building a new plant; we are making steel such as South America has never known. I cannot let go even for an afternoon of golf. My office boy has better leisure."

"Señor," I said, "do you know why I am in South America?"

"Because," he said, "because perhaps you had not too much to do and had the necessary time and money to permit it."

"No," I replied, "I had a great deal to do and I did not have too much of either time or money. We are sitting here on your lovely terrace because a few weeks ago a woman whom I wouldn't know if I saw her looked at a brass plate in a Chinese wall in the city of Peking in the heart of China."

I told him the story. Like Shorty, he made me repeat the words: "Enjoy yourself. It is later than you think." During the rest of the afternoon he seemed a bit preoccupied.

The next morning I met him in the corridor of our hotel. "Doctor," he said, "please wait a moment. I have not slept well. It is strange, is it not, that a casual acquaintance, which you yourself would say you are, could change the current of a very busy life? I have thought long and hard since I saw you yesterday. I have cabled my wife that I am flying to join her."

He put his hand on my shoulder. "It was a very long finger indeed," he said, "that wrote those words on the garden wall in China."

Many years have been added to the average expectation of life, but each individual's fate is still a hazard. The most valuable people around us have lived largely for others. This seems the time to remind them that they will have more years, and happier ones, to do good for others if they start right now to do something for themselves; to go places and to do things that they have looked forward to for years; to give those who love them the happiness of seeing them enjoy some of the rewards that they have earned; to replace competition with a bit of contemplation.

The "Shorty" in this story lived only a few years more. I spent the last hours at his bedside. Over and over again he said, "Fred, I am so happy that we went to South America together. I thank God we did not wait too long."

The Golden Moment

Author Unknown

It didn't take long for Elizabeth to guide the old man across the busy street. He thanked her by introducing her to "golden moments."

He was a very old, very appealing little man, and he stood hesitantly upon the corner of two streets, both congested with traffic, and looked wistfully across to the opposite corner. Once he started forward toward the curb, but shaking his head decidedly, he drew back and glanced up and down the street.

Elizabeth was standing perhaps 20 feet above him, waiting for her car [streetcar], and it was not until she saw it coming and stepped forth to signal it that she noticed the undecided figure wavering upon the edge of the walk. She signaled the car to go on and impulsively ran back to the little old man's side.

"Let me help you across," she said.

His face lighted up, his cheeks glowed rosily, and his eyes shone as he clung to her strong young arm and was ferried through the stream of traffic safely to the other side.

"There!" Elizabeth said and smiled her brightest smile.

"Bless you, child! But," he said self-reproachfully, "I made you miss your car."

"It doesn't matter in the least."

"I'm very glad of that," he said simply. "You've given me my golden moment, child—with your help and your smile."

"Your golden moment?" Elizabeth was frankly puzzled.

He nodded. "Yes, my golden moment," he answered. "You know, there is one golden moment in every hour for everyone—if we only look for it."

"Is there?" Elizabeth stammered. "I didn't know it."

"No?" It was the old man's turn to look surprised. "Why, of course there is, my dear. Look out for your golden moments, and you will see."

He smiled, lifting his hat and disclosing his thin, white, curly hair, and was gone down the street. Elizabeth stood a moment at the corner, letting another homeward-bound car go past.

"A golden moment in every hour!" she mused. "That dear old man—perhaps there is, for him. But someone doesn't do something nice for me every hour; I'm sure of that. No, nor for any of us. I know Mother doesn't have a golden moment in every hour."

As she spoke, her eyes rested on the window of a florist's shop beside her. One window was filled with bunches of purple violets and maidenhair fern. Elizabeth's eyes lighted up as she looked at the flowers. Violets were her own as well as her mother's favorite flowers.

"If I only had a bunch of them to take to Mother," she said wistfully, peering into her purse and closing it with a sigh. She had nothing but car fare—one bright silver dime. And her car was coming.

She stepped to the edge of the curb, then halted. Her mind skipped

nimbly over the blocks between herself and home. There were a great many of them.

"But I often walked farther before we came to the city," Elizabeth said. "I believe I'll do it!"

Turning her back on the approaching car, she hurried into the shop with its perfumed interior and came out with the violets and their fringe of maidenhair wrapped in green oiled paper. Holding them carefully, she turned toward home.

"How pleased Mother will be! No one has brought her flowers in . . . I don't know how long. I know she'll be pleased."

And Mrs. Horton *was* pleased. Her face flushed with surprise and delight when she carefully opened the package and the violets were revealed.

"And you walked home that I might have them!" she cried brokenly. "Oh, Elizabeth!"

"That's all right, Mother," Elizabeth said briskly. "I enjoyed the walk. I don't believe I get enough exercise anyway. Why, Mother—Mother—you are crying!"

Mrs. Horton hid her face in the flowers for a moment. "Don't mind me, dear," she said a little quaveringly. "It's just because I've been such a dreadful and ungrateful mother. I'm ashamed to admit it, but I was nearly ready to give up this evening. The children have been so restless today, and everything has gone wrong. I thought I was a failure as a mother, and I couldn't stand it. Then you came with your violets—and oh, I can't tell you any more!" She buried her head upon Elizabeth's shoulder and sobbed a little, then went with shining face to put the violets in water.

"She has her golden moment—when she needs it so much," Elizabeth whispered to herself as she removed her coat and hat. "Yes, who is it?" she called in response to a timid rap on the door.

"It's Teddy," said a disconsolate little voice as the door opened. "I've got a story here, but there wasn't anyone to read it to me. I don't suppose you have the time?"

Elizabeth hesitated. She did so want to work a little on her new frock. But what of Teddy's golden moments—had he many during the day? She looked at his wistful and questioning little face and gathered him into her arms.

"Where is the story?" she demanded. "Let's not let it go unread another instant. And after I've read it, we'll see if you cannot learn to read just a tiny bit."

She read the story and patiently taught him the sounds of several letters to remember until the following evening, when she would read him another story and teach him a few more letters. Then they went down to supper.

Mr. Horton sat under the light, looking old and careworn. Elizabeth threw her arms around his neck, holding his cheek against her own. "Dear old Daddy," she said, "he works so hard for us all. I wish you didn't have to work so hard, Father."

His eyes lighted up, and the tired lines seemed magically erased. "You work pretty steady yourself, little daughter," he said. "It isn't the work that a person minds so much—it's just the feeling a man gets sometimes that maybe no one cares. It lifts his burdens to have a couple of arms around his neck like—" He choked and broke off.

Elizabeth kissed him and went slowly to her chair.

After supper, when she had praised Harvey until his boyish cheeks glowed redly, for some point wherein he deserved praise, and made Betty, the real helper of her mother, the sweeping cap of pink-and-white lawn that she had wanted for so long, she told them about the old man and his golden moment.

"You've given each of us at least one of pure 18-carat gold," her father said. "But I don't see where you come in. You have not had a single one."

Elizabeth stared breathlessly for a moment. "Why—yes—I have," she cried. "Why it seems as if they *all* have been golden! I believe you can't give a golden moment without getting one in return. I've had more than my share—more than the rest of you."

Her father looked at her shining face. "It sounds like a good investment," he remarked. "Suppose we all try to see if it works with us, too. I believe we shall be a happier family if we do."

"I know we shall!" Elizabeth cried.

"Sing for Me"

Arthur A. Milward

Seven children in a London hospital, all victims of cancer, band together to give an incredible gift to another patient—before it's too late.

In addition to my son, Adrian, there were seven children in his ward at the Hospital for Sick Children in London. They ranged from Adrian's four years, through Carolyn, Elizabeth, Joseph, Hermie, Miriam, and Sally, to 12-year-old Freddie.

All of the young patients were victims of leukemic diseases and didn't have long to live. All, that is, except one—beautiful, green-eyed, golden-haired Elizabeth, who was about 10 years old. After completing a common regimen of therapy with the other children, she would go home to live a healthy life. Yet the other children felt a genuine and profound sympathy for the little girl, as I learned when I paid my daily visits to my son and talked—but not only with him. Companions in distress, the children shared everything, even their parents.

Elizabeth, who had undergone complicated surgery in the region behind her ears, was going deaf. The process was quite advanced, and it would be only a matter of months before her hearing loss was complete—and irreversible. That Elizabeth was an ardent music lover, who possessed a clear and delightful singing voice and showed promise as a pianist, made the prospect of her inevitable deafness all the more tragic. But she never complained. Occasionally, though, when she thought no one was looking, silent tears would form in her eyes and slowly roll down her cheeks.

Elizabeth loved music more than anything else, and she enjoyed listening as much as she enjoyed performing. Frequently, after I had helped my son prepare for bed, she would beckon me into the playroom, which was quiet after the day's activities. Seating herself in a big, leather armchair, and making room for me to sit beside her, she would take my hand and say, "Sing for me."

Certainly no Pavarotti but capable of carrying a tune, I could not deny her request. Facing her so she could see my lips, and enunciating as clearly as I could, I would sing a couple of songs for these special "command performances." She would listen intently and with obvious enjoyment, then thank me gravely with a quick kiss on the forehead.

The other children, as I have said, were disturbed by the little girl's plight and decided to do something to cheer her up. Under Freddie's leadership they came to a decision, which they took to staff nurse Hilda Kirby.

"Kirby," as she was known to parents and children alike, was a tall, angular young woman, whose formidable manner had been known to strike terror in the casual observer. The children, however, were not deceived by her brusque efficiency. They knew that Kirby was their friend.

Initially, Kirby was taken aback by their announcement. "You want to give a concert for Elizabeth's eleventh birthday?" she exclaimed. "And it's in three weeks' time? You're mad." Upon seeing their crestfallen faces, she added, "You're all mad. But I'll help you."

Kirby lost no time in keeping her promise. She hurried to the telephone in the nurses' sitting room and dialed the number of a conservatory of music, not a great distance away in north London. "Kindly give a message to Sister Mary Joseph," she instructed the receptionist. "Tell her to expect a visit this evening from Hilda Kirby on important business."

As soon as she was off duty, Kirby took a cab to the conservatory to see her friend Sister Mary Joseph, who was a voice and choir teacher. After a brief greeting, the nun came right to the point.

"Kirby," she asked, "what harebrained scheme do you intend to involve me in now?"

"Mary J," replied Kirby, "is it possible to transform a small group of children, none of whom has had any musical training, into a passable choir capable of giving a concert in three weeks?"

"It is possible," replied Sister Mary Joseph. "Not very probable, but possible."

"Bless you, Mary J," exclaimed the nurse. "I knew you would."

"Just a minute, Kirby," said the bewildered nun. "Tell me more. Maybe I am unworthy of your blessing."

Twenty minutes later, the two parted on the steps of the conservatory.

"Bless you, Mary J," repeated Kirby. "We'll see you on Wednesday at three."

"Called what?" demanded Freddie incredulously as Kirby confronted him and the other children while Elizabeth was undergoing her daily therapy. "Is she a man or a woman, then? How can she be called 'Mary Joseph'?"

"She's a nun, Freddie. She teaches at one of the best music schools in London. It'd cost you two guineas an hour to take lessons from her. And she's going to train you—for free."

"Blimey!" interjected Hermie, who knew the value of a shilling because his mother kept a stall in London's Sunday-morning market in Petticoat Lane. Brushing aside Freddie's objections, Hermie said, "We'll take it."

So it was settled. Under Sister Mary Joseph's able direction, the children practiced each day while Elizabeth was undergoing therapy. There was only one major problem: how to include nine-year-old Joseph in the concert. Clearly, Joseph could not be left out, but, following surgery, he could no longer use his vocal cords.

"Joseph," the nun told him after she had noticed him watching wistfully as the others were assigned their singing parts, "I believe our Lord wants you to help me in a very special way at the concert. You have the same name as I have, and He wants you to work quite closely with me. You will sit beside me and turn the music pages as I play the piano."

For a brief moment, Joseph's eyes shone. Then, close to tears, he scribbled frantically on his note pad, "But Sister, I can't read music."

Sister Mary Joseph smiled down at the anxious little boy. "Don't worry, Joseph," she assured him, "you will. Our Lord and I will work on it."

Incredibly, within the three-week deadline, the Lord, Sister Mary Joseph, and Kirby transformed six dying children, none of whom had any noticeable musical talent, into an acceptable choir, and a little boy who could neither sing nor speak, into a confident page-turner.

Equally remarkable, the secret was well kept. Elizabeth's surprise as she was led into the hospital chapel on the afternoon of her birthday and seated on a "throne" (a wheelchair) was genuine. Her pretty face flushed with excitement, and she leaned forward to listen.

Although the audience—10 parents and three nurses—sat only a few feet from the platform, we had some difficulty in seeing the faces of the choristers clearly. But we didn't have any trouble hearing them as they worked through a somewhat incongruous repertoire that ranged from "Jesus Loves Me" to "Danny Boy"—all favorites of Elizabeth's.

"Remember to sing *loud,*" Sister Mary Joseph had admonished the choristers just before the program began. "You know she can hear very little, so give it all you've got." And they did.

The concert was a great success. Elizabeth said it was the best birthday she had ever had. The choir almost burst with pride. Joseph beamed. The rest of us, I'm afraid, shed more tears.

Anyone who is close to desperately ill or dying children realizes that it is not the hopelessness of their situation, nor even their physical suffering, that is so devastating. It is their indomitability, their courage in the face of overwhelming odds, that breaks your heart.

I have no printed program to show for the most memorable of all the concerts I have ever attended. No rave reviews were written. Nevertheless, I have never heard, nor do I expect to hear, more beautiful music. If I close my eyes, I can still hear every note.

Those six young voices have been stilled now these many years. All seven members of the choir—the six choristers and the silent page-turner—are sleeping. But I guarantee that Elizabeth, now married and the mother of her own golden-haired, green-eyed daughter, can still hear, in the ear of her memory, those six young voices that were among the last sounds she ever heard.

When Lincoln Passed

Mabel McKee

When young Richard Trowbridge met the tall, ungainly stranger, he had no way of knowing that this humble, serving man would someday be considered the greatest American of his age.

When Richard Trowbridge walked across the dining room of the Eagle and Lion Inn that morning, Ezra Ross, the merchant, thought of a young prince. The youth carried his head like one. His dark eyes flashed as if giving a challenge to A. Beste, the innkeeper, who gave him some terse orders about directing the service in the room.

But Ezra Ross didn't dream that the lad who was serving him was related to a king. The flash in the boy's eyes merely accompanied a bitter surging in his heart because he had to take orders from the innkeeper. Though no one knew it, the surging promised a time of reckoning with the man who had refused the boy credit at his inn until his uncle could arrive. Instead, the innkeeper had told him

31

that he would have to work for his room and board or find other lodgings.

Black Cindy came in from the kitchen to gather up the empty dishes on the table. Then Ezra Ross left the room, Richard Trowbridge following a little later. His work was over until dinnertime. He wandered out to sit on a bench in front of the tavern and watch the stagecoaches come in.

Two judges walked up and down in front of the inn, discussing politics. They talked of the Kansas-Nebraska bill and the new party—Republicans, its supporters called it. Often both of them quoted Col. Richard Thompson's opinion of different leaders in those turbulent times.

Mention of Col. Richard Thompson brought a smile to Richard's lips. When his uncle or the colonel arrived, it would become known who he was. He imagined these men, who had called him "Boy" and ordered him to do their most menial tasks, would treat him with honor. His heart beat exultantly. *I, who am related to a king, will then come into my own,* he thought proudly.

His uncle wanted Richard to read law in Colonel Thompson's office when they had become settled. He himself was to buy one of the packing houses on the other side of the river. An advertisement that it was for sale had been inserted in a Philadelphia newspaper, and this it was that had interested John Seymour in the little town on the Wabash. Long before his nephew had come from England, John had wanted to leave New York City and Philadelphia and journey to the Northwest Territory, reported by Western settlers to be the garden spot of the world.

Suddenly, there was a commotion among the men in front of the inn. A cloud of dust from down the street, the scattering of small boys playing in the road, and the rushing of the Negroes who carried the luggage of travelers into the inn told one story—the coach from the West had been sighted.

A few minutes later, it was in front of the inn. A wave of disappointment went through the crowd of watchers. There was only one occupant, a man asleep on the backseat. Scant attention was given him by the young dandies who were watching for the return of the town's two belles. Immediately, they scattered, and the boys ran around the tavern to play in the backyard. Richard Trowbridge, the habitual "loafers," and the judges were the only watchers left. Richard turned toward Charles Lesser, the driver of the coach, who had started to climb from his high seat to get water for his horses.

He slumped into a heap when his feet touched the ground. One of the men and Richard ran to him. The boy who was related to a king liked the kindly stage driver. He had brought him on the last lap of his journey to the Wabash and allowed him to drive his horses much of the way. His illness now distressed Richard.

The blueness of the driver's face and trembling of his hands told the story. He had contracted that deadly disease of early settlers along the river—the ague. His teeth chattered so much they could hardly understand his request for a driver to take the coach on to Indianapolis. Finally, he managed to ask, "Will you drive it, young mister?"

Unconsciously, Richard threw up his shoulder. "Young mister" was a title the old driver had given him on their trip over as the boy drove and the old man pointed out different trails along the way. Now he answered in a sturdy fashion, "I'll be glad to drive for you." His dark eyes flashed with pride. "You know I can manage the horses, sir. I'll see that they have food and water and care, exactly as you do."

The old man was helped into the inn, and Richard made ready to mount the driver's seat. But just then he became aware of some commotion at the coach itself. The two judges who were going to Indianapolis had opened the door and were surveying a long, lanky Westerner who was asleep, sprawled on the backseat. Another traveler had climbed on the front seat. Their intention of talking politics on their way to the capital city could not be carried out if they were required to occupy different seats.

One of them prodded the sleeping man—prodded him until he awoke with a jump. He yawned, and it seemed to Richard that his mouth was at least a yard wide. Then he smiled sleepily, and instantly his homely face became beautiful to the boy.

He drawled out in nasal tones that grated on one's nerves, "Howdy, friends! What can I do for you?"

Rather imperiously, Judge Hammond stated their request for the backseat of the coach so their talk would not be interrupted. He suggested that the stranger sit on the front seat with the other passenger. His request brought a still broader smile to the Westerner's lips. Slowly and with difficulty, he managed to move his long legs and then the rest of his body from the coach. He reached under the seat and brought out a stovepipe hat, which he fitted on his head.

Tall, lanky, with ill-fitting clothes, the man stood then. His rugged features were crooked and angular and indescribably homely. His shoes were ill-fitting. So was the collar of his shirt. His neck was extremely long and reached far above it. His hands hung from his sleeves and dangled like those of a scarecrow. Many of the people who were coming out of the candy store across the street stopped in front of it to stare at the strange-looking person.

Richard was sure he would never forget this man so long as he lived. He had seen no other that looked like him. He visualized the word "Yankee," which he had heard applied contemptuously in New York to the pioneers of the Middle West.

The tall man, who had started to climb into the coach's front seat, suddenly stopped. "Why, here's a new driver," he exclaimed, and he smiled his rare smile again. "He doubtless will need some instruction about the road. I'll ride with you, young man, if you don't object."

He swung himself onto the high seat beside Richard, and soon they were driving down the dusty road, past children who shouted at them and women who stared and waved. The beautiful bay horses pranced as if on parade. Richard lifted his head with the same pride he had shown back in

England when he and his mother had driven with their cousins to Buckingham Palace to see their relative, the queen.

Soon they were out of the town and passing through a woods of sycamore and poplar trees. Thick underbrush grew all around. Wild vines covered the trunks of the trees nearest the road, which was so rough that Richard on the high driver's seat had a terrible time keeping his balance. After a time they reached a district in which it had rained the night before. Soon they were in a region where the road was muddy and water stood in the deep ruts.

Once Richard gave a terrific lurch, and just then the tall, ungainly man reached out his strong hand and clutched him.

"Sit closer to me, son," he said kindly. "It takes more than a jolt to unseat a backwoodsman. That made me think of Tom Harden and the time he tried to ride the oxen. Never heard that story, I reckon?"

He himself laughed at the story of disaster and fun he told. His voice was squeaky at times; then deep and soft again. His laugh was still stranger than his voice. But his story was good and told so well that Richard laughed uproariously and forgot all his former troubles.

Ahead of them lay a stretch of corduroy road. The tall man told Richard that it had been built by laying logs crosswise in the road where swampy land prevented filling in. He told of cutting down the trunks of such trees and of splitting rails for all the fences on his father's farm.

"Pretty nice little village—that Terry Hut," he said after a time. "Reckon you're going to live there. I went through there when I was a boy, moving a family from Boonville over to Illinois. I made three dollars that way. I stayed all night in the Spencer wagon yard. I reckon it's still there."

Richard was interested in this man in spite of himself. The expression "wagon yard" had caught his fancy back at the inn when he first heard it. He had gone down to the place they called wagon yards, watched the farmers drive their loads of corn and other produce into them for the night and make their beds in the wagons filled with straw. It was always amusing to

see them crawl into this straw, drawing heavy covers around them, ready to sleep all night.

He could imagine the tall stranger crawling into such a wagon bed, folding up his legs for the night, and then sleeping soundly the sleep of the just.

On and on the stranger talked, telling stories about the people who had lived in the Hoosier county that had been his boyhood home and about the men who kept store or were attorneys in Springfield, Illinois, which was then his home. When he mentioned the fact that he, too, was a lawyer, Richard sat up straight.

"Do you know Col. Richard Thompson?" he asked excitedly. "He's a lawyer back there where we came from."

"Dick Thompson!" chuckled the stranger. "Reckon I do know him. He's the brightest, keenest lawyer in the whole Middle West. He's up at Indianapolis now, lookin' after the legislature there, I should say."

"I'm going to read law in his office." Richard raised his head proudly. "My uncle, who met him while he was in Washington, arranged for that."

"You are!" The tall Yankee seemed delighted. "Reckon you'll know all the rudiments of law then. Up at Indianapolis they say what law Dick don't know ain't ever been written. That reminds me of a story Abner Williams told about his schoolteacher. Don't suppose you ever heard that?"

Richard shook his head. When it was finished and the boy had laughed many hearty laughs, he in turn began to talk. He went back to England and told of his royal relations there, of the deaths of his parents, and of the urge for adventure that had brought him to America. He told of his journey across the prairies to Indiana and of the innkeeper who had made him work when his money gave out. He admitted that he was too proud to ask for credit in his uncle's name at the packing establishment. Almost vindictively, he added the information that his uncle would see that this innkeeper was properly humiliated for his treatment of him.

"Reckon I wouldn't do that, son." The tall man spoke slowly, persuasively, sweetly. A beautiful smile came over his rugged face. "He didn't mean to be rude to you. He's often been cheated that way. When people have been cheated, they can't be blamed for doing as he did. Guess he didn't know the story about the man who went to a feast and took a high seat only to be sent down lower, and about the one who took a low seat and was sent higher. That's in the Bible, son. Think you'd better read it someday."

At his own suggestion, Richard allowed the man to take the lines. He drove like an experienced horseman, not talking much, but watching the rough, muddy road ahead of him. When he did speak, he told of how the national highway over which they were driving had been built and improved during the last 20 years.

Once they stopped the coach at a little gully to get a drink. The tall driver told Richard the spring was the finest in that district. He led the way through a thicket where tall ferns grew and to the rocks from which trickled a stream of cold water. They drank from their hands like boys. When they came back to the coach, Judge Hammond had his head out of the window, frowning impatiently.

"We want to get to Indianapolis before dark," he said. "Will we have time to stop at the Half-Way Inn for dinner, do you think?"

Richard hesitated. He had almost forgotten there was a hostelry by this name on the road. The tall stranger, who was studying the position of the sun, finally answered.

"Reckon we shall, Judge. They'll have dinner ready any time they see us." He added to Richard, "We'd better eat there, too. I'm as hungry as Enoch Rent's bear. Now I must tell you that story."

After they had climbed back onto the top of the coach, they heard Judge Hammond's stentorian voice talking about "Whigs" and "Butternuts" and "slaves."

"Slaves! Men and women and children sold like cattle!" The man who was driving grew stern. "The judge says they should be allowed in Indiana to work in the fields. Slaves here! The ordinance of the Northwest Territory fixed that."

Richard was completely absorbed in the man's talk. He would have to know about Indiana's laws and ordinances if he became an attorney like the famous Colonel Thompson, as his uncle desired.

Finally, they were at the Half-Way Inn—a long, low frame-and-log building set back in a big yard. Here all coaches that traveled along the National Road stopped for meals or to stay overnight. A fat, jolly-looking host ran out to ring a dinner bell. He waved his hand at the coach, calling a greeting to the old driver, who he thought was driving. The tall stranger waved back, cordially, cheerfully, kindly.

Richard had driven the coach as near the side of the yard as he could, but still a muddy space intervened between it and some boards that were laid to the inn door. Before he could descend from the high seat to open the door of the coach for his passengers, the tall man was out of the seat and onto the ground. He jumped across the mud puddle, spattering his long coat, and was in the yard where some loose boards lay. He picked up two or three, carried them to the end of the board walk, and made an extension to the coach door so the passengers were able to walk to the inn without getting their feet muddy.

When Judge Hammond complained of a touch of ague and said that the drizzling rain would make him bedfast, the tall man ran into the inn and came back carrying a heavy coat for him.

Who is he, anyway? Richard asked himself. *He acts like a servant but speaks like an educated person. I wonder if it would be rude to ask his name. I told him mine, but he didn't offer to tell me his. I'll wait a little while longer. Perhaps he'll tell me later.*

Surmising that the boy had no money, the tall man graciously asked him to be his guest for dinner, and together they went into the dining room.

The rest of the trip was a quieter one for the man and the youth. The drizzle became a slow, pronounced rain, which seemed to sadden the tall man still more. He dropped into a silence, broken suddenly when his voice seemed fairly to wail, "I can't bear to think of the rain falling on the lonely graves of the people you love."

Richard's eyes filled with quick tears as he thought of the two new graves in England that held his father and mother. He drove on and on, through mud puddles and water at times. Trees loomed tall on each side of the road. Sometimes the woods were so dense that it seemed like night as they passed through them. The coach jolted from one side of the road to the other. A feeling of elation rose in the boy's heart as he thought of the two pompous men inside the coach, still talking politics. He hoped they were jolting from one side of the seat to the other.

Just before they reached Indianapolis, the stranger talked again. Richard, according to his advice, was not to worry if his uncle didn't arrive soon. The work at the hotel was not hard. Indiana was a democratic state; and when he did get started in law, people would give him extra praise for having worked his way in time of emergency. "Remember this, son," he added with a kindly smile, "if you try always to serve, you can't go wrong."

Richard noticed the man's awkward hands, showing by their callused spots and their roughness that their owner had worked at the hardest manual labor. He listened with more interest then as the stranger spoke of honest labor scars.

Soon they were at the little hostelry in the capital city at which the coach stopped. Richard noticed that the tall man remained in his seat while he sprang to the ground and opened the coach door for his passengers. The two judges hurried toward a distinguished-looking little man whom everyone seemed to know.

While he was watching the three talk together, Richard noticed that his tall, ungainly friend was unfolding his legs and coming to the ground with a single jump. The noise of his landing drew the attention of other people in front of the inn, particularly that of the distinguished-looking man who was talking to the judges. Hurriedly, he came toward Richard's friend.

"Why, Mr. Lincoln," he began, "I had no notion you were coming by stagecoach."

"Dick Thompson!" The tall man clutched his hand, and his face was wreathed with 100 smiles. "I'm glad to meet you so soon. And here"—his other hand reached out for Richard's—"is my young friend who has come all the way from England to see you. Since I've come only from Illinois, I reckon that gives him the first chance to talk to you."

Richard Thompson, who had heard that the young Britisher was coming and who knew all his sad history since the death of his parents, at once gave the boy a cordial handclasp. "Abraham Lincoln," he said, turning to the tall stranger, "is the best lawyer and the most intelligent man in the country. You'll always be glad to have him for a friend."

Judge Hammond and his companion were staring at the Westerner with open mouths. Abraham Lincoln, the lawyer who was then stirring the country through his debates with Stephen Douglas, had given them his seat in the coach at their request. He had carried boards and made a walk so they would not step in the mud. They could not speak, so great was their amazement and confusion.

Richard stood speechless, too. But through his heart went one sentence: *He served like a king.*

Some years later, Richard Trowbridge stood in Indianapolis again. This time he was a man, with a pretty young woman, dressed in long, hooped skirts, tight basque, and tiny hat, clinging to one arm as they waited at the station. The sleeve that should have held his other arm hung empty. He had left that at Gettysburg.

It was raining as it had been that day back in the long ago when Richard had driven the coach along the National Road. Crowds thronged the station—crowds that were tragically silent and restless. Women sobbed and men were grief-stricken.

Abraham Lincoln was passing—on his last journey from Washington to his hometown, Springfield, Illinois. He was coming more quietly than he had ever traveled before, coming in a casket wrapped in flags, for he had been killed by an assassin's deadly bullet.

Richard Trowbridge turned to his wife. "I shall never forget how he carried that board to the coach," he said softly. "I shall never forget that he told me always to serve like a king."

A sound of weeping rose, mingled with the noise of an engine. Slowly it came—the dark, snorting steel creature on the back of which Abraham Lincoln lay. Richard Trowbridge saw it through the mourning people around him and the station building, draped in black. And he said softly, to himself more than to the woman by him, "Years from now they'll know that the greatest American of them all is now passing."

A Boy Who Loved Lincoln

Kathleen Read Coontz

**Had 13-year-old Osborne Oldroyd
not set out on his quest when he did,
much of what he would leave for
posterity nearly 70 years later would
have been lost forever.**

On a summer's evening in 1926, in the house where Abraham
Lincoln died, sat an old man holding in his trembling hands a little
piece of paper.

He did not have to glance at the check to know that it bore the
signature of the Treasurer of the United States, that it was made out
to himself—Osborne H. Oldroyd—and that it called for the
payment of $50,000. A great deal of money! More than the old man
had ever had even a passing acquaintance with in all of his 82 years.
The worn, neatly brushed coat and the carefully mended socks
peeping above the low shoes were mute witnesses to the fact that
funds were welcome—really needed—here.

Yet it was not of the amount of the check that Captain Oldroyd was dreaming this quiet August evening. Something far more wonderful than anything that dollars can buy had just happened to this veteran—a dream that he had held in his heart for more than 60 years had at last come true. *Think of it! Wanting something with all your soul and might, living for it, working and sometimes going hungry for it—and then—suddenly one day to have it happen!*

It all started back in 1857, when the old man was a boy of 13. His long name, Osborne Hamiline Ingham Oldroyd, was a little bunglesome to write at the end of his compositions at school, yet he was proud of it, for did not the initials spell the name of his beloved state—O-H-I-O—a state to which he longed to bring honor someday?

Osborne's father kept a little drugstore on the corner in the village of Mount Vernon, and Osborne was allowed to run a newsstand on one side of it. Every week the Pittsburg News Company shipped a package of books and magazines to their young agent in Mount Vernon. One day he found in the weekly budget a little paper-covered book containing a speech of a certain lawyer in Springfield, Illinois, by the name of Abraham Lincoln. Always curious as to the contents of his periodicals, Osborne opened the little pamphlet and glanced over it. There was something in the forceful yet simply worded lines that caught and held the boy's interest. He turned to the back of the book and there found a brief summary of the life of the speaker. This man Lincoln had been born in a cabin in Kentucky, had attended school only a few days in his whole life, and had educated himself by reading and by studying law. He was now practicing law in Springfield.

How could anybody write like that who had never been to school! Osborne turned back and read the speech all over again. His father coming up behind him had to call him twice to supper before the boy heard, so engrossed was he in the words of this Kentucky rail-splitter. It was then—and only then—that Osborne Oldroyd met Abraham Lincoln, but between

the boy and his hero there sprang up an association that was to last all of his life and become the moving spirit in his career.

Osborne was by nature a collector. He was all the time collecting something—marbles when he was a little boy, stamps and pressed flowers when he grew older. His resolution to collect Lincoln mementos, however, was the beginning of a collection that was to last a lifetime.

He wrote to the news company and asked them to send him everything that came their way about this man Lincoln. It was not long before he had other speeches and news items about him. He was thrilled later to receive a Springfield newspaper containing a picture of his hero and another lawyer by the name of Stephen Douglas, who had debated Lincoln upon the subject of slavery.

Great things were beginning to happen in the nation at this time. Osborne—better, perhaps, than many of the men tucked away in this little Ohio village—was able to keep up with the happenings because of the information brought him through the Springfield paper he received.

Then came Lincoln's election as president of the United States, and the boy's heart thrilled with pride and admiration. Close upon the inauguration came the cry of "War! War!" and soon the quiet streets of the village were echoing to the tramp of marching regiments of soldiers.

Osborne was strangely restless to join them, but the elders said, "Wait. You are too young now; your time will come." But the boy was not content to wait long. The patient, worried man in the White House at Washington needed many soldiers in the field. So one night when the moon was rising over the little drugstore, Osborne, not yet 18, slipped away to join the boys in blue.

Before he went, however, he tied up all of his Lincoln mementos, wrapped around them a little flag that had flown from a recruiting station nearby, and laid them reverently in the drawer of the old highboy up in his room.

Many times in camp or on the battlefield he thought of his treasures and of the man for whose sake they were collected. Through all of the horror and suffering of those long months, one desire burned in the breast of the young soldier—to look upon the face of Abraham Lincoln!

Once this almost happened. Toward the close of the war, his company was passing through Washington. Someone cried, "There goes Lincoln!" The young captain looked up with fast-beating heart, but a great wagon loaded with army paraphernalia rolled in front of him just then, and when it had passed, Lincoln was gone. Two weeks later while his company was celebrating the end of the war, in Memphis, Tennessee, the adjutant rode up and in a loud voice read the notice of the president's assassination.

The world reeled for Osborne Oldroyd, the gallant young captain who had faced shot and shell undaunted. He crept off by himself, where he might hold communion with the great, gentle soul that had passed. Oh, that he might do something—something great for this man who had laid down his life for suffering humanity! There flashed through his memory the modest Lincoln collection reposing in the old highboy drawer up in his little room at home.

Captain Oldroyd remembers even now that he said aloud, "I shall go home and give my life toward collecting everything in the land to do with this friend of mankind. I shall raise to him a great memorial!"

The years that followed found him true to his resolution. While he was earning a livelihood in his Ohio town, he spent all of his spare time acquiring new Lincoln relics. Every editorial, every memorial service, every account of those last sad days was zealously gathered up by the young collector. With a burning desire to walk and live where Lincoln had walked and lived, Captain Oldroyd moved to Springfield, Illinois. Here, with a Springfield girl for his wife, one who had seen Lincoln many times and who was in hearty sympathy with his ambition, Osborne rented the Lincoln homestead and opened up a modest Lincoln museum.

There was not a great deal of interest in his undertaking, however, and many people thought the young man rather strange to give up so much of his time to collecting old, worn-out furniture and other articles—even though they had belonged to Abraham Lincoln. They did not then dream that someday a great nation would rise up and bless the man for his sacrificial work. Each addition to the collection meant a real sacrifice to the young couple starting life together on limited funds. But nothing seemed too hard for the ardent hero-worshiper. When money was not forthcoming for railroad fare, he made his pilgrimages of collecting on foot. Many a dress for the devoted wife and a smoke for her husband went into some addition for the collection.

It was at this time that collector Oldroyd acquired the furniture from the Lincoln homestead: the cradle that had rocked the Lincoln children, the cookstove in which Mrs. Lincoln had baked cookies for little Tad and Willie before they went to the White House, the precious old office chair in which the young lawyer sat when he wrestled with intricate terms in law and later wrote the speeches that Oldroyd knew almost by heart.

A collector of anything must know his subject thoroughly. Although Captain Oldroyd was never permitted to look upon the face of "Father Abraham," he nevertheless knew Lincoln better than many people who had been so privileged.

In the long winter evenings, he read and reread every line that the martyred president had ever written. He tramped for miles around the town, visiting homes that had known Lincoln and listening to the narratives of the inmates. From the many favorite jokes repeated to him, he gained his knowledge of Lincoln's famous sense of humor; from Lincoln's son Robert, and others who had come in intimate contact with him, he learned of Lincoln's likes and dislikes—in food, dress, and personal characteristics. In other words, Oldroyd the collector became intimate with Lincoln the man who had long ago entered his life.

A collection is valuable only when it is undeniably genuine. Realizing this, Captain Oldroyd determined that every article added to his collection must undergo a rigid test. Accordingly, he sifted all evidence carefully and traced every new acquisition back to its place in Lincoln history before he added it permanently to his museum.

He was besieged with offers of "Lincoln walking-canes," but always met the fakers with, "My dear sir, Abraham Lincoln never carried a walking-cane in his life!"

By this time, interest was aroused in Captain Oldroyd's Lincoln memorial. The great man had been dead for 20 years, and people frequently dropped into the little museum and paid the small admittance fee to look upon the personal belongings of the man who appeared to grow greater as time passed. But the fees were not enough to keep the wolf from the door where Lincoln himself had once scrimped and saved.

With necessity pressing him hard, Captain Oldroyd went one day to the state officials and proposed to present the museum to the state, in return for a salary that would permit him to enlarge the collection without such severe deprivation to his family, which now included a little daughter. But the state was busy with more important things and was not interested in his proposition. Some enterprising Easterner who had seen the collection offered the captain $500 for it. Five hundred looked mighty big to Captain Oldroyd, and he might have taken it had not the prospective buyer announced his intention of taking the collection to some other state. The collector felt that this would be like selling his birthright for a mess of pottage. Lincoln's things belonged here, in his adopted state or—here it was again, that old resolution about a national museum—at the capital of the United States.

Accordingly, in 1893, the determined man packed up his treasures and, together with his wife and daughter, made his way to Washington. Here he met many who were interested in his enterprise, and soon he had his museum established in what to him was the most hallowed spot of the capital city: the house opposite Ford's Theatre, where Lincoln was carried the night he was shot and where he died on April 15, 1864. The whole city was pregnant with memories to the man who had clasped Lincoln's hand by means of that little paper-covered book, before his name was on every tongue.

Here was the great White House, with its portico under which the carriage had driven that last fatal night; the box at the theater, over which the flag Oldroyd had just bought had been draped; the little toy shop out on Pennsylvania Avenue where the same woman who had sold little Tad and his father leaden soldiers wept as she told of his wondrous sympathy. In the sanctuary of the house where Lincoln had quietly breathed his last, Captain Oldroyd was permitted to live.

Spurred on by these new intimate reminders of the life of his hero, the collector rapidly added to his accumulation of relics. The exhibit, which first required one room, soon spread to two, later taking up the entire lower floor of the house; for the museum became popular with tourists, and the growing fees enabled the owner of the exhibit to buy extensively. Many articles, too, were donated from time to time.

One day a woman visitor stopped before going out of the museum and said to Captain Oldroyd, "You have many beloved things, but I have something of Lincoln's that is dearer than any of these."

"And what may that be?" inquired the old captain, jealous of this unknown treasure.

"The old plaid shawl that he wore," quietly answered the woman.

The shawl! Here it was nearly within his grasp, and he had searched all over the country for it. He offered the woman a price. She refused. He pleaded with her for the shawl, but she only shook her head.

"I cannot part with it. It has meant so much to me, this big, homely shawl that he wore around his stooped shoulders. You see, my mother was a friend of Mrs. Lincoln's. When Mrs. Lincoln came back, after the president's death, she asked my mother to name something of Lincoln's that she would like to possess. My mother always thought of him in the plaid shawl, and she hesitantly asked if Mrs. Lincoln would part with it. The shawl was sent her a few weeks later, and I have always loved it. I have had sorrow in my life and disappointments, but somehow that old plaid shawl just seemed to breathe patience and to stand for all of the goodness and charity in the world. It may come to you someday; but I couldn't live without it now."

Realizing that here was a kindred spirit in her love and admiration for Lincoln, the old collector refrained from urging the lady to part with her keepsake. Two years afterward, he received a registered package from

Chicago and, opening it, found the plaid shawl and this little note: *My mother died and in her will left her beloved Lincoln shawl to your museum.*

So also came to Captain Oldroyd other Lincoln relics that had been precious keepsakes in a family and made valuable additions to his collection.

The last bit of Lincoln's writing he bought from the White House guard who had preserved it, but not before dire poverty drove the family to part with it. The guard, too, had memories connected with his treasure. Broken in health and spirit, he loved to tell of the night when President Lincoln wrote that last line.

"He was all ready for the theater. Mrs. Lincoln was in the carriage, impatient for him to join her. A soldier outside requested a pass, and I took the request to the president. Always considerate of others, he sat down and wrote that line—the last he ever wrote: 'No pass is necessary to authorize anyone to go or return from Richmond. People go and return just as they did before the war.' "

Down in Kentucky one of the Hanks family, hearing of the Oldroyd collection, was instrumental in sending an interesting souvenir of his great cousin. It was a rough, black locust rail taken from the fence that Lincoln built with his father around the log cabin on Goose Neck Prairie, Illinois, in 1830.

Captain Oldroyd hung it from the ceiling in the museum, where the eyes of all the young Americans who visited there might fall upon it the first thing: a reminder of the toil and frugality of the boyhood days of the great Lincoln.

Every nine-year-old boy enjoyed in the museum a certain privilege that was denied to others. He was allowed to hold in his hands the big Bible from which the child Abraham Lincoln learned to read, and to trace with his finger the scrawl in the front: *Abraham Lincoln, February 1818*—the proud announcement of a nine-year-old birthday boy who never knew a birthday cake!

The worn, old Bible had had a long, roundabout journey before it finally fell into the hands of Captain Oldroyd. The old man liked to tell about it to the interested boys and girls who came to him.

"Some of my friends gave me a trip to Chicago to the World's Fair in 1893. I had seen all there was to be seen—so I thought—and was getting ready to go home when I came across the greatest treasure in the whole exposition: the old Lincoln family Bible. It was brought to the exposition by some Kentucky men and was being exhibited in a tent outside of the grounds. This was one of the Lincoln relics that I had long wanted to obtain. I began to bargain for the Bible, but they wanted $150 for it and I hadn't that much money in the world. But I couldn't go home without the Bible. I wired to one of my friends and asked to borrow the money. It came, and I went back the happiest man in the land, carrying the beloved and long-sought-for Bible safe in my bag."

The old collector loved to tell his stories about the relics and found happiness, as always, in his work; but as the years began to go by, an ache in his heart deepened. He was getting to be an old man and still the dream of his boyhood was unrealized—the dream of a national museum for Lincoln, one owned and cared for by the government.

Each year some senator or congressman introduced a bill in Congress providing for the purchase of the collection, and each year brought some disheartening delay in its passage. If the old collector had been in comfortable circumstances, he might have presented his museum to the government; but, he argued, if they appreciate the worth of the collection, they will be willing to buy it. Then, too, Captain Oldroyd could ill afford to part with his lifework collection without pay.

Many times he might have sold the collection had the main motive been a mercenary one. The collection had become famous, and offers from all over the United States came to him. Illinois, finally awake to the fact of its loss, offered $50,000 for the Lincoln relics to add to their museum in

---

Springfield. "Lincoln no longer belongs to Illinois. He belongs to the ages—and to the American people. The capital must have this museum," was the answer the collector sent back. A New York museum offered $100,000 for the collection a little later, but it received the same answer: "The collection must stay in Washington."

Following that came an offer from Henry Ford, as well as individual offers for certain articles, that would have kept the old man in luxury. But it was not money that he wanted.

When President Harding dedicated the magnificent structure of white stone known as the Lincoln Memorial, the old captain, standing near, looked out across the beautiful Potomac River whose misty shadows form a strangely fitting background for the building and, shaking his white head, murmured to himself, "A wonderful memorial, a costly and beautiful thing; but I am offering them a more precious one—a thing that is a part of Lincoln himself!"

The collector had almost lost hope that he would ever live to see the fruits of his labor recognized by his government, when one wonderful day in April there came the news that Congress had passed the bill for the purchase of the Oldroyd Lincoln-Memorial Collection. There then followed the August day that introduced Captain Osborne Oldroyd to our readers at the beginning of the story. Do you wonder that he sat like one in a trance? Can you picture now some of the things that went through his head—some of the memories that crowded upon one another as he looked around at the 3,000-odd Lincoln relics he had accumulated?

The Oldroyd Lincoln-Memorial Collection, which has recently come into the possession of the United States, is the largest collection devoted to a single individual in the world. It is all the more remarkable when we consider that it was not made by committees with large funds behind them, but by one man over a period of 70 years of patient, unselfish searching.

Had one born in Shakespeare's time gathered into one collection such an assortment of articles pertaining to the poet, he would have rightfully won the gratitude of all generations. This work of love is what Osborne Hamiline Ingham Oldroyd has done for his boyhood idol, Abraham Lincoln.

The museum contains a library of more than 1,000 volumes, all relating to Lincoln; there are invaluable magazine and newspaper files; 5,000 clippings; hundreds of sermons delivered throughout the nation at the time of the funeral; 253 portraits; 25 busts and lifelike masks; 171 memorial medals struck in honor of the martyred president; and countless letters addressed to or written by the man who in his greatheartedness never turned a deaf ear to sorrowing humanity. There are also the many personal articles that lead the visitor step-by-step along this career from its humble origin to the White House.

You may think of the old collector as happily spending the remainder of his life among his treasures as their custodian. Sometimes he glances up at a worn, brown-paper-covered pamphlet in a frame above his desk; sometimes he reads a bit from the volume containing every poem that was ever written about Lincoln—the last contribution of Captain Oldroyd to his memorial museum.

When you go to Washington, you will want to look him up and hear from his own lips other stories of his adventures in collecting. He will tell you that the collection is a memorial to the hero of his boyhood and manhood, but as he talks, you will feel—as I did—that it is also a memorial to the unswerving loyalty of a 13-year-old boy nearly 70 years ago.

The Spirit of Valley Forge

Wallace Dunbar Vincent

"So, you're that lazy, good-for-nothing Lawrence Forman's boy, eh?" he said. "Like father, like son." With such a reputation, Victor felt defeated before he could begin. What possible chance did he have? His mother reached back 148 years to give him the answer.

"What's the use of trying?" exclaimed Victor Forman. "I can't fix the old sled, and that's all there is to it!"

He threw down his hammer and stood scowling in disappointment. Tomorrow would be Washington's Birthday, and all the boys and girls of Trumbull would be coasting on Long Hill. The combination of February 22 and snow-covered roads always meant a glorious time for the young folks of the town—it had come to be a cherished annual event.

"What's the trouble, Victor?" came the gentle voice of Mrs. Forman from the kitchen.

"Oh, nothing, Mother," replied the boy, "except that this old wreck of a sled won't stay together, no matter what I do to it. And tomorrow's the big day on Long Hill."

"I'm sorry, dear," said his mother. "Are you quite sure you've tried hard enough? I wish you had more patience. Your father was like that. Suppose I threw down my sewing as soon as it didn't turn out well, where would the rent money be? As it is, Victor, I just don't know where I'm going to get the last two dollars for Mr. Dodge the day after tomorrow. I almost begged Mrs. Denner to pay me for the sheets I hemmed last week, but she declared she couldn't spare anything before the end of the month—and she wasn't a bit nice about it."

"Oh," cried Victor, coming in from the woodshed, his face red with anger, "she's just like—"

"There, there!" interrupted Mrs. Forman, pressing a needle-pricked finger against her son's lips. "Calling hard names never does any good."

"I don't care," persisted Victor, brought to a sudden realization of how hard his mother worked by the feel of that rough finger. "I'd have gotten a job at the clock works only for Mr. Denner! 'So you're that lazy, good-for-nothing Lawrence Forman's boy, eh?' he said. 'Like father, like son. No, we don't want any shirkers in the Gilbert Clock Shop.'"

The boy's voice shook with shame and indignation. A warm arm went around his shoulders.

"Never mind, dear," soothed Mrs. Forman, her thin cheeks very pink. "Your father's worst fault was a lack of grit. He was always starting with enthusiasm and stopping in despair. He couldn't seem to swim against the current. That's why I'm so anxious for you to be brave and persistent. Life doesn't hold much for the man or woman who gives in. There's something splendid about fighting against odds—and winning!"

"I know there is, Mother," agreed Vic eagerly. "And I'm going to be that kind. See if I'm not! Now listen. You know how hard it is to get an odd job in this town. Most everybody does their work, and people like the Gilberts have a lot of servants. But I'm going out now, and I won't be back until I've captured that two dollars for the rent."

"That's fine of you, dear," smiled Mrs. Forman, wondering how long that resolution would last. "But I'd rather have you keep on at that sled, now you've begun it! Conquer the sled today, and you'll be better prepared to find work tomorrow."

Half an hour later, a very downhearted boy found his mother up in her room. She laid down her work and had him sit beside her, snuggled up, just as he used to when a small boy in trouble.

"I've tried my very best," he declared, "and the old thing just won't stay together. Perseverance won't conquer everything!"

"Perseverance and brains usually will," smiled Mrs. Forman, running her tired fingers through his tumbled hair. "What is the real difficulty?"

"Well, you see, a sled gets a lot of slamming and wrenching, and nails won't hold. That's all. I'd use screws, only I haven't any way of boring a small enough hole. So, there you are!"

Mrs. Forman closed her eyes and seemed to see her husband standing before her, making his old excuses.

"Suppose," she said, thinking hard, "suppose you were to find a piece of wire, or an awl, of the right size and heat it red-hot and burn a hole for the screw?"

"Mother! You've struck it! Why didn't I think—" and Vic was out of the room like a rocket.

In another hour he was back with the mended sled, jubilant. He had not only made it firm and strong, but had put his initials—*V. F.*—on it with brass-headed tacks. Heartened by his bit of success—for nothing cheers a fellow like the sense of work well done—Vic was eager to prove that he could earn that two dollars before night.

Taking his sled along, for he could coast part of the way, he started for the Gilbert place. The mansion of John M. Gilbert, in its spacious grounds, was the showplace of Trumbull, just as John M. Gilbert himself was its leading manufacturer and richest resident. His huge factory, locally known as the "Clock Shop," loomed up against the distant hills as one looked from the station; and some day to be employed by the Gilbert Company was the dream of most of the boys for miles around. Mr. Gilbert was a thickset man with close-cropped gray hair and beard, who inspired the stranger with awe, his acquaintances with respect, and his family and intimates with real affection.

As Vic started to coast down the first short hill, who should appear but Sid Denner, whom he always tried to avoid.

"Hello, Vic!" he said with his twisted smile. "Still using the same old sled? Look at mine! Just bought it down at Clark's for seven dollars. Ain't she a beauty? Flexible steerin' gear and everything. It'll be the finest little slider on Long Hill tomorrow, eh?"

"Sure will," assented Vic, who never was small about what others had.

"Where you goin'?" asked Sid, mightily pleased with himself.

"Well," frankly replied Vic, "I'm going to see if I can get some kind of a job at the Gilberts' for tomorrow."

"Aw, come on and coast with the rest of us, even if you don't own anything better than that old, busted egg crate." And Sid threw himself upon his sled and flew down the snow-packed road.

The temptation was too much. Vic followed five seconds later. The new sled seemed scarcely to touch the icy road, as it gathered speed with every yard. Vic felt as if he were pushing his old one with every muscle in his body. But it, too, went faster and faster with every second, until he could hardly see or breathe. He was gaining—he knew he was! Oh, if only—!

The end of the hill, where the road turned to the right, was coming toward him like an express train. Then Sid's long legs were only 20 feet ahead. Then their sleds were even. The old one shot ahead, although on the outside of the turn, and darted on for another 100 yards. Sid stopped just beyond the curve, and the fellow was childishly kicking his sled in futile rage.

"The silly!" chuckled Vic.

It was after six o'clock when he got home. The table was spread with a simple but inviting supper, and the open door of the oven showed biscuits keeping warm. Mrs. Forman, in a neat blue dress and spotless apron, sat with folded hands, waiting. It occurred to Victor how seldom he had ever seen his mother idle.

"Sorry to be late," he cried, hurrying to wash. "But I was bound to come home with some money, even if it had to be very little. It's little, all right! Ten cents for filling Granny Slocum's wood box. I tried everybody I ever worked for. Went first to the Gilberts', but Banks, the gardener, said there was no need for outside help. He was decent about it, though. Looks like more snow tonight."

"Did the sled go all right?" asked his mother as they sat down. She never forgot the things nearest to her boy's heart.

"Out-coasted Sid Denner's seven-dollar one!" he boasted, but he told her no more, fearing a mar to a peaceful meal.

After a while, Mrs. Forman referred again to the Clock Shop.

"If you'll try hard enough," she said, "I do believe you'll find employment there yet. And when they see what an intelligent, dependable young man you are—"

"Now, Mother!" broke in Vic. "There you go, building air castles again. I tell you—"

"I believe that if you went straight to Mr. Gilbert—"

"Why," gasped Vic, swallowing a big piece of biscuit, "I'd—I'd sooner go straight up to a hungry lion! Now, see here, Mother, stick-to-itiveness is all right; but everyone's against me—"

"Victor," interrupted the mother earnestly, "do you ever realize why we're privileged to live in this free country, under the blessed Stars and Stripes? It's all because of the unconquerable spirit of the man we honor tomorrow, and of his little army. If ever men had the right to be discouraged, to say, 'It's no use trying,' *they* had the right. But they were built of better stuff!

"My grandfather's father was one of the heroes of Valley Forge in 1777. Tomorrow I'll show you a letter he wrote to his wife in the winter of 1777–78—just 148 years ago. The soldiers were but half clad, and many had no shoes. Their poor frozen feet left blood prints on the snow as they marched. Then, your great-great-grandfather wrote, his company had been issued no rations for four days. Many of the men were so sick they could not stand. Did they talk of surrender? Not they! Washington, unable to do more than keep demanding relief from the government, walked among his suffering men and tried to cheer them up. The glorious fellows—some not more than boys—struggled up on their poor freezing feet, raised their blue hands to salute, and tried to cheer *him*. That was the spirit of Valley Forge! It always wins because it never knows defeat."

Victor stood with clenched fists, staring at the opposite wall. In a vision he saw the starving, freezing, cheering little army that had saved their country, his country, by persevering to the end. With head held high, he went slowly to his mother's side and put his arm protectively about her shoulders. He tried to tell her all that his heart was resolving, but could only say, "Tomorrow, Mother, tomorrow—"

February 22 brought more snow to Trumbull. By two o'clock that afternoon, when Vic trudged up the long path to the Gilbert mansion, it lay a foot deep on the level and shoulder high in drifts.

As he turned toward the back of the house, a window of the enclosed porch opened and a deep voice said, "Well, boy, what do you want?"

Just above him was the stern face of John M. himself.

"I—want work, sir," stammered Vic.

"I see," nodded Mr. Gilbert. "Come inside and tell me all about it."

Vic stamped the snow from his boots and brushed what he could from his shoulders and cap. It was strange, but standing there facing the man so many feared, Vic felt perfectly at ease. The hard face and deep voice certainly had a terrifying quality, but underneath there seemed to be a very kindly spirit. In hardly any time at all, Mr. Gilbert had drawn from the boy all about his mother, her sewing, the rent, and his endeavor to get steady work.

"I guess that mother of yours is quite a woman, isn't she? Now, here's the reward for your persistence: Today you are needed. This morning Banks slipped on the ice and broke a leg. All the other servants are too busy to clean off this path. A number of guests will be coming at six o'clock tonight. The road around the house being snowed under, they will have to walk from the gate to the porch. I want that path clear of snow at six o'clock, to the minute. I'll pay 50 cents for every cubic yard of snow you remove, if the path is clean at six. Understand?"

"Yes, sir," replied Vic, staring at the path as he calculated. It was about 75 feet to the gate and about four feet wide. The snow was fully a foot deep. That made 300 cubic feet. Divide that by 27 to find the cubic yards. His eyes flew back to Mr. Gilbert's, wide with excitement.

"Then I'll get about five dollars and a half!" he cried.

"If you do the job," was the reply. "It's still snowing, remember. By the way, you're not so bad at mental arithmetic. You'll find shovels and brooms in the toolhouse. Throw the snow around those young maples bordering the path on either side—it will do them good. Now, my boy, go to work!"

For a while, Vic worked away like a well-oiled machine, scooping up the snow in big shovelfuls and tossing it first on one side, then on the other. There was no wind, it had stopped snowing, and the sun felt pleasantly warm.

When a little more than halfway to the gate, his arms began to ache and he slowed down a bit. The path was of concrete, and it seemed to get rougher as he went on. Oftener and oftener the edge of his shovel would

catch in the uneven surface, impeding him. His back began to ache across the shoulders. He straightened up and leaned on the shovel, panting a little. As he rested, the sun went behind a cloud, and a sharp wind sprang up.

"Hello, Vic!" called someone from the road. It was his particular chum, Ben Larsen, with his bobsled. "What you doing, having fun? Why aren't you over on the hill with the crowd? Don't you know what day this is? Looked for you all morning."

"I'll be over soon's I get this done," shouted Victor. Shouted, for the wind had begun to shrill through the trees.

"Hurry up," advised Ben, going on. "There's more snow coming, and too much'll spoil our coasting."

Vic nodded and went on shoveling. The young trees along the path now bent in the wind, and a sudden gust caught up a mass of snow and dashed it into his face. Momentarily blinded and half smothered, Vic dropped the shovel, stepped on it, and went sprawling on his back.

"Well!" he sputtered, trying to rub the snow from his eyes with a snow-filled mitten. "Guess I'll earn my money by the time I'm through."

Glancing back over what he had done for encouragement, his knees seemed to give way under him at the sight. The path that had been so clean a minute before was now white with snow that blew across it in billows.

Something seemed to stick in his throat, and something made his eyes smart as he looked at the ruin of all his hard work. Aching back, weary arms, time that could have been spent in jolly coasting—all for nothing! "What's the use?" he groaned as he turned toward the house with lagging step and hanging head. There were tears in his eyes—almost.

Mr. Gilbert looked out of the porch window.

"Well, my boy," he said sternly, "have you finished?"

Victor's voice wasn't quite steady.

"No, sir, it's no use. I'd cleaned more than half when this gale started up and undid all my work. The snow blows on faster than I can shovel it off. I'll put the shovel back."

"Wait a moment!" snapped the other. "Is it your way to quit a job as soon as it gets hard?"

Vic felt himself lashed by the very vehemence of the man.

"When I made my bargain with you, I took into consideration the probability of more snow, of shifting winds, of difficulties to be encountered. Otherwise why should I agree to pay five dollars or more for clearing such a path? But if you want to quit, I'll give you two dollars for what you've done."

"No, sir!" objected the boy, flushing painfully. "I won't take a cent if I stop now. But I'm not going to stop. I hate a quitter, really. Only I—well, it seems like trying to bail out a boat with the water coming in faster than you can scoop it up."

"Even in such a case," suggested Mr. Gilbert, a warmer light coming into his gray eyes, "if I had to go down, I'd go down bailing, wouldn't you?"

Well, look who's here!" cried Ben Larsen. The fellows and girls grouped about the bobsled waved or sang out to Vic. "Greetings to our conscientious, horny-handed son of toil."

Vic grinned somewhat wearily. He had pulled his sled through the woods, a shortcut to the top of Long Hill, determined to enjoy one coast at least before going home.

"How much did you get paid?" yelled someone.

"It wasn't over a quarter!" called another.

"Say, Vic," said Ben, "did you get it all done? Some job, I'll say it was!"

"Thought I would quit," admitted Victor honestly, "when it started snowing and blowing again; but Mr. Gilbert—"

He stopped abruptly as a big snowflake landed on his nose.

"Say! What time is it?" he asked.

"Nearly half-past five," answered someone.

"Can you beat that? I promised to have that path clean at six, and here's snow again. This wind must be blowing snow all over it. I'll have to go back through the woods, as I came, and do what I can."

"Don't be an idiot!" stormed Ben, grabbing him roughly by the arm. "You did your job to suit, got paid for it—the deal's closed. You can't help what happens now!"

Then Vic did the thing that took consummate courage. He turned without another word and hurried into the woods.

Stumbling, sliding, crashing through snow-laden brush, he ran till he reached the road. Almost directly before him was the Gilbert estate. Panting with a strange pain catching him in the side, he hastened up the path, now white with eddying snow. Around to the toolhouse he went for a broom.

Grabbing the broom, he started around the house, and the swirling snow struck him full in the face. Again he was shaken by the apparent foolishness of keeping up the fight. "Perseverance won't conquer everything," came his old saying. Then came his mother's reply, "Perseverance and brains usually will!"

Brains! Well, what more could he do than—

Suddenly, his own excited brain seemed to leap out and fasten upon a possible solution to his problem. On the sheltered side of the toolhouse stood a pile of wooden shutters used for boarding up the house when it was closed for a season. With his broom handle, he pried off the top one. One by one he dragged them to the path and leaned them, overlapping, against the young maples, until the whole path was sheltered on the windward side. The snow, scudding low across the lawn, banked up against this barrier, holding it securely, but did not rise above it.

His heart throbbing as much from exultation as from exertion, Vic grabbed the broom to complete his good work. But the wind left him little to do; and as the first sleigh drove up with its load of guests, he had the satisfaction of looking down at a path as clean as anyone could wish.

He was opening the gate when Mr. Gilbert called to him.

"I see the boat didn't sink after all," he said, and he looked at the boy with something of admiration.

"Well, sir," laughed Vic happily, "I found a way to plug the leak."

"Yes, you surely did!" affirmed John M. "By the way, my boy, I shall expect to see you in my office tomorrow morning at nine precisely. Tell that mother of yours that some of your spirit of Valley Forge is needed in the Clock Shop."

For Better or Worse

Lynnette Baughman

This is the unforgettable, true story of a man who loved enough to court the same woman twice!

Their spirits were soaring as the newlywed couple, Kim and Krickitt Carpenter, headed toward Phoenix to spend Thanksgiving with her family. They were driving their new Ford Escort and chatting about the Cowboys, the university baseball team that Kim coached back in their hometown of Las Vegas. With them was Milan Rasic, Kim's assistant coach.

It was pitch-dark at 6:30 P.M., and by then Krickitt had taken the wheel. Kim, who had a head cold, had gotten in the backseat of the car so he could lie down. Six miles west of Gallup, New Mexico, on Interstate 40, a flatbed truck traveling ahead of them at about 30 miles per hour was obscured by exhaust smoke. Kim woke to Krickitt's scream of terror and Milan's shout: "Watch out!"

Krickitt hit the brakes and attempted to swerve left, but collided with the flatbed. A pickup truck that had been behind them slammed into the driver's side of the Escort. The little car flew through the air and came down on its roof, skidding more than 100 feet before it stopped.

Kim was squeezed against the roof of the car, which was underneath him. He couldn't move his legs, and the pain in his back was excruciating.

"Krickitt!" Kim screamed. There was no answer.

He couldn't see that Krickitt was suspended above him, held by the seat belt and the steering wheel, her head swelling grotesquely as fluid flooded her brain.

It took a half-hour for rescuers to extract Krickitt from the crumpled metal. Since she was critically injured, the first ambulance took her to Rehoboth McKinley Christian Hospital in Gallup. Shortly after, a second ambulance followed with Kim and Milan, who was not badly injured. Krickitt was then flown to University Hospital in Albuquerque.

Kim Carpenter and Krickitt Pappas had met by phone, a chance business call in September 1992. As head baseball coach at New Mexico Highlands University, Kim, 27, received lots of catalogs for customized sportswear. When something caught his eye, he dialed the toll-free number, and in Anaheim, California, a sales associate answered. Her voice was animated, sparkling with laughter.

"Your name is really Krickitt?" he teased.

"And you're from Las Vegas but not Nevada?" she responded, laughing. She explained that her real name was Krisxan, a Greek name, pronounced *Kris-ann*, and that an aunt nicknamed her Krickitt when she was two because she never stood still.

Over the next three months, Kim's interest in sportswear increased remarkably, but only if a certain 23-year-old sales associate was available to answer his calls. A gymnast, Krickitt knew a lot about sports, and she seemed genuinely interested in Kim's team.

Pretty soon their conversations turned deeper. Both were dedicated

Christians who believed marriage vows were a sacred promise. It seemed that, at every turn, each was finding something more to love in the other.

In April 1993 Krickitt accepted Kim's invitation to visit New Mexico and see his team play. Two weeks later, Kim met Krickitt's friends and parents.

Kim asked Krickitt's father for his daughter's hand that June, a formality she insisted upon.

"You have our blessing," Gus Pappas said.

Kim then flew to California and went to Krickitt's apartment. Dressed in a suit and tie despite the sweltering heat, he called her name until she came out on her balcony.

"Well, will ya?" Kim yelled.

"Will I what?" Krickitt responded, then raced down to him.

Kim knelt on one knee and held out a bouquet of flowers. "Will you be my lifetime buddy?" Kim asked.

"Yes!" she said. "Yes, I will."

On September 18, 1993, Krisxan Pappas and Kim Carpenter were married in Scottsdale, Arizona. The couple honeymooned in Maui and, on their return, squeezed into Kim's small apartment in Las Vegas.

Only 10 weeks later, Kim listened in shock as a doctor told him that Krickitt was in a coma, completely unresponsive. There was possible brain damage. She might die.

Around 5:00 A.M., Kim, despite his own severe injuries, had arrived in Albuquerque to see Krickitt. She had a plastic hose in her mouth and a device stuck in her head to measure intracranial pressure. Plastic bags hung on metal stands, all draining fluids down clear tubing into her arms.

This can't be Krickitt! Kim thought as he felt the room sway and go dark.

Krickitt's athletic body started fighting back. Though still comatose, she was able to breathe on her own by the first week in December. She was transported by air ambulance to Barrow Neurological Institute in Phoenix, deemed the best place for her recovery.

Krickitt gradually came out of her coma, and three weeks after the accident it was time for a professional assessment of her mental abilities. Kim stood by anxiously as a therapist asked Krickitt questions.

"Where does the sun rise?" the therapist said.

Answer, babe, Kim urged silently. *Show us you're getting well.*

Krickitt looked puzzled, then satisfied. "North," she said with certainty.

"Who is the president?"

"Nixon."

"Where do you live?"

"Phoenix."

Phoenix was where she had lived before she was married. Kim was encouraged. *Yes, babe! We're going home soon, and everything will be all right.*

"Who are you married to?"

Krickitt's blue eyes drifted around the room. Her voice was flat and emotionless, and her words stabbed at Kim's heart: "I'm not married."

Stunned, Kim backed out of the room. In the hallway, he wept openly, slamming his fist against a wall. *God, help me! Help Krickitt and me.*

As Krickitt became more responsive, it gradually became clear that she had lost all memory of the year before the accident. She didn't remember their courtship, wedding, or honeymoon, or their short time together as husband and wife. Kim Carpenter was a complete stranger to the woman he had fallen madly, hopelessly in love with.

For the next month her parents and friends would ask, "Who are you married to, Krickitt?"

She would seem to concentrate, but then say any of a half-dozen men's names—her gymnastics coach, old friends, a doctor.

Once Kim showed her a video of their wedding. When the camera panned on Kim's face, he said gently, "That's me, Kimmer. And the girl is you, Krickitt." But Krickitt showed no reaction.

Every day Krickitt worked with a physical therapist, speech therapists, and others at Barrow. Once an accomplished gymnast, she had to be taught to walk. At first she would jerk her right foot forward and drag the left foot, unable to lift it even an inch off the floor. Her brain had sustained injuries in the frontal lobe, which controls personality, emotions, and decision-making, and in her parietal lobe, which governs language and mathematical comprehension.

Krickitt's memory of being a child, a teenager, and a college student gradually returned. But Kim continued to be "that guy," just one more person who made her try to walk, feed herself, and hit a ball with a paddle.

Often her reaction to him was anger and rejection. "Why don't you go back to Las Vegas?" she said more than once.

"Because I love you," was Kim's unwavering response.

In February 1994, Krickitt was able to move into her parents' house and go to Barrow as an outpatient. In March Kim began a physically and emotionally exhausting commute, flying to Las Vegas to coach the college baseball team half the week, and back to Phoenix on Sundays to prod Krickitt the rest of the time.

Sometimes there were clear signs of improvement, like the day when Kim pitched a ball to her. Instead of missing it by several feet, she scored a direct hit. In her sudden laughter, Kim could hear the echo of the Krickitt he'd fallen in love with.

There were comical moments, too. One day after Kim had returned to Las Vegas, she told a Barrow therapist, "I miss that guy who was here."

When Krickitt got home, her mother phoned Kim and said, "Krickitt wants to talk to you."

Kim was thrilled that she'd thought of him. "How are you?"

"Fine," she said. "I gotta go now."

Her short attention span was evident when people visited her, too. She'd greet them warmly with "Hi, how are you? I'm glad to see you," and follow it with "Well, bye now" in the next sentence.

For the most part, however, Krickitt had to cope with confusion, unfocused anger, and physical pain. Kim turned to the Bible and to prayer for strength. *Lord, please let Krickitt remember me. Please, God, bring her back to me.*

On March 12, 1994, Kim and Krickitt went to their apartment for an "orientation" visit. In the small living room, Krickitt picked up an 11-by-14-inch photo and studied it with a quizzical look. It was their wedding picture, but it didn't mean a thing to her.

A month later, Krickitt went "home" to stay. It was not easy. Her brain injuries didn't heal like a broken leg mends, with steady improvement. Her continual confusion over where to find things in the apartment and how to find her way around, her anger at Kim for being tough about her therapy—all this caused temper outbursts that were completely unlike the woman Kim had known and loved. This new Krickitt was like an unruly adolescent, not caring about anyone's feelings. A young woman known for patience and compassion before the accident, she now lacked both.

For the first time they got into arguments, and after one of these Krickitt ran out of the apartment. Worried, Kim drove around until he found her outside a fast-food restaurant.

"You promised me you would not run off!" Kim scolded her.

"I can't *promise* anything," she cried, as dismayed by her erratic behavior as he was.

"I can't live like this anymore," Kim said. "I can't see me without you, and I can't see you without me, but maybe that's the way it has to be."

There was one promise that was bred in Krickitt's bones: She had grown up believing that marriage was forever. It was a promise she and Kim had each made to God before they even met. And when neither of them felt they could go on as they were, that promise kept them together.

In the fall of 1995, Kim went to see a professional counselor. During one session the therapist asked him, "What made Krickitt fall in love with you?" At first he gave the counselor a glib answer, describing himself as "funny, clever, handsome." But then he took the question seriously. *What had made Krickitt fall in love with me?*

He thought of all the love and affection he'd shown her during their courtship. He was her sweetheart. Then he considered how he had acted since her injury. He was more like a parent or coach. Finally, it struck him: *Start over! Win her back!*

"Would you like to go to a movie tonight? We could get some pizza afterward." It felt awkward courting Krickitt again, but Kim made "date night" a part of their weekly routine.

They tried golfing together, but they often didn't make it past the second hole. Kim had to learn patience, to let go and not criticize. They knew they were on the right track when they could laugh and say, "Wow! We made it to the fourth hole without fighting!"

Although Kim set out to reawaken love in Krickitt, he couldn't foresee the result of their dating. She was the same woman and yet different. Kim came to love her as the person she had become.

Krickitt began to notice how compassionate and generous Kim was. Gradually, she felt herself "growing into love," which she described as "sort of like falling in love, only better."

Kim's counselor planted the seed of an idea: Would it be meaningful to renew their vows?

"Oh, yes!" was Krickitt's reaction. "And if we're going to have a wedding, I want a proposal, too," Krickitt said, her jaw set.

On Valentine's Day 1996, Kim once again went down on one knee and, with a bouquet of flowers in one hand, asked Krickitt to be his bride.

"People think we're getting married a second time to make my memory come back," Krickitt would say. "But I have accepted that that part of my life is erased."

The reason for the wedding ceremony, Krickitt adds, was because "every woman should have that moment to remember."

On May 25, 1996, Krickitt Carpenter held out her hand to Kim. "I thank you for being true to your original vows," she said, "and I pray that I might be the wife you fell in love with."

They gave each other their original wedding rings. Then, unaware of the other's plan, each brought a second ring to commemorate this second vow of love.

Kim and Krickitt emerged from the chapel, posed for photos, and then made their way through a crowd of family and friends. It was the beginning of a new life for them, a moment that Krickitt could now remember and treasure forever.

Could You Have Loved This Much?

Bob Considine

Once in a while a story comes along with such Velcro power that you can't possibly dislodge it from your memory once you've read it. This is one of them.

This is the story of a woman's love for her husband. Whether he deserved that love—and why he acted the way he did—are questions I can't answer. I'm not going to write about Karl Taylor. This story is about his wife.

The story begins early in 1950 in the Taylors' small apartment in Waltham, Massachusetts. Edith Taylor was sure that she was "the luckiest woman on the block." She and Karl had been married 23 years, and her heart still skipped a beat when he walked into the room.

Oh, there'd been tough times during those years, times when Karl had been depressed, unable to keep a job; but she had helped him through the low times, and she only loved him more because he needed her.

As for Karl, he gave every appearance of being a man in love with his wife. Indeed, he seemed almost dependent on her, as if he didn't want to be too long away from her. If his job as government warehouse worker took him out of town, he'd write Edith a long letter every night and drop her postcards several times during the day. He sent small gifts from every place he visited.

Often at night they'd sit up late in their apartment and talk about the house they'd own . . . someday . . . "when we can make the down payment."

In February 1950, the government sent Karl to Okinawa for a few months to work in a new warehouse there. It was a long time to be away, and so far!

This time, no little gifts came. Edith understood. He was putting every cent he saved into the bank for their home. Hadn't she begged him for years not to spend so much on her, to save it for the house?

The lonesome months dragged on, and it seemed to Edith that the job over there was taking longer and longer. Each time she expected him home, he'd write that he must stay "another three weeks," "another month," "just a couple of months longer."

He'd been gone a year now, and suddenly Edith had an inspiration. Why not buy their home now, before Karl got back, as a surprise for him! She was working now, in a factory in Waltham, and putting all her earnings in the bank. So she made a down payment on a cozy, unfinished cottage with lots of trees and a view.

Now the days sped past because she was busy with her wonderful surprise. In two months more, she earned enough to get the floor laid for one of the bedrooms.

The next month, she ordered the insulation. She was getting into debt, she knew, but with what Karl must have saved . . . She worked feverishly, almost desperately, for now there was something she didn't want to think

about. Karl's letters were coming less and less often. No gifts she understood. But a few pennies for a postage stamp?

Then, after weeks of silence, came a letter:

> *Dear Edith,*
>   *I wish there were a kinder way to tell you that we are no*
> *longer married. . . .*

Edith walked to the sofa and sat down. He'd written to Mexico for a
divorce. It had come in the mail. The woman lived on Okinawa. She was
Japanese—Aiko, maid-of-all-work assigned to his quarters.

She was 19. Edith was 48.

Now, if I were making up this story, the rejected wife would first feel
shock, then fury. She would fight that quick paper-divorce; she would hate

her husband and the woman. She would want vengeance for her own shattered life.

But what I am describing here simply did not happen. Edith Taylor did not hate Karl. Perhaps she had loved him so long she was unable to stop loving him.

She could picture the situation so well. A penniless girl . . . a lonely man who—Edith knew it—sometimes drank more than he should . . . constant closeness . . . But even so (here Edith made a heroic effort to be proud of her husband)—even so, Karl had not done the easy, shameful thing. He had chosen the hard way of divorce, rather than take advantage of a young servant-girl.

The only thing Edith could not believe was that he had stopped loving her. That he loved Aiko, too, she made herself accept. But the difference in their ages, in their backgrounds—this couldn't be the kind of life she and Karl had known! Someday they would both discover this; someday, somehow, Karl would come home.

Edith now built her life around this thought. She wrote Karl, asking him to keep her in touch with the small, day-to-day things in his life. She sold the little cottage with its view and its snug insulation. Karl never knew about it.

He wrote one day that he and Aiko were expecting a baby. Marie was born in 1951, then in 1953, Helen. Edith sent gifts to the little girls. She still wrote to Karl and he wrote back: the comfortable, detailed letters of two people who knew each other very well. Helen had a tooth, Aiko's English was improving, Karl had lost weight.

Edith's life was lived now on Okinawa. She merely went through the motions of existence in Waltham. Back and forth between factory and apartment, her mind was always on Karl. Someday he'll come back. . . .

And then the terrible letter: Karl was dying of lung cancer.

Karl's last letters were filled with fear. Not for himself, but for Aiko and especially for his two little girls. He had been saving to send them to school in America, but his hospital bills were taking everything. What would become of them?

Then Edith knew that her last gift to Karl could be peace of mind for these final weeks. She wrote him that, if Aiko were willing, she would take Marie and Helen and bring them up in Waltham.

For many months after Karl's death, Aiko would not let the children go. They were all she had ever known. Yet what could she offer them except a life like hers had been? A life of poverty, servitude, and despair. In November 1956, she sent them to her "dear aunt Edith"!

Edith had known it would be hard to be a mother at 54 to a three-year-old and a five-year-old. She hadn't known that in the time since Karl's death they would forget the little English they knew. But Marie and Helen learned fast. The fear left their eyes; their faces grew plump. And Edith—for the first time in six years, Edith was hurrying home from work. Even getting meals was fun again!

Sadder were the times when letters came from Aiko. *Aunt. Tell me now what they do. If Marie or Helen cry or not.* In the broken English Edith read the loneliness, and she knew what it was to be lonely.

Money was another problem. Edith hired a woman to care for the girls while she worked. Being both mother and wage-earner left her thin and tired. In February she became ill, but she kept working because she was afraid to lose a day's pay; at the factory one day she fainted. She was in the hospital two weeks with pneumonia.

There in the hospital bed, she faced the fact that she would be old before the girls were grown. She had thought she had done everything that love for Karl asked of her, but now she knew there was one thing more. She must bring the girls' real mother here, too.

She had made the decision, but doing it was something else. Aiko was still a Japanese citizen, and the immigration quota had a waiting list many years long.

It was then that Edith Taylor wrote to me, telling me her story and asking if I could help her. I described the situation in my newspaper column. Others did more. Petitions were started, a special bill was speeded through Congress, and in August 1957, Aiko Taylor was permitted to enter the country.

As the plane landed at New York's International Airport, Edith had a moment of fear: What if she should hate this woman who had taken Karl away from her?

The last person off the plane was a girl so thin and small Edith thought at first it was a child. She did not come down the stairs, she only stood there, clutching the railing; and Edith knew that if she had been afraid, Aiko was near panic.

She called Aiko's name, and the girl rushed down the steps and into Edith's arms. In that brief moment, as they held each other, Edith had an extraordinary thought.

Help me, she thought, her eyes tightly shut. *Help me to love this girl as if she were part of Karl come home. I prayed for him to come back. Now he has— in his two little daughters and in this gentle girl that he loved. Help me, God, to know that.*

Today, Edith and Aiko Taylor and two little girls live together in the apartment in Waltham. Marie is the best student in her second-grade class; Helen's kindergarten teacher adores her. And Aiko—she is studying to be a nurse. Someday she and Edith would like a house of their own. At night they sit up late and make plans. Today Edith Taylor knows she is the "luckiest woman on the block."

Spring
to
Summer

The Heart's Beginning

Pearl S. Buck

Mary Lou wondered why her mother was not happy about Grandfather's coming to live with them. Then she overheard a discussion having to do with Grandfather's fate.

When Mary Lou came home from school, she found her father doing something new. He had put a big piece of white paper on the kitchen table, and he was drawing lines on it with a ruler and a black pencil. Mary Lou had skipped into the kitchen to get an apple and found her father there.

"Where's Mother?" she asked first of all.

"She's getting Timmie up from his nap," her father said, frowning at the white paper.

"What are you doing?" she asked next, but after she had taken a rather large bite of apple.

Her father pursed his lips. "I am going to build something."

"A playhouse?" She was always wanting a playhouse, and since her father was a carpenter, it would be easy for him to make one for her.

"That comes next," her father said.

"Then what *are* you doing?" she asked again. Sometimes her father made her impatient because he was such a terrible tease.

"I am going to build a room onto our house," her father said softly.

"For me?" she asked.

Her father looked at her then and made a funny face. "Can't you think of somebody else?"

"But who else?" Mary Lou asked. "Oh Daddy, please tell me! Don't just be funny."

"Well," her father said, "your grandfather is coming to live with us."

This was such news that Mary Lou took three bites of apple before she asked another question. "You mean my grandfather from Kansas?"

"The same," her father said. He leaned over the paper and drew a line very carefully.

"Why is he coming to live with us?" Mary Lou asked.

"Well, he's getting old and he needs us."

"It's a long way, isn't it?" Mary Lou asked.

It was such a long way that she had never even seen her grandfather, because she lived in Pennsylvania.

"When is he coming?" Mary Lou asked.

"When your summer vacation begins," her father said.

"That," Mary Lou said, "is two whole months away."

She leaned over the paper on the table, where her father had drawn a big square and a little square.

"Bedroom," her father pointed out, "and bathroom. Nice, isn't it?"

"Why can't he sleep in the room with Timmie?" Mary Lou asked.

"He needs a room to himself," her father said, "and so does Timmie."

Mary Lou felt that she had to think things over, and so she skipped away to find her mother, who was still upstairs with Timmie. Her mother was sitting in the rocking chair, holding him and rocking back and forth. But she wasn't smiling.

"I was wondering where you were," she said when she saw Mary Lou.

"I was downstairs talking to Daddy," Mary Lou said. "Mother, Grandfather is coming to live with us. Isn't that wonderful?"

"I hope he will be happy here," her mother said.

"Why wouldn't he be happy?" Mary Lou asked.

"Well, he's old," her mother said.

"Very old?"

"Yes, very old."

"Fifty?" Mary Lou guessed.

"That's not old," her mother said. "At least not very old."

"Sixty?"

"Older than that."

"Whew!" Mary Lou whistled. "Seventy!"

"And more," her mother said. "But you mustn't ask him how old he is."

"Why not?"

"Because it's not polite."

"Why isn't it polite?" Mary Lou asked. "I like people to ask me how old I am."

"You won't when you get older."

"But why not, Mother?" Mary Lou asked.

Her mother suddenly got a little cross. "Oh, I don't know, Mary Lou. I wish you wouldn't keep asking questions."

Mary Lou knew her mother was not really a cross woman, and when she was cross, it was because something had happened that she did not like and it was better not to ask her what it was. So Mary Lou said, "I will take Timmie outside for you, Mother. It's nice and warm."

"Thank you," her mother said. "That would be a real help."

Mary Lou asked no more questions for that day, and she put Timmie's coat and cap on, which she could do very well because she was already eight years old and in the third grade, and then she took him outdoors into the yard to play in the sand pile.

When Grandfather came, she could ask him all the questions she wanted to, except of course how old he was.

Every day it was exciting to see how much of the new room her father had made. Every day as soon as he came home from his job, he worked on the new room, and soon it began to look very nice. When the floor was done and the walls papered, Mary Lou's mother put down a green rug, and at the windows she hung some green-and-white curtains.

"It's a nice room," Mary Lou's father said proudly.

"I hope Grandfather appreciates it," her mother said, and she was not smiling again.

Mary Lou waited until her mother had gone into the kitchen for something and then she asked her father, "Daddy, why isn't Mother happy about Grandfather's coming to live with us?"

"She's afraid she won't be able to take good enough care of him," her father said.

"But I'll help her, the way I do with Timmie," Mary Lou said.

"Good girl," her father told her. "You do that and everything will be all right."

This made her so happy that she could not keep from telling her mother that night when she was being tucked into bed.

"Mother," she said, "I am going to help you take care of Grandfather when he comes here to live."

But still her mother did not smile. "You had better wait and see how he likes children."

Mary Lou was surprised. "Why wouldn't he like children?" she asked.

"Sometimes old people don't," her mother said.

"Why don't—" Mary Lou began.

Her mother did not let her finish. "Go to sleep," she said. "It's late."

So there was another question not answered.

Oh, well, Mary Lou told herself, *when Grandfather comes I'll ask him that one, too.*

When Grandfather finally came, there were quite a lot of questions that Mary Lou had saved up, but of course she could not ask them all at once. She had to wait until she knew him. They went to the station to meet him, and soon the train came rushing in. Doors opened, steps were let down, and people began pouring out.

Toward the back of the train, an old gentleman, very tall and thin, with white hair and a white beard, was getting down from the train. He carried a cane to help him. Mary Lou heard her father shout loudly, "Father, here we are!"

It made her feel strange for a moment to hear her father call somebody else "Father." She felt mixed-up. Suddenly, for the first time, she understood that her father had once been a little boy. She knew it, of course, for he had told her stories about living in Kansas, but it always seemed to be another boy he was talking about. Now she knew it was really he, because here was his own father, this old, old man.

"Well, son," Grandfather said in a quiet sort of voice, "it's nice to see you." He stood leaning on his cane while they all came to shake hands with him. "And this," he said, "is Mary Lou, and this is Timmie."

Grandfather was speaking their names in a low voice. Then he turned to their mother and smiled. "Marian, my dear, it's very good of you to let an old man share your home."

"You're welcome, I'm sure, Father," she said.

They got into the car, and Grandfather did not say anything more. At last they were home, and Mary Lou's father got out of the car first and took Grandfather's suitcase to the new room. They all went to the new room with Grandfather to see how he liked it.

"It's not quite finished," Mary Lou's father said. "I want to put in some bookcases."

"I hope you like the rug," her mother said.

"It's very nice," Grandfather said. "Very nice, indeed. I thank you all."

"Then why don't you smile?" Mary Lou asked.

"Mary Lou!" her mother cried. "You shouldn't ask such questions."

"That's all right," Grandfather said. "Children have to ask questions because it's the way they learn. I'll be smiling when I catch my breath, Mary Lou."

"We'd better let Grandfather rest," Mary Lou's mother said, and she took the children away with her, and Grandfather shut the door.

"Why does he shut the door?" Mary Lou asked.

"Old people like to be quiet," her mother said.

"All the time?" Mary Lou asked. She was quite astonished because the one thing she did not like was to be quiet.

"I'm afraid so," her mother said. "But no more questions!"

There was something very different about the house now that Grandfather had come to live with the family. Mary Lou felt happier than she had ever been before, but she did not know exactly why. Sometimes Grandfather was quite a lot of trouble. He had aches and pains in his bones and then he could not walk very well, and there were even days when he had to stay in bed and Mary Lou's mother had to take his meals into his room on a tray. This made her a little cross again.

"Mother," Mary Lou asked her mother one morning when they were having breakfast together and Grandfather could not get up, "do you wish that Grandfather hadn't come here?"

"Mercy no," her mother said. "It's just that I am too busy."

"We'll all help you more," Mary Lou's father said.

"Then I needn't be cross," her mother said and smiled quite nicely.

"May I take the tray to Grandfather?" Mary Lou asked, getting up.

She carried the tray carefully, and when she went in, there he sat in his bed, looking very nice and clean, his hair brushed and even his beard brushed.

"Here is your breakfast, Grandfather." Mary Lou put the tray on the table by his bed.

"Thank you, my dear," he said. "I wish I could use my legs instead of yours, but this morning they decided not to work."

"Why?" Mary Lou asked. One nice thing about having Grandfather in the house was that he always had time to talk. There ought to be one grown-up in every house who has plenty of time to talk and especially to answer questions.

"Well, my legs have walked me around for a very long time," Grandfather said. "I suppose we can't blame them if they feel tired now. They do their best."

"Will my legs ever feel that way?" Mary Lou asked.

"Certainly," Grandfather said cheerfully. "But don't bother about it now. Just you run and have a good time."

There were other days when Grandfather's legs felt better and then he liked to walk with Mary Lou. On such days, he joked. He said, "I really have three legs, for I think I should count my cane, don't you?"

Mary Lou laughed. "But that is a wooden leg, Grandfather!"

"All the better," Grandfather said. "It doesn't get tired."

Mary Lou felt warm and quiet and happy when she talked with Grandfather. Especially since they never had to hurry. Even walking with Grandfather was quiet and happy. If she felt like running, she ran ahead and then came dancing back to him.

"I do like to see you run," Grandfather said one day. "It's a pretty sight."

Mary Lou thought of something. "Does it make you feel sorry that you can't run, Grandfather?"

"Oh, no," Grandfather said. "I have run many miles in my time. When I was your age, I ran everywhere I went. I had my turn at running. This is your turn. And when you're old like me, it will be other children's turns."

Mary Lou stopped. Here was something she had never thought of before. "Will I be old like you, Grandfather?"

"I hope so," Grandfather said.

"But Grandfather!" Mary Lou cried. It suddenly seemed frightening to think that she must one day be old and stay in bed whole days because her legs ached. Oh, and her pretty brown hair would grow white, and her smooth skin be wrinkled like Grandfather's!

"You won't mind," Grandfather said. "It will be natural. The years slip along just as day and night slip along now and you hardly notice it, do you?"

"No," Mary Lou said solemnly. Then that was what *time* meant, something that just slipped along. "And then you die, Grandfather?"

"Well, yes and no," Grandfather said.

While they walked, they had come to the edge of a field and there was a big beech tree. Mary Lou knew it well because in summer the children on her street would play in the shade there. It was a very old tree, more than 200 years old, her father said, and the top was dying.

"Look at the old beech," Grandfather said, pointing at it with his cane. "What do you see, Mary Lou?"

"Just an old, old tree."

"Is that all?" he asked.

She looked again. "That's all. And some little switches of trees growing around it."

"It's those little trees I see," Grandfather said. "Do you know where they come from?"

"Just wild, Grandfather."

"No," he said. "They come from the beech. That old tree knows that its time is about over, and so what does it do? It tells its roots to send up a lot of little new trees. At first the new trees drink in the earth-water from the old tree's roots, and then they start roots of their own. By the time the old tree dies, they don't need it anymore. They have their own life. Still, if it hadn't been for the old tree, they wouldn't be alive. So the old tree keeps on living in them."

Mary Lou knew that Grandfather wanted her to understand something.

"You mean you are like the old tree?"

"I am, Mary Lou," he said.

"And Daddy is the new tree—and Mother?"

"And you and Timmie," he said. "It's the way life goes. You see, it never stops."

They stood for a moment, looking at the great old beech. Then Mary Lou remembered a question she had forgotten to ask.

"Grandfather, you love children, don't you?"

"I do," he said. "I love them very much."

"I can feel it," Mary Lou said, and she put her hand into his.

Then Grandfather said, "That's enough for one day, Mary Lou. We've been thinking big thoughts."

They walked home again, and when they got there Grandfather went to his room to rest and Mary Lou skipped out to play. She felt happy because it was interesting to talk to Grandfather and she was beginning to love him very much, too.

But that same night after supper she heard a strange conversation between her mother and father. She was up in her room, getting ready for bed. Timmie was already asleep, and so was Grandfather. He always went to bed right after supper, the way Timmie did. But it was a beautiful, warm night, and Mary Lou found it hard to go to bed, and after her bath she leaned out of her window. It was just above the porch, and on the porch her father and mother were sitting and talking. Mary Lou did not mean to listen, but she could not help hearing what her mother suddenly said.

"Donald," her mother said, "I really think we should consider putting your father into a nursing home. He is getting too feeble."

Her father did not answer for a while. Then he said in a strange voice, "Whatever you say, Marian. I know the burden falls on you."

"It's not that," her mother said. "It's that I don't think it's good for the children to have an old person in the house. He is failing and it will make them sad. Besides, I have to tell them to be quiet in the mornings when he's asleep, and when he is sick, they have to keep quiet all day, and that's hard on them. After all, it's their home, not his."

Her father said in the same strange voice, "Whatever you say, Marian."

For a minute Mary Lou could not believe it. Send Grandfather away just when she was beginning to love him? Oh no! She crept into bed and lay on her back, her arms under her head, and she could not sleep. Who would have time to talk with her and answer her questions if Grandfather went away? Why, Grandfather was hers and Timmie's, and how could Daddy and

Mother send him away? Tears came into her eyes. How could they believe that he made Timmie and her sad? Maybe it was because Grandfather spilled things and Mother had to wash more shirts and table mats. Once when he had breakfast in bed, he upset his whole tray and the sheets had to be changed. Maybe Mother was tired.

Then I'll take care of him, Mary Lou thought. *I'll tell him to hide his clothes if he spills on them, and when I come home from school I'll wash them in his bathroom.*

She could not go to sleep for thinking, and when at last she did sleep, it was not for all night. Her trouble woke her up in the middle of the night. Everybody was in bed now and the house was still. She got up and went to the window. The moonlight was shining down, not brightly, for the moon was low, an old moon her father said, and it was slipping down behind the hills, beyond the field where the great beech stood.

Suddenly, a light shone out of a window downstairs. It was in Grandfather's room. Then he was awake, too. It would be a good time to tell him that she was going to wash his things. She tiptoed down the stairs and knocked softly on his door.

"Come in," Grandfather said.

He was sitting up against his pillows, reading a book. She shut the door behind her.

"Grandfather," she said, "we must talk softly so nobody can hear us. We have to keep it a secret. I am going to wash your clothes now if you spill anything on them."

Grandfather looked astonished.

She had to tell him then what she had heard her mother say on the porch. "It isn't that Mother doesn't want you here," she said. "It's just that she is too busy and she thinks you would be more comfortable in the nursing home."

"I see," Grandfather said in a low voice.

"But I don't want you to go," Mary Lou said. She was quite surprised to find that suddenly she had to cry, and she began to sob. "I like you to live here, Grandfather—it makes me feel better—"

"Thank you, dear," Grandfather said in the same low voice. "And it is sweet of you to want to wash my things, Mary Lou. But I think maybe your mother is right. I may live a long time yet, and some day you would find it troublesome, too, to wash my things, and that would make me feel bad. Don't cry, dear."

"But the little trees like to stay with the old beech," she sobbed. "They don't send it away."

"Hush, my child," he said. "Trees are not human beings."

She was kneeling by the bed now, and he stroked her hair. "It's time for you to be asleep," he said.

"Aren't you going to sleep, Grandfather?"

"Old people don't need to sleep so long," he said. "Good night, Mary Lou, and don't you worry about me. Wherever I am, you can come and see me."

"You shan't go," she said. "I won't let you."

"Thank you, dear child, for wanting me to stay," Grandfather said. "And good night again."

The next day when she came home from school, her father was bringing Grandfather's trunk down from the attic. Mary Lou stopped where she was just inside the door and dropped her books on the floor.

"Grandfather is *not* going," she said in a loud voice.

"How did you know, Mary Lou?" her father asked, much surprised.

"I say he shan't go," she said and stamped her foot.

Her mother heard the noise and came out of the kitchen. "But Grandfather wants to go," she said. "This morning after you went to school, he told us that he would be happier if he went to a good nursing home, not too far away so that you could come and see him."

"No," Mary Lou said, beginning to cry. "No, no, no!"

"Why, Mary Lou!" her mother said.

"The child is upset," her father said. "Come here, Mary Lou. What's the matter?"

They sat down on the bottom step of the stairs, and she cried on his shoulder.

"Now then," her father said, patting her back, "what's it all about?"

Mary Lou told him everything then. "I heard you," she said. "I heard you talking last night. It's not true about Timmie and me being sad. I like Grandfather to be here. He is so interesting. And he isn't busy all the time. And he explained about the big beech and the little trees."

"What is the child talking about?" her mother said. "The big beech?"

"You come with me," Mary Lou said, crying very hard indeed. "Come see the big beech and I'll tell you what Grandfather explained—"

There was nothing for it except to go with her. Timmie was playing in Grandfather's room where it was quiet and he could make a house with his blocks that he kept under Grandfather's bed, and Mary Lou and her father and mother went down the road to the field where the old beech stood, sheltering the little ones.

"There it is," Mary Lou said. "Grandfather is just like that beech. He's old, too, but he's ours. We're the new trees, don't you see, growing out of his roots."

"Roots?" her mother said, not understanding at all.

"Oh Mother," Mary Lou said impatiently, "I know Grandfather isn't really a tree, but he's something like it. Can't you feel how Grandfather is like the old beech? And how you and Daddy and Timmie and I are the new trees? You have to feel it—I can, can't you?"

"I can," her father said gently. "I feel exactly what you mean, Mary Lou." But her mother said nothing.

"Those little trees will grow old someday, too. Grandfather said they would," Mary Lou went on. "There will be other new trees then."

Still her mother said nothing.

"Mother," Mary Lou said, "would you like it if someday Timmie and I sent you away? When you are old?"

"No," her mother said thoughtfully, "no, I wouldn't like that."

"Oh Mother," Mary Lou said, "now you know how I feel about Grandfather! Please don't let's send him away. I'll wash his things, I'll sweep his room. But I want to keep him because he's ours."

"Well," her mother said, "this is all very strange."

"There is a good deal in what Mary Lou is trying to tell us, Marian," her father said.

"If that's the way she feels," her mother said, "then I was completely wrong last night."

"Thank you, my dear," he said. "We'll all be happier, I think."

So that was the way it ended. They walked home together, and as soon as they got there, Mary Lou's father took the trunk upstairs again. Then they went into Grandfather's room. Timmie was putting a steeple on a church he had built while they were away, and Grandfather was sitting in the rocking chair, watching him. On the bed were some neat piles of clothes he had got ready to put in the trunk.

"You may as well put those clothes away again, Father," Mary Lou's father said. "We have decided that we can't spare you. You'll just have to stay with us."

Grandfather looked up, surprised. "But I thought—" he began.

"No buts, Grandfather," Mary Lou's mother said in a nice, bright voice. "Mary Lou took us down to the big beech tree and explained how she felt."

"Oh Grandfather," Mary Lou said, "please, please, stay with us."

Grandfather's cheeks were suddenly pink above his white beard. "Well," he said, "well, well, well—if that's the way you feel—"

"Oh, I do," Mary Lou said.

"Then so do I," Grandfather said.

An Easter Song

Grace Ethelyn Cody

> **Gretta couldn't bring herself to do it. How could Father expect it of her, so soon after Mother's death? But she could not get his wan face out of her mind. Perhaps she might find an answer in a house where darkness was total—always.**

In the doorway, Kenneth Barnes paused to look back at Gretta. Perhaps he expected a farewell glance, but the black-gowned girl at the library desk did not stir. For a minute, he watched her in silence as she sat there, pen in hand, gazing dully out of the window.

"By the way, sister," he said at last, in a tone of determined cheerfulness, "it's past the time when Mother always brought her amaryllis up from the basement. Shan't I carry it up for you?"

Gretta started. "How did you know I was thinking about that?" she asked.

"I didn't know it."

"Then whatever made you speak of it?"

At first her brother hesitated. Then he came over to the desk and sat down. "I've been thinking about it myself, Gretta," he said. "I'll tell you. I saw that Bridget had gone to tending it down there in the sunny basement window."

Gretta nodded. She had noticed, too.

"I guess she thought it might hurt us—make us remember too much—to have it upstairs," Kenneth went on softly. "Yet she wanted to take care of it and make it blossom, because Mother always did. And—well, the thing I can't forget is that last year, when Mother asked me to carry the big, heavy thing upstairs for her, I said I was in too much of a hurry and went off downtown and"—the boy's voice choked—"she brought it up herself."

For answer, Gretta suddenly buried her face in her arms on the desk and began to sob bitterly.

"Don't, Gretta, don't—dear!" he begged. "It doesn't do any good."

"Oh, I can't help it!" she cried passionately. "You haven't anything to be sorry for, compared with me, Ken! Everyone knows how good you are. But I came home from school that same day, and she was so tired, and I never even noticed the cover she had been putting on the amaryllis jar, or anything like that. I just said the plant was a straggling, overgrown old thing, and I wished we could have some decent house plants like other people, and oh, I was horrid—horrid! I can see her face now with that hurt look, and I can't bear it, Ken—I can't! If I could only go back and begin over—but she's gone! I've lost my chance! Oh, I wish I could die!"

"Hush, Gretta! Father'll hear."

"I can't help it. I can't always keep it in. I try and try! I was just sitting here, wondering if Father would like to have me put that plant in the bay window, the way Mother always did, and thinking that I couldn't bear to have it here, reminding me every day how I'd lost my chance. Oh, I was always thinking about myself instead of about her when she was here, and I never even knew it until she was gone!"

Kenneth patted her shoulder and wondered what he could answer.

"I'm pretty sure Father would like it," he said presently in a tone of decision. "I'm going straight down to bring it up now."

He was gone before she could object, and when he reappeared with the
heavy jar in his arms, Gretta hastily wiped her eyes and cleared the little
stand in the window.

"There goes Father to the post office!" exclaimed Kenneth, hearing the
front door close. "He likes to have me walk down with him, so I'll run and
catch up. You put some kind of a cover around the old jar and take care of
it, won't you, Gretta? He'll be pleased if you do."

"I'll try, Ken," she said brokenly, but the tears had come again, and she
could only shake her head, without a word, when Kenneth said, "Don't cry
anymore now. Brace up. We must, for Father, you know."

Mr. Barnes was shut into his study until late that afternoon. He was writing
his Easter sermon, and when at last he came out, there was the shining look
of victory after struggle on his pale, worn face. The first words he spoke were:

"Mother's amaryllis! That's your work, I know, daughter."

"No, Ken did it," said Gretta, hardly looking up from the stocking she
was darning because she wished to hide the tears that stood in her eyes. She
was a pathetic little figure as she sat there with head bowed over her work,
and her father felt it. He crossed the room and laid a tender hand on the
yellow braids wound around her head.

"Ken may have brought it upstairs," he said, "but 'twas Gretta who put
the pretty cover on it, I'm sure. And it's well started already, isn't it? Look
at those buds! I believe it will blossom before Easter day!"

Gretta could not answer, but the father understood, and drawing up a
chair, he went on, with a brave attempt at brightness.

"There's good news for us all tonight. Aunt Elsie writes that she can get
away at last. She'll be here a week from Saturday, the day before Easter, and
she'll stay as long as we need her. Aren't we thankful?"

Aunt Elsie was Mr. Barnes's youngest sister, dearly loved by him and both his children, but Gretta could not echo the brightness in his tone. She could only falter, still with downcast eyes, "I suppose we are, Father—as thankful as we can be for anything—now."

Then Kenneth came in, and Bridget called the lonely trio to dinner, and at last one more of the hard days came to an end.

They were so long, those days! There was no special hope in Aunt Elsie's coming because there was no special hope in anything anymore, and yet it seemed months to Gretta before 10 days dragged away.

"My precious!" That was all Aunt Elsie said when Gretta met her at the door the morning before Easter, but the little figure in the black dress was clasped close, and Gretta suddenly found comfort.

Then the study door opened behind them.

"Stephen—dear, *dear* boy!" cried Aunt Elsie to the Reverend Mr. Barnes, and with one arm still around Gretta, she put the other about her brother's neck. "And Kenneth, too! Another dear boy!" she added a minute later as the tall fellow caught his aunt in a boy's loving hug. That was all. In a few minutes, it was as if she had always been there, except for the sudden hint of warmth and brightness through the lonely house.

The greetings were scarcely over before someone called to consult with Mr. Barnes, and he came back to the group with a troubled expression on his face.

"Miss Holbrook has been taken ill suddenly," he said. "They have tried everywhere to find someone to sing the solo in her place tomorrow, but there seems to be no one who can do it. Daughter," he added with a new thought, "I've been planning that the service tomorrow should be for Mama, specially. Not that others should know about it, of course, but I have been thinking about her beautiful life all the time I was writing my sermon, and I wanted it all to be just as she would like it. For the solo I was going to have that little Easter song that she used to love to hear you sing. Could you—do you suppose you could sing it for me?"

Gretta shrank back. "Oh Father!" she said. She felt two pairs of appealing eyes—Kenneth's and Aunt Elsie's—but neither of them knew what this meant to her. "Father—you couldn't expect—oh, I can't sing! It's gone out of me. I never, never can sing anymore! Don't you know that?"

With the question, she was sobbing in his arms—great, racking sobs, such as it hurts the heart to hear—while he patted and soothed her gently.

"There, daughter, I shouldn't have asked it! It was selfish of me. I had a sudden thought that it would help me so much—give me more strength to go through it all—and I spoke before I thought. I know you can't."

He was no sooner out of the house than Aunt Elsie turned to Gretta with tears welling into her eyes.

"He breaks my heart, Gretta!" she cried. "To see him, so thoughtful of others while he's missing her so at every turn himself! When he stood there, brushing his own coat collar, it came over me how she always watched for the chance to do those little things for him—and I could hardly bear it."

"But I've tried to do all I could to take care of him, Aunty," protested Gretta, surprised out of her tears. What she had expected was a heart's outpouring of sympathy for herself. "You'll find every one of his buttons sewed on, and his stockings mended, and—"

"Yes, yes, dear, I know, but it's the heart that always thought of him before herself—always, always—don't you know? He's starving without it—and so quiet and brave!" Then, after an instant, she added in a different tone, "There's her beautiful amaryllis, blossoming away, just as if she were here. I'm glad of its warm brightness for us all. We must keep trying to be bright, too, Gretta, for his sake—and for hers."

"But I hate that flower for being red!" said Gretta bitterly. "It ought to be black this year. How can it be bright?"

Elsie Barnes looked steadily at her niece for a minute or so. "Do you know the story of that amaryllis?" she asked.

"No—or yes. Mother has told me something about it, I think, but it's so long ago that I've forgotten."

"That seems strange. She has had it as long as she has had you, I do believe. Why, you must know Mrs. Meredith, the quaint little lady who gave it to your mother because she was so grateful for kindness to a little daughter of hers who had died! She was the one who said, 'Mrs. Barnes, I'm going to give you this bulb, and I want you always to remember, when the flower comes out, that it's the blossom of kind deeds.' I suppose the reason I remember it so plainly is because your mother told me the story again when I was here last summer, and she took me out to Bloomingdale with her to see Mrs. Meredith. Don't you remember our going out there, Gretta?"

"Y-yes, I think I do. Wasn't it the day of my class picnic up the river?"

"I believe it was. And I believe you know about Mrs. Meredith, too, don't you—the blind lady who has been out West for 10 or 12 years and who lost her husband, all her children, and nearly all the money she had, and then she lost even her eyesight? There's a brother who supports her, and he wanted her to come and live with his family, but she said she would rather go back to her own little cottage, where she knew her way around in the dark; so he pays a woman to look after her there. The day your mother and I went to see her, the lilacs were all in bloom, and she was sitting in the doorway, smiling to herself because she could enjoy their fragrance, even though she couldn't see them. Don't you remember her now?"

"Well, I knew there was a blind Mrs. Meredith and that Mother used to go to see her, but she was one of so many that Mother visited! I had forgotten that the amaryllis had anything to do with her."

"Mrs. Meredith wasn't 'one of many.' I should almost think your mother would have taken you out there with her sometime."

A look of painful remembrance crossed Gretta's face. "I think she did ask me to go there with her and sing for Mrs. Meredith one day last fall," she confessed, "but I had something else on hand. I was always so taken up with school and my own affairs that I didn't have any time for Mother's plans. I never tried to help her, Aunt Elsie. I was just selfish. That's why I can't bear it now! I can't bear it—I can't!"

Aunt Elsie said nothing, but sat looking at Gretta, waiting for the gust of sorrow to spend itself. She was hoping for something—and it came.

Gretta suddenly lifted her tearstained face. "I want to go out to Bloomingdale and see Mrs. Meredith this afternoon!" she exclaimed. "Why can't I, Aunt Elsie?"

"No reason in the world. The new trolley line takes you close to her cottage. And I'll put up a basket of fruit and good things, if you're really going, dear."

"I am going," decided Gretta, with a new look on her listless face.

She found the lilac hedge on each side of the path leading from the gate to the cottage, just as Aunt Elsie had pictured it, except that the blossoms had not come yet, and when she was admitted to the cottage sitting room, she found the little blind woman, with her hands folded on her white apron. There was an anxious look on her face at the sound of the strange footsteps, but that faded as soon as Gretta spoke her name.

"Why! It's the singing girl, isn't it?" she asked, searching the doorway with sightless eyes; and then, as Gretta came close and told her who she was, the old lady gave a cry of joy.

"Ah! Kneel down by me, dear! Come close," she begged. "Let me pat your cheeks—they're pink, I know they are! And your hair—yes, take off the hat, so . . . your braids are soft and smooth, just like the mother's! Ah, child, the world was black to my eyes before, but I could feel it grow blacker the day I heard that your dear mother had gone over before me!

"There, dear, your cheeks are wet! I should not have said that—it hurt you. You see, I'm so used to sitting here in the dark alone and thinking, thinking about the ones who are gone, that I don't realize how it seems to the young. Don't cry, dear! Listen. Did you notice how I asked, when you came in, if you were the singing girl?

"I'm afraid you'll think I'm a strange old woman, but really, you know, there isn't any singing girl at all. She's just a little dream that I comfort myself with, and when I'm alone here, I fancy she comes in and takes me by the hand, and leads me into my parlor there, and puts me in the armchair, and opens the old piano, and sings and sings—just as your mother always did when she came. And—do you know, deary, it was because your voice seemed like your mother's, only younger, that I thought for a minute my singing girl had come true? Now do you think I'm a foolish old woman?"

Gretta's tears had stopped falling as she listened to the story of the "singing girl," and when it ended, she surprised herself by saying, "Shall we go into your parlor, Mrs. Meredith, and may I sing to you—for Mother?"

"Oh deary, *could* you?" came the answer in a flutter of delight, and a moment later they were on their way across the room, the weak, little old woman leaning for strength on Gretta's arm as they entered the old-fashioned parlor with its gaily flowered velvet carpet, long French windows, and rows of family portraits.

The young girl had a strange feeling that it was someone not herself who opened the lid of the square piano and touched its tinkling keys. It seemed to be another voice—not hers—that rang out sweetly in the dim, old room. First she sang some tender little songs of summertime and the outdoors. Then, before she realized that it was coming, she heard from her own lips the melody of the little Easter song that her mother had loved.

Softly, the words began:

> If some hand is quite still
> That we have loved and kept in ours until
> It grew so cold;
> If all it held hath fallen from its hold,
> And it can do
> No more, perhaps there are a few

Small threads that it held fast
Until the last,
That we can gather up and weave along
With patience strong
In love.

If we bend close to see
Just what the threads may be
Which filled the quiet hands,
Perhaps some strands
So golden, or so strong, may lie there still
That we our empty hands may fill
And even yet
Smile though our eyes be wet.

Then came a change in the music—a refrain of Easter gladness—and as Gretta's voice filled the room, she suddenly felt her own heart thrilling with its joy.

A sound made her turn. There, halfway across the floor, stood the little blind woman, with arms outstretched, groping her way toward the singer.

As Gretta sprang to help her, the wavering arms closed around her neck, and Mrs. Meredith cried, "Oh deary, you don't know what you've done for a lonesome old heart! You don't know what you've done! First you sang me roses and lilacs. I could feel them against my face and smell their sweetness—and *then* you sang me an Easter lily, and I saw it! Child, child—God sent you here!"

And Gretta kissed the old face over and over as she whispered, "Yes, He sent me. And I'll come again. I'll—I'll be your singing girl!"

When Gretta left the car on her way home and started up the street to the parsonage, she saw her father a little ahead of her. There was a tired droop about his figure, and for the first time she thought with a pang that he was growing old. Hurrying to catch him, she slipped a hand through his arm.

"Father, I've been out to see Mother's friend Mrs. Meredith this afternoon, and while I was there, I found out that I haven't lost my chance—I mean that I can do things for Mother yet. And, Father, I've found out that I *can* sing. I'll sing for you tomorrow, if it will help."

They had reached the parsonage door, and he turned and looked at her searchingly. "It would be too hard. You would break down."

"No, I'll not break down."

Another straight gaze into her eyes. They met his bravely, and to his unspeakable comfort, he saw them reflecting the clear courage of his own.

"Thank you, my child," he said, bending to kiss her. "It will help. The song is part of my sermon."

The next morning in church a slender girl in a white dress stood up among the Easter lilies and sang. It was not a great voice, but sweet, and it went to the hearts of all who heard.

Its spirit of Easter gladness was still glowing in the pastor's face as he came forward and began to speak to his people. Gretta had never heard her father preach like this. Eloquent, tender, courageous, he stood there, the embodiment of a living Hope, and his listeners forgot all sorrow in the beautiful inspiration of his message.

The service was over. One by one the friends who had pressed forward to clasp his hand in thankfulness had gone away, and at last, in the tender hush of the old church, with the fragrance of flowers all about them, the father turned to his child.

"Daughter," he said, "your song gave me strength to speak."

"Oh Father," she answered, her eyes shining with joy, "not *my* song! It was *Mother's.*"

In an Artist's Studio

Author Unknown

This is the story of a great artist, a lovely gypsy girl, and a powerful painting of Christ's love.

Years ago a painter stood in his studio, his right thumb to the belt of his blouse and his left hand holding the pipe he had withdrawn from his lips, in honor of his visitor, Father Hugo, the vicar of the rich Church of St. Jerome. The artist, Stenburg, had not yet reached middle age. He was famous in Düsseldorf, and some said that his name would someday be known worldwide. When that day came, Stenburg ruefully thought, he would be past the enjoyment of riches that tarried so long. He loved his art. Now and again he became so absorbed in his work that he forgot all else than the picture upon his easel. Still, though good work he had done, he had never satisfied himself, nor reached his own ideal. His was good work, but he desired something more. Thus Stenburg was not a satisfied man. Otherwise, to the world, he appeared a jolly, prosperous man, who displayed, on occasion, a shrewd business capacity and who knew his own interests well. He was speaking now.

"No, Reverend Father, the sum you offer would but ill repay me for the labor of so large an altar-piece as you honor me by naming. It must have many figures, all carefully studied. The crucifixion is not an easy subject, and it has been so often portrayed that it would be difficult to compose a picture different—as I should wish it to be—from others."

"I will not limit you to the price. You are an honest man, Sir Painter, and the Church of St. Jerome will not pay for the altar-piece. It is to be the gift of a penitent."

"So! That makes a difference. Return, Reverend Father, a month from today, and studies for the work shall be ready."

So they parted, both well pleased, and during the following weeks Stenburg studied the composition of the altar-piece and penetrated into the Jewish Strasse for models for his figures.

Father Hugo was satisfied. He desired the central point of the picture to be the cross of the Redeemer and left the grouping of the accessories to the artist. From time to time, the vicar dropped in to inspect the progress of the work.

With the bursting of the young green leaves and the upspringing of the first flowers, a hunger had seized upon the artist's soul to leave Düsseldorf and, with his sketchbook, wander over the surrounding country. On the borders of the forest he came one day upon a Gypsy girl plaiting straw baskets. Her face was beautiful; her coal-black hair fell in waving ripples to her waist; and her poor, tattered red dress, faded and sunburned to many hues, added to her picturesque appearance. But her eyes were the feature that caught the artist's regard—restless, limpid black eyes, whose expression changed every moment: Pain, joy, fun, and roguery were reflected in their depths as swiftly as the cloud shadows chase one another across a lake.

What a capital picture she would make! thought Stenburg. *But then, who would buy a Gypsy girl? No one!*

The Gypsies were looked upon in Düsseldorf with hatred, and even to this day the fact of being a Gypsy is, in the eyes of the law, a punishable offense.

The girl noticed the artist, and flinging her straw down, she sprang up. Raising her hands above her head and snapping her fingers to keep time, she danced lightly and gracefully before him, showing her white teeth, her glance sparkling with merriment.

"Stand!" cried Stenburg, and he rapidly sketched her.

Quickly though he drew, it was a weary position for the girl to maintain, but she never flinched. A sigh of relief as her arms dropped and she stood at rest before him attested to the artist the strain the attitude had been.

"She is not only beautiful, she is better—a capital model. I will paint her as a Spanish dancing-girl."

So a bargain was struck. Pepita was to come thrice a week to Stenburg's house to be painted. Duly at the appointed hour she arrived. She was full of wonder. Her great eyes roved around the studio, glancing on the pieces of armor, pottery, and carving. Presently, she began examining the pictures—and soon the great altar-piece, now nearing its completion, caught her attention. For days she gazed at it intently.

At last, in an awed voice, she asked, "Who is that?" pointing to the most prominent figure.

"The Christ," answered Stenburg carelessly.

"What is being done to him?"

"Being crucified," exclaimed the artist. "Turn a little to the right. There! That will do."

Stenburg, with his brush in his fingers, was a man of few words.

"Who are those people about him—those with the bad faces?"

"Now, look here," said the artist, "I cannot talk to you. You have nothing to do but stand as I tell you."

The girl did not dare speak again, but she continued to gaze and speculate. Every time she came to the studio, the fascination of the picture grew upon her. Sometimes she ventured an inquiry, for her curiosity consumed her.

"Why did they crucify him? Was he bad, very bad?"

"No, very good."

That was all she learned at one interview, but she treasured each word—and every sentence was so much more known of the mystery.

"Then if he was good, why did they do so? Was it for a short time only? Did they let him go?"

"It was because—" The artist paused with his head on one side, then stepped forward and arranged her sash.

"Because—" repeated Pepita breathlessly.

The artist went back to his easel; then looking at her, the eager, questioning face moved his pity.

"Listen. I will tell you once and for all, and then ask no further questions."

And he told her the story of the cross—new to Pepita, though so old to the artist that it had ceased to touch him. He could paint that dying agony, and not a nerve of his quivered; but just the thought of it wrung her heart. Her great black eyes swam in tears, which the fiery Gypsy pride forbade to fall.

The altar-piece and the Spanish dancing-girl were finished simultaneously. Pepita's last visit to the studio had come. She looked upon the beautiful representation of herself without emotion. Then she turned and stood before the altar-piece, unable to leave it.

"Come," said the artist, "here is your money and a gold piece over and above, for you have brought me good luck. 'Dancing Girl' is already sold. I shall want you sometime perhaps again, but we must not overstock the market with even your pretty face."

The girl turned slowly.

"Thanks, Signor!" But her eyes, full of emotion, were solemn. "You must love Him *very* much, Signor, when He has done *all that for you*, do you not?"

The face into which she looked flushed crimson. The artist was ashamed. The girl, in her poor, faded dress, passed from his studio, but her plaintive words rang in his heart. He tried to forget them, but it proved impossible. He hastened to send the picture to its destination; still he could not forget "*. . . all that for you.*"

At last the pain was not to be borne. He would face it and conquer it. He went to confession: Father Hugo questioned Stenburg. He believed all the doctrines of the church. So the vicar gave him absolution and assured him that "all was well." The artist allowed a liberal discount on his altar-piece, and for a week or two felt at ease. But then up rose the old question, "You must love Him very much, do you not?" and *would* be answered. He grew restless and could not settle to his work. So wandering about, he heard of things that had not come under his notice before.

One day he saw a group of persons hastening to a house near the walls, a poor place, and then he noticed others coming in the opposite direction, and they, too, passed into its low doorway. He asked what was happening there, but the man he questioned could not satisfy him. This aroused his curiosity.

A few days later he learned that a stranger, one of the "Reformed," lived there—one of those despised men who appealed on every occasion to the Word of God. It was hardly respectable, hardly safe, even to know them. Yet perhaps here he might find that which he sought. They might possess the secret of peace. So Stenburg went to observe, perhaps to inquire, certainly not to join them; but a man cannot approach fire and remain cold. This Reformed preacher spoke and looked as one who was walking the earth with Christ—yes, one to whom He was all. Stenburg found what he longed for: *a living faith*. His new friend lent him for a time a precious copy of the New Testament, but hunted from Düsseldorf after a few weeks, he left and had to take the book with him; but its essence remained in Stenburg's heart.

Ah! No need to question now. He felt in his soul the fire of an ardent love. "Did all that for me! How can I ever tell men of that love, that boundless love, which can brighten their lives as it has mine? It is for them, too, but they do not see it, as I did not. How can I preach it? I cannot speak. I am a man of few words. If I were to try, I could never speak it out. It burns in my heart, but I cannot express it—*the love of Christ!*"

So thinking, the artist idly drew with a piece of charcoal in his fingers a rough sketch of a thorn-crowned head. His eyes grew moist as he did so. Suddenly, the thought flashed through his soul: *I can paint! My brush must proclaim it. Ah! In that altar-piece His face was all agony. But that was not the truth. Love unutterable! Infinite compassion! Willing sacrifice!*

The artist fell on his knees and prayed to paint worthily and thus speak.

And then he wrought. The fire of genius blazed up—up to the highest fiber of his power; nay, beyond it. The new picture of the crucifixion was a wonder, almost divine.

He would not sell it. He gave it as a freewill offering to his native city. It was hung in the public gallery, and there the citizens flocked to see it. Voices were hushed and hearts melted as they stood before it, and the burghers returned to their homes knowing the love of God and repeating to themselves the words written so distinctly beneath:

All this I did for thee;
What hast thou done for Me?

Stenburg also used to go there, and watching far back from a corner in the gallery the people who gathered about the picture, he prayed God to bless his painted sermon. One day he observed, when the rest of the visitors had left, a poor girl standing and weeping bitterly before it. The artist approached her.

"What grieves thee, child?" he asked.

The girl turned; she was Pepita. "Oh, Signor, if He had but loved *me* so," she said, pointing to the face of yearning love bending above them. "I am only a poor Gypsy. For *you* is the love, but not for such as I." Her despairing tears fell unrestrained.

"Pepita, it was also all for *thee.*" And then the artist told her all.

Until the late hour at which the gallery closed, they sat and talked. The painter did not weary now of answering her questions, for the subject was the one he loved best. He told the girl the story of that wondrous life, magnificent death, and crowning glory of resurrection and also explained to her the union that redeeming love effected. She listened, received, and believed His words: *"All this I did for thee."*

Years after, when both the painter and the Gypsy girl had gone to rest, a merry young nobleman drove in his splendid equipage into Düsseldorf, and while his horses were baited [fed and watered], he wandered into that famous gallery. He was rich, young, intelligent. The world was bright, and its treasures within his grasp. He stood, arrested, before Stenburg's picture.

He read and reread the legend on the frame. He could not tear himself away—it grew into his heart. The love of Christ laid its powerful grasp on his soul. Hours passed; the light faded. The curator touched the weeping nobleman and told him it was time to close the gallery. Night had come— nay, rather for that young man, the dawn of eternal life! He returned to the inn and reentered his carriage. He turned his back on Paris and sought again his home. But from that moment, he threw life, fortune, and fame at the feet of Him who had whispered to his heart:

> All this I did for thee;
> What hast thou done for Me?

This young nobleman was Zinzendorf, the father of the Moravian Missions, who answered that question by his devoted life and his welcomed death.

Stenburg's picture no longer hangs in the gallery of Düsseldorf, for when, some years ago, the gallery was destroyed by fire, it perished; but it preached, and God used it to tell of His gift—Calvary's Substitute—of whom Paul said, "Who loved me, and gave Himself for me."

Can you, reader, say, "And for me"?

Hero in Feathers

Ella A. Duncan

Little did they know what a courageous heart beat in the little ball of quacking fluff left on their doorstep one spring morning.

When the doorbell rang that spring morning, two-year-old Susie found a small duck nestled in a basket on the front step. It was just a round, yellow ball of fluff with two black, shiny beads for eyes and a curious ebony bill that went poking about constantly into everything. It had always seemed extremely cruel to give children such small, helpless beings; too many such defenseless creatures are tortured to slow death. Surely Susie would be no exception among children. John declared emphatically that the bit of down would be nothing but a nuisance; it was to be taken to the pet shop the next morning.

Then came the ordeal of separating one small, unreasoning being from another. From the moment she found him, all of Susie's other

117

interests had been discarded for the tiny bit of quacking life. She was ecstatic when the duckling scrambled from his basket and waddled at her heels about the room. I tried to explain that he was just a baby duck and must go to his mother, but when I put him in a box on the back porch, Susie's howls from the front porch and the duck's clatter rent the air. We had to relent, but, of course, only temporarily.

Surprisingly, the little girl was gentle with the soft, fragile body of the duckling. As for him, from the very beginning there was no one else in the house but Susie. When she walked, he waddled at her heels; when she ran, he rolled over and over like an animated yellow tumbleweed, trying to keep up with her and protesting such speed in high, hysterical quackings.

Susie spent hours, that first day, showing the birdlet her possessions. As the little girl displayed storybooks and blocks, the small duck nestled by her side, quacking contentedly. In her eagerness to make him understand, she bent her head to his level, chattering earnestly. In response, the yellow neck would stretch up and the beady eyes sparkle while the little duck talked in his own baby language. I have always thought that there is some canny or uncanny understanding between the young of the earth, something sadly impossible between adult animals. Watching the little blonde girl and the baby duck, I was sure that there was not only a sort of spiritual blending, but also a definite mutual understanding of language. There was no doubt of it in the weeks and months that followed.

Within the first hour Susie named the duck. She chose "Waddles," truly an appropriate name for an embryo hero. But I anticipate.

It was raining the next morning, so it was easy to grant Waddles a day of reprieve. I think we knew then that he would never see the inside of a pet shop. Each morning after that we made feeble excuses for not sending him, until finally John exclaimed over his coffee, "Let's keep the little fellow. It would break Susie's heart to take him away now. Besides, I sort of like him myself," he finished sheepishly.

At last Susie had a playmate—her first. There being no children her own age near us, she had been alone among adults all her short months on earth. There had been no name in Waddles' basket, so we never knew where he came from. I am sure, however, some friend much older and wiser than we must have brought him—someone who knew that everything on earth longs for something its own age, something with which to share like experiences and joys. To Susie and Waddles, everything on earth was still shiny-new and wonderful beyond belief—things for exploring and exclaiming.

Together that summer in the high-fenced backyard, daughter and duck found a complete world of magic. To Ann, the maid, and to me, it was amazing how that funny little duck so quickly and completely took over what at times had been a real task for two adult human beings.

The two chased butterflies, built castles in the sandbox, played hide-and-seek among the shrubs and lawn furniture, or just sat in the sun and chattered about things beyond the ken of a grown-up world. There were hilarious games of their own invention, over which Susie went into spasms of laughter and Waddles quacked his glee in a voice that began to "change" as the summer wore on. His yellow down had given way to a thick coat of slate-gray feathers marked with black. Because we knew nothing of his ancestry, we had no way of knowing what his breed line might be. He grew to be larger than most ducks, however, and was a strong, handsome fellow as he waddled proudly about the yard, head and shoulders held high.

Waddles had been with us two years when Baby Carol came and Susie was ready for nursery school. We brought the baby home from the hospital in her bassinet, and Ann went to call the two playmates from the backyard. They stood silently, side by side, for a few seconds, studying the new red mite.

"Where are her teeth?" Susie wanted to know. But it was Waddles that surprised us most. Except for his various degrees of quacking, he had never made any other sound. Now he suddenly beat his great wings against his sides, let out a trumpeting honk, and sat down purposefully beside the bassinet. We did not know it then, but with that wild, foreign cry, Waddles was proclaiming to the world that he was at last an adult. On his shoulders had descended the grave responsibility of guard for a new, helpless being.

It was amusing, at first, to see the big duck there beside the bassinet, his neck held stiff and high, his keen black eyes darting in search of danger. Worn out from play with Susie, he had usually gone willingly to his box on the back porch. That night John had to pick him up and carry him—protesting and hissing—outside.

Early the next morning Waddles was at the back door, quacking urgently to be let in. After breakfast, to get rid of his infernal noise, I sent Susie out to play with him. Soon she was back.

"He won't play with me anymore!" she wailed.

"It's the truth," said Ann. "He just ignored her."

I was torn with sympathy for my eldest daughter in this first tragedy of life, and she was utterly bewildered by it. But before the week was over, a little boy and a little girl, near her age, moved into the neighborhood. Then came the glorious experience of nursery school—and Susie was no longer a baby.

As for Waddles, it finally seeped through his small duck brain that the only time his guarding act was necessary was when Baby Carol was put in the backyard for her sunbath. The rest of the day he waddled majestically about the yard, muttering philosophically to himself, or sat in the sun and brooded contentedly. The only time he resembled his former animated self was when the time for the sun bath drew near. He was always at the back door, waiting. If Ann or I were late getting Baby Carol out, Waddles set up a demanding clatter. In a restrained frenzy of excitement, he would waddle beside the carriage until it was stopped. Then, always facing the house, he settled beneath it, every inch of his body at trained attention.

Once more, I was having reason to give thanks for Waddles as an aid to child-rearing. It was impossible to teach Susie and her newfound friends to close the back gate as they should, but as long as Waddles was around, neither man nor beast could come near his baby. The dogs and cats of the neighborhood soon learned to avoid that gate. Even the milkman asked if he might leave the milk at the front each morning, rather than battle the big duck.

It was Waddles himself I worried about at first. I was afraid he might get out and wander off, or be run over in the street. After the second venture up the driveway to the front of the house, however, he evidently decided that the outside world held little of interest for him. He returned to his big backyard and never again left it. It was his kingdom, and woe betide the trespasser!

It was that very vigilance, however, that nearly caused his banishment; I shudder yet to think how very near we came to disposing of him.

Because of an illness, Ann had to leave us, and a new girl was employed in her place. The first morning that she took the baby outside, Waddles flew at her in a veritable fury of beating wings, snapping beak, and clawing web feet. Before I could come to the rescue, he had ruined the girl's hose and left her legs bruised and bleeding. In shock and anger, she quit. Two others followed in quick succession. It was impossible for them to avoid the backyard entirely. It was even more impossible to convince Waddles that they were to become a part of the family. Up until then, he seemed to have had an uncanny instinct for doing as he should. We had never punished him, and I had no idea how to go about it now. The only solution seemed to be exile.

Then—miracle of miracles—Ann came back. All was peace in the backyard once again. I was thankful for that and for her help. A plague of rabies had broken out among the dogs of the town, and Ann would guard the children as no strange girl could be expected to do. Still, we mothers lived in a nightmare of dread. We tried to cooperate in keeping the youngsters entertained, but it was difficult to restrain them.

One morning when there was no school, I had all the youngsters for a morning picnic. After the picnic Ann herded them into the house, to get them ready for the moving pictures we were going to show. I took Baby Carol to the backyard for her belated nap. Making sure that the gate was closed and Waddles settled in his usual fighting stance beneath the carriage, I went back into the house.

The phone rang. A friend down the street said, "I just saw a dog turn into your driveway, and if I know a mad dog, that one is."

Every time a stray dog had been seen in the neighborhood for weeks, everyone was sure it had rabies. Nevertheless, prickles of fright were breaking out along my spine. Then I thought, *The back gate! One of the children might have gone back for something.*

On legs that threatened to buckle, I started for the yard. Before I was halfway through the house, for the second time in his life came that high, wild honk . . . and I *knew!*

Screaming for Ann, I burst through the back door upon a scene that will remain with me the rest of my days. Not three yards from the baby was a misshapen, shaggy dog with a swollen head, red, unfocused eyes, and dripping mouth. Flying to meet him was Waddles, wings outspread and neck stretched forth, ebony beak snapping and cracking like a small, angry machine gun. I knew that Ann was close behind me with the broom; then I lost sight of everything, except the desire to gather my baby in my arms and race for safety.

Somehow I made it, with Ann and her broom as flanking support. She slammed the back door behind us and ran to call the police. Too weak and paralyzed with fear to move, I leaned against the closed door and listened to the uncanny battle outside. The blood-chilling growls and muttered barks of the mad dog told me that Waddles was doing his best, but I knew that his best was not going to be enough this time. I was too frightened to look, but from the sounds coming through the opened windows, the shaggy dog and the big duck were fighting all over the backyard. Their bodies bumped and threshed against the side of the house and porch; then, except for the slapping of Waddles' big wings, the snapping of his beak, and the duller sound of the dog's jaws, the fight would dim out. Waddles' first squawk of pain brought me to with the frenzied urge to do something.

"I can't just let him stay out there and fight alone when he doesn't have a chance!" I told Ann desperately.

"You certainly can't go out there and fight that mad dog bare-handed. Think of the children," she declared.

There was not a gun in the house, and the police could not possibly get there in time. I prayed that Waddles would somehow realize his danger and fly up on something out of reach before it was too late. But all the time I knew he would not. His stout little heart simply would not let him stop fighting until his enemy was driven from that yard. This time, however, his opponent lacked sense enough to flee, no matter what the punishment.

The pain-filled squawks and barks gradually lessened, as did the sound of the fight, until once again, all was quiet in the backyard. It was an ominous, deadly quiet, and through it Ann and I clung together until the police came.

There was a muffled shot out back, then one of the officers came to the door. "I want you to see a sight you will never see again," he said.

The backyard was a shambles. Chairs had been upset. Flowers and shrubs were beaten down. Baby Carol's carriage had been overturned, and criss-crossing the sandbox, which had once held so much happiness for a small blonde girl and a little duck, were dark red stains. In the open gateway, a wing tip touching the fence on either side, lay Waddles—his broken neck outstretched and ebony beak turned scarlet. Just beyond him, in the drive-way, lay the body of the great yellow dog.

"I don't think the bullet was necessary," said the second officer, still absent-mindedly holding his gun and looking with wonder at the mutilated head of the dog.

Somehow Waddles had managed to hold out until he drove his last enemy from the little plot of earth he held sacred and dear above all others. Some inborn instinct from his wild, dim past must have warned him that this mad invader meant death and destruction to everything he loved, and, like heroes the world over, he gave his life to preserve his little world and the happy way of life within it.

There were no medals or citations for Waddles—only a small grave in the corner of the yard he loved so well and the deep, undying devotion in the human hearts that knew him.

Influence Unawares

Frances Greenman

This is a story about a pothole-riddled road, a country dinner, and the many guises influence can take.

"I calculate," said Pa Dallas, "that the commissioners ain't asking odds of no one. Goodness knows both roads are far from good, and there's not a mite of use to try to make them decide on our west road. I feel it in my bones they're going to pick the east route."

Pouring two buckets of foaming milk into a big pan in the milk house, he looked inquiringly at his wife.

Ma Dallas took her time to finish the skimming; she plunged the skimmer into a pail of water and hung it on its own particular nail before she demanded, "Why?"

" 'Cause we don't know what sort of influence to bring to bear."

" 'Influence'—what a word! I'd think it would be dead from overwork. Why don't you menfolks *try!*"

"We can't think of anything to do," said Pa as he picked up his pails. "Billy Mix ain't one to ask nor take advice. Tom Hart's 'most as bad, and neither of 'em wants to be reelected. Besides, they've called in a highway engineer and a good-roads expert. I calculate we'll have to let matters take their course."

Mr. and Mrs. Jed Dallas had neither "chick nor child" of their own, but, like George Washington, they owned many children. To the whole countryside, they were Pa and Ma; their house door was the easiest one to swing open, and no one ever passed a dull hour within the four walls of the old farmstead.

Mrs. Dallas gazed speculatively through the open door of the milk house upon the flowering trees and the sheen of spring grasses. A lilac bush beside the door swayed in the morning breezes, pigeons fluttered from the barn roof, and Good Fellow, the best churn dog in Pretty Meadow township, thumped his tail on the wide stone step.

"Your turn's coming," said Ma. "I'm going to start you churning right off. You can 'influence' the machinery, and the machinery'll 'influence' the churn, and the churn'll 'influence' the cream, and—" Ma Dallas laughed.

She was 60-odd years old and, in spite of her weight, as spry as a girl. All the countryside loved Ma Dallas and the butter she made. The proprietor of the Great Eastern Emporium at the county seat paid his highest price for the firm golden balls with a deer stamped neatly on each one.

"Only fault I find with your butter, Ma," he told her, "is you don't bring in enough."

"I'd come oftener, Mr. Swift, if it wasn't for the road. There are forty-'leven kinds of bumps and hollows in it. I'll own I'm considerable upset by the time I reach your store."

Ma lingered awhile in the milk house that morning. Everyone who came to the farm said the milk house was the *"nicest* place." A cool little brook rippled among the stones; big pans, "four-foot square," stood on iron legs at a convenient height for Ma and Clarissy Ann to skim the lakes of milk topped with yellow cream. The lattice windows were wreathed in vines; shining tins and implements ornamented the walls; and on a shelf was a row of steins with Delft-blue boys and girls and cats chasing around and around them. Outside, a big cottonwood whispered, and in the friendly shade of the tree, Good Fellow paced around and around, "influencing" the butter to "come."

While I'd love to have the paved road past our place, I've got no time to worry this morning, Ma said to herself. *Sugar cookies and bread to mix and a pot of beans to look after! Mercy, I'd better be flaxing [move more quickly] around a bit swifter!*

When Ma reached the kitchen, Clarissy Ann was just hanging up the dish pan.

"Aunt Dell," began Clarissy, "Uncle Jed ventures the commissioners'll pick the east road. My, what wouldn't it mean to us west-roaders to have a decent highway clear to town! I wish we had some influence."

"Run down to the cellar, Clarissy, and 'influence' the lard and that dish of berries to come up into the kitchen."

"But don't you care about our getting the paved road, Aunt Dell?" wailed pretty Clarissy.

"You know well's I do, child, how I'm all but jounced to a jelly after a trip to town. However, I'm real busy now, thinking about 'influence.' "

While Ma made cookie dough, she pondered her subject. She got out the crimp-edged cookie cutter and began to make circles in the sugar-sprinkled dough on the molding board.

"Let's see," she mused, "I spanked Ted McCool once when I caught him in my May cherry tree, and now he's real important—a highway engineer, been called on to go over both roads and advise the commissioners. Now I'll wager—"

What she would wager she did not say, for the dining-room door opened, and a tall, thin woman with a silk bag on her arm came into the kitchen.

"Why, Mittie Brewster!"

"I knocked at every door, Ma. I told Henry I'd rather sit a spell with you than look at the best Duroc ever penned. Henry's daft on pigs. He's gone over to Charley Stetson's to try to buy another."

Mrs. Dallas plumped up the cushion in the calico rocker by the morning-glory window. "I'm glad you did, Mittie, but I'm right in the midst of cookies."

"Go on, Ma. You know I can tat and talk same as you can bake and talk. My, you sure own the homiest kitchen in the country! I tell folks if I was collecting kitchens, like we used to collect buttons, I'd have yours on my charm string sure."

Ma laughed and tested the temperature of the oven with her hand before sliding in a pan of cookies. "It's just a pot or so of geraniums and cheerful paint, Mittie."

The visitor shook her head. "Your kitchen has a soul, Ma. I suppose you have heard the commissioners are going over our road Saturday. They have a Mr. Paul, a good-roads expert, down from the city."

"Better get a bad-roads expert," said Ma dryly. "If anyone can show two worse roads than the east and west ones our commissioners are inspecting, I don't want to view 'em. There's not one reason why we shouldn't get the paving on our road, nor, so far as I know, why the east road shouldn't neither."

"Every time it rains, I tell Henry I'd about as soon be tossed up in a blanket as to go to town over our road. Sam Sprout's going to be a widower one of these days, it takes so long to get a doctor when Mary has those spells. On a smooth road, Doc Kilroy could make it in a quarter of the time. Think what a good road would mean to us all."

Ma placed a plate of cookies on the broad window ledge near her guest, rested her hands on her hips, and surveyed the woman in the rocker. "I'm real pillowy, Mittie," she said, "but I own feelings, especially when I'm trying to reach town with my butter and my disposition in the same condition they were when I left home."

Mittie Brewster held forth on roads until a long call from an auto horn broke the quiet of the morning.

"That's Henry!" she exclaimed. "I got to go. Ma, if you can think of one thing to do . . . You use your influence."

The rest of the day Mrs. Dallas reflected on "influence." "Haunts me like a composition subject!" she murmured. "Now, I wonder what sort of a man this good-roads expert is."

A whiff of mingled odors from the kitchen came to Ma as she rested in a comfortable rocking chair in the living room. There were fresh bread and baked beans; a large pot of "good luck" simmering for supper on the back of the range added its pleasant aroma.

Ma was putting a plate of Sally Lunn bread on the table when an idea came to her. Hastily crossing to the telephone, she called a number.

"That you, Mr. Thorp? You acquainted with Mr. Paul? Yes, the good-roads expert. What sort is he? No, no, I suppose he is honest. City man? Lived on a farm when a boy. Oh! What? Friend of Ted McCool's? Sho! I don't even know him. A little rheumatic! We all are. Thank you."

All during supper, Peter and Clarissy talked about the road.

"It won't do a mite of good to try to influence men like Billy Mix and Tom Hart," said Pa.

"Jed," asked Ma, passing around dishes of strawberries, "just what do you mean by 'influence'?"

"Oh, sort of talk 'em over. You know I'm no elocutor, Ma. I can't."

"I wouldn't try, then," said Ma cheerfully.

That evening Ma Dallas's mind reverted to a long-gone year when she had spanked a very little boy for eating cherries. *It seems dreadful now,* she told herself. *I never see a cherry to this day but I also see that youngster's brown eyes that looked at me so reproachful. I was ashamed right off. If he hadn't broken a limb from my best tree, I don't suppose I'd have touched him. My, how he put for home! Kept looking back as if I was going to chase after him. Left his hat and never did come back for it.*

Ma laughed softly. Her memory, like her butter, was excellent. She continued to rock and to "visit" with herself. *Ever since I heard Ted had come back, I've wanted to make some sort of reparation, though I don't have any notion he's one to harbor grudges. I've 'most a mind to do it. I've an idea he's a real lovable chap, and I'd like to see him again. I believe that little straw hat of his is up in the garret this very minute, and I'll ask him to come get his hat.*

Getting paper and pen and ink, Ma wrote a letter. As she put on the stamp, she said aloud, "I'll not try to use one mite of 'influence,' either. There shan't be a word said about roads, not one word." She sighed as she pushed up her spectacles. "Seems sad when my body can only live once in the world that it has to ride over the sort of road it does; but we 'lected Tom Hart and Billy Mix, and now we'll have to abide by their decision. I've thought all day, and I don't get any nearer 'influence' than I was this morning. I'll lay it away in lavender, that road, and tend to the business of making it up to Ted McCool."

In two days the mail carrier on R.D. 4 left a letter for Mrs. J. Dallas. Every line of her face expressed satisfaction as she read it.

I'm not so sorry I spanked him now, she said to herself. *No, I'm not sorry at all.*

"Folks," announced Ma as she poured coffee at the foot of the dinner table, "day after tomorrow we get company for dinner."

"*We* do!" Clarissy held a plate of raised biscuits aloft. "Who?"

"Never you mind," said her aunt. "A friend or so of mine. I want every one of you to bridle your tongues all the time they are here. I don't want one word said about roads, either foreign or domestic. No matter what comes up, or *who*, roads are to rest all day. And I'm considering killing John J. Pershing."

"Why, Aunt Dell!" Clarissy Ann set down the old blue plate so suddenly and violently that a biscuit bounded off and landed in the pickle dish.

"I thought," said Pa Dallas, "John J. was for Thanksgiving. Must be real special guests."

"Extra," agreed Ma.

The next morning there was assembled in the Dallas kitchen a wonderful assortment of "cookeries"—a term that Peter and Clarissy had coined for lard and flour, eggs and cream, and other wherewithals needful for the creations for which Ma was famous.

Clarissy ran down and up the cellar stairs until she felt like a squirrel. She creamed butter, beat eggs, and made six trips to the spring house. While on a flying visit to the barn for strictly fresh eggs, she confided to Peter that from indications the king of all the Belgians was to dine with them on the morrow. "But she's weakening on John J.; she says she doesn't want to overdo her reparation."

"Overdo *what!*" Peter laid down a monkey wrench and stared at his sister's flushed cheeks and tousled curls.

"I don't know, and if she'll only leave John J. alone, I don't care. He'll weigh a good 25 pounds by Thanksgiving."

"Beats me," said Peter. "There's a joker somewhere."

"It isn't like Aunt Dell to be so secretive, but I've got to hurry. I do need a pair of wings this day."

Later Ma ordered Peter to round up the three pullets that the Dominique had brought off so early.

"I was 'most provoked to anger," said she, "when that hen sprung her hatch on us—and snow still lingering in the hollows and under hedges. But now I can see *why* they shelled out so early; they're prime fries right now. After all's said, a platter of crusty spring chickens with mashed potatoes and cream gravy is hard to beat. But I'm some unsteady in my mind whether it is steamed brown bread or plain johnnycake I'll need; one hot bread's enough along with fresh salt risin's."

"Let's make ice cream," coaxed Clarissy.

"No, Clarissy, ice cream is just fixings. I'm going to serve victuals—apple dumplings and cherry pie."

"Shall I dress up," asked Clarissy, "and must Peter wear a stiff collar?"

"Mercy to me, why? If there is one thing I want tomorrow, it is for us all to be natural and casual. If it's the least bit chillsome, Peter, you build a scrap of a fire on the living-room hearth, 'long 'bout half past eleven. A fire on a hearth, even when it's not real necessary, is cheerful as a robin. You know the kind I mean, Peter—not hot but heartening. Clarissy, you leave that braided rug right where it is and the candlesticks on the chimneypiece. I'm going to use the willow ware.

"I can see right into the back of your head, Clarissy," Ma Dallas went on. "You're going to ask me not to pour the coffee at the table and not to heap up platters. Now, Clarissy, this is *my* company. When you have *your* company, I've not a mite of objection to your dishing up to suit yourself and drinking coffee with the pie and interluding with a salad and so forth, but tomorrow we serve a bountiful country dinner in true country style. And no matter what happens, don't any of you act surprised—and pick me some 'laylocks' for bouquets."

The next day when a smart gray automobile drove into the farmyard about noon, Mr. Dallas, Peter, and Clarissy Ann were as curious as quails.

"Well, I do say!" exclaimed Peter as four men climbed out of the car. "If it isn't the commissioners!"

"Who are the other two?" asked Clarissy.

"I calculate," said their uncle, "that I better go right down to meet them—and find out."

Ma suddenly appeared in the doorway, enveloped in a very clean, very much starched gingham apron over her neat, sprigged calico dress. Ma looked "folksy," but not at all "companified."

"Now, I wonder what Ma's up to?" said Pa as he started down the steps.

"Remember," cautioned Clarissy, "not to be surprised even if it's a French general and an extra king. This is Aunt Dell's day, and we've got to mind."

In the farmhouse living room, the guests were aware that a cozy little fire flared on the hearth, that the lilacs filled the air with sweet fragrance, and that comfortable chairs, braided rugs, and sunny windows made a welcome resting place for weary travelers who had been riding over a rough road since early morning.

The good-roads expert settled himself in a padded chair near the fireplace. Young Ted McCool made conversation. He was full of reminiscences of the days when his family had lived on the Dickey place and when Ma had chastised him. Finally, he slipped out to the kitchen and frankly confided to his hostess that Paul and he were as hungry as 17-year locusts.

"I bet my new spring hat, Ma Dallas, that it would be fried chicken. Who wins?"

"You do this time, son. And now you carry it in and put it by Pa's chair."

"You're going to give us all we want? You're not going to serve it hotel style?"

"Hotel style!" Ma exclaimed with derision in her voice.

With a grin of delight, the famished engineer bore in the heaping platter. When the good-roads expert passed his plate for "more," humorously admitting that in the matter of fried chicken and gravy he was a direct descendant of Oliver Twist, Ma felt that her dinner was successful.

The commissioners were astonished that roads were not a topic of conversation. They were fully persuaded, however, that no one except the two experts they had hired could exert a bit of influence. Thinking how kind Ma Dallas had been to invite young Ted McCool to dinner and to bring with him any friends he wished, they showed their gratitude in a way that pleased Ma.

It takes her *to cook a round dinner,* thought Pa Dallas. *Some women make a meal too square. I hope Mr. Paul can swim, for he's liable to drown himself in cream if he don't watch out.*

The day was older by three hours when the gray automobile passed through the big gate. As the car neared the county-seat town, Billy Mix, at the wheel, called to the two men in the tonneau, "Well, which road are you for? You have seen both."

"That was a rattling good dinner we ate at Dallas's," remarked Mr. Tom Hart, "and she told us the latchstring was out whenever we happened along."

"We'll have to go out that west road to inspect the work from time to time—if we choose that road," said Ted McCool.

"Considering that one road is about as bad as the other," said the good-roads expert, "why, I vote west. I thought such a dinner had vanished along with my boyhood."

"I'd just as lief decide on the west road," said Billy Mix.

In the late afternoon, a young man was diligently searching through the postcard rack in a variety store while he softly whistled, "Can she make a cherry pie, Billy Boy, Billy Boy."

The next day Ma Dallas found a postcard in her mailbox; there was a picture of a fine bunch of cherries on one side, and on the other, beside the address, was a message written in lead pencil.

"Mercy me!" said Ma as she read it. "My dinner won us the road!"

She sat down very suddenly upon a bench by the flowering-almond bushes; a bewildered expression crossed her round, plump face. "Now I'm some surprised! I never had a notion of serving any 'influence'—just a good country dinner."

The old Dominique that had furnished the pièce de résistance for the meal of yesterday came walking by, holding her head pertly on one side.

"Chick'-biddy," said Ma softly, "chick'-biddy, I calculate I'll adorn you with a name. I calculate hereafter I'll call you 'Influence.'"

The Hardest Lesson

Fulton Oursler

When Frank Dudley checked into a Boston hotel, he never dreamed that three short telephone calls would change his life forever.

Some psychologists believe that character is fixed in childhood and can never be changed. But my friend Dr. Edwin declares that any man who wants to can change himself at any age—if he has the courage. To illustrate, he tells about Frank Dudley.

Dudley, born poor, put himself and his younger brother through college. Then, on sheer nerve, he formed his own advertising agency in New York and earned a modest fortune. One day Dudley checked in at a Boston hotel, never dreaming that three brief telephone calls were about to change his life.

First he called his brother's home and asked his sister-in-law, Agnes, if she and his brother could have dinner with him.

"No, thanks," Agnes said briskly. "Eddie has a business appointment tonight, and I'm going to be busy, too. When he calls, though, I'll tell him to give you a ring."

Was there a faintly acrid undertone in her voice? Shrugging off the suspicion, Dudley called an old college friend and asked him to join him at dinner.

His friend's answer made Dudley reel: "We're going to the party Eddie and Agnes are giving tonight. I'll see you there!"

Bewildered, Dudley had scarcely replaced the receiver when the telephone rang.

"Frank? This is Eddie. How are you? Sorry I'm tied up tonight. How about lunch tomorrow?"

Scarcely knowing what he said, the older man mumbled assent.

Since high school days, when both of their parents had died, Frank had been father and brother to Eddie. Naturally, they had not been so close since Eddie's marriage. But never once had the older brother betrayed his disappointment in the match. Agnes could never be an intellectual companion for Eddie, who was a scholar, a teacher of history. Nevertheless, Frank had always treated his sister-in-law with tender gusto.

Why had they lied to him? After a sleepless night, he drove to his brother's house.

When Agnes opened the door, he blurted out, "Why didn't you and Eddie invite me last night?"

"Frank, I'm terribly sorry. Eddie wanted to ask you, but I told him I'd rather not have the party. You'd have ruined everything."

"How can you say such a thing?"

"Because it's true, Frank. Why do you suppose we came to Boston except to get away by ourselves? You hurt Eddie every time you come around. You're the big, successful man who has to impress everybody. You top everything Eddie says, every opinion he expresses, every story he tries to tell; you

contradict him and make him look foolish. Well, last night the president of the college was coming to dinner. We hope Eddie's going to be promoted. Why should you take the spotlight and spoil everything? That's why I put my foot down. I've always known what you really think of me. But there's one thing I can tell you: I try to make Eddie happy, and that's more than you ever do!"

"I'm not like that at all," Dudley cried.

"Aren't you, though?" Agnes said miserably. "You ought to get wise to yourself."

Eventually, Dudley appeared in the office of his friend Dr. Edwin.

"I can't get this thing out of my mind, and I can't decide what to do," said Dudley. "That woman is my mortal enemy. I won't let her separate Eddie and me. There must be a solution."

Dr. Edwin looked at his friend. "There is," he declared flatly. "But you won't like it. Your sister-in-law gave you the best possible advice when she told you to get wise to yourself. Like everybody else, you are not one person but three: the man you think you are, the man other people think you are—and the man you really are.

Generally, the last one is the man nobody knows. Why not make his acquaintance? It may change your whole life."

A haunted look settled on Dudley's troubled face. "How do I start?" he asked finally.

"Why don't you play the game I call spiritual solitaire?" the doctor suggested. "Listen to yourself. Weigh your thoughts and impulses before speaking or acting."

That night Dudley went to dinner with several men he knew. Presently, one of the group began to tell a joke. Dudley had heard the story before, and his eyes wandered away. He thought of another yarn, much funnier than this one, which he meant to tell the moment the narrator finished.

With a jolt, he remembered Dr. Edwin's game. And suddenly the words of Agnes resounded in his mind: *"You top everything Eddie says, every story he tries to tell."*

As a shout of laughter followed the story, Dudley blurted out, "My, that's a good one! And how magnificently you told it!"

The storyteller turned to him with a grateful glance.

This little experience was the beginning of Dudley's adventure with himself. At lunch with a business associate the next day, he learned that a certain man wanted to be elected vice-president of a trade association.

"That won't be easy," Dudley objected.

"Why not?"

Dudley hesitated. He was learning to make hesitation a habit. He had intended to reveal how often the association's directors came to him for advice; he meant to hold forth, to expound . . . Again Agnes's voice echoed in his memory: *"You're the big, successful man who has to impress everybody."*

"That man," he stammered, "is too good for vice-president. He'd make a great president."

"Dudley," cried the other with joy, "you talk like a statesman! He's my closest friend, and with your help we can put him over."

Dudley was inwardly astonished at the meanness he had come so close to committing. And why? Simply because he wanted people to think how important he was.

There were many such discoveries. It startled him to detect the gossip with which he spiced conversation, the little distractions his tongue uttered against men whom he called friends. He found, to his horror, that he was capable of rejoicing over one man's misfortune and grieving over another's success. The more he learned about himself, the easier it was to forgive others.

Two weeks later, he returned to Dr. Edwin, a package under one arm, and related his discoveries.

"What about your brother's wife? Are you still angry with her?"

"Doctor, I am so sore at myself I haven't room to be sore at anybody else. And I'm on my way to Boston. In this package is my young nephew's birthday present. I was going to buy him a $200 camera until I realized that would be more expensive than anything his father could give him. This is something no money could buy for him."

At his brother's door, Agnes looked at him uncertainly. Presently, he sat with Eddie Jr. in the living room, the gift package opened on his knees. It was a stout black book; the worn cover had no title.

"This scrapbook," Dudley began, "is something I've been keeping for years. It's filled with things about your father: clippings from the sports pages when he was high school swimming champion; snapshots; and letters people wrote me when he was reported missing overseas. Here's a note about that from my second-best friend in the world: 'You,' he said, meaning me, 'have a brilliant mind, but your brother, Eddie, has splendor of the heart, and that's a lot more important.' "

In the silence, as the child read the letter, Agnes turned her back and went to the window.

"Who is your very best friend?" asked Eddie Jr.

"The lady at the window," said Dudley. "A good friend tells you the truth. Your mother did that for me when I needed it most, and I can never thank her enough for it."

Agnes did something for the first time in her life. She put her arms around Dudley and gave him a sister's kiss.

Matilda

Author Unknown

Many people assume that top grades will guarantee career success and that low grades will guarantee career failure. Miss Pillsbury belatedly learned that other qualities may be more significant than mere grades.

"I'm sorry, Miss Haggett," said President Dacey.

The sun, dropping to the west, shone full through the big window, slanting long, dusty beams across the president's desk. Matilda gazed dully at the scintillating motes that danced in the light, but nothing sparkling or lively had any message for her just then. She gave no sign, however, and stared so fixedly ahead of her that the president made a mental observation to the effect that the information he was imparting to Miss Haggett was not likely to disturb that stolid individual much.

"It cannot be a surprise to you," went on the president. "You were fully warned at the midyear examinations that your standard would have to be very much raised to allow you to graduate. We have done what we could for you through your course, but somehow you have failed to respond. Perhaps you have done your best?"

From the upward inflection and the inquiring look on the speaker's face, Matilda felt that something was expected of her; so she answered, "Yes, sir."

"Well," continued the president, rapidly shifting his papers as if he could not stop working even to talk, "if you have honestly done your part, you have nothing with which to reproach yourself. Do not regret your time here. All you have learned will be of use to you, and there are many other paths in life besides that of a teacher. I suppose you will hardly care to stay for graduation."

"No, sir," answered Matilda.

"Then I must bid you good-bye, Miss Haggett, and repeat that I am heartily sorry we cannot grant you a diploma."

The president spoke kindly, but he went back to his work with the air of one who has finished an unpleasant duty. He became absorbed in the pile of documents before him and hardly noticed that Miss Haggett left the room, or that Miss Pillsbury entered. When the presence of his mathematics teacher did dawn upon his consciousness, he leaned back in his chair with a sigh.

"I've just disposed of Miss Haggett," he said. "She did not seem to regret the situation very much. I am afraid all the pushing and pulling we did in her case are thrown away. What do you make of her, Miss Pillsbury?"

Miss Pillsbury laughed. "Not a success in mathematics, at all events. She will be much more in keeping on her father's farm, feeding the hens and scrubbing floors."

When Matilda Haggett left the president's office, she felt that the end of the world had come—that is, the end of *her* world. Two years before she had entered the state normal college with hopes high and happy, and this was the end—failure.

She walked slowly away between the long lines of elms that shaded the campus path with their lofty, graceful branches. No one knew what those trees meant to that silent, awkward girl.

Then her thoughts went over the hills to her home by the quarry. She must go back and take up life again with its purpose gone. She could never be a teacher. Who would hire one who had failed to take her diploma? She wondered what the other girls had that she lacked. They did not study as hard as she, yet they had no trouble with their grades.

No more awkward or unattractive student had ever presented herself at Westlake Normal College than Matilda Haggett. Her appearance was as unprepossessing as her name. The social life of the place was to her a mystery into which she never penetrated. She longed for it with all the strength of her shy nature, but she did not know how to make it hers. She loved the college, and it was to her as if she were banished from paradise when she packed her poor little wardrobe and bought her ticket home.

Matilda thought over the whole situation as she sat bolt upright on the car seat. Her mother would say that she was glad of it; the place for a girl was in the kitchen. Her father would grumble at the expense that had brought no return. There would be many questions asked and comments made all over the village, and the girl was not so stolid as she looked; she even winced at the thought.

It was a very wretched Matilda who climbed into the stage for Quarry Hill. Hanson Mires, the driver, slapped the reins on the back of his rusty old pair as they started on their slow pull.

"Well, there, Tilly," he remarked, "I wasn't calculating to see you back quite so soon. Your pa told me you wouldn't be along for quite a spell yet. Ain't sick or anything?"

"No," said Matilda.

"Got your graduating, or whatever you call it, done up before you expected, eh? I reckon you took all the prizes, now, didn't you, Matilda?"

A deep red mounted to Matilda's cheeks. Hanson was a diligent dealer in small news, but the truth might as well come out now as any time, and Matilda was not one to shirk.

"Oh, no, Mr. Mires," she said. "I'm home because I didn't pass."

"Didn't what?" inquired the merciless Hanson.

"Didn't pass my examinations. I've failed."

"Sho, now! You don't say so. Well, that's too bad. Better have stayed home in the first place, hadn't you?"

Matilda almost admitted in her heart that she had. She thought it again as she washed dishes that night in the hot, steamy little kitchen, under the fire of her mother's questions and her father's complaints, and it was forced upon her mind many times during the next few days as she fell into her old place in the household. It was not the work Matilda minded. She gave to her domestic duties the same slow but faithful labor that she had expended upon her algebra. But the girl had taken a glimpse into another world, a world of thought, of gentleness and courtesy, of high aims and beautiful ideas. Would it be better to have remained ignorant of that world, now she could have no share in it? However it might appear to others, her heart answered, *No!*

Matilda's mind was busy with the question one bright September day as she sat on the rickety little back porch, shelling peas for dinner. Over the rock ledge that cropped out behind the house bobbed two little towheads, their owners busy at play.

Suddenly, a shriek of infantile warfare broke the silence. Matilda put down her pan and went to the rescue. She separated the belligerents, shook them into good order, and returned to her work.

If there was something for them to do, they wouldn't fight so, she said to herself. *Those Peck twins are scratched up all the time, and they don't even know their letters. The Quarry Hill children are just going to the bad. If I had a diploma, I'd set up a school right away. Of course those babies can't walk all the way to Centerville.*

Here a pea intended for the pan took an erratic leap into space, impelled by a surprised action of Matilda's thumb as an idea seized her.

"Why!" she exclaimed aloud. "Why, I believe I will!"

Nearly two years after that autumn day, Miss Pillsbury was sent out from Westlake on a tour of educational inspection. She visited large towns with their well-graded systems and imposing buildings, and small villages with their country schoolhouses. In both fields she found graduates of the normal college doing good and acceptable work.

She was stopping in a mountain village in the western part of the state when she was told that three miles farther on, there was a small settlement known as Quarry Hill.

"A forsaken place," said her informer. "They're a real wild lot up there, those quarrymen are. Foreigners most of them, and they don't care anything about learning. Some of their young ones used to walk down here every day, but it's a long tramp, and I believe they've got some kind of a school of their own now. You'd better not think of going, Miss Pillsbury; it's a rough road, and you won't find much."

Miss Pillsbury was tired. She had hoped to turn her face homeward that day, but instead she took passage in the stage for Quarry Hill.

Those struggling little schools are the very ones that need our help and encouragement, she said to herself.

The Quarry Hill schoolhouse was an old, unpainted barn. It stood upon the crest of a hill and had for its outlook a whole world of rise and dip, of wooded slope and green valley, away to the purple mountains of the horizon.

Miss Pillsbury knocked at the rough entrance. A white-headed tot with a clean face and a ragged apron opened the door; then, abashed by the presence of a stranger, it introduced one stubby finger into its mouth and stared.

"What is it, Ingra?" asked a voice from within, and a young woman appeared, book in hand. The book fell to the floor as the young woman cried, "Miss Pillsbury!"

"Matilda Haggett!" exclaimed the visitor.

It was the rudest kind of a schoolroom, with its sagging floor and its unfinished walls. The desks were made of rough boards nailed onto crossed legs, and the benches were lower editions of the same. The children were of all sorts of ages. They looked happy, quiet, and docile.

"I hope you don't think it wrong of me," said Matilda when she had dismissed her pupils to their recess.

"Wrong of you? I don't understand."

"Teaching without any diploma, Miss Pillsbury. It does seem presumptuous of me. I don't feel that I have any right to a school when I failed so; but this place does need it, and there isn't anyone else to do it. Of course I wouldn't take pay like a regular teacher."

"My dear Matilda," said Miss Pillsbury, "what do you mean? Are you not paid to do this work?"

"Oh, no; the children give enough to get some books. I couldn't take anything when they are so poor. You see, it isn't as if I were a real teacher who had graduated."

"What do your parents think of such an arrangement?"

Matilda's face fell. "They don't like it much. Father says I've got to go earning next fall. I don't know what I shall do. There's a factory at Centerville, but I can't bear to leave here."

Miss Pillsbury looked at the girl before her in amazement. Could this be the stupid and unresponsive Matilda Haggett of the algebra class? Clumsy and plain as ever, and even more shabbily dressed, but she was actually dignified. When she spoke to her former teacher, she was the shy, awkward girl of old; when she confronted her scholars, there was no doubt but she was "Miss Haggett," absolute and supreme.

All that afternoon Miss Pillsbury watched Matilda and her school closely. She made almost no comment on what she saw; but once she asked, "How did you learn to be so clear, Matilda?"

Matilda's answering flush was born of astonished delight.

"Do I make things clear? Oh, I am so glad, Miss Pillsbury! I don't know, unless it's because I have to study things myself, and I'm so stupid, you know."

Miss Pillsbury went back to Westlake Normal College. At the first meeting of the faculty, she gave an account of her journey. When she finished her report, she paused for a moment, then began to speak again, not from her paper this time.

"I have yet to tell of a school," she said, "that, it seems to me, is accomplishing valuable and practical results. Beginning with five pupils in an ignorant and lawless community, it now numbers about 30. The children, instead of running wild, are orderly and interested. The tone of the place has been changed. Some of the parents, who are foreigners, have formed an evening class, where they may learn to read and write. The teacher carries on her work, if not in accord with the latest pedagogical methods, at least with admirable simplicity and judgment. In humble circumstances herself, she gives her services. Her name is Matilda Haggett."

The president screwed up his eyebrows.

"Matilda Haggett! Was that not the girl who couldn't get her diploma?"

"The same Matilda," replied Miss Pillsbury, dropping her official manner. "The girl we all thought hopeless is working on in a humble, patient way, feeling actually guilty because she thinks she is not worthy to teach, apologizing to me for presuming to teach school without a diploma, yet single-handedly making over the rough little village. And the most wonderful part of it all is that she really is a good teacher. She has to go down to the very bottom of things to understand them herself, and that is just what those children need. Of all the classes I visited, I enjoyed none more than I did Matilda Haggett's in that tumbledown shanty."

It was graduation day at Westlake. Most of the students were from country towns, and their families came by rail or stage, or drove in their own wagons to see their girls graduate. College Hall was well filled with an admiring audience of interested relatives and friends, and on one of the very front seats sat Matilda Haggett. She had come in response to a letter from Miss Pillsbury.

> *I want you to visit me during commencement week, and as I*
> *will not take no for an answer, I enclose a ticket for your journey.*
> *It will do you good to come, and perhaps you may get some*
> *points for your school.*

Matilda winced as she read this last sentence. The thought of her school touched a sore spot. Her father had told her decidedly that when the summer was over, she must "quit playing" and go to work. Matilda admitted the justice of his decision, but her whole heart was in her school.

She shrank, too, from visiting the scene of her failure. But Miss Pillsbury's word was law to Matilda. She was too young and simpleminded not to be excited by the prospect; besides, there was the ticket! So once more she packed her trunk.

I'm so glad my best dress is all right, she thought as she laid it in the tray. The "best dress" was a cheap muslin bought two years before in happy anticipation of her own graduation. But in Matilda's eyes it was beautiful, and she spread out its clumsy folds with entire satisfaction as she took her seat in College Hall. Miss Pillsbury, with true delicacy, had made no suggestions in regard to the ungainly gown, but she had added a fresh ribbon here and a few flowers there, and had fluffed up the hair that, when allowed to curve into its natural waves, was Matilda's most attractive feature.

Matilda could not help feeling a pang of envy when the graduating class came on the platform, but she crushed it as unworthy. She listened to the exercises with great respect.

I never could have done it, she thought. *I wish one of them would teach in Quarry Hill. They'd know how so much better than I.*

President Dacey presented the diplomas with his usual felicity.

He's so handsome, thought Matilda. *My, wouldn't I like to have him look at me that way, as if he was proud of me!* she added, in painful recollection of that dreadful day when she last stood in his office.

"When a soldier in the British army distinguishes himself by special bravery," said President Dacey, "he is given a badge of honor called the Victoria Cross. It has no value in itself; no price can be set upon it. Its worth lies simply in its sentiment; it is the symbol of bravery. Like that plain iron cross, these certificates that I give you have no intrinsic value. They are of no possible use to you save in showing that you have honorably done your work. They are the 'Well done' pronounced upon your labor. It is with great pleasure that I have presented you with these diplomas. It is with special gratification that I bestow one on a young lady, not a member of this class, but one who has earned it by faithful and successful endeavor. Will Miss Matilda Haggett please step up on the platform?"

"*I?*" responded Matilda disbelievingly from the front seat.

It took considerable pushing, encouragement, and explanation to get the bewildered Matilda up on the platform. Finally, she stood before the president, surprised out of her awkwardness into the simple dignity of perfect unself-consciousness.

"I congratulate you heartily, Miss Haggett," said President Dacey with his most stately bow.

And then Matilda, not knowing what else to do, broke down and put her face in her hands and cried.

She cried once more that night, when Miss Pillsbury told her that an appropriation would be granted for the maintenance of a school at Quarry Hill and that if she wished the position of teacher, it should be hers.

"You can earn quite as much as you could at the factory, Matilda," said Miss Pillsbury, "so I think you may feel certain that your father will be satisfied."

"But it doesn't seem right that I should have it," said Matilda. "I don't know a bit more about algebra than I did, Miss Pillsbury."

"Perhaps not, but you have learned a great deal about some other, higher things," responded the teacher as she tenderly kissed the girl good-night.

Her Greater Privilege

Josephine DeFord Terrill

Why had Pastor Allen asked her to sing? Didn't he know she and Roger had broken their engagement? And hadn't Roger told him why?

"Well, well! You're looking just as fine as ever!" exclaimed Uncle Abner, grasping Grace's hand in his fatherly way. "I've been so eager to see you."

Grace could only smile faintly in reply, her face suffused with embarrassment. She had not dreamed that Pastor Allen would come over to the dormitory to see her. A cool, reproachful nod was all that she felt she had the right to expect from him on his visit to the college.

"But I am surprised that you aren't planning to sing for me tonight," he chided affectionately. "You know I always expect you to sing every time I come."

"Why—I thought—" began Grace, her embarrassment mounting higher.

The old man cut her short, a twinkle in his keen blue eyes. "You thought I'd lost my love of good singing while I was sick? Well, I assure you I haven't." A mistiness veiled the brightness of his eyes. "We won't get to hear you very much longer, you know."

Just then a group of girls on their way to evening worship called out, "Oh, there's Pastor Allen!"

He turned to greet them. "Well, well! There are Miss Leonard and Mary and Helen. How are you all? So good to see everyone again."

Then to Grace he said, "Well, I must be getting back to Roger. I promised the dean I'd say a word to his boys in worship." He started toward the door and then called back with the pleasant informality of his 70 years, "Now, don't plan any special song, Grace. I'll just select one and call for it when I want it."

Grace turned and went into the girls' parlor for the evening worship. Could it be possible, she asked herself, that Uncle Abner did not know that she and Roger had broken their engagement? He certainly did not act as if he knew, for he treated her in the same proudly possessive manner that he always had. She had hoped to avoid him on this visit and meant to keep out of his way, for she did not wish to see the disappointment that she knew would be on his face. But he had come himself to see her almost immediately upon his arrival, showing no trace of disappointment. She could not understand. Why had Roger not told his uncle? Surely he must have written the news sometime during his long illness! But perhaps, she concluded with a pang that she would not have acknowledged, Roger had not thought it important enough to write about now, especially since he seemed to have found someone to take her place.

She dreaded the thought of having to sing for Pastor Allen. She had always enjoyed giving him the pleasure before, but now she feared that it would only renew the buzz of gossip among the students. If only she dared remain away from the meeting. She did not wish to see Roger and his uncle appear together on the platform. They meant nothing to her now, either of them, so why must she sit there before them, remembering things that were past? As soon as worship was over, she hurried to her room and dropped wearily down on her window seat, to continue wondering why the old man's attitude toward her was not changed.

Grace Woodman and Roger Allen were to graduate with the senior class at Wellworth College in June. They had been friends since their sophomore year and planned to be married immediately after graduation and go as missionaries to Africa. Grace had grown up in a small Western city, where she had made an early reputation for herself with her voice. In college she had continued her training under the music instructor, who was a graduate of a foreign conservatory. During her summers at home, her popularity in musical circles had increased, and after she returned to school in the fall of her last year, she received an offer to become assistant vocal instructor at the college in her hometown, at a surprisingly high salary. Thrilled over the opportunity to make a name for herself, and appreciative of the honor bestowed upon her, she had asked Roger to let her have three years in which to satisfy her musical ambitions in America before going to Africa.

That she should be tempted by such an offer had stunned her fiancé into inarticulate amazement. His life had been dedicated to Africa since childhood, when one of his greatest pleasures was listening to the reading of the wonderful letters that came regularly from Uncle Abner, who had grown old in that field. Disappointment and hurt pride blinded his eyes to the force of the temptation to which Grace had yielded, and, likewise, her ambition closed to her the realization of the devotion and the spirit of service to which Roger clung. A quick clash was inevitable. Each withdrew in bewildered silence, holding the firm conviction that it was the other who had fallen short.

The news of the break spread rapidly over the college, but the reason for it was never told. Whether pride or loyalty sealed Roger's lips, Grace did not know; and why Grace did not announce her acceptance of the instructorship, Roger may have often wondered. For a few months they went their separate ways, crushed, proud, unshaken. Roger plunged more deeply into his study of the Bible and homiletics, while grim lines etched themselves about his lips and brows.

Grace multiplied the hours before the piano, and a more poignant quality crept into her voice. When Roger relaxed his ascetic seclusion and appeared to respond to the persistent friendliness of Verabelle Taylor, acknowledged leader of the school's inevitable flapper class, Grace grew more aloof, more proud, and more determined to go far in her career. And when it was announced in chapel that Pastor Allen, returned missionary and now an itinerant pastor, was resuming his work following months of illness and was coming through Wellworth to speak at the general meeting of the Foreign Missionary Band, of which Roger was leader, Grace felt a strange confusion deep within herself. She had been resting in the hope that he would not visit the college again until after her departure from it in June, for though she still was firm in her desire for local fame, she shrank from standing before the bar of Uncle Abner's disapproval. He had strongly endorsed his nephew's choice of a life-partner, and always on his visits, the three of them were seen together walking about the campus or sitting in church. They had made an interesting trio, and faculty and students alike seemed inspired by their friendship.

Grace aroused herself from her reflections and prepared for the meeting. A few minutes before it was time to go over to the auditorium, she went up to the floor above in the dormitory, to return a borrowed book.

As she passed Verabelle Taylor's room, she heard the usual chatter of voices inside. A remark caught her attention, and she paused for a moment, stupefied.

"Why, we've *got* to go to the meeting! Don't you know that Vera's 'Uncle

Abner' is going to talk?" There was no mistaking the subtle derision behind the words.

Another voice added, "And Roger will be on the platform. *He'll* know if Vera isn't there."

There was a wild scramble, and bureau drawers were banged open and shut. "How does my hair look?" "Let me get a peek, will you?" "Don't put on too much powder, Vera." More shuffling and then an amused giggle: "Say, can't you just see Vera ministering to some little African soul?"

There was an appreciative laugh all around, and then came Verabelle's easygoing drawl. "I'll let Roger do the ministering, thank you."

"Better not tell him that until you get him," advised a knowing voice.

Sick at heart, Grace hurried away. Surely the Roger she had known could not be seriously interested in a girl like Verabelle. Conscious of a sudden feeling of responsibility, she went into the auditorium and took her place in the front row at the left, where she always sat when she sang. She had just found the page and was preparing to join in the song service already in progress, when the door at the side of the platform opened and Pastor Allen motioned her to come in to him. She dreaded being alone with Roger in the presence of his uncle; nevertheless, she went in. Roger greeted her with a strained half smile, but it seemed to Grace that his eyes were not so studiously indifferent as they had been at their occasional encounters during these last tense months.

The older man explained hastily, "Roger tells me that someone else is going to sing also; so I thought I'd better tell you that I want your solo at the end in place of the usual closing song."

She wondered why he should call her in for this unnecessary bit of information, but she answered quickly, "Anyway you like, Uncle Abner," unconscious of having called him "Uncle" until too late. She flashed a frightened and apologetic look at Roger, which he answered with another inscrutable smile.

The old man's face suddenly lighted up, and he placed a hand on the shoulder of each, saying impulsively, "My, it's just like old times, being here again with my two children! You can't know how I've missed the inspiration of your young enthusiasm."

He looked fondly at his tall nephew and then turned to Grace with so deferential a smile that her eyes fell before it. She turned quickly and went back to her seat in the rapidly filling auditorium.

Roger, as chairman, made the opening announcements. At the close of the opening song, a wave of perfume and the swish of taffeta announced the arrival of Verabelle Taylor and her coterie of faithful followers. Since Roger Allen's apparent interest in her, they had graduated from the extreme back of the room to the extreme front. But their habit of arriving late had not altered. While Roger stood waiting to introduce the speaker of the evening, the girls pushed down the seats one by one, traded back and forth to their satisfaction, and finally settled themselves. Then, as Roger began to speak, they engaged themselves in nudging one another, with covert glances toward the platform.

As Grace followed Pastor Allen through his talk, she became conscious of a strange stirring in her heart. And then, precipitously, the truth flashed upon her that this talk was all for her. *Uncle Abner knew!* He had known all along of her refusal to go to Africa. And he was taking this way to win back her heart to her first desire. And knowing that although she felt deeply, she was not sentimental, he appealed, not to her heart, but to her sense of justice. He knew that she could not truly desire personal glory when there were unfortunate ones who needed her help.

As Grace listened to his words, a little of the rebellion and antagonism in her heart against she knew not what began to slip away. She felt herself growing more and more receptive as he spoke of the meaning of true glory, of the depth of true satisfaction, of the value of true service. He traced the lives of many who chose the path of easy glory with its inevitable and deadening discontent and then of some who reaped the rewards of unselfish service for

others. There were a few
gripping personal stories,
with a heart pang in each
one of them. How thank-
ful Grace was that no one
in the audience knew
what lay behind the tense
pleading of the minister's
words. Occasionally, she
sought Roger's face, but
his eyes were fixed on a
spot somewhere in the
back of the room, his face
set and pale.

When the talk was over,
there seemed to be only
two faces in the room
untouched by tears. Roger
stared grimly ahead. Grace sat motionless, like one in a nightmare who felt
herself lifted higher and higher until everything was dizzily far below. Only
the face of the minister rose before her. Each word that he spoke had been
like a hammer beating against her brain. And then, across what seemed a
wavering abyss, she heard Pastor Allen asking her to sing. In a daze she
opened the book to the number and walked to her place.

When the music began, in a sudden sweeping panic she felt that she could
not sing the song he had chosen, but her years of training conquered her
fears, and her voice began:

> O Jesus, I have promised
>   To serve Thee to the end;

Be thou forever near me
    My Master and my Friend.

And with those lines, all her long-cherished objections fell from her heart like heavy garments slipping from weary shoulders. She wondered how she could ever have thought of giving up the work that once she had been so eager to do. For a moment, her voice held in a sustained sob, then floated smoothly on:

I shall not fear the battle
    If Thou art by my side;
Nor wander from the pathway
    If Thou wilt be my guide.

There was an electric silence in the large auditorium as Grace sang, and more than one discerning person suddenly understood the reason for the unusual emotion in her voice. A load lifted from the hearts of several faculty members as they saw the new consecration in her face after these last months of unyielding coldness.

I see the sights that dazzle
    The tempting sounds I hear.

At these words, a bright spray of tears splashed Pastor Allen's grizzled cheeks, and he lifted his face heavenward with a smile of serene thankfulness. The set lines on Roger's face had relaxed, and he endeavored unsuccessfully to hide the trembling of his lips. Even Verabelle and her chums sat speechless, puzzled at the unaccountable awe that they felt.

As Grace sang on in her clear, lovely voice, to which was added the new note of anguished repentance, she remembered that her surrender had come too late to rectify all of her mistake. It was too late to go to Africa with the one whose dreams had once united with hers. Someone else had been chosen to share in his service there. With a heartache comparable to her self-determination, she dedicated herself to go to Africa—alone—to some dark corner to "serve Thee to the end." The last lines,

> Oh give me grace to follow,
>   My Master and my Friend,

were a prayer for strength to fulfill this new resolution.

She hardly knew how she got away from the auditorium when the meeting was dismissed. Running hastily through the dormitory hall to her room, she snatched her coat from her closet and slipped down the back stairs and out into the shadows behind the building. Circling around to get to the main street, where she could walk alone and yet in safety, she passed a car whose motor had just begun to whir.

"Grace!"

Roger sprang out and came around to where she had stopped. "Where are you going?"

"Why—just for a walk," she replied weakly, too surprised to demand in turn what he was doing out here in Professor Morley's car.

"Uncle Abner went up to find you. He thought maybe . . . " Roger hesitated a second. " . . . you would like to go with us to the train."

"Oh!"

They faced each other, and only the pounding of their hearts broke the stillness. It was in silence that they had parted, a bewildered, unyielding silence; and now in a silence pulsating with a new understanding and a stronger devotion, all those months of proud loneliness were swept away.

"Would you like to come?" he asked in a voice husky with emotion.

"Yes, I would," she answered quietly.

It was as if he had asked, "Will you go with me to Africa?" and she had answered softly, "Yes, I will."

The Captain Who Did Not Play

Ira Rich Kent

Sometimes the greatest battles are neither seen nor heard—for they take place within the soul. Sid Dunham was in the throes of such a battle: Did his team deserve the best player it could get?

Ask any Bedford man who is the best baseball player his college has ever had, and he will answer without a moment's hesitation, "Sidney Dunham." A quest for details puzzles the inquirer. *Strange sort of star ballplayer, that,* I thought when I had heard them; and I ferreted out his story.

Dunham was a student primarily, it seemed, who had a perfectly normal liking for the game and tried to play it in school. At college he failed to make a regular place on his freshman team. But he stuck to it, and in his second year played with more or less regularity on the second nine, where he was tolerated because no better man appeared. As a junior, he attained the "varsity" under much the same conditions. The only good thing the coach of that year had to say about him was that he did not get "rattled" in a tight place and that he seemed to have a steadying influence on the rest of the nine.

There was a bitter struggle for the captaincy at the close of that season. When election came, Cameron and Willets fought in a deadlock for many ballots. Rather than see his rival win, Willets, in a spasm of hopeless rage, threw his strength unexpectedly to Dunham. The meeting had broken up in riot. The athletic council, knowing Dunham for a boy of character about whose scholarship standing there was no doubt, ratified the election.

Spring practice began in a turmoil. Cameron, the disgruntled, did not come out at all. Willets, who had caused the mischief, found himself on probation; he could not have been captain, anyway. To make things worse, the "first-string" pitcher, a friend of Cameron's, quit after a few days' practice. That left Burke, the catcher, and Dunham himself, the only veterans on the team. The new material was ordinary; that was the very best that could be said of it.

The nine—*a* nine—played its first game. It was nervous and disorganized—no Bedford team in the memory of the college janitor had taken such a beating.

That evening, Dunham was trying to forget—and succeeded only in forgetting his Greek composition—when the coach and the manager came in. Although he did not know it, it seems that interview was what made him a great ballplayer. Floyd did most of the talking. Barnet, the manager, was the sort to sit on the window seat and put in, "That's right!" "You see that, don't you, old man?" "That's the way we all feel about it."

"Pretty tough start, Sid." Floyd pulled a long face. He was harrowing the ground, preparatory to planting his seed. "Everybody's mighty sore about the game. It raises rats with me to turn out such a bum team!"

"I suppose so," said Dunham dejectedly. He was thinking more of the college than of the coach.

"Of course something's got to be done."

"You see that, don't you, Sid?" put in Barnet.

"I see we need to improve a lot, if that's what you mean. What else can we do? This isn't a league team, where you can go out and hire a lot of new men. If Cameron and McDougal would come out—"

"Yes, that's it." Floyd was quick to seize his opportunity thus presented. "I have some reason to think Cameron and McDougal *would* come out again, now that Willets is out of it, if—that is—"

Dunham sat up straight. "If I would resign and help put them in?"

Floyd laughed nervously. "Well, they would, in that case, Sid, if you want to know. I have every reason to think they would, both of them. And it would be a great thing for you to do—the finest sort of sacrifice for you to make for the college. Everybody'd think you were doing a mighty fine thing."

"How about its being a mighty fine thing for them to come out and play anyhow?" Dunham could not help snapping out that much.

"Well, it would, of course," Barnet came in again.

"But they don't choose to do it," Floyd finished the sentence. "And they're two, anyway, and both stars, and—"

"And I'm not," said Dunham quietly. "I know."

He seemed to have grown suddenly more mature—more experienced, sober, and wise—even as Floyd watched him. The older man felt himself put on the defensive.

"You think I should turn the place over to a man who, for a petty spite, has been willing to sacrifice the team. I'd do anything in my power to make the nine a credit to the college. I'd do this—"

"Well, then—" Floyd broke in.

"Wait. I'm not sure that the college, the real college, would think as you do—would think that knuckling down to that sort of spirit *is* creditable."

"We've *got* to have a winning team!" declared the coach.

Dunham got up and stood with his back to the empty fireplace, stretching his arms along the mantel.

"No," he said. "I used to think that, but it isn't so. What we've got to have is a creditable team.

"I know I stand in a dubious light," he went on. "So I'll say this: If you want any other man who is now in the squad, you may have my resignation. But—" He stood a little straighter. "I don't believe I'll make way for Cameron."

One look at the boy told Floyd the uselessness of argument. It was as if something bigger than Dunham himself was speaking with his tongue. His decision seemed as impersonal as it was final.

"Then I shall resign myself!" cried the coach wrathfully. "If you want to throw the whole season in the ditch, go ahead! I'm done with it. A nice mess you'll make of it!" If a man can be said to "flounce" out of the room, Floyd did it.

Barnet followed more slowly.

"I hope you won't quit, too," said Dunham with a touch of irony that failed to penetrate.

"Perhaps I have made a mess of it," said Dunham as he turned out the light. "But somehow it looks so clear to me that way and not clear at all any other."

He lay awake a long time. And the more he thought, the clearer his mind became. The sting Floyd had administered seemed to have wakened all sorts of dormant traits of mind and character in the boy. It was near dawn when he went to sleep; but he slept then, like a child, untroubled.

Floyd did resign, and on the whole Dunham was rather relieved. There was raging in some quarters, and the stubborn captain had to hear some bitter words. But, to his surprise, he got a little encouragement and support that was comforting. The council accepted Floyd's resignation without demur and, to general undergraduate consternation, gave Dunham permission to take charge of the coaching himself.

A day or two later, a junior named Bingham, whom the captain barely knew as a sober chap who was working his way through college, reported with the squad and asked for a chance to pitch for batting practice.

"I haven't been out before," he said in explanation, "because I've been too busy working. But I think you're right about this matter, Dunham, and if I'm good enough, I'm willing to let my outside work go this spring, for the sake of helping you out."

Dunham thanked him heartily—for his spirit, rather than for anything he really expected of the recruit. But when the final cut in the squad was made a week later, the newcomer was left on it. He had shown himself a better pitcher than even the vanished McDougal. Another man left as well was Smith, a sophomore trying for third, whom Floyd had rather ignored because of his weakness on ground balls. Dunham, after spending a half-hour with him on two mornings, put him in right field for the fourth game of the schedule. And with Bingham pitching, Bedford broke its string of defeats. Smith, who had already made two clever sacrifices, drove in the winning runs in the eighth, with a smashing two-bagger to left.

Dunham smiled that night, although his team had made five errors.

"There are two men on the squad, though, who bother me," he said. The captain had brought Bingham to his room for what he called a "council of war."

"Dorsey and Small?"

"They're the ones. They can't get it through their heads that Cameron isn't an issue any longer. I want to be perfectly fair, but I've got to do the best thing for the nine. What do you say?"

"Drop them both," was Bingham's unhesitating reply. The spirit that had brought him to the team carried him far.

"Why not compromise?"

"Compromise?"

"Drop one of them. I think I can have it out with Dorsey and get him to see things straight—if Small goes."

"Who'll you put on first?"

"Dorsey." The captain chuckled at Bingham's fallen jaw. "It's a sort of ruse, maybe; but I want to keep Dorsey and keep him *with* me. So I'm bribing him, if you choose, with a change from substitute outfielder to regular first baseman. That's where we need him—and he'll be pleased to pieces!"

The "ruse," if such it was, at any rate worked well. Dunham rid himself of one troublesome malcontent and transformed the other into a pretty devoted follower. Even the stern Bingham admitted the success of the move.

There was another man on the squad who gave Dunham uneasiness; but of him nothing was said to Bingham. Burke, the veteran catcher, was an irresponsible, redheaded lad, impatient of restraint and amiable enough so long as he did things in his own way. Dunham knew that a crisis must come with him, and he wanted it to come as soon as possible.

Burke was naturally enough a slugger. He took with ill grace the captain's directions to "lay down a bunt" or "wait it out." Dunham tried argument and reasoning without avail. Then one day in a game, the catcher went to bat, with one out and a man at first, with definite instructions for the hit-and-run. The runner at first started with the pitch. Burke lunged at the ball with all his might, sending a high fly to the right fielder, who had plenty of time to get it to first for a double play.

When Burke came in, the captain went to meet him.

"Jimmy," he said good-humoredly, "that's one too many times."

Burke started to reply belligerently, but Dunham stopped him.

"There isn't going to be any blowing up, or firing from the squad, or anything like that. But you and I are going to meet in the gym with the gloves after the game. If you beat me, you can play your own game the rest of the season without a word from me; if I win, you're going to obey to the letter every order I give from now on." And Dunham held out his hand.

Burke looked a little bewildered; then he laughed. "Sure thing!" he said. "That's fair."

They faced each other with the thickly padded gloves, and the captain knocked Burke down three times.

"I'm your man," said the catcher when he got up from his third descent. "You're square, Sid, and you know more than I do. Put it there!"

They tore off the gloves, shook hands again, and went laughing to dinner.

After that, Burke joined the "board of strategy," as he called it, that met every night in the captain's room to plan the campaign. And woe to any luckless fellow who missed a signal or disobeyed it after that. Between Bingham and Burke, discipline was rigorous.

So the captain, by such various means, found himself—a third of the season gone—with a team that, whatever its technical shortcomings, was wholeheartedly with him. Things began to go more smoothly, and the team began to win—not always, but most of the time.

Then Dunham, having won these battles, found his hardest one still ahead of him.

One afternoon he stopped on the way from practice to watch the exciting finish of a class game. He went on to his room, a quarter of an hour later, knowing that he had just discovered the best infielder in college.

Borland, the sophomore captain and second baseman, had unmistakably brought his team through a winner partly by his own batting and fielding, but mostly by that strange "baseball sense" that made all his plays look easy, by putting him always in the right place half a second before another would have been there. He was rather a slender, even frail lad, and Dunham remembered that his apparent lack of muscle had been the reason for Floyd's abrupt dismissal of him in the early spring practice.

Bingham and Burke would not come in for the board meeting till nine o'clock. Before that time, Dunham fought the hardest fight of all.

He knew at the beginning how it was coming out. The end was clear as crystal, but it took all his grit to make himself look at it squarely. He knew that without a shadow of doubt he was himself the weakest player of the Bedford infield, and he knew without a shadow of doubt that he must find a place for Borland in that infield. He went over the whole thing time after time, weighing the possible value of his own presence on the field as against the sophomore's skill, dissecting every argument for or against himself with the same impersonal power that Floyd had seen and that Burke had recognized—and the answer was always the same.

No use, he thought. *There isn't any way for me to get by.*

His mind was made up when Bingham and Burke came in, and he told them.

Burke burst out in wild, incredulous protest, while Bingham looked at him soberly. Then, to Dunham's surprise, Bingham came over and put his hand on the captain's shoulder.

"Are you quite sure about this?"

Dunham smiled up at his sober face. "Quite sure," he said.

Bingham's fingers tightened on his shoulder, but he did not say anything more.

And by and by he helped quiet Burke down—which was the biggest help he could give the captain just then, for the Irish boy was almost in tears with rage and loyalty and incoherently threatening to "go out and smash young Borland's leg" as a desperate cure for the situation.

Borland was called out with the squad the next day and given a trial at second. "In case I need a substitute," Dunham told the team. The last hope left him when he watched the boy at work, saw how much more smoothly the play went, how brilliant the newcomer was, and at the same time how intelligently he fitted into what had become the complex mechanism of the infield.

"The coaching lines for me," Dunham said, with a sorry little laugh, as Bingham joined him there.

The pitcher nodded. "You were right, I guess, Dunham."

The Bedford nine had two championship series to play—two games in three with Corliss and Drayton. It was not really until the first of these—when they met Corliss on the enemy's grounds—that the team showed its final form. That game was fairly close, but in the second Bedford ran away from the other team. Since there was no third game necessary, there was a chance for a good rest before the first meeting with Drayton, much stronger that year than the Corliss team.

So Bingham was fresh and at his best again, and Drayton went down before him, fighting gamely, but beaten. But in the last inning a swift-pitched ball struck him on the contracted muscles of his right arm. Dunham took him out instantly, and Bradley finished the inning.

The pitcher's injury seemed to respond to treatment, and he went into the next game confidently—or, at least, with outward confidence. He knew, as the team did, that Bradley could not take his place against Drayton, fighting in the last ditch.

Crouched on the coaching lines inning after inning, the captain watched the game go by. The fine instrument he had made responded to his touch as readily as if it had been a violin upon which he played.

But inning after inning, he watched Bingham grow weaker and the shadow of pain appear and deepen on his face. Yet the courage of the man was magnificent. "Making them hit it," relying on the team behind him, Bingham pitched as few balls as possible. The seventh and eighth innings passed; Drayton was still a run behind, but growing ever more threatening. In the eighth, only Borland's clever turning of a double play stopped what looked like a fatal batting rally.

But in the first half of the ninth, the storm broke. Bingham was steady as ever—they hit him, that was all. Six hits rattled off the Drayton bats, five runs came tumbling in, and the stands were in an uproar.

The captain was waiting for his men when they came in to the bench. With a laugh, a pat on the shoulder, a word of direction, he went down the line, then trotted out to his place in the coach's box. This inning would show if he had failed; whether they won or not, this inning would show the team!

Miller was up. "Wait!" signaled Dunham, and Miller waited, although he was finally called out on strikes. But he and the captain smiled at each other reassuringly. Dahlgren, the fast third baseman, was next. "Wait!" signaled the captain again. And Dahlgren waited—to better effect, for he got his base.

Bacon came up. The captain dropped on one knee and waved his hand. Dahlgren was off like a streak and slid neatly behind the second baseman— safe. He was up in a flash. Dunham stood up. Bacon drove the next ball sharply to right; the fielder, coming in fast, made a fine stop. Dahlgren sprinted hard past third, slowed up, drew a throw to that base, then dashed home. Bacon, paying attention to nothing but the captain's signals, had never stopped running. He was nearly at third when the startled catcher discovered him. The hurried throw was a bit high; his long slide was beyond the fielder's reach.

Dorsey raised a high-curving foul, which the right fielder foolishly caught, and Bacon came like a shadow across the plate. But Bedford was still two runs behind, the bases were empty—and two out!

"Wait!" signaled Dunham.

Burke grinned at him grimly—and waited. He got his base. The infield stayed back for the play at first, and Souther, shortstop and sprinter, tipped the ball softly toward third. The baseman came rushing in on it, but his throw was too late. Souther, plunging feet first, was indisputably safe. And meanwhile Burke, starting with the pitch, had gone straight on to third. The startled shortstop could not handle the first baseman's hurried throw in time to get him.

"Wait!" signaled the captain.

The Drayton pitcher, unsteadied a little by events, could not get the ball over for Stone.

And Smith, Floyd's outcast, was the next batter.

"Wait!" signaled Dunham for the last time.

The Drayton pitcher gave him two balls, then a called strike; then Smith fouled one, another strike. Then the pitcher "wasted one," in vain.

"Three and two!" called Dunham, his voice rasping just a little.

With the pitcher's motion, all three of the runners were off. The pitcher had to "put it over." Smith did not hit it hard, but his short, sharp swing drove it swiftly down the "groove" and over third base. By the time the ball passed out of the diamond, Stone was turning second and Burke had scored. Souther came sprinting in at his heels.

"Go on!" signaled the captain, and Stone never slackened in his rush for the plate. Smith's hit was only a long single; but the left fielder had to run almost to the foul line to get it, and with the runners already under way, it was long enough.

The captain waited only for the umpire's assuring signal; then he walked slowly toward the bench. It was over, and he was satisfied; the men had played wonderfully well. But *they* had done it; he felt somehow tired and rather useless.

Suddenly, he felt Bingham's arm on his shoulder. The junior's stern face was working oddly.

"Dunham, Dunham, don't you think *we* know?" he cried.

Then a redheaded, dusty tornado burst upon them. "Here's the man who won it!" it shrieked as it came. "Here he is! Don't talk about us! Hurray for Dunham!"

And after him came the others, Smith and Dorsey at their head, stirred to great things, even in a game, by one man's example—and knowing he had done it.

And after that the avalanche of the stands.

So that is the story of the captain who did not play. The best player of them all!

Summer to Autumn

My Life as a Black Man

Jesse Owens, with Paul G. Neimark

As a black man in 1930s America, Jesse Owens faced many obstacles, but none more formidable than the one he faced at the 1936 Olympics.

No one called me "nigger" until I was seven. That was because in Oakville, Alabama, in the World War I years, a sharecropper's child like me—a great-grandson of slaves—almost never saw the white man who in effect owned his every breath. In our case, it was John Cannon, who lived in a big house on top of the hill and had eight Negro families sharecropping 250 acres of cotton for him.

My father, Henry Owens, had the largest spread, 50 acres, because he had four sons to work it. But I couldn't help, because I was so sickly that every winter I came down with pneumonia. A couple of those winters, when my father couldn't find enough wood to keep the fireplace going in our little cardboard house, I came close to never seeing spring. Yet somehow my mother always managed to pull me through. When I was well again, she'd take my father aside and plead with him to go North. "Little J.C.'s going to die unless we do something, Henry."

My father resisted the idea. He felt too old to change, and his fear of the unknown was greater than the fear of poverty. But I got sick again; this time blood came up every time I coughed. . . .

Finally, one night in February 1921—I was eight—John Cannon sent for Father. We'd had a particularly good cotton crop that year and had got out of debt at Cannon's store. That threatened Cannon's hold on us, I guess, so he sent for my father to come up to the big house on the hill, and there his assistant proposed that the 50-50 deal be revised to 60-40, Cannon's favor—retroactive.

For Henry Owens, 42 years of silent resentment finally became words. "That ain't fair," he said.

"Fair?" the assistant replied. "What does fair have to do with you?"

Those words stuck in my father's craw, and the next Sunday after church he told us we were leaving Oakville for Cleveland.

He couldn't find steady work in Cleveland. But my three brothers got jobs in the steel mills, and we managed not to starve. My health improved, and soon even I held jobs, though sometimes for pennies, while going to grade school.

There still wouldn't have been a Jesse Owens story, however, without Charles Riley, a physical-education teacher and the first white man I really knew. When he asked me to go out for the track team in the fifth grade, it wasn't because he saw any potential track champion in me, but a potential corpse. My legs, and the rest of me, were so thin that I looked like a malnutrition case.

"I can't," I told him. "I work after school."

"Well, Jesse [my real name was James Cleveland, but people changed J.C. to Jesse], how about *before* school, then?"

So, every morning, 45 minutes before the opening bell rang, this shy, bespectacled little teacher would meet me out on the sidewalk by the school and work with me. . . . He was like a father to me. Charles Riley put me on the first step not only to athletic fame but to escaping the sickness of black-think—the hatred that black militants today make a profession of. He showed me beyond all doubt that understanding and love can exist between races.

We never talked about white and colored. There was no reason to. He taught *that* by example. And his example taught me a lesson I'll never forget, even if the blackthinkers line up from here to China, shouting that it isn't so. The *blackthink*—pro-Negro, anti-white bigotry—of some extremists today is not much different from John Cannon's *whitethink*.

After several months, my legs still looked like pieces of straw. I wanted to quit. "I'll never make the team this year, Mr. Riley," I said dejectedly.

"Who says we're trying to make it *this year?*" Riley answered me. "You're training for four years from Friday, Jesse."

Without the pressure of having to change overnight, I learned to enjoy running. I was relaxed out there. By the time I reached [high school], I was running close to the national high-school record in the 100-yard dash. Then one day in 1933, . . . I tied the world's record, running the distance in 9.4 seconds.

Suddenly, the whole world was at my door. Reporters wanted interviews. Colleges started writing, sending people, making offers—free tuition, a new car, a six-room apartment. I hated to say no, but I turned the offers down. I wanted to believe in the American dream. But the scene was tearing me apart. I was scared of moving into a world where I would live like a millionaire while my father nearly starved. He had just been laid off a job, loading 100-pound crates, that paid him $12 for a 60-hour week. I began to go to pieces inside. Finally, I protested in the only way I could. I quit the track team.

One day at school, Riley took me aside. "Jesse, I respect you for what you're doing. But if I could get your father a permanent job, would you go to college—on *your* terms?"

"There are no permanent jobs for Negroes, Mr. Riley," I answered.

"But if there were?"

That weekend, Charles Riley drove to Ohio State University and talked with Larry Snyder, the best track coach in the country. On Sunday night, Riley was back with two letters. One was from the dean's office. They wanted me to attend college there, and they offered me three jobs—waiting tables, working in the library, and running an elevator—to pay my tuition and modestly support my family (at 17, I had married my childhood sweetheart). The other letter offered my father a permanent job with the state of Ohio. I was five inches taller than Charles Riley, but I threw my arms around him and kissed him.

It wasn't easy at the university; the experience left plenty of scars. The other Negro athletes and I had to take our meals in the one ramshackle house where all the Negroes lived. En route to track meets, our white teammates always went into restaurants first, to see if the rest of us could come in. If the answer was no, they brought food out to us. Once when a diner-owner saw what was happening, he ran out and jerked the plates of food away from us, yelling, "I don't want money to feed no niggers!" After soul-shattering hurts like that, I would run my head off in the track meet, trying to run out all the frustration and anger and fear that was inside of me—fighting back, fighting to prove something.

In the summer of 1936, when I boarded a ship for Germany and the Olympic Games, . . . that same agonizing fear-reflex cramped my soul. Negroes had gone to the Olympics before and won before. But so much more was expected of me. Adolf Hitler, arming his country against the entire world, had perverted the Games into a test between dictatorship and freedom. In a way I was competing against Hitler himself and his myth of "Aryan supremacy." I was entered in four events, and Hitler had been grooming his best athlete, Lutz Long, to beat me in one of them. Long— a tall, sandy-haired, perfectly built fellow (the ideal specimen of Hitler's "Aryan supremacy" idea)—had been known to jump over 26 feet in preparing for the Games. No one knew for sure what he could really do because Hitler kept him under wraps. But stories had filtered out that he had gone as far as I had, farther than anyone else in the world. I was used to hearing rumors like that and tried not to think too much about it. Yet the first time I laid eyes on Long, I sensed that the stories hadn't been exaggerated. . . .

August in Berlin was muggier than May in Ann Arbor or Columbus. Yet the air was cool, and it was hard getting warmed up. The ground on the runway to the broad jump pit wasn't the same consistency as that at home. Long was used to it. I wasn't.

His first jump broke the Olympic record. In the trials!

Did it worry me a little? More than a little. He was on his home ground and didn't seem susceptible to the pressure. In fact, he'd already done one thing I always tried to do in every jumping event and race I ran: discourage the competition by getting off to a better start.

Well, there was only one way to get back the psychological advantage. Right off the bat I'd have to make a better jump than he did. I didn't want to do it that way—it wasn't wise to use up your energy in preliminaries. Long could afford to showboat in the trials. This was his only event, the one he'd been groomed for under Hitler for years. I had to run three races besides, more than any other athlete on either team.

But I felt I had to make a showing right then. I measured off my steps from the takeoff board and got ready. Suddenly, an American newspaperman came up to me.

"Is it true, Jesse?" he said.

"Is what true?" I answered.

"That Hitler walked out on you? That he wouldn't watch you jump?"

I looked over at where the German ruler had been sitting. No one was in his box. A minute ago he had been there. I could add two and two. Besides, he'd already snubbed me once by refusing the Olympic Committee's request to have me sit in that box.

This was too much. I was mad, hate-mad, and it made me feel wild. I was going to show him. He'd hear about this jump, even if he wouldn't see it!

I felt the energy surging into my legs and tingling in the muscles of my stomach as it never had before. I began my run, first almost in slow motion, then picking up speed, and finally faster and faster until I was moving almost as fast as I did during the 100-yard dash. Suddenly, the takeoff board was in front of me. I hit it, went up, up high—so high I knew I was outdoing Long and every man who ever jumped.

But they didn't measure it. I heard the referee shout "Foul!" in my ears before I even came down. I had run too fast, been concentrating too much on a record and not enough on form. I'd gone half a foot over the takeoff board.

All the newspaper stories and books I've ever seen about that Olympic broad jump had me fouling on the next of my three tries, because the writers felt that made the story more dramatic. The truth is I didn't foul at all on my second jump.

I played it safe. Too safe. I was making absolutely sure I didn't foul. *All right*, I said to myself. *Long has won his point. But who will remember the preliminaries tomorrow? It is the finals that count.* I had to make sure I got into those finals. I wasn't going to let him psyche me out of it. I wasn't going to let Hitler anger me into throwing away what I'd worked 10 years for.

So I ran slower, didn't try to get up as high during my jump. *Surely*, I said to myself, *if I can do 26 feet trying my best, I certainly ought to be able to do a foot less without much effort.* That would be enough to qualify for the finals, and there I'd have three fresh jumps again. That's where I'd take apart Lutz Long.

It's funny how sometimes you can forget the most important things. I forgot that I wasn't the kind of guy who could ever go halfway at anything. More than that, no sprinter or jumper can really take just a little bit off the top. It's like taking a little bit off when you're working a mathematical equation or flying an airplane through a storm. You need the total concentration and total effort from beginning to end. One mistake and you're dead. More than that, my whole style was geared to giving everything I had, to using all my speed and energy every second of what I was doing. Once or twice I'd tried a distance race just for kicks. I was miserable at it. If I couldn't go all out all the time, I was no good.

So my second jump was no good.

I didn't foul. But I didn't go far enough to qualify either. It wasn't just Long and Owens in the event anymore. There were dozens of other participants from other countries, and a bunch of them—too many—were now ahead of me.

I had one jump left.

It wasn't enough.

I looked around nervously, panic creeping into every cell of my body. On my right was Hitler's box. Empty. His way of saying I was a member of an inferior race who would give an inferior performance. In back of that box was a stadium containing more than 100,000 people, almost all Germans, all wanting to see me fail. On my right was the broad jump official. Was he fair? Yeah. But a Nazi. If it came to a close call, a hairline win-or-lose decision, deep down didn't he, too, want to see me lose? Worst of all, a few feet away was Lutz Long, laughing with a German friend of his, unconcerned, confident, *Aryan*.

They were against me. Every one of them. I was back in Oakville again. I was a nigger.

Did I find some hidden resource deep within me, rise to the occasion and qualify for the finals—as every account of those Olympics says?

No, I did not. I found a hidden resource, but it wasn't inside of me. It was in the most unlikely and revealing place possible.

Time was growing short. One by one the other jumpers had been called and taken their turns. What must have been 20 minutes or half an hour suddenly seemed like only seconds. I was going to be called next. I wasn't ready. I wanted to shout it—*I wasn't ready!*

Then the panic was total. I had to walk in a little circle to keep my legs from shaking, hold my jaw closed tight to stop my teeth from chattering. I didn't know what to do. I was lost. . . . If I gave it everything I had, I'd foul again. If I played it safe, I wouldn't go far enough to qualify. *And this is what it all comes down to,* I thought to myself. *Ten years and 4,500 miles to make a nigger of myself and not even reach the finals!*

And then I couldn't even think anymore. I started to feel faint, began to gasp for breath. Instinctively, I turned away from everyone so they couldn't see me. But I couldn't help hearing them. The thousands of different noises of the stadium congealed into one droning hum—*ch-ch-ch-ch ch-ch-ch-ch*, louder and louder in my ears. It was a though they were all chanting ["Choke!"] Hatefully, gleefully. *Ch-ch-ch-ch. Ch-ch-ch-ch. CH-CH-CH-CH.*

Suddenly, I felt a firm hand on my arm. I turned and looked into the sky-blue eyes of my worst enemy.

"Hello, Jesse Owens," he said. "I am Lutz Long."

I nodded. I couldn't speak.

"Look," he said. "There is no time to waste with manners. What has taken your goat?"

I had to smile a little in spite of myself—hearing his mixed-up American idiom.

"Aww, nothing," I said. "You know how it is."

He was silent for a few seconds. "Yes," he said finally, "I know how it is. But I also know you are a better jumper than this. Now, *what has taken your goat?*"

I laughed out loud this time. But I couldn't tell him—him above all. I glanced over at the broad jump pit. I was about to be called.

Lutz didn't waste words, even if he wasn't sure of which ones to use.

"Is it what Reichskenzler Hitler did?" he asked.

I was thunderstruck that he'd say it. "I—" I started to answer, but I didn't know what to say.

"I see," he said. "Look, we talk about that later. Now you must jump. And you must qualify."

"But how?" I shot back.

"I have thought," he said. "You are like I am. You must do it 100 percent. Correct?"

I nodded.

"Yet you must be sure not to foul."

I nodded again, this time in frustration. And as I did, I heard the loudspeaker call my name.

Lutz talked quickly. "Then you do both things, Jesse. You remeasure your steps. You take off six inches behind the foul board. You jump as hard as you can. But you need not fear to foul."

All at once the panic emptied out of me like a cloudburst.

Of course!

I jogged over to the runway. I remeasured my steps again. Then I put a towel parallel to the place half a foot before the takeoff board from where I wanted to jump.

I walked back to the starting spot. I began my run, hit the place beside the towel, shot up into the air like a bird and qualified by more than a foot.

The next day I went into the finals of the broad jump and waged the most intense competition of my life with Lutz Long. He broke his own personal record and the Olympic record, too, and then I—thanks to him—literally flew to top that. Hours before I had won the 100 meters in 10.3, and then afterward the 200 meters in 20.7 and helped our team to another gold medal and record in the relay.

During the evenings that framed those days, I would sit with Lutz in his space or mine in the Olympic Village, and we formed an even more intense friendship. We were sometimes as different inside as we looked on the outside. But the things that were the *same* were much more important to us.

Lutz had a wife and a young child, too. His was a son. We talked about everything from athletics to art, but mostly we talked about the future. He didn't say it in so many words, but he seemed to know that war was coming and he would have to be in it. I didn't know then whether the United States would be involved, but I did realize that this earth was getting to be a precarious place for a young man trying to make his way. And, like me, even if war didn't come, Lutz wasn't quite sure how he would make the transformation from athletics to life once the Olympics were over.

We talked, of course, about Hitler and what he was doing. Lutz was torn between two feelings. He didn't believe in Aryan supremacy any more than he believed the moon was made of German cheese, and he was disturbed at the direction in which Hitler was going. Yet he loved his country and felt a loyalty to fight for it if it came to that, if only for the sake of his wife and son. I couldn't understand how he could go along with Hitler under any circumstances, though, and I told him so.

He wasn't angry when I said it. He just held out his hands and nodded. He didn't explain because he didn't understand completely himself, just as I couldn't explain to him how the United States tolerated the race situation. So we sat talking about these things, some nights later than two Olympic performers should have. We didn't come up with any final answers then, only with a unique friendship. For we were simply two uncertain young men in an uncertain world. One day we would learn the truth, but in the meantime, we would make some mistakes. Lutz's mistake would cost him too much.

Yet we didn't make the mistake of not seeing past each other's skin color to what was within. If we couldn't apply that principle to things on a world scale, we still could live it fully in our own way in the few days we had together, the only days together we would ever have.

We made them count. We crammed as much understanding and fun as we could into every hour. We didn't even stop when we got out on the track. Lutz was at my side cheering me on for every event, except the broad jump, of course. There he tried to beat me for all he was worth, but nature had put just a little more spring into my body and I went a handful of inches farther.

After he failed in his last attempt to beat me, he leaped out of the pit and raced to my side. To congratulate me. Then he walked toward the stands pulling me with him while Hitler was glaring, held up my hand and shouted to the gigantic crowd, "Jesse Owens! Jesse Owens!"

The stadium picked it up. "Jesse Owens!" they responded—though it sounded more like *Jaz-eee-ooh-wenz*. Each time I went for a gold medal and a record in the next three days, the crowd would greet me with "Jaz-eee-ooh-wenz! Jaz-eee-ooh-wenz!"

I'd had people cheering me before, but never like this. Many of those men would end up killing my countrymen, and mine theirs, but the truth was that they didn't want to, and would only do it because they *had* to. Thanks to Lutz, I learned that the false leaders and sick movements of this earth must be stopped in the beginning, for they turn humanity against itself.

Lutz and I vowed to write each other after the Games, and we did. For three years we corresponded regularly, though the letters weren't always as happy as our talks at the Olympics had been. Times were hard for me and harder for Lutz. He had had to go into the German army, away from his wife and son. His letters began to bear strange postmarks. Each letter expressed more and more doubt about what he was doing. But he felt he had no other choice. He was afraid for his family if he left the army. And how could they leave Germany? It was Lutz's world, just as the South had been the only world for so many Negroes.

The last letter I got from him was in 1939. *Things become more difficult,* he said, *and I am afraid, Jesse. Not just the thought of dying. It is that I may die for the wrong thing. But whatever might become of me, I hope only that my wife and son will stay alive. I am asking you who are my only friend outside of Germany, to someday visit them if you are able, to tell them about why I had to do this, and how the good times between us were. Lutz.*

I answered right away, but my letter came back. So did the next, and the one after. I inquired about Lutz through a dozen channels. Nothing. A war was on. Finally, when it was over, I was able to get in touch with Lutz's wife and find out what had happened to him. He was buried somewhere in the African desert.

Lutz Long had been my competition in the Olympics. He was a white man—a Nazi white man who fought to destroy my country.

I loved Lutz Long as much as my own brothers. I still love Lutz Long.

I went back to Berlin a few years ago and met his son, another fine young man. And I told Karl about his father. I told him that, though fate may have thrown us against one another, Lutz rose above it, rose so high that I was left with not only four gold medals I would never have had, but with the price-less knowledge that the only bond worth anything between human beings is their humanness.

As I look back over my 57 years, I must admit that at times I have come close to violence, to crossing over into the camp of the black-thinkers, the militants. I came closest on the day that Martin Luther King, Jr., was shot. I had known and loved Martin long before he came to national prominence. As I sat grieving, the long-buried smell of the Oakville cotton fields rose to stifle my senses. We'd spent centuries slaving in manure to grow one man like that, and he'd been snuffed out as if he were a dime-store candle. I wanted to hate. At the same time, seeing what was inside me made me hold back. For what I saw there was the same thing that drives every militant blackthinker today: a desire for revenge.

American Negroes have made tremendous progress away from that Oakville we've all lived in. Today we're *making it*. Believe it or not, most black men today start just about equal with the white. We may not begin with as well-off a set of parents, and we may have to fight harder to make that equality work. But we *can* make it work. I know what is usually said— that black men and women don't have much chance. It's a lie. If the Negro doesn't succeed in today's America, it is because he has chosen to fail. Yes, there are exceptions. But there are exceptions for whites, too.

The black militants of today, often talking from integrated highrises, restaurants, and universities, don't know what it is to be really shut out, as we were in our Oakvilles. The soapboxing blackthinkers, the angry extrem-ists, the nationalists, represent a very small minority of today's Negroes. The violence, hate and self-pity they preach are the easy way out. What we need is self-control, true assertiveness and long-range planning. We can't expect to undo hundreds of years in a month or two.

Not every man can have a Charles Riley [or a Lutz Long], but every Negro has a Martin Luther King. If the black man is owed a debt from the past, he owes a debt, too. He owes the men who have come before him, the ones who helped him personally, and the many more who helped him by standing up when it counted and not copping out. He owes it to them not to give in to violence and anger, owes it to a lot of men as yet unborn. He owes it to himself to be a man, a human being, first and last, if not always.

You see, black *isn't* beautiful. *White* isn't beautiful. Skin-deep is never beautiful.

Bobbie Shaftoe

Author Unknown

Teachers usually reward quiet, compliant students. Yet, more often than not, the so-called troublemakers are the ones who succeed and go on to blaze new trails. Bobbie Shaftoe was one of those troublemakers— until the sudden storm.

Bobbie Shaftoe's gone to sea,
Silver buckles on his knee.
He'll come back and marry me.
Pretty Bobbie Shaftoe.

This old and musical nursery rhyme had been ringing in my head all day as I went about my work. My work was teaching a district school halfway between Garret's Mills and Bentley's Dam—so situated in order to accommodate children from both villages.

Why that ancient nursery rhyme should have been singing itself in my head all day, I do not know, unless it was because one of my pupils, popularly known as Bobbie Shaftoe, had that morning given me an unusual amount of trouble. How and when he received the nickname, I never heard. Perhaps it was because of his oft-declared ambition to be a sailor and to go to sea; possibly it was because of a similarity of sound between this name and the real one. He was 10 years old, bright and active, and the most mischievous child I had ever seen—not maliciously mischievous, but good-naturedly, irrepressibly, unceasingly mischievous. Such mild punishment as his mirthful misdemeanor deserved had but momentary effect on him, and one must have had an unusually hard heart to have chastised Bobbie with any degree of severity.

On the June day of which I write, Bobbie was more than ordinarily full of pranks and practical jokes. He had been busy with them all the bright morning, and he was holding his own steadily through the hot and sultry afternoon. I had reprimanded him, times without number; I had punished him mildly time and again, without lasting effect. Finally, I seated him on top of a cold stove in order to humiliate him, but from that conspicuous perch his comical motions and strange grimaces, when my back was turned, kept the entire school snickering until I took him down. After that he made an amusing picture on his slate, of himself sitting on the stove, and held it up to be laughed at by the boys in his vicinity; but before I could capture it, his sponge had obliterated forever this triumph of his art. His next achievement that afternoon was the production of little pasteboard figures of men, pinned to a stick and fighting each other furiously as his deft fingers pulled the string attached to them. I caught him at it squarely.

"Let me have them, Bobbie," said I.

He turned them over to me without a murmur, explaining as he did so, "You pull thith thtring w'en he knockth 'em down. I'll thow you, thee? Don't they jutht lambatht each other, though?"

It is needless to say that the school was again diverted; everyone, save Bobbie and me, grinned broadly. He was sober and I was annoyed.

"Give them to me at once," I said sharply. "What am I going to do with such a boy? How shall I punish you? I have tried everything except a severe whipping. Shall I give you that? Or can you suggest something else?"

He cast his eyes to the ceiling and screwed up his mouth comically, as if in intense thought. The school broke out in renewed laughter. Finally, he said, "You might put me up in the loft, Mith Mitchell. I haven't been up there yet."

"Very well," I replied quickly. "Up into the loft you go."

He was a little staggered at the suddenness of my decision. I don't think he really expected me to adopt his suggestion, for the loft was not a pleasant place to go into. It was dark, hot, and empty, with the roof sloping down on each side, so that only through the middle of it could a boy stand erect.

"Here, Bobbie," I continued, "help me to set this table under the opening—that's it. Now give me that chair."

The horizontal aperture that led to the loft was just over the high platform that stretched across the rear end of the room, and with the aid of a chair placed on the table, one could readily climb up to it.

"You hold fatht to the chair an' don't let her thlip," cautioned Bobbie as he hitched up his suspenders, screwed up his face, and made ready for his grand ascent.

He climbed to the table, mounted the chair, and thrust his head and shoulders through the opening, out of sight. He drew them down again in a moment to say, "It'th dark up there, Mith Mitchell."

"I know it," I replied calmly.

"An' hot."

"I know it."

"An'—an'—lonethome."

"That's why I'm sending you up there."

"Well," he sighed, "here goeth. Good-bye."

He reached up, grasped the framework of the opening, and in the next instant he had drawn his pliant little body up out of sight. I lifted the chair down, removed the table, and tried to go on with the routine of recitations. There was some scrambling above in the loft; once I saw a bare brown foot twinkling down through the opening for a second, for the edification of all of Bobbie's fellow pupils; and once a dust-begrimed face, inverted and comical, looked carefully down and set the school in a new roar.

"Bobbie," I called out to him finally, "put the cover down on the opening at once." I had not thought to have this done—it would make it so dark up there—but his irrepressible mischief left me no recourse.

"Yeth'm," he replied still cheerfully. "Thall I thit on it to hold it down?"

"Certainly."

The cover, which was on hinges, was carefully let down, and this movement was immediately followed by a thud, which indicated that Bobbie was "thitting on it." After that, save certain indefinable sounds, all was quiet in the region of the loft.

The afternoon tasks went on monotonously. The day grew more sultry as it drew to its close. Just before it was time to dismiss school, one of my pupils, a little girl, after looking out a moment through the open door into the dusty road, rose quickly from her seat, threw up her hand, and began to snap vigorously with her finger and thumb to attract my attention.

"Well, what is it, Rosie?" I inquired.

"Please, Miss Mitchell, Bobbie Shaftoe is out there in the road."

"Who?" I asked in amazement.

"Bobbie Shaftoe. He's out there hiding behind a tree."

Of course, everyone turned and looked out of the door. At that moment a little figure darted out from the shadow of one tree and sought shelter behind another. It was indeed Bobbie Shaftoe. How he managed to make his escape from the loft I could not conjecture.

I went to the door and called, "Bobbie! Bobbie! Bobbie Shaftoe!"

He left the protection of the tree at once. "Yeth'm," he replied, "I'm coming."

He had evidently hurt his foot in some way, as he limped slightly as he came up the steps.

"Take your seat, Bobbie," I said sternly, "and don't move out of it until I give you permission to do so."

He hung his head a trifle as if he were ashamed at last of his deeds, dropped into his seat, and sat there in perfect quiet during the few minutes that intervened before school closed. I dismissed the pupils somewhat ahead of time, as there seemed a thundershower coming in the west and I wished them to get to their homes before it rained; but Bobbie I kept with me to punish him. I had my monthly report to make out. I had thought of keeping him in his seat during the hour that I should be thus occupied. He sat quietly but had taken up a book and begun to study.

After a while my curiosity got the better of my determination, and I said to him, "Bobbie, will you tell me how you escaped from the loft?"

He answered, "Yeth'm, I opened the thcuttle hole in the roof—it'th right up there, you know—and I climbed out on the ridgepole. There'th a limb of that big elm hangth right down there, and I got on that, and then it was eathy to thlide down to the ground."

The escape shorn of its mystery was simple enough after all. A low, ominous roll of thunder ended in a bass so deep and powerful that it sent a tremor through the building.

"Bobbie," I said with sudden resolution, "I wish you wouldn't give me so much trouble. I don't want to be scolding and punishing you all the time. I like you too well for that."

Bobbie looked at me with calm seriousness in his deep blue eyes. "I've been thinkin' about that, Mith Mitchell," he replied. "I like you, too. I'm goin' to thtop it. I am goin' to try to be better."

"Oh, will you, Bobbie?"

"I will."

I saw by the quiet look of resolution on his face that he meant it.

"Thank you, Bobbie," I exclaimed, taking both his little brown hands in mine.

I was going to say something else to him, but a sharp flash of lightning, followed in a second by a crack and a crash of thunder, interrupted me. I hastened to shut the doors and close the windows and lower such apologies for shades as we had. Sudden darkness fell upon us, and thunders were incessant. I sat on the steps of the platform and held Bobbie's hand, thankful for human company and sympathy. The rain came and fell, not in drops, but in sheets and layers. In a minute the public road in front of us was a dashing torrent. In another, the schoolhouse lot was a miniature lake. But the terrible stormbursts soon passed us by. The roar of the rain died away toward the east. After a little while the sky began to brighten, and I gained courage to look from the window on the washed and flooded landscape. Bobbie had behaved like a hero. Not one word had passed from his lips, and beyond the slight pallor of his face, one could see in it no signs of fear.

"I gueth it'th gone by now, Mith Mitchell," he said. "Wathn't it a big one, though?"

The words were scarcely out of his mouth when a new sound came to our ears—a sound more ominous than any we had heard yet, increasing in volume with every passing second. Bobbie stood for a moment intently listening, then dashed to the platform and tore back the shade from the window. We both looked out.

"It'th Bentley'th Dam," he cried. "It'th burtht."

Far up the ravine, where Coulters Creek came dancing through in the summertime, a solid mass of water was sweeping down toward us, crested with the debris of its journey. It would strike the pond, flood the narrow valley, and wash the schoolhouse from its foundation. This was inevitable, yet there was no escape. Before we could cross half the distance to the nearest house, the water would be upon us. I started back into the room and covered my face with my hands.

Bobbie stood for a moment in fearful indecision; then he flung his arms toward the ceiling and cried, "The loft—the roof—the tree!"

I grasped the idea at once. In it lay the only hope of safety. We seized the table, placed it in position, and flung the chair on it. The next moment Bobbie was shoving up the cover with herculean strength. It yielded and fell back. He plunged upward into the darkness of the loft and had his hands down to help me before I had fairly gained the chair. The next moment we were both climbing out at the scuttle to the ridge of the roof. Even as we did so, the flood came down. It was deafening to hear and so frightful to see. On its crest were the wrecks of houses, and in its foam, dead bodies were tossed. It struck the pond and then swept on to the dam, the bridge, and then the narrow gorge below us; then, checked in its progress, it came leaping, flooding, up the bank and across the road, rising with fearful rapidity to the windows of the schoolhouse, rolling a boiling, foam-flecked wall of death and destruction out into the field.

"Grab it, quick! Go up!" Bobbie was calling as he held the limb of the tree within my reach.

I was weak from fright, and the swirling waters made my head swim. I grasped the limb and pulled myself along on it, but so slowly and awkwardly that Bobbie, losing his hold, caught my foot and pushed me upward. The water was at the eaves; the schoolhouse was swaying on its foundation.

I caught and clung wildly to the next branch above my head and cried out, "Save yourself, Bobbie! Hurry, save yourself."

The building lurched ponderously to one side as Bobbie grasped for the limb, missed it, and fell back onto the ridgepole of the roof. He caught hold on the framework of the scuttle to save himself from falling into the waves and clung to it desperately as the building, loosed from its bearings, went sailing out upon the flood. Already the waters were beginning to recede. The schoolhouse, rising and falling, dipping and twisting, went swimming down toward the gorge.

"Good-bye," called Bobbie as he went past, "good-bye, and hang on tight, Mith Mitchell. I'm goin' to thea."

"Good-bye," I called back to him. "Oh Bobbie, good-bye!"

The waves dashed over his head now and again as he floated out of sight; and even in that dreadful moment, the words of that sweet, old nursery rhyme came back to my mind:

> Bobbie Shaftoe's gone to sea,
> Silver buckles on his knee.
> He'll come back and marry me.
> Pretty Bobbie Shaftoe.

The flood went down, and the ruined landscape lay bare of water, save in pools and ponds. Twilight descended beautiful as a dream, and through it came the men from the village, seeking the lost and dead; they helped me down from the tree that had saved me. I went shivering to Bobbie Shaftoe's house. At midnight they brought him home. They had found him far down the stream, tangled in the wreckage of the flood. He was not dead, but that was the most hopeful thing one could say of him.

At dawn, he flung out his arms from the coverlet. "Hang on tight, Mith Mitchell," he cried weakly. "Good-bye, I'm goin' to thea."

"Oh Bobbie!" I cried. "Come back to me, brave Bobbie!"

He seemed to hear me and to understand, for he opened his eyes and answered, "Yeth, Mith Mitchell, I have been thinkin' about it, an' I will."

And he did. Night and day I sat by him and nursed him back to health and strength. But when he grew to be well again, his mischievous nature had left him. He was a changed boy. He was sober and studious. And even before the years of his youth had wholly passed, earnest manhood rested on him like a crown.

When Tulips Die in the Spring

Ruth Garren

Jenny knew that tulips shouldn't be pulled from the ground until they died down completely. Strangely enough, she was to discover another application for that statement—one that had to do with Old-Timers' Day fiddling.

Only nine o'clock in the morning, and already it was hot. Jenny looked out of her bedroom window. The fields and trees around the house had gone from spring green to the deeper green of summer in one rainless week.

Her grandfather, whom everyone called Papa John, was working in the garden. She could hear the *tick-tick* of his hoe against the dry earth and the chirping of a few birds.

Last week Jenny had gotten out of school for the summer. Already she knew it was going to be long.

She turned from the window to her dresser, which was covered with trophies: six years of Presidential Fitness awards; a handful of ribbons from Field Day events at school; seven firsts, three seconds, and one grand prize trophy for fiddling in Mountain Youth festivals.

She picked up the newspaper clippings from the Benton *Beacon*, sealed in plastic to keep them from yellowing. Jenny was five years old in the photograph, and her great-grandfather, whom she'd always called Grandpa, was 75. The photographer had caught the two of them, dappled in sunlight, through the leaves of a huge oak tree, holding their fiddles and smiling into each other's faces.

The paper read: "Five-year-old Jenny Burrows is a fifth-generation fiddler. Her great-grandfather Clive Sprague, of Benton, and his brother Gus, of Hiwassee, were taught by their father when they were about Jenny's age. Clive, in turn, taught his daughter Helen (now deceased) and his grandson Philip, Jenny's father, who died in Vietnam. 'Jenny's got real talent,' Mr. Sprague comments. 'You've either got it or you don't, and Jenny's got more of it than any young'un I've ever taught—in or out of the family.' Jenny's mother plays the mandolin. Other family members play the bass fiddle, guitars, and banjos. The family group entertains regularly in the Polk County area. Look for them on Old-Timers' Day at Big Ridge Park at the same spot under the big oak where family members have gathered a crowd on Old-Timers' Day for 70 years."

Jenny studied the photograph. Grandpa's face was crisscrossed with lines. Now the lines had turned to furrows, giving his face character and making him a natural subject for photographers who showed up at every Old-Timers' Day.

Jenny set the clippings back on the dresser. *Well, they're in for a surprise this year*, she thought, *because Jenny Burrows, award-winning fiddler, will not be fiddling on Old-Timers' Day. She's had enough.* She tied her hair back with a ribbon to lift it from her neck.

Jenny went outside. Her mother was digging holes in the dirt and planting flowers. A drop of sweat balanced on the tip of her nose. Streaks of dirt showed where she had wiped her forehead.

"You look as if you've been out here awhile," Jenny said.

"A couple of hours."

"And you're going to get one of those redneck tans again, Mom. Just like last year."

"Well, Jenny, the only way to avoid that is to work outside in my bathing suit, and I don't believe I'll be doing that."

Again this spring Mom was mixing petunias and impatiens, snapdragons and begonias, without much thought for color or design.

"Mom," Jenny asked her, not for the first time, "why don't you do all pink things, or all pink and white? This is going to look like a crazy quilt."

"Well, honey, it's the way I like it."

Jenny knew she would say that.

"Mom, I want to talk to you about something."

"Go right ahead."

"I don't want to play for Old-Timers' Day Sunday."

"Why not?"

"Because I don't play the fiddle anymore."

"Since when?"

"Since now. I'm beginning to get good on the violin, and I don't want to get myself mixed up."

"What does your teacher say about that?"

"Nothing. He doesn't know I play the fiddle."

"You mean to tell me you've been taking lessons from him for two years and you didn't tell him?"

"No."

"And he's never caught on?"

"No."

"He never thought you were a bit gifted for a beginner?"

"He said I had good tone for a beginner, but I just said thank you and let him teach me technique and everything else, just like I'd never held a bow or a violin before."

"Well, Jenny Burrows"—the spade was furiously stabbing the earth—"that is deceitful. That is right next door to an outright lie. Do you think your grandmother would have done that, or your father?"

"I don't know, and I don't care. Fiddling is a hokey thing to do anyway."

"Hokey? Where did you get that idea? You are going to break your great-grandfather's heart, young lady, and your uncle Gus's, too."

"They'll get over it."

"They're in their eighties. They may not have another Old-Timers' Day."

"You're trying to lay guilt on me, Mom. I hate it when you do that. Grandpa and Uncle Gus might as well get used to playing without me. Besides, there's Uncle Gus's family."

"But they've never been as good as you are, and they never will be. And you know it." Mom paused a minute and stood up to confront Jenny at eye level. "You know you can't put your 'hokey' mountain traditions behind you any more than you can deny the fact that you're a fourth-generation Christian."

"Well, the jury is still out on that one."

"Jenny Burrows!" her mother said, shocked.

"What are those ugly things there?" Jenny asked, trying to change a subject she wished she'd never started.

"Those are the last of the tulips."

"Why don't you dig them out?"

"Because it's not time yet. They have to die down completely; then you can just pull the stems out of the ground. I figure I'll put these impatiens there, and pretty soon they'll be big enough so you won't even notice the tulips."

"I'd pull them out."

"I know you would."

Old-Timers' Day dawned bright and clear, the kind of weather Jenny used to pray for in the old days. In the kitchen her mom was packing sandwiches and potato salad into the cooler. Mom's mandolin and Jenny's fiddle stood at the back door, ready to be carried to Papa John's van.

"My fiddle's there," Jenny pointed out. "I told you not to pack it."

"It's Papa's van, Jenny, and he'll take it if he wants to."

"Well, do what you want, but you're just taking up space for nothing."

The scene at Big Ridge Park was as noisy, colorful, and confusing as in past summers. Some groups were already playing music. Others were standing around talking. People who had come to listen waited with their lawn chairs to see which groups might be worthy of their sitting-down attention.

Grandpa began tuning up. Papa John, who said he'd married his wife, Helen, to get music genes into his family, not because he had any talent to bring to hers, sat in a chair in the shade. He and Helen had had only one child, Philip. Philip and Madge had had only Jenny, and only Jenny was left.

The music began. Grandpa led with a slow, gentle ballad. Jenny noticed that his fingers were stiff and his tone no longer as warm or rich as she remembered it. Still, he was one of the best fiddlers around.

Then someone asked for "Foggy Mountain Breakdown," a fast-clogging number. Grandpa started out playing first fiddle, but his fingers faltered. He nodded toward Gus's son Axel. Axel took over, fumbling a little in the beginning, but not doing too badly. Still, Jenny could see the frustration on Grandpa's face. He was used to being the best.

Jenny remembered how in the old days, when she was just learning, Grandpa's expertise had covered for her immature playing. Could she do any less for him?

She went to the van and got her fiddle. She tuned it as she walked back, holding the instrument, made by Grandpa himself, gently under her chin.

She slid in at the edge of the group and began playing second fiddle with Grandpa, her bowing sure and strong, her tone as mellow as his had been in his best years.

He nodded to her, and she took the lead. Her fingers had become stronger and more flexible from violin lessons and typing classes. The music filtered up among the leaves of the oak tree and wafted off toward the mountains that made up Big Ridge. People set their lawn chairs down to relax and listen and watch.

Jenny was taking over for her great-grandfather, covering his weak tones with her strong ones as he had once done for her. Yes, it was right *not* to pull out the tulips—her roots. As the cameras clicked, she again smiled up into Grandpa's furrowed face.

The Story of a Stepmothering

Annie Hamilton Donnell

**The day young Elizabeth married
John Hyder, she would become
a stepmother to his five children.
What if she couldn't handle it?
Then Aunt Hannah gave her
some advice.**

"Sit down," Aunt Hannah said, smiling welcomingly; but the girl—
she seemed scarcely more than that—shook her head. She stood in
the doorway, stretching out imploring hands.

"Help! Help! Aunt Hannah, save me! I'm scared."

The smile upon Aunt Hannah's sweet old face broadened to a
laugh that gently shook her body.

"I should know it, my dear; you look scared. Sit down; things don't
look half so bad sitting down. Then begin right at the beginning,
and out with it. What are chair-ridden old aunts for if not to listen
to young lovers' troub—"

"Don't put John in, Aunt Hannah. He doesn't seem 'troubled' in

207

the least; and, besides, he isn't a young lover, poor boy! I haven't told him, but I think I've found a thin place on the top of his . . . Aunt Hannah, I ought to be middle-aging, too. Here I am, the giddiest young thing on Essex Street. I haven't disgraced you and John yet; but I'm going to. I feel it in my bones."

There was a short space of silence in the old-fashioned, sunny room, except for the soothing tick-tocks of the clock on the mantel, like strokes of a gentling hand. The young voice was quieter when it began again.

"It's this way. I don't dread the baby—bless his three years!—nor the next two, three. It's the Girl at the Top I dread, Aunt Hannah. What shall I do? John is—why, just a man. He can't see why the mere word 'stepmother' should set my heart flitter-flutter and take away all my courage. What would you do, Aunt Hannah?"

"Marry John."

"Of course I shall do that, but then what?"

"Go home with him, and mother his children."

"But they'll call it—everybody will call it—*stepmothering* them. And the Girl at the Top won't love me; I know she won't, Aunt Hannah! I dreamed she hated me. Why, I'm only nine years older than she is, and John says she's old for her age."

More silence and soothing tick-tocks, while in her invalid chair sat Aunt Hannah, dreaming a sad little past dream of her own. A John was in it, and motherless little children that she had shrunk from mothering. Long years after, when old age and invalidism came hand-in-hand to meet her, the loneliness ahead appalled her; and the thought of her John and his sons and daughters, who might have been hers, too, was dreary company for her.

"My dear"—Aunt Hannah's old eyes were wet; her old voice shook a little—"take a lonely old maid's advice. Marry your John, and bring up his babies; and the Lord help you. Don't be afraid anymore, my dear."

"No," Elizabeth Armstrong said, oddly strengthened and comforted, "I

won't be afraid. John and the children are what matters, not I. I'll do my best, Aunt Hannah."

"Sew on their buttons," Aunt Hannah said softly, thinking of little buttons she might have sewed on. "Sew 'em on strong, my dear. Bind up their little wounds and bumps. Give 'em time to love you, but love them right off. It will all come out right."

"But the oldest one, the Girl at the Top," Elizabeth murmured. "If she hasn't any bumps to bind—"

"She will have! *Find* 'em and bind 'em, my dear."

The young woman rose and stood before the little gray person in the invalid's chair. "I will, Aunt Hannah," she said humbly and went away relieved.

At the home of John Hyder, five children waited for the new mother. The Girl at the Top drilled them every day like this: "Be nice *always* to her. Take off your caps, boys; Judy, say 'Ma'am.' Remember she will be Father's wife."

"But she won't be our mother," Judy persisted.

"No"—sharply—"nobody said she would. If Father says to *call* her so, you'll have to. But that won't make her a mother. Only . . . "—here the Girl at the Top always spoke with slow emphasis—" . . . *only, be nice to her."*

The day the new wife was expected, the drill was more elaborate and protracted. The children were apportioned parts of a stiff little ceremony of welcome. As soon as wheels sounded on the drive, the boys were to hurry to the front door and stand, one on either side, caps in hand. Judy was to stand just inside the door and smile, only smile. As for herself, the Girl at the Top straightened her young shoulders and girded herself for the ordeal. Her fresh face whitened at its near approach. To the baby alone was not apportioned a part in the grim little welcome ceremony; whatever the baby at the dread moment willed to do, he would do. He would have to be left to his own devices. But, "Oh Bobby, Bobby, Bobby, don't kiss her!" besought the Girl at the Top of the family. And so together they all waited.

"John," the young bride was saying rather tremulously, "you'll have to hold up my hands. I'm getting fainthearted. Is 'Stepmother' written on my face, John? It must be; for I can feel the letters—s-t-e-p and the rest. This minute the people on this train are saying, 'Stepmother, stepmother; look at her!' I wish Aunt Hannah had come, too."

They were getting close now. Only a few more miles of shining track and a little riding behind a horse—then the lights, the house, and the children! Elizabeth Hyder's sweet face was full of anxiety. So much depended on the beginning, she had been told.

"Here we are!" John Hyder announced cheerfully as the train stopped. He looked so capable and unafraid and happy that Elizabeth took belated courage and followed him spryly out to the platform. They took a carriage and rode away in the moist, pleasant darkness. Hand found hand in the little shut-in space, and new husband and new wife silently renewed their vows.

Wheels! The boys sprang to their posts and swept off their caps. Judy stationed herself and put on painfully her pale, little smile. The straight young figure of the Girl at the Top leaped straighter yet. Only the baby sat on, unconcerned, upstairs among his toys.

They came up the steps together, hand-in-hand, walked between the capless sentinels up to the steady smile of Judy. Then the Girl at the Top came forward, her careful little speech trembling on her lips. "We bid you— bid you welcome," she said. "We hope you will find—find—will find—"

But she never found it, for at that instant the ears of the new mother were greeted by shriek on shriek, bump on bump. The baby was coming down to meet her. From stair to stair bounded his little body. Instant confusion reigned, and the ceremony of welcome ended, scarcely begun.

It was the new mother who received the little bounding baby at the foot of the stairs. Her outstretched arms caught him. Quivering and shrieking, he lay against her breast. Instantly, her trained senses—for she had been a nurse—perceived that more than fright and bruising was the matter. She blanched at the sight of a dangling little arm.

"Go for a doctor, John," she whispered, too low for little ears. She lifted a smiling face to the frightened children about her. "Don't anybody say a word; everybody smile, *smile!* I'm going to tell this baby a story, here, right in this cushiony chair. Hush, hush, darling; don't you want to hear what the Balloon Man did? Don't move one little inch, and I'll tell you; it was such a funny thing to do."

The shrieking trailed out piteously into sobs. The new mother, wincing herself at the baby's pain, held the tiny body absolutely still. "Well," she began cheerily, "the Balloon Man bumped into a little cloud and made it cry. It was a baby cloud, you know—not three years old and brave, like you. And way down, down below on the earth, what do you suppose people began to do?"

The quiet voice waited. The little sobs almost stopped.

"Well, they began to put up their umbrellas. 'Why, it's raining!' they said; for the baby cloud was crying, you know. 'Excuse me,' the Balloon Man begged, for he was a very polite Balloon Man—there, there, darling, don't cry, don't move! Don't you want me to sing a funny little song about the kitty that couldn't spell 'cat'? It begins this way—"

She hurried into a merry little tune, tilting her head in time and making funny faces. Then another story, another song—would the doctor never come? The moments seemed hours.

When he came, the other children were sent away. They went with scared, pale faces; and the girls covered their ears. The Girl at the Top of the family had hers still buried in her pillows when, after what seemed a great while, someone touched her arm. She sat up rigidly.

"Is he dead?" she demanded.

"He is sound asleep," her father answered quietly. "The doctor has gone. It is a very bad break, and it will take the greatest care to keep him perfectly quiet. My dear"—the big hand stroked her hair lightly—"your new mother would like to see you. Will you go to her? She cannot leave the baby."

Laura—the Girl at the Top was named Laura—sank back among her pillows. Not alone; she did not want to go alone. She was frankly afraid. What did stepmothers say to stepdaughters? Did they make fine speeches? And oh—oh, if they kissed—

"I don't want to go," she cried into her pillows.

Her father, patiently waiting, did not hear. He touched her arm again.

"Laurie, will you go? For my sake, Laurie?"

And for his sake she went. The room where Bobby lay, very white and still on the bed, was dim in the twilight. It was quite a moment before the girl saw the slight figure bending over Bobby.

"Oh, I'm glad you've come!" whispered a sweet voice. "*Will* you take off my hat for me? One of the hat pins in it aches! I don't dare to move; this blessed baby went to sleep holding my thumbs. Oh, thank you!" an instant later as the girl's deft fingers removed the dainty bridal creation. "Now I can take some comfort. Your father wanted to take it off, and I wouldn't let him.

A *man* can't take hat pins out. It takes womenfolk to do critical things like that—and like this, dear." Her eyes sought the girl's eyes and drew them to the little, wan face on the bed. "We must take care of him together, don't you see? I am so glad you are grown-up. You see, the doctor was very imperative about our keeping him from moving his poor little arm. He *mustn't*. It's up to you and me, dear—"

The bit of harmless slang was oddly reassuring to Laura. She had not expected stepmothers to talk like girls. She moved a little nearer in the twilight, straining her ears for the soft whisper. It came very soon.

"If you could get me a drink of water . . . I think it makes a person thirsty to sit in one position so long."

The Girl at the Top hurried noiselessly away. When she came back with the glass of water, a faint, rather shaky, whispered laugh greeted her. "You'll have to 'drink' me!" the new mother said. "I don't dare to move an inch. Every minute he sleeps is worth so much, poor little broken boy! Would you be willing to hold the glass to my lips?"

Here was another unexpected thing. Who would have thought a stepmother would do this? Laura held the glass with unsteady little fingers. A drop splashed onto them, another onto the new mother's cheek. The softest possible laugh followed, and without at all meaning to, the Girl at the Top joined in.

After a little, Laura lighted a lamp and shaded it carefully from the bed. Father came tiptoeing in and whispered something about supper, but no, no, the stooping figure beside Bobby would not listen to him. What did she need of supper? She must not move yet, not yet awhile.

She had her way. Laura, at her father's instigation, brought in a cup of hot milk and a plate of toast and fed her like a little child. It made them both laugh in the soundless way they had so quickly learned. Then Laura was sent away for her own supper.

The long night set in. The new mother's face grew strained and white, but she refused to move. No, Laura might *not* take her place, not yet; yes, oh, yes! she might *stay.*

"I'll be so glad to have you! You may put a pillow behind my back; there, that is a blessing. How handy you are! Now sit in that easy chair opposite and get three winks, like a good little—girl."

It almost seemed as if she had started to say "good little daughter." Laura found herself wishing a strange thing—that she *had* said it! It would have sounded good in the hushed, half-lighted room with Bobby, the baby they both loved, there in a little white heap on the bed. The new mother must love Bobby; Laura, watching her, was sure of it. The position was very hard to keep; she was certainly growing whiter. Laura got up and hurried to her.

"Let me come, please, please!" she begged.

"Not yet. He is sleeping so blessedly, dear."

"Dear"—it sounded sweet to Laura. She sat in the great chair, thinking new thoughts about stepmothers. A long time seemed to pass. Only the ticking clock spoke. Then, "Laura! Laura, come!"

The girl sprang to her feet. Just in time she got to the new mother, in time to catch her in strong young arms. She was fainting; Father must come.

Bobby's clinging fingers relaxed and curled again sleepily; he did not wake.

"I shall be all right in a minute; don't call anyone. Just—just hold me. You have such good arms. I couldn't bear it another minute. . . . Oh, isn't it good I didn't wake him up?"

The girl's arms around the new mother trembled. A sudden yearning came over her. All wise young theories and dreads fled in shame before this sweet presence of love. Laura stooped her humbled little face to the pinched white lips and voluntarily kissed them. It was more than a kiss. It was a surrender.

Aunt Hannah, wrote the young wife by and by, *you knew. It is all "coming out right." I'm glad I married my John, and I'm glad I married my John's family.*

Interview with an Immortal

Arthur Gordon

He came looking for an answer, but was too timid and awed by greatness to ask the question. When the day was over, the question he never asked had been answered.

The month was June; the English weather was blue and gold. The world was young, and so was I. But driving down from Oxford in the old Sunbeam I had borrowed for the occasion, I felt my assurance deserting me.

The great man was almost a recluse now, and it was said that he did not care for Americans. Through a mutual friend, I had managed to secure permission to visit him. Now as I neared the little village of Burwash, where he lived, I began to experience something like stage fright. And when I found the somber seventeenth-century house and saw my host walking down to the gate to meet me, I grew so flustered that I hardly knew whether to shake hands or turn and run.

He was so small! The crown of the floppy hat he wore was not much higher than my shoulder, and I doubt if he weighed 120 pounds. His skin was dark for an Englishman's; his mustache was almost white. His eyebrows were as thick and tangled as marsh grass, but behind the gold-rimmed glasses, his eyes were as bright as a terrier's. He was 69 years old.

He saw instantly how ill at ease I was. "Come in, come in," he said companionably, opening the gate. "I was just going to inspect my navy."

A Scottie came bounding down the path and stopped short when he saw me.

"Now, this," his master said, "is Malachi. He's really quite friendly. But of course, being a Scot, he hates to show it."

He led me, still speechless, to a pond at the end of the garden, and there was the so-called navy: a six-foot skiff with hand-cranked paddle wheels. "You can be the engine room," he said. "I'll be the passenger list."

I was so agitated that I cranked too hard. The paddle wheel broke, and there I was, marooned in the middle of a fishpond with Rudyard Kipling. He began to laugh, and so did I, and the ice was broken.

A gardener finally rescued us with a long rake. By then my host had me talking. There was something about him that drove the shyness out of you, a kind of understanding that went deeper than words and set up an instantaneous closeness. It was odd; we couldn't have been more different. He was British; I was American. He was near the end of an illustrious road; I was at the beginning of an obscure one. He had had years of ill health and pain; I was untouched by either. He knew nothing about me—there was nothing to know. I knew all about him, and so to me he was not just a fragile little man in a toy boat. He was Kim and Fuzzy Wuzzy and Gunga Din. He was Danny Deever and the Elephant's Child. He was the dawn coming up like thunder on the road to Mandalay; he was the rough laughter of the barracks room, the chatter of the bazaar, and the great organ tones of "Recessional." To me he was, quite simply, a miracle, and no

doubt this showed in my dazzled eyes, and he felt it and was warmed by it.

I had had an ulterior motive in coming, of course. I wanted to meet him for himself, but I was also a puzzled and unsure young man. I had in my pocket a letter offering me a job as instructor at an American university. I didn't really want to be a teacher; I knew I didn't have the selflessness or the patience. What I wanted to be, ultimately, was a writer. But the teaching job was the only offer I had. I had no other prospects, no money at all. At home, the dead hand of the Great Depression still lay heavy on the land. Should I play it safe and say yes to the offer?

What I wanted desperately was for someone of great wisdom and experience in the field of letters to tell me what to do. But I knew this was a preposterous responsibility to thrust upon a stranger. And so I waited, hoping that somehow the heavens would open and the miracle of certainty would descend upon me.

While I waited, he talked. And as he talked, I began to forget about my problems. He tossed words into the air, and they flashed like swords. He spoke of his friendship with Cecil Rhodes, through whose generosity I had gone to Oxford. "They say we were both imperialists," said Kipling a little grimly. "Well, maybe we were. The word is out of fashion now, and some Englishmen are weak enough to be ashamed of it. I'm not."

He questioned me almost sharply about some poets of prominence: Eliot, Stein, Cummings. I said I thought they were good.

"Do you?" he asked guilelessly. "Quote me a few lines."

I sat there, helpless, and he laughed.

"You see," he said, "that's the trouble with verse that doesn't rhyme. But let's not be too harsh where poets are concerned. They have to live in no-man's-land, halfway between dreams and reality."

"Like Mowgli," I said impulsively, thinking of the brown-skinned boy torn between village and jungle.

He gave me a look with his blue eyes. "Like most of us," he said.

He talked of ambition, of how long it took to fully master any art or craft. And of secondary ambitions: The more you had, he said, the more fully you lived. "I always wanted to build or buy a 400-ton brig," he said reflectively, "and sail her around the world. Never did. Now, I suppose, it's too late." He lit a cigarette and looked at me through the smoke. "Do the things you really want to do if you possibly can. Don't wait for circumstances to be exactly right. You'll find that they never are.

"My other unrealized ambition," he went on, "was to be an archaeologist. For sheer, gem-studded romance, no other job can touch it. Why, right under our feet here in Sussex . . . "

He described how he had decided to sink a well. A few feet down, they found a Jacobean tobacco pipe. Below that, a Cromwellian latten spoon. Still farther down, a Roman horse bit. And, finally, water.

We went back to his study, a large, square room lined with bookcases on two sides. There were his desk, his chair, an enormous wastebasket, and his pens—the kind you dip in ink. At right angles to the fireplace was a small sofa.

"I lie there," he said with a smile, "and wait for my demon to tell me what to do."

"Demon?"

He shrugged. "Intuition. Subconscious. Whatever you want to call it."

"Can you always hear him?"

"No," he said slowly, "not always. But I learned long ago that it's best to wait until you do. When your demon says nothing, he usually means no."

Mrs. Kipling called us to lunch, and afterward I felt I should take my leave. But Kipling would not hear of it.

"I'm still full of talk," he said. "You've eaten my salt, so now you must be my audience."

So we talked. Or rather, he talked while I made superhuman efforts to remember everything. He had a way of thrusting a harsh truth at you and then, in the next breath, beguiling you into a wry acceptance of it.

"If you're endowed," he said at one point, "with any significant energies or talent, you may as well resign yourself to the fact that throughout your life you will be carrying coattail riders who will try to exploit you. But instead of fuming and fretting about this, you'd better thank God for the qualities that attract the parasites and not waste time trying to shake them off."

We talked of friendship; he thought young ones were best and lasted longest. "When you're young," he said, "you're not afraid to give yourself away. You offer warmth and vitality and sympathy without thinking. Later on, you begin to weigh what you give."

I said, somewhat diffidently, that he was giving me a lot, and his eyes twinkled. "A fair exchange. You're giving me attention. That's a form of affection, you know."

Looking back, I think he knew that in my innocence I was eager to love everything and please everybody, and he was trying to warn me not to lose my own identity in the process. Time after time he came back to this theme.

"The individual has always had to struggle to keep from being over-whelmed by the tribe. To be your own man is a hard business. If you try it, you'll be lonely often, and sometimes frightened. But no price is too high to pay for the privilege of owning yourself."

Suddenly, the shadows were long on the grass. When I stood up to go, I remembered the letter in my pocket and the advice I had thought I wanted. But now there was nothing to ask. *Do the things you really want to do. . . . Don't wait for circumstances to be exactly right. . . . When your demon says nothing, he usually means no. . . . No price is too high to pay for the privilege of owning yourself.*

I knew now that I would refuse the teaching job and wait for my demon to speak clearly to me.

We walked to the gate, Malachi scampering ahead of us. My host held out his hand.

"Thank you," he said. "You've done me good."

The thought that I could have done anything for him was beyond my grasp. I thanked him and climbed into the old Sunbeam. I looked back once. He was still standing there in his floppy hat, a great little man who forgot his own illness and his own problems and spent a whole day trying to help a troubled and self-conscious boy from across the sea.

He had a gift for young friendships, all right. He gave me much more than advice. He gave me a little bit of himself to carry away. After all these years, I feel the warmth of it still.

The Canopy Bed

Temple Bailey

Diminutive Van Alen wished he could be tall so that lovely Mazie Wetherell would be impressed with him. He had not yet learned that a man's stature isn't necessarily determined by his height.

"My great-grandfather slept in it," Van Alen told the caretaker as she ushered him into the big, stuffy bedroom.

The old woman set her candlestick down on the quaint dresser. "He must have been a little man," she said. "None of my sons could sleep in it. Their feet would hang over."

Van Alen eyed the big bed curiously. All his life he had heard of it, and now he had traveled far to see it. It was a lumbering structure of great width and of strangely disproportionate length. And the coverlet and the canopy were of rose-colored chintz.

"I think I shall fit it," he said slowly.

Mrs. Brand's critical glance weighed his smallness, his immaculateness, his difference from her own great sons.

"Yes," she said with the open rudeness of the country-bred, "yes, you ain't very big."

Van Alen winced. Even from the lips of this uncouth woman the truth struck hard. But he carried the topic forward with the light ease of a man of the world.

"My grandfather had the bed sawed to his own length," he explained. "Did you ever hear the story?"

"No," she said. "I ain't been here long. They kept the house shut up till this year."

"Well, I'll tell you when I come down." Van Alen opened his bag with a finality that sent the old woman to the door.

"Supper's ready," she told him, "whenever you are."

At the supper table, the four big sons towered above Van Alen. They ate with appetites like giants, and they had big ways and hearty laughs that seemed to dwarf their guest into insignificance.

But the insignificance was that of body only, for Van Alen, fresh from the outside world and a good talker at all times, dominated the table conversationally.

To what he had to say the men listened eagerly, and the girl who waited on the table listened.

She was a vivid personality, with burnished hair, flaming cheeks, eyes like the sea. Her hands, as she passed the biscuits, were white, and the fingers went down delicately to little points. Van Alen, noting these things keenly, knew that she was out of her place and wondered how she came there.

At the end of the meal, he told the story of the canopy bed.

"My great-grandfather was a little man and very sensitive about his height. In the days of his early manhood, he spent much time in devising ways to deceive people into thinking him taller. He surrounded himself with big things, had a big bed made, wore high-heeled boots, and the crown of his hat was so tall that he was almost overbalanced.

"But for all that, he was a little man among the sturdy men of his generation, and if it had not been for the Revolution, I think he would have died railing at fate. But the war brought him opportunity. My little great-grandfather fought in it and won great honors; then straight back home he came and had the bed sawed off! He wanted future generations to see what a little man could do, and his will provided that this house should not be sold and that, when his sons and grandsons had proved themselves worthy of it by some achievement, they should come here and sleep. I think he swaggered a little when he wrote that will, and he has put his descendants in an embarrassing position. We can never sleep in the canopy bed without taking more upon ourselves than modesty permits!"

He laughed, and instinctively his eyes sought those of the girl who waited on the table. Somehow he felt that she was the only one who could understand.

She came back at him with a question: "What have you done?"

"I have written a book," he told her.

She shook her head, and there were little sparks of light in her eyes. "I don't believe that was what your grandfather meant," she said slowly.

They stared at her—three of the brothers with their knives and forks uplifted; the fourth, a blond Titanic youngster, with his elbows on the table, his face turned up to her as to the sun.

"I don't believe he meant something done with your brains, but something fine, heroic—" There was a hint of scorn in her voice.

Van Alen flushed. He was fresh from the adulation of his bookish world.

"I should not have come," he explained uncomfortably, "if my mother had not desired that I preserve the tradition of the family."

"It is a great thing to write a book," she said, leaning forward, aflame with interest, "but I don't believe he meant just that—"

He laughed. "Then I am not to sleep in the canopy bed?"

The girl laughed, too. "Not unless you want to be haunted by his ghost."

With a backward flashing glance, she went into the kitchen, and Van Alen, pushing back his chair, decided to explore the old house.

Except for the wing occupied by the caretaker, nothing had been disturbed since the family, seeking new fortunes in the city, had left the old homestead to decay among the desolate fields that yielded now a meager living for Mrs. Brand and her four strapping sons.

In the old parlor, where the ancient furniture showed ghostlike shapes in the dimness and the dead air was like a tomb, Van Alen found a picture of his great-grandfather. The little man had been painted without flattery. There he sat—Lilliputian on the great charger! At that moment Van Alen hated him—that hop-o'-my-thumb of another age, founder of a pigmy race, who, by his braggart will, had that night brought upon this one of his descendants the scorn of a woman.

And even as he thought of her, she came in, with the yellow flare of a candle lighting her vivid face.

"I thought you might need a light," she said. "It grows dark so soon."

As he took the candle from her, he said abruptly, "I shall not sleep in the canopy bed. There is a couch in the room."

"Oh!" Her tone was startled. "You shouldn't have taken all that I said in earnest."

"But you meant it?"

"In a way, yes. I have been in here so often and have looked at your grandfather's picture. He was a great little man—you can tell from his eyes—they seem to speak at times."

"To you?"

"Yes. Of how he hated to be little, and how he triumphed when fame came at last."

"I hate to be little—"

It was the first time that he had ever owned it. Even as a tiny boy he had brazened it out, boasting of his mental achievements and slurring the weakness of his stunted body.

"I know." She had shut the kitchen door behind her, and they were standing in the hallway alone. "I know. Every man must want to be big."

She was only the girl who had waited on the table, but as she stood there, looking at him with luminous eyes, he burned with dull resentment, envying the blond boy who had sprawled at the head of the supper table. After all, it was to such a man as Otto Brand that this woman would someday turn.

He spoke almost roughly: "Size isn't everything."

She flushed. "How rude you must think me," she said, "but I have been so interested in dissecting your grandfather that I forgot—you—"

Van Alen was moved by an impulse that he could not control, a primitive impulse that was not in line with his usual repression.

"I am tempted to make you remember me," he said slowly.

After that there was a startled silence. And then she went away.

As he passed the sitting room on his way upstairs, he looked in and spoke to Otto Brand.

More than any of the other brothers, Otto typified strength and beauty, but in his eyes was never a dream; his brain had mastered nothing. He was playing idly with the yellow cat, but he stopped at Van Alen's question.

"Her great-grandfather and yours were neighbors," the boy said with his cheeks flushing. "They own the next farm."

"The Wetherells?" Van Alen inquired.

The boy nodded. "They ain't got a cent. They're land poor. That's why she's here. But she don't need to work."

"Why not?"

"There's plenty that wants to marry her round about," was the boy's self-conscious summing up.

With a sense of revolt, Van Alen left him, and undressing in the room with the canopy bed, he called up vaguely the vision of a little girl who had visited them in the city. She had had green eyes and freckles and red hair. Beyond that she had made no impression on his callousness. And her name was Mazie Wetherell.

He threw himself on the couch, and the night winds, coming in through the open window, stirred the curtains of the canopy bed with the light touch of a ghostly hand.

Then dreams came, and through them ran the thread of his hope of seeing Mazie Wetherell in the morning.

But even with such preparation, her beauty seemed to come upon him unawares when he saw her at breakfast—and again at noon, and again at night. But it was the third day before he saw her alone.

All that day he had explored the length and breadth of the family estate, finding it barren, finding that the population of the little village at its edge had decreased to a mere handful of laggards, finding that there was no lawyer within miles, and but one doctor; gaining a final impression that back here in the hills, men would come no more where once men had thronged.

It was almost evening when he followed a furrowed brown road that led westward. Above the bleak line of the horizon the sun hung, a red-gold disk. There were other reds, too, along the way—the sumac flaming scarlet against the gray fence rails; the sweetbrier crimson-spotted with berries; the creeper clinging with ruddy fingers to dead tree trunks; the maple leaves rosy with first frosts.

And into this vividness came the girl who had waited on the table, and her flaming cheeks and copper hair seemed to challenge the glow of the autumn landscape.

She would have passed him with a nod, but he stopped her.

"You must not run away, Mazie Wetherell," he said. "You used to treat me better than that when you were a little girl."

She laughed. "Do you remember my freckles and red hair?"

"I remember your lovely manners."

"I had to have nice manners. It is only pretty children who can afford to be bad."

"And pretty women?" he asked, with his eyes on the color that came and went.

She flung out her hands in a gesture of protest. "I have seen so few."

His lips were opened to tell her of her own beauty, but something restrained him, some perception of maidenly dignity that enfolded her and made her more than the girl who had waited on the table.

"You were a polite little boy," she recalled, filling the breach made by his silence. "I remember that you carried me across the street, to save my slippers from the wet. I thought you were wonderful. I have never forgotten."

Neither had Van Alen forgotten. It had been a great feat for his little strength. There had been other boys there, bigger boys, but he had offered and had been saved humiliation by her girlish slimness and feather weight.

"I was a strong little fellow then," was his comment. "I am a strong little fellow now."

She turned on him reproachful eyes. "Why do you always harp on it?" she demanded.

"On what?"

"Your size. You twist everything, turn everything, so that we come back to it."

He tried to answer lightly, but his voice shook. "Perhaps it is because in your presence I desire more than ever the full stature of a man."

He was in deadly earnest. Hitherto he had been willing to match his brain, his worldly knowledge, his ancestry, against the charms of the women he had met; but here with this girl, standing like a young goddess under the wide, sunset sky, he felt that only for strength and beauty should she choose her mate.

He wondered what he must seem in her eyes—with his shoulder on a level with hers, with his stocky build that saved him from effeminacy, his carefulness of attire, which is at once the burden and the salvation of the small man.

As for his face, he knew that its homeliness was redeemed by a certain strength of chin, by keen gray eyes, and by a shock of dark hair that showed a little white at the temples. There were worse-looking men, he knew, but that, at the present moment, gave little comfort.

She chose to receive his remark in silence, and as they came to a path that branched from the road, she said, "I am going to help take care of a child who is sick. You see, I am mistress of all trades—nurse, waitress, charwoman when there is nothing else."

He glanced at her hands. "I cannot believe that you scrub," he said.

"I sit up at night to care for my hands"—there was a note of bitterness in her tone—"and I wear gloves when I work. There are some things that one desires to hold on to, and my mother and my grandmother were ladies of leisure."

"Would you like that—to be a lady of leisure?"

She turned and smiled at him. "How can I tell?" she asked. "I have never tried it."

She started to leave him as she said it, but he held her with a question: "Shall you sit up all night?"

She nodded. "His mother has had no sleep for two nights."

"Is he very ill?"

The girl shrugged her shoulders. "Who knows? There is no doctor near, and his mother is poor. We are fighting it out together."

There was something heroic in her cool acceptance of her hard life. He was silent for a moment, and then he said, "Would you have time to read my book tonight?"

"Oh, if I might," she said eagerly, "but you haven't it with you."

"I will bring it," he told her, "after supper."

"But—" she protested.

"There are no 'buts,' " he said, smiling. "If you will read it, I will get it to you."

The sky had darkened, and as he went toward home, he faced clouds in the southeast.

"It is going to rain," Otto Brand prophesied as they sat down to supper.

The other three men hoped that it would not. Already the ground was soaked, making the cutting of corn impossible, and another rain with a frost on top of it would spoil all chance of filling the silo.

Van Alen could not enter into their technical objections. He hoped it would not rain because he wanted to take a book to Mazie Wetherell and he had not brought a raincoat.

But it did rain, and he went without a raincoat!

The house, as he neared it, showed no light, and under the thick canopy of the trees, there was no sound but the *drip-drip* of the rain. By feeling and instinct, he found the front door and knocked.

There was a movement inside, and then Mazie Wetherell asked softly, "Who's there?"

"I have brought the book."

The bolt was withdrawn, and in the hall, scarcely lighted by the shaded lamp in the room beyond, stood the girl, in a loose, gray gown, with braided, shining hair—a shadowy being, half-merged into the shadows.

"I thought you would not come," she said in a hushed tone, "in such a storm."

"I said I should come. The book may help you through the long night."

She caught her breath quickly. "The child is awfully ill."

"Are you afraid? Let me stay."

"Oh, no, no. His mother is sleeping, and I shall have your book."

She did not ask him in, and so he went away at once, beating his way back in the wind and rain, fording a little stream where the low footbridge was covered by water, reaching home soaking wet but afire with dreams.

Otto Brand was waiting for him, a little curious as to what had taken him out so late, but getting no satisfaction, he followed Van Alen upstairs and built a fire for him in the big bedroom. And presently, in the light of the leaping flames, the roses on the canopy of the bed glowed pink.

"Ain't you goin' to sleep in the bed?" Otto asked as he watched Van Alen arrange the covers on the couch.

"No," said Van Alen shortly, "the honor is too great. It might keep me awake."

"My feet would hang over," Otto said. "Funny thing, wasn't it, for a man to make a will like that?"

"I suppose every man has a right to do as he pleases," Van Alen responded coldly. He was not inclined to discuss the eccentricities of his little old ancestor with this young giant.

"Of course," Otto agreed, and his next remark was called forth by Van Alen's pale-blue pajamas. "Well, those are new to me."

Van Alen explained that in the city they were worn, and that silk was cool, but while he talked, he was possessed by a kind of fury. For the first time, the delicate garments, the luxurious toilet articles packed in his bag, seemed foppish, unnecessary—things for a woman. With all of them, he could not compete with this fair young god, who used a rough towel and a tin basin on the kitchen bench.

"Maybe I'd better go," the boy offered. "You'll want to go to bed."

But Van Alen demurred. "I'm not sleepy," he said, and wrapped in his dressing gown, he flung himself into a chair on the opposite side of the fireplace.

And after a time he brought the conversation around to Mazie Wetherell. He found the boy rather sure of his success with her.

"All women are alike," he said. "You've just got to keep after them long enough."

To Van Alen, the idea of this hulking youngster as a suitor for such a woman seemed preposterous. He was not fit to touch the hem of her garment. He was unmannerly and uneducated; he was not of her class— and even as he analyzed, the boy stood up, perfect in his strong young manhood.

"I've never had much trouble making women like me," he said. "And I ain't goin' to give up, just because she thinks she's better than the rest round about here."

He went away, and Van Alen stared long into the fire, until the flames left a heart of opal among the ashes.

He had not been unsuccessful with women himself. Many of them had liked him and might have loved him if he had cared to make them. But until he met Mazie Wetherell, he had not cared.

Desperately, he wished for some trial of courage where he might be matched against Otto Brand. He grew melodramatic in his imaginings and saw himself at a fire, fighting the flames to reach Mazie, while Otto Brand shrank back. He stood in the path of runaway horses, and Otto showed the white feather. He nursed her through the plague, and Otto fled fearfully from the disease.

And then having reached the end of impossibilities, he stood up and shook himself.

"I'm a fool," he said to the flames shortly. Then he went to bed, to lie awake, wondering whether Mazie Wetherell had reached that chapter of his book where he had written of love, deeply, reverently, with a foreknowledge of what it might mean to him someday. It was that chapter which had assured the success of his novel. Would it move her, as it had moved him when he reread it? That was what love ought to be—a thing fine, tender, touching the stars! That was what love might be to him and to Mazie Wetherell, what it could never be to Otto Brand.

At breakfast the next morning, he found Mrs. Brand worrying about her waitress.

"I guess she couldn't get back, and I've got a big day's work."

"I'll go and look her up," Van Alen offered; but he found that he was not to go alone, for Otto was waiting for him at the gate.

"I ain't got nothin' else to do," the boy said. "Everything is held up by the rain."

It was when they came to the little stream that Van Alen had forded the night before that they saw Mazie Wetherell.

"I can't get across," she called from the other side.

The bridge, which had been under water when Van Alen passed, was now washed away, and the foaming brown currents overflowed the banks.

"I'll carry you over," Otto called, and straightway he waded through the stream, and the water came above his high boots to his hips.

He lifted her in his strong arms and brought her back, with her bright hair fluttering against his lips, and Van Alen, raging impotently, stood and watched him.

It seemed to him that Otto's air was almost insultingly triumphant as he set the girl on her feet and smiled down at her. And as she smiled back, Van Alen turned on his heel and left them.

Presently, he heard her running lightly after him over the sodden ground.

And when she reached his side, she said, "Your book was wonderful."

"But he carried you over the stream."

Her eyes flashed a question, then blazed. "There, you've come back to it," she said. "What makes you?"

"Because I wanted to carry you myself."

"Silly," she said. "Any man could carry me across the stream—but only you could write that chapter in the middle of the book."

"You liked it?" he cried radiantly.

"Like it?" she asked. "I read it once, and then I read it again—on my knees."

Her voice seemed to drop away, breathless. Behind them, Otto Brand tramped, whistling; but he might have been a tree, or the sky, or the distant hills, for all the thought they took of him.

"I want to beg your pardon," the girl went on, "for what I said the other day. It is a great thing to write a book like that—greater than fighting a battle or saving a life, for it saves people's ideals; perhaps in that way it saves their souls."

"Then I may sleep in the canopy bed?" His voice was calm, but inwardly he was much shaken by her emotion.

Her eyes, as she turned to him, had in them the dawn of that for which he had hoped. "Why not?" she said quickly. "You are greater than your grandfather—you are—"

She stopped and laughed a little, and in this moment of her surrender, her beauty shone like a star.

"Oh, little great man," she said tremulously, "your head touches the skies!"

Father

Edith Hoffman James

Lovely Katie's big night was coming— her recital, which would announce her success to the world. Wouldn't Father love to be there, too? But he'd be dressed in that shabby old suit of his, and wear those ugly shoes. No, she just couldn't admit to her friends that he was her father!

"Hello, Uncle Harry!" piped a childish voice from a nearby porch. "When's Katie comin' home?"

The old man passing along the sidewalk stopped and turned toward the speaker with a smile.

"Hello there, Dottie! Katie's comin' home next month. Helpin' Mother, aren't ye? Bless yer little heart!"

"Yes, I'm helpin'," answered Dottie in a matter-of-fact tone; then added, "My, but we're anxious to see Katie. Won't she be a grand lady, though!" And then she turned to her task of sweeping the big, old-fashioned veranda with a broom taller than her own sturdy self.

Uncle Harry walked on, but slowly now. *Be glad to see her!* he mused. *I guess I will! Precious child! The world may sometime call her great, but she'll always be just my own little Katie—so like her dear mother!*

Wrapped in thought, he almost collided with a little urchin who stood at the corner, crying.

"Why, Sammy, what's the matter?"

"O-o-o-o!" wailed Sammy. "I'm hungry I am, an' Ma—Ma she said I couldn't have no supper!"

"Sammy, have ye been bad?" questioned Uncle Harry sternly.

"No!" And the little boy sobbed aloud.

"What's the trouble, then? Come, tell Uncle Harry," he said as the youngster hesitated. And then the gray head bent lower while Sammy confided his secret.

"We ain't got nothin' to eat!"

The furrow in the old man's brow grew a bit deeper. He made a move as if to give the child the groceries he carried. But upon second thought, he took the dirty little hand in his own and said kindly, "Come on, sonny, I'll go home with ye and see about things."

Sammy dried his tears and trotted along trustfully. Uncle Harry was a friend true and tried. He had come to this home of trouble and poverty to "see about things" before.

When the white wicket gate opened an hour later, and the old man walked up the flagstone-lined path that had led him home for a quarter of a century, his market basket was empty and his meager bank balance materially lessened.

"Hello, Fannie!" he greeted a little white, stub-tailed dog bobbing up and down between his elbow and the ground.

On the porch he stopped to peer anxiously into the mailbox.

"Ho, there's a letter," he exclaimed. "Down, Fannie!"

Trembling fingers drew out the envelope and tore it open; misty eyes strained to see the words in the fading light.

" 'Tis short," he said to himself as he folded the one brief page, "but then Katie's busy. Guess I'll have to get the lamp before I can see to read it."

The low door opened into the gray shadows of an old-fashioned sitting room. The clock on the shelf ticked loudly as the rough hand fumbled along the wall, searching for the match holder. Then as the blaze was struck, a red flame flared up and sent wild forms swaying along the walls and bending to the ceiling.

"Let me see now! Let—me—see! Where'd I put the lamp? Guess my memory's failin' me. Oh, here 'tis! My, the chimney's black! It never looks so when Katie's home."

A newspaper crumpled under his big hand was pushed in and twisted about.

"There! 'Tis streaked, but I can see!" Stooping so that the dull red rays struck the paper, the father's dim eyes read and reread the brief note.

Finally, Fannie's patience gave way with a whine.

"Poor little pal!" he exclaimed. "Hungry? I'd clean forgot 'twas suppertime! Let's see what we can find to eat. I gave Widow Lane what I was bringin' home for us, but we'll unearth somethin'!"

With joyful little barks, Fannie ran back and forth as her master prepared their humble meal. When the dog was satisfied, Uncle Harry sat down to eat his own "bite," with Katie's letter propped up against the milk pitcher in front of him.

" 'Only four weeks more,' she says," he mused, " 'until I'll be home, Daddy.' Let me see—I'll mark it on the calendar, that's what I'll do, Fannie. There!" The little dog barked her approval. "Now we'll mark off every day as it goes by. Then the time won't seem so long, will it, Fannie?"

An added sparkle in the bright eyes looking up at him and several understanding twitches of the stump tail were her answer.

"An' she says she's goin' to give her recital next Tuesday—Tuesday! Why, that's six days from today! Wish I could go and surprise her! The fare's eight dollars, Fannie. Wonder if I could spare the eight dollars there and the eight dollars back again? Sixteen in all! That's a lot, Fannie," he said to his dog.

Drawing a worn bankbook and a stub pencil from an inner coat pocket, he began to figure laboriously.

"Ought to have Katie here right now to do my figurin' like she used to," he said to himself. "Now let's see! Her trainin' at that music school has put a perty big hole in my savin's, and I ain't had much work this winter, and there's next month's tuition an' all. But she's all I have to do for, an' she's worth it, isn't she, Fannie?"

The stump tail wagged vigorously.

Cross furrows checked the old man's forehead for a half hour while he figured painstakingly. Suddenly, his hand came down on the table, jingling the dishes.

"I'm a-goin' to go, Fannie! I'm a-goin' to go! Only six days till I'll see her! Think of hearin' her play to that big crowd of people! Wouldn't her mother be proud of her, though! She coulda played that way, too, if she'd had a chance. But we're givin' Katie a chance, ain't we, Fannie? You an' me, an' her Aunt Harriet! An' she's succeedin', too. Someday maybe she'll be a music teacher herself—an' famous, but she'll always be just Daddy's little girl! 'Tis sure good of Aunt Harriet to board her for nothin'—"

The fond father sat musing over the twist of fortune that had brought his wife's elder sister—married years before to a wealthy, titled Englishman and whom he had never seen—back to her native land and caused her to open her heart and home to his one ewe lamb, that she might improve her really exceptional musical talent under the direction of a famous professor.

Suddenly, he roused with a start. "If I'm a-goin' to Chicago, I'll have to fix up a bit so's Katie won't be shamed. Let—me—see. My old brown suit's kind of shabby—I've had it 10 years—but I guess this here new-fashioned 'cleaner and presser' down by the drugstore can fix it up all right. An' I must have a new tie. An' shoes? Guess my old ones'll do if I shine 'em good. Just think, Fannie, I'm a-goin' to go see Katie an' hear her play! An' I'll see Aunt Harriet and Uncle Thomas, and thank 'em for all they've done for her!"

Tears of gratitude came to the father's eyes as he went about his evening duties.

"There, Katherine, your dress is perfect! You look like a dream!"

The radiant girl turned away from the reflection in the long mirror toward the speaker. "Oh, Aunt Harriet, you're so good! But for you I never could have had this chance to study music at all. And now, just think of it, I am going to give a recital all alone. Truly dreams come true. They do—they do! And I'm so happy, Aunt Harriet."

"How lovely it would have been if your father could have come for tonight! That would make your joy complete."

"Yes," the girl answered, "Dad would enjoy it." She bent over the flowers that had just come for her, to hide the flush that came to her face at the mere thought of her plain, humble old father in these luxurious surroundings.

As her aunt left the room, Katherine turned once more to the vision in the mirror. But somehow instead of her own beautiful reflection, she saw a stooped, gray-haired man in a faded brown suit.

"Oh," she exclaimed impatiently, "I just *couldn't* have Dad come here. I didn't mention his coming on purpose in my letter. Dear old Dad! I'd love to see him, of course, but what would Aunt Harriet and Uncle Thomas think of him in those old clothes, and I know well enough he hasn't any new ones. He'll just *have* to stop supporting that shiftless Lane family and helping all the other poor folks in town and fix up some, if Aunt Harriet insists on his spending a week with us at North Shore this summer!"

"The motor [automobile] is at the door, Miss Katherine," announced the maid, interrupting the girl's musings, and Katherine soon found herself entering the great concert hall.

As she walked across the platform, the sea of faces struck terror in Katherine's heart. Tremblingly, she seated herself at the piano, but with the first few notes came confidence and self-forgetfulness. She went through her program, living in the melodies she played, and finished with the satisfaction that she had done her best.

The cheering throng began to disperse, and a group of admiring friends gathered around the girl.

"I am proud of you," said the good professor Heinz. "You must meet Hardiman soon. He is interested in future programs. You have the gift, my dear, *you have the gift!* There is a great future before you."

As Katherine turned to receive other congratulations, her eye caught sight of a familiar figure pressing forward through the crowd. It was a bent, gray old man dressed in a rough, threadbare brown suit. Perhaps a rod away he stopped and looked at her uncertainly, longingly, and oh so lovingly. His eye caught hers, but she gave no sign of recognition. A few moments he stood there, his heart fairly bursting with fatherly pride and love, but at last, glancing from his radiant, beautifully gowned daughter to his rough shoes and shabby clothes, he turned and with one more glance, slowly followed the last stragglers through the door and out into the darkness of a strange city.

Katherine's father had arrived only just in time for the concert. He had meant to stay overnight, but now there was no use. He found his way back to the big, dingy La Salle Street station and waited there for the midnight train that would take him home—back into the obscurity of the country, where he knew now that he belonged.

And Katherine? As she saw her father turn away, her heart cried out with love and longing, but pride—and what a false pride it was!—kept her from making his presence known, and she kept saying over and over to herself, *I just couldn't bear to have my friends see him! I just couldn't!*

Alone at last in her own room, she burst into tears. "Oh Dad," she sobbed, "dear old Dad! You came all this way just to see me—and how horrid I've been! Oh, Daddy, I wanted to see you! I did! I did! You're so good! Always working for me. When I get home, I'll play and play for you, and I'll stay all the long vacation. I won't go to the shore with Aunt Harriet and Uncle Thomas. I'll do everything I can to make you happy!"

The last weeks of her stay in the city were filled to the brim with work and pleasure. The usual

home letters came, but her father never mentioned his trip to the city; and when she described her recital, she did not hint that she had seen him there.

And then the day of leaving came. She wrote her father just when she would arrive, and all the way home she was thinking of ways to atone for the deep wrong she felt she had done that loving heart.

It was raining when the train finally puffed in and stopped at the little red Rock Island station. Gathering her baggage, Katherine hurried out to the platform, but her father was not there.

Surprised, she thought, *Well, perhaps he didn't get my letter.*

Leaving her grips [suitcases] with the ticket agent, a friend from childhood days, she hurried up the familiar street in the gathering dusk.

"Why," she exclaimed, coming in sight of home, "what are all those people doing in our yard?"

The front door was open, and by the light that streamed out, she could see neighbors coming and going. Her heart filled with a nameless fear, she began to run.

"Something must be wrong," she panted as she flung open the old white gate. "There's Mrs. Walters, and she's wiping her eyes!"

Just then someone saw her. "Oh," exclaimed a kindhearted woman. "It's Katie come home! What shall I tell the poor child?"

As in a dream she heard that her father had been suddenly stricken with apoplexy, and how the deliveryman had found him just a few minutes before her arrival, where he had fallen in the doorway, apparently just as he was starting to the station to meet her.

The girl's grief was heartbreaking. "Oh Dad!" she cried and fled toward the still house.

Hearing a familiar voice, Fannie darted to her side and led the way to the quiet bedroom. Katherine dropped on her knees beside the still, cold form of her father and sobbed out her confession of love and appreciation and her prayer for forgiveness. But the kindly eyes were closed; the heart, always so full of love for her, had ceased its beating; and the lips that in life would have reassured her with, " 'Tis all right, Katie, all right!" were dumb.

"Oh," she cried as good Dr. Neill came to take her away, "if he would only come back just long enough for me to prove to him that I love him better than all the world besides!"

But alas, it was too late.

At the Close of His Career

Grace S. Richmond

Judge Anthony was old, and power, events, and time had passed him by. Then came the invitation to speak before the illustrious Pocasset Club at their annual dinner. But, wondered his daughter, should he? What if it turned out to be an embarrassment?

"Emily, my dear."

Judge Anthony leaned forward in his easy chair as he caught a glimpse of his daughter passing the library door. She came in obediently, and her father held out a note that he had just received. His hand shook a little as he extended it; the judge's hand was seldom steady now.

His daughter read the note and looked down at him with a glance of joyful sympathy.

"Why, Father dear," she said, "how very pleasant this is for you!"

"Well—yes, yes," said Judge Anthony, a little smile touching his lips. "It is pleasant—very pleasant, I confess."

The note was from a distinguished lawyer of the city, and a part of it ran thus: *It will give the members of the Pocasset Club great gratification if you will kindly consent to speak to the toast, "The Effect of the Hague Conference on the Peace of the World," at their annual dinner, to be given at the Irondequoit House on the evening of December 10th.*

Emily's eyes lingered on the note. "I am so glad they have honored you," she said, "though I think they have honored themselves still more." After a moment, she added with a little hesitation, "Shall you—do you think it best to—to accept?"

"To accept, my dear?" The judge straightened himself in his chair, held his fine old head erect, and looked up at his daughter in surprise. "Why should I not?"

"Oh—I—" Her eyes fell away from his gaze; she studied the note again. "I merely thought—while of course you would enjoy doing it—it might be—possibly—a little hard for you—"

But she dared say no more, for the old gentleman was regarding her in a way that showed he was hurt.

"I trust," he said with the somewhat stately air that he could still assume and which sat well upon him, "that you do not consider me mentally incompetent to perform the task. My physical disabilities have not yet turned my brain, I hope."

"Oh, Father dear," the girl cried, dismayed and kneeling by his chair, "you know I was thinking only of the labor it would be to get up such a speech— the mere fatigue—and the exertion!"

"Emily," said the judge slowly, "you perhaps know that it has been to me a matter of some regret—I may say sorrow—that I should have been forced to retire from an influential and honored position several years before the age limit would have made it necessary. It will be a gratification to me to address my fellow jurists once more upon such a subject as this."

She was looking earnestly up into his face. He seemed so like himself as he returned her gaze, his black eyes under their heavy white eyebrows were so full of light, his voice was so firm and his manner so dignified, that the misgivings which had seized her gave way before his appeal—she felt that it was an appeal—and she rose, saying more lightly, "I can see just how you feel, sir, and I'm sure the pleasure of the work will make it easy for you. I'll only ask you to let me lighten your labors all I can. Let me copy the speech for you when it is done—if you—I suppose you—"

She stopped, dreading to give him pain again. But he anticipated her with a smile and a courtly little wave of the hand.

"You are quite right, my daughter," he said. "I shall not, at my age and with my infirmities, attempt to speak extemporaneously. Those who have known me will make excuses for me and allow me the latitude due my years. If you will copy my manuscript from my poor handwriting and have it typewritten, I shall be exceedingly grateful to you, my dear."

And so Emily wrote for him a graceful note of acceptance, kissed him with her heart in her lips, and went away to think it all over anxiously.

She had no mother now, and there was only one person to whom she felt she could tell her fears. This was her young brother, Horace, who, although several years her junior, was her most trusted confidant. He listened to her news with an expression of great surprise.

"Why, it's—it's not possible for him, is it?" he asked. "Think of the days when he seems so—so—*foggy!* Do you suppose, even on his best days, he's capable of it—now? The Pocasset Club—none of the members are anything but Ph.D.'s and LL.D.'s—and mighty distinguished ones at that. Was it Doctor Lockwood who wrote, did you say? That's a great compliment in itself. Emily, suppose he should fail!"

"Oh, yes, I've thought it over till I don't know what to think," she answered, her delicate eyebrows contracting with anxiety. "We can only wait to see if he is able to write at all as he used to do. Oh Horace, what a difference for eight years to make in him! When Judge Underwood defeated him,

I thought Father was just in the prime of his powers. Sometimes I think his disappointment over that made him fail so fast. Horace, he ought not to be a broken old man at 76."

"Perhaps he'll prove he's not," said Horace hopefully, and Emily hoped with him for a week. Then she saw her father's manuscript, and her heart died within her.

He had been very busy over it. She had found him bending over his desk hour after hour, sometimes appearing to be writing with ease, sometimes to be laboring painfully. She watched and waited eagerly for the completion of the task, but when at last he gave her the manuscript, she had not the courage to look at it in his presence. With the best excuse she could offer, she went away to her own room, and there she found what she had feared.

The manuscript began coherently enough, with an apparent attempt at his old style of elaborate introduction. With a rising hope she went on to the second page, then suddenly floundered in a mass of words in which she could find no sound meaning. She hurried on, looking for a clue, until she was forced to acknowledge to herself that the sense was hopelessly lost in a jumble of incoherent verbiage.

She had graduated from college the preceding June, and she was no mean critic of literary work. She began to study her father's manuscript with an eagerness that she had never before given to any task. When she came upon a page of clearer thought, in which the argument the author was struggling to make shone out like a crimson thread in a mass of dark wool, her heart leaped. Then, as the meaning of the sentences became obscured again, her face lost its light, her lips quivered with pain, and at last she laid her head down upon the manuscript, sobbing as a mother might over a just-discovered mental defect in a beloved child.

A step sounded behind her, and a voice with a note of sympathy in it said softly, "Is it so bad, sister?" Her brother's hand came gently upon her hair.

She lifted a tear-stained face, nodded without speaking, and then, as he bent to look over her shoulder, covered the sheets with both hands, whispering, "Don't look at it, dear, please don't! I can't bear that even you should see. Oh—poor Father!"

Horace waited silently for a moment, his young face stirred with the same emotion that shook the slender shoulders below him. Suddenly, he said eagerly, "Sister, don't take it so hard. It's a tremendous test for him to write such a speech as that now. But if it were in shape, I believe he could read it all right. Don't you suppose you could fix it up—straighten it out? He'd never notice the changes. And when he's a little excited, he acts and talks as well as ever. Try it, Emily—do!"

She looked up doubtfully. "I thought of it—if I could ever do it! But think, Horace, what an audience that will be!"

"But it would be a speech they could respect," he urged. "There wouldn't be any breaks in it, even if it weren't quite equal to one of Father's old efforts. And it would be good, I know it would. You can study up on the subject. The magazines and papers are full of the Hague Conference. Think what it will be to him to make that speech!"

Emily rose with the manuscript in her hand. "I think I'll try," she said.

"You're a trump!" cried Horace. "I'll hunt up every article to be had."

He was as good as his word. He brought copies of the leading American reviews, and when on top of these he laid copies of the best foreign reviews also, she laughed outright.

"You are a dear," she said. "You've brought the brightest minds of the world to the rescue. I should be a dunce if I couldn't learn something from them all. There is a genuine idea—a fine idea—running all through Father's work. If only I can find out what he meant to say and say it for him in some sort . . . " Then she plunged in.

She had told her father that she would copy his paper before reading it with him, and she had led him to understand that this would take her some days. He had said he hoped she found the paper such that she should not be ashamed to have it read, and she had colored deeply, kissed him, and murmured, "You know we're always proud of you, Father dear."

To find out what he would have said, then say it for him as he would have said it in the old days when clearness, conciseness, and force were the notable characteristics of his work, was an effort that tried her very soul. She brought out scrapbooks containing copies of his past speeches; she recalled as vividly as she could the descriptions she had heard of some of his great hours; she even kept his photograph before her as she wrote.

During this time it might almost be said that the girl tried to assume her father's personality, think as he thought, feel as he felt, breathe into her work the spirit of his life. It would have been hopeless, had she not lived in such constant sympathy with him.

When it was all done she did not know whether she had succeeded or not. She carried the manuscript to him with a faintness of heart that nearly forbade the carrying out of her purpose. She read aloud the opening sentences with a voice that shook perceptibly. She felt like an apprentice who had attempted the work of a master.

There had been a peculiar expression upon his face as she began to read, one that might almost have denoted anxiety. It was one of his "good days," and Emily was sure that his mind was working clearly. As she went on, the expression changed to one of relief, then to eagerness—pleasure. When at last she looked up doubtfully, his eyes were very bright and he was smiling.

"It will do," he said. "When I wrote it, I fancied that there might be points that I had not made quite clear, but this seems entirely so. It expresses perfectly the argument I had in mind. The language is simple; I supposed I had used some rather more forcible words toward the close than those you have read me, but perhaps I have unconsciously assimilated the tendency of the times toward less pretentious construction. At any rate, my dear, I am quite satisfied—quite satisfied. They cannot say the old man's hand has forgotten its cunning—eh, Emily, my dear? It seems a long day since I have addressed such an assemblage as that will be."

She kissed him and got away before she broke down. The strain had been great upon her nerves and sympathy, but the worst was safely over. The judge's eyesight, by the aid of the gold-rimmed spectacles, was very good, his enunciation distinct, and his manner always faultless. With the type-written pages before him and the stimulus of the occasion to keep him up, she felt that she had nothing serious to fear.

Yet, in spite of this confidence, when the day of the dinner arrived, Emily realized that she had dared much. She looked anxiously for her father's appearance at the breakfast table and noted with relief that he seemed at the threshold of another of those "best days" in which he was so entirely himself. She watched over him all day, saw that nothing occurred to disturb or excite him, and had her reward at evening when he stood before her, dressed for the dinner, the carriage waiting at the door.

He had always looked his best in evening clothes; and she said to herself, as she noted the unwonted vigor expressed in every line of his still fine figure and the look of pleasure and anticipation on his face, that the risk was not too great to take and that whatever impression he might make on others, for himself it was to be an evening of delight.

By the courtesy of the club, Emily and other ladies were to have seats in the balcony that extended around the dining hall. They were to enter in time for the speechmaking.

When at the hour appointed she found herself, with the friends who had brought her, scanning the brilliant scene below, her first thought was of gratitude. She had secured a position where she could look directly down upon her father and could see into his face. She felt somehow as if from this point of vantage she could still help him, if he should need help.

His name upon the list of speakers came almost at the close. It seemed to the girl, as speech followed speech, that the strain upon him must be very great. She watched him anxiously, but assured herself after a time that he was listening and enjoying with the quiet poise and perfect command of himself that in the past had characterized him.

When he was called upon at last, Emily felt her heart beating to suffocation. She was alive to every movement and expression, not only of her father, but of the men about him. She watched to see them turn in their chairs to face him, heard with a throb of pleasure the hearty and prolonged applause they gave the name of "the Honorable Horatio Anthony," and then listened breathlessly for the first words from his lips.

They came in a clear, steady, assured tone—*her* words.

"The assembling of the Peace Conference distinctly marks an era in the world's history. The fact of its existence, the gathering together of the chosen men of all the great nations, and their thoughtful, intelligent, and, it is to be believed, impartial discussion of the things that make for peace must, without question, have a great and lasting influence upon the progress of the world's affairs."

Yes, these distinguished men were listening with the close attention and courteous deference that men give to one another on occasions like this. As Judge Anthony went on, his daughter felt that they were listening with interest, even with absorption. Could it be possible that she had really found the scarlet thread and separated it entirely from the tangled wool?

As he read on, Judge Anthony's voice grew still stronger and clearer. It took on the ringing tone that used to penetrate the consciousness of his hearers like the vibration of a bell. As he neared the conclusion, Emily suddenly recognized with a startled thrill that he was using words, phrases, and sentences that were not in the manuscript and that they were strong words, effective phrases, telling sentences.

She leaned farther forward over the balcony with an utter absorption that her friends noticed, smiling in empathy. Her cheeks were very pale, her lips parted, her eyes burning.

Judge Anthony reached the last paragraph of his manuscript and flung the sheets down upon the table. Standing erect, his white head thrown back, his black eyes flashing, his voice sounding through the hall, he burst into a peroration equal to the most stirring that those present had heard from his lips in other days. Men moved in their chairs, leaned forward—several of the older ones who had known him best glanced at one another in astonishment—but all listened as if to one inspired. There was no question in any mind but that Judge Horatio Anthony, with all his old-time brilliancy and power, was bringing a strong and effective speech to a magnificent conclusion.

Up in the balcony, the girl who had saved the day heard with quickened breath the great storm of applause that greeted Judge Anthony's last words. She saw those about him eagerly congratulating him; she recognized the expression of sincere admiration upon their stirred faces; she felt that if they had invited him to speak out of courtesy and regard, they were moved now by genuine pleasure. She gazed down smiling, with returning color in her face.

Just then the orchestra, which had played throughout the dinner but had been silent during the speechmaking, began softly the air of "Auld Lang Syne." Instantly, every man was on his feet, with the warm old words upon his lips. When they had sung it through, Judge Anthony rose and bowed in his courtly way. The black eyes under the white eyebrows were not flashing now, and his simple "Thank you, gentlemen!" had in it a note that brought moisture to more eyes than Emily's.

It was only a week later that Judge Anthony's friends heard of his sudden death. When Emily, after her first sharp grief, asked the physician if the excitement of the dinner had killed her father, he answered in his grave, gentle way:

"I will not say that is not possible. But I can assure you death might have come as readily at any time within the last year, or the year to come. You have this to comfort you, Miss Emily. He went at a moment when he had made men appreciate him again. I myself had not supposed him capable now of such an effort as that address. It was great; it was wonderful. Men will not forget it. The younger men who did not know him in his prime will remember him by it. Don't regret your consent to his acceptance, my dear. I think your father himself would have had it precisely as it was. It gave him perhaps the greatest pleasure of his life; to us who heard him it was his farewell—a fitting farewell, Miss Emily."

Ready for Heaven

Ewart A. Autry

The Grim Reaper was coming for Grandpa. His heart was signaling him that his life was over—or would be before nightfall. Looking around the place, he decided there were a few things that needed fixing before folks came over for the funeral.

It was ten o'clock on a hot June morning when Grandpa Hawkins decided he was about to die. He didn't tell anyone just then, but Grandma knew something was wrong when she saw him grab the lawn mower and start cutting grass. Just a few minutes before she had seen him playing with five of the grandchildren in the shade of the big apple tree. The yard had needed mowing for 10 days. She had mentioned it to him several times without visible results. It wasn't like him to suddenly leave the cool shade and go to work just as the sun was getting hot.

She put on her glasses and watched him through a window. Even the grandchildren had left the apple tree and were staring at him in amazement. But he wasn't paying any attention to them. He wasn't noticing anything except the grass. The dog flopped down in front of him and almost got his tail mowed before he could get out of the way.

Grandma smiled and went back to her work. *That won't last long,* she said to herself. *He'll be back under the apple tree in no time at all.*

But when she looked out an hour later, the yard was almost finished and he was still doggedly pushing the mower as if nothing else in the world mattered. A puzzled frown creased her forehead. It always worried her when Grandpa failed to run true to form. It usually meant that some unheard-of scheme was forming in his mind. Like the time he went deer hunting on stilts and fell into a hole. Or the time he dressed like a woman and killed a buck and got his picture in the county paper. Or the time he took the doo-jingle off her new hat and used it for a lure to catch the biggest bass ever caught in the county. Or the time he had become the first skin diver in the county and scared the daylights out of the fishermen up the river. News had circulated that there was a strange creature in the river, and folks had come from miles around to see the monster of Corkscrew Bend. No sir, Grandma had never found life dull with the little sawed-off man with the bristling mustache who was now so industriously mowing the yard.

It is little wonder that she worried as she saw him finishing up the last corner of the yard. There might be something bubbling in his head that would have the whole county laughing. Sometimes his weird ideas had proved downright embarrassing.

In a moment, however, she smiled again. *He's probably planning another fishing trip,* she said to herself, *and wants to leave with a clear conscience.*

When the yard was finished, Grandpa came into the house. "Take a peep at the yard, Ma," he said, "and see if it satisfies you."

"I was watching you," she said. "Seems to me that you did a good job."

"Mighty few men, and no boys at all, could beat it," he said briefly.

"Why did you take such a sudden notion to cut it?" she asked curiously. "I've been reminding you that it needed cutting for several days."

"I don't do things when folks keep reminding me to do them," he said testily. "That's plain nagging. I cut it because I got to thinking that I'd hate for a crowd to come in and see the yard looking like a rabbits' den."

"Well, it looks nice, but I don't suppose there'll be a crowd coming in," she said.

"There may be a crowd coming in before you know it," he said significantly.

"You've never before seemed to care what the neighbors thought about the yard," Grandma remarked. "You've always said if they didn't like it they didn't have to look at it."

"There comes a time when a man starts caring for things," he said. "Where's the hammer?"

"In the hall closet where it always stays," she said. "What do you want with it?"

"You always have more questions than I have answers," he snorted. "But if you must know, I'm aiming to fix that back screen door."

She stopped dusting and looked at him closely. "Are you feeling well, Lem?" she asked.

"Maybe I am, and maybe I'm not," he said. "If I am, it's my business. If I'm not, it's the same."

Grandma smiled and went back to her dusting. For 40 years, she had been accustomed to his crusty, belligerent ways and knew that beneath that rough exterior there was a faithfulness and tenderness of heart that had made life with him very wonderful. Folks had always said that she spoke softly like the dripping rain, while he roared like thunder, and that thunder and rain went well together.

He pecked away at the screen in silence. There was no muttering and no sudden explosion even when he mashed a finger. When it was finished, he called Grandma to see it.

"Now I guess folks won't be saying I just let things go around here," he said.

"It's a good job," Grandma told him, "but hardly anyone sees the back door except me."

"There'll probably be a lot of other folks seeing it," he said. "They'd better come!" he added vehemently.

"Lem, have you invited some folks to our house?" she asked. "If you have, I'd better do a little extra cleaning up."

"I haven't invited anybody," he said emphatically, "but there are times when folks come without being invited. I think I'll shave."

Grandma dropped into a chair. "Well, this beats all," she said. "You just shaved last night, and here you are ready to shave again. I don't know what's on your mind, but there's bound to be something—something very unusual."

"Is there any law against a man shaving any time he gets ready?" he demanded.

"Of course not," she said. "It's just that I don't understand it." She shook her head slowly and went into the kitchen.

He followed her, opened the refrigerator, and took a package from the freezer compartment. "Let's have this steak for dinner," he said.

"But that's those nice T-bone steaks," she said. "I thought we were saving them for some special occasion."

"This *is* a special occasion," he said. "Let's have the T-bones." He scratched his chin for a moment. "We could invite Milt Huggins over to eat them with us," he added.

Grandma dropped a plate and stared at him in amazement. "Now I *know* there's something wrong, Lem Hawkins," she said. "You and Milt Huggins have been feuding for years, and now you're ready to invite him over for a steak dinner!"

"Oh, I guess Milt's all right," he said. "He can't help being hollow-headed, simpleminded, and dumb. I ought not to hold it against him."

"You two are just alike," Grandma said. "It's about time you quit that silly feuding. It makes you the laughingstock of the community."

"I wonder if he'll send flowers?" Grandpa said thoughtfully.

"What on earth are you talking about, Lem?" Grandma asked, now completely baffled and beginning to wonder if perhaps Grandpa was a little touched in the head.

"I was just wondering if Milt would send flowers to my funeral," he said simply.

"Did you get too hot out there helping the kids catch bugs and things for their circus?" she demanded.

"If I got too hot at all, it was mowing the yard," he said shortly. "Anyhow, my heart was acting up before I cut the grass."

"Your heart?" cried Grandma in alarm.

"Yes, my heart," he said. "It's been thumping and jumping and cutting all sorts of shines. I'm sure I'll go to glory this very day. That's why I thought

I'd better cut the yard and fix the screen. If I go suddenly, there'll be a crowd in to sit with you."

Grandma was already pulling off her apron. "You're going to see a doctor, Lem!" she said firmly. "And you're going at once!"

"Now, hold your horses, woman. I aim to eat some of that T-bone steak before I go anywhere. Even when a man's going to the electric chair, he gets to choose his last meal. Well, I choose T-bone steaks, and T-bone steaks I aim to eat. No use to leave them around for somebody else to gobble up when I'm lying in the dirt. Think I'll read a chapter in the Bible while you're finishing dinner."

He started for the next room, but stopped in the door and turned. "That's what I'm talking about," he said solemnly, pointing toward the region of his heart. "You can see it acting up even through my shirt."

Grandma took one look and burst into tears. "Oh, Lem," she sobbed, "we've had such a good life together."

Just then Johnny, the six-year-old grandson, ripped into the room like a tornado. "I want my frog, Grandpa!" he cried.

"Your frog, Johnny?" questioned Grandpa. "I don't know anything about your frog!"

"It's in your shirt pocket, Grandpa," said Johnny. "I put it there this morning."

Grandpa looked at the boy for a moment, then reached into his shirt pocket. His face brightened, then broke into a broad grin. "So *that's* what's been thumpin' and jumpin' and actin' up!" he said. "Did you hear that, Ma?" he half shouted. "It's not my heart at all. It's just this ornery little frog! Here, take your frog, boy, and get out of here," he said as he tousled Johnny's hair.

Grandma dried her tears, laughed, and hugged Grandpa all at the same time. "Bless that frog, bless that frog!" she said over and over.

"I ought to kill the ornery little rascal," Grandpa snorted. "He sure heaped a lot of work on my shoulders." He scratched his chin for a moment. "And about Milt Huggins," he said slowly, "we'll just feed him some other time."

Autumn to Winter

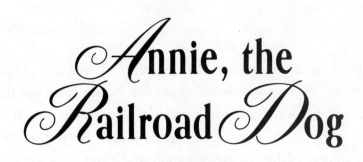

Annie, the Railroad Dog

Phil Walker

A whole city in love with a dog?
Hard to believe, but it's true.

This is a story about a dog and a city's love affair with her.

In the early 1930s, the twin colossus of the Depression and the Great Dust Bowl stood astride a prostrate Colorado and had brought the city of Fort Collins to its knees. In the embattled homes, stores, and offices of the city, the lights burned around the clock as the dust storms marched endlessly across the plains, blotting out the sun. There was no money, no jobs, no crops, no credit, and no end in sight. The two or three thousand families in town had a tendency to band together and focus on living a day at a time. Traditions ran deep. No matter how hard things were, people felt they could count on each other. Life was still pretty simple.

The most modern transportation that people had was the railroad. Certainly, there were a fair number of cars in town by this time, but there were no interstate highways, and cars were a local phenomenon. If you wanted to really get somewhere, you took the train. This meant that a lot of people went in and out of the main train station, and it was a popular meeting place.

In 1934, a train heading for Fort Collins steamed into the little town of Timnath, several miles to the east, on a cold winter morning. Across the street from the station was a blacksmith shop, and a couple of the railroad men happened to have business there.

"Hey, Frank! Come here a minute. Look at what I found!"

Hiding in the back of the shop was a little collie, barely more than a puppy. She was cold and shivering and starving. However, she must have been a real personality because she charmed those tough old railroad guys right out of their bib overalls. Times were hard in 1934, and a stray dog just didn't attract a lot of attention amid the general misery of the Poudre Valley. This one did.

"Cute little thing," said Frank, and he reached down and scooped the dog into his arms.

The dog raised her nose toward his face and eked out a tiny, forlorn bark, followed by a slurpy, wet kiss.

"Awww, gee," said the man. "You're a good girl." He scratched her ears and smoothed her fur.

"Let's take her home with us," suggested the other man.

"I don't dare bring home another animal to feed," declared Frank. "My wife wouldn't allow it."

"She can live at the depot," said the other man. "She'll be our mascot."

So the railroad men took the little dog onto the train and brought her back to Fort Collins and gave her a home. They also gave her a name. They called her Annie. Annie lived at the depot on Laporte Street, just off College

Avenue, and she turned out to be one of those rare individuals who charmed everybody.

From then on, Annie was a permanent fixture at the Fort Collins railroad depot. She was known and loved by the whole town. Whenever a train chugged into the station, Annie would faithfully march out to the platform and greet every passenger. Annie was the unofficial ambassador of the city, and newcomers were often amazed to see local people get off the train and run to greet the little dog before they would their own families! She never strayed very far from the station. It was her empire, and she was the reigning queen.

You see, Annie had come at the worst part of the Depression and the dust storms. She was a bright little light in otherwise drab and dreary days. People had come to think of her as a symbol of better times. She represented something permanent, reliable, and beautiful. The citizens of Fort Collins cherished her. For the next several years, people just gritted their teeth and propelled themselves, along with Annie, into an unknown future.

By 1941 things had begun to look up. Business was better, agriculture was improving, and the dust storms had come to an end. The future was bright. But the world outside had grown a little unlovely, and much of it was at war. When Pearl Harbor was bombed in December, the United States was drawn into World War II.

Very soon, young men from Fort Collins and the Poudre Valley started to leave for the military bases. The scenes were all the same: Little clusters of friends and family would gather around a young man on the platform of the downtown train station and say their last tearful good-byes. Almost always, just as the train was about to pull out of the station, the young man would reach down and give the faithful little collie a final pat and admonish her, "Annie, you be a good dog until I get back."

Annie would bark an encouraging farewell, and then the young man would be gone. Annie, the railroad dog, said good-bye to them all . . . some of them for the last time.

The years passed. By the end of 1945, the boys who had gone away to war now began returning to Fort Collins—older, wiser, and eager to get on with their lives. Every day, they could be seen staring anxiously through the windows of the trains as they pulled into the station in Fort Collins.

Once again the scenes of families, friends, and loved ones gathering around the soldiers and sailors were repeated, but now with a much happier outcome. And in the midst of all this, the faithful railroad collie, Annie, was there to bark a greeting and welcome home each favorite son. It was not at all uncommon to see tough, battle-weary veterans sink down on the station platform and take the little dog in their arms and cry, while Annie licked their faces and dried their tears. In those moments, each man knew that he was really home, and the war was truly over.

Now the exciting years of expansion and growth began. Prosperity brought an expanding population. New homes and businesses were built. Fort Collins was busy shaking off the ravages of all the terrible things the townspeople had been putting up with for so many years: dust storms, depressions, drought, war, rationing, and hoping somebody in your family didn't get killed. There was a great sense that the future potential for Fort Collins was nothing less than spectacular.

But there was one soul in town whose work was now finished and whose life was near its end.

Although railroad engines continued to chug into the station on Laporte Street, just off College Avenue, they came less often and they pulled fewer passenger cars. Most people now were finding it more convenient to use their cars, since the roads had been enlarged and improved. They had even started to build a thing called a "freeway" in Denver.

Nevertheless, the arrival of a train was always the signal for Annie, the railroad-station collie, to struggle to her feet and valiantly meet every passenger with a little woof and a wag of her tail. Her arthritis had gotten so much worse in the last couple of years that it was getting harder and harder for her to get around.

At last, the tough, old railroaders just could not let her suffer anymore. In her fourteenth year, she was put to sleep.

Fort Collins wept.

Annie had seen them all through the tough times. There had been times in the past when the only thing that seemed right about the city was that little dog. The men of the Colorado and Southern Railroad broke all the rules and buried her right next to the tracks where she had spent her life. And they also put up a three-foot-tall headstone that said, "From C and S Men to Annie . . . Our Dog." Half the town showed up for the funeral.

The grave site was destroyed some years later when the tracks were repositioned, but the gravestone is preserved today at the Fort Collins Museum, where it can be seen and the story told over and over again.

It is the story of a dog—and a city—and a love affair that never ends.

A Matter of Honor

William T. McElroy

**Years before, not to have followed
Vance Carter's example would have
been unthinkable in a society where
one's personal and family honor
were both held sacred.**

Mr. Clayton, president of the Greenvale National Bank, stared at his
secretary, a puzzled expression on his face.

"What does this man look like?" he asked, running his thumb over
the card she had just handed him. "Vance Carter died bankrupt two
years ago. Yet this card bears his name."

"It may be his son, sir. It is a young man."

"Didn't remember that he had a son. Well, show him in; I'll see
him."

A moment later, a tall, calm-eyed young man stood in the presence
of the banker.

"It was good of you to see me, sir," were his opening words. "You probably remember my father and his misfortunes. I've just finished college and have come back to Greenvale to find a job and pay off the debts he left. I hoped you might need a man here in the bank."

The abrupt unexpectedness of the young man's statement took Banker Clayton off his guard for a moment.

"Er-er-yes, we do need a clerk. But let that stand for a moment. I remember your father, but I don't remember that he left any debts. He was forced unexpectedly into bankruptcy, wasn't he?"

"Yes, sir. And it broke his heart. He gave up everything, even our home—Mother had died years before—but all the sacrifices didn't quite clear up the indebtedness. He died within a month. I have had to work my last two years through college, but I've graduated now and am ready to go to work, whenever I can get a job, to pay off the remaining indebtedness."

"But you don't owe anything," said the banker impatiently. "The courts settled the matter once and for all."

"I don't owe anything *legally*. I understand that. But I'm not giving much consideration to that. *Morally* the debt stands. It's a matter of honor, you see, sir."

"Hmm! Yes, I see. A matter of honor. How much was the indebtedness?"

"About $5,000."

"And you have nothing?"

"Nothing but an education and a willingness to work."

"Well, that's not a bad start. But, young man, the position we have open pays only $30 a week. It'll take you a long time to save enough out of that to pay off $5,000. You have to live, you know."

"Yes, sir, but I'll live very inexpensively. Anyway, it's a start. Perhaps I may be able to make more money later on. I'll work hard. That debt must be paid sometime."

"When can you start to work?"

"Right now," was the prompt reply.

Thus it was that the vacancy in the clerical force at Greenvale National Bank was filled. And it soon became evident that it was well filled. Mr. Clayton, whose curiosity had been aroused, kept a close watch over his new employee. The bank's force was composed of picked men, but none of them worked harder or more faithfully than the new clerk.

And none saved half so much in proportion to income. Out of his first paycheck, Vance deposited half of the amount in the bank's savings department. So with the second, and the third, and so on, as President Clayton took pains to discover. How it was accomplished the bank president never could find out, though he argued with himself that it was the interests of the bank rather than personal curiosity that led him to investigate.

He found that the boy lived in a little room at the YMCA; that he denied himself most, if not all, of the ordinary pleasures of youth; and that to earn a little in addition to his salary he spent his evenings addressing envelopes for a circular letter company. Even so the bank president could not conceive of a young man of attractive personality as denying himself so uncomplainingly and persistently solely as "a matter of honor." He watched him closely, expecting to see him "break over," as he expressed it to himself, sooner or later.

But his expectations were doomed to disappointment. Vance did not "break over." As his salary increased, his savings account grew proportionately. At the end of three years, he had $3,000 on deposit. In the seclusion of his private office, Banker Clayton studied in quiet amazement the report a clerk had just placed before him.

"He's going to do it!" he exclaimed, slapping the desk with his open palm. "As I live, he's going to do it! He's the pluckiest chap I ever saw. For a son like that I'd give a million dollars and think I'd got a bargain."

Three more years passed. By this time Vance had become one of the most valued employees of the great banking institution. At last the day came toward which he had been working so long. As nearly as he could compute, he had money enough in the bank to meet the old debts in full and, in addition, to pay interest on them at the regular legal rate. It was with a feeling of great relief and thankfulness that he sent out carefully worded invitations to all of his father's creditors to attend a dinner to be given a week or so later.

As he sealed and stamped the last envelope, he leaned back in his chair and took a deep breath. *I know now how a man feels who has just been let out of prison where he has been punished for something he did not do*, he told himself. *My, what a load is off my shoulders!*

For six years he had worked day and night to earn the money. Many an ambitious young man is willing to do that for himself. But to continue working so hard and denying himself so rigidly simply to satisfy a debt that the courts have decided one does not owe is a different matter. But through the years he had worked and saved. Now he had reached the first of his life's goals—the satisfaction of all the claims that he felt were moral, even if not legal, obligations on him and the clearing of his father's name as well. Now that the invitations were in the mail, another week would see the culmination of his long years of hard work and self-denying saving.

The next evening at a dinner party, President Clayton heard of the invitations from one of his friends who had received Vance's surprising note. The following morning, in the midst of his duties, the clerk got a peremptory summons to come at once to the president's office. The banker looked up expectantly as the young man entered.

"Vance," he said, "I've heard of your dinner next week. I wonder if you'd consider me presumptuous if I asked for an invitation to it."

"No, sir. I'd be glad to have you there."

"Well, I'll come on one condition. That is, that you will let me pay half the expenses of the dinner as a mark of my appreciation for what you are doing."

"I'm sorry, sir, but I can't do that."

"Why not?"

"Well, I guess it's just a matter of honor, sir."

"Hmm! Still as keen as ever on these matters of honor, are you?"

"Yes, sir, I hope so."

The shrewd bank president looked his clerk over for a long moment. After the silence and scrutiny had become embarrassing, he spoke again.

"Well, I'll come anyway—on your condition. I'll admit, Vance, though it's a sad admission for a man of my age, that I have a big lump of curiosity in this matter."

Vance grinned. "I'll be glad to have you come. I'd have invited you in the first place if I'd known you were interested."

"Interested! I didn't know such things ever happened outside of storybooks. I wouldn't stay away for $1,000."

The information that Vance had given in his letters of invitation was sufficiently thrilling to those who had received them to bring practically a unanimous acceptance. There were further surprises awaiting the guests as they went to their places at the long table. Beneath the usual place cards, each guest found at his plate an envelope containing an oblong slip of blue paper. There were none of these unopened two minutes after the men were seated. A hum of surprised conversation buzzed through the dining room, and many interested glances were turned in the direction of the quiet young man at the head of the table.

The dinner was a great success. It was not the quality of the food served, for Vance had not ordered an elaborate spread, but rather the unusual circumstances that had brought the group together. Probably the prevailing good humor could have been traced more particularly, if the truth were told, to the fact that each man present felt that he had found again a sum of money he had long ago charged off his books as gone forever. There are few members of the human race who will not expand under such circumstances.

At last Vance shoved back his chair and rapped on his water glass with a spoon to gain the attention of his guests. Amid the profound silence that

ensued, he began to speak. He reviewed briefly the circumstances of his father's heartbreaking failure in business. Then he spoke even more briefly of his own struggles; of his resolution six years before to pay off the last cent of his father's debts; and how by hard work and careful saving he had come to this hour when he could present to every guest a check for the full amount of his loss, plus six percent interest for the entire period.

"It has not been easy," he concluded. "Of course, I knew that legally I owed nothing. That made it harder for me, when I grew discouraged, to go on. I admit that. But I feel sure my father would have fulfilled these obligations as a moral debt, had he lived; and I could do no less. From now on I can face the world, feeling that I have done my duty to my own conscience and to my father's memory. It has not been a legal matter to me; it has been, rather, a matter of honor. I thank you for coming tonight as my guests. Whatever your pleasure has been this hour, I wish to assure you that mine has been greater."

As he ceased speaking, pandemonium broke loose. To an outsider it would have seemed more like a political convention than a gathering of dignified businessmen. Cheer after cheer rang through the room, and men almost climbed over each other to shake hands with their host.

When some semblance of order had been restored, Mr. Hillis, president of the great Hillis Manufacturing Company, began to speak. His words were to the effect that in a long business career this was the first time he had ever known such a thing to happen. But the point of his remarks, as he himself emphasized, was in his closing words.

"Greenvale should be proud to have such a citizen," he said. "And that no other town may be able to take him away from us, I wish in the presence of this company to offer him a position with my own firm at $5,000 a year."

There was another outburst of cheering; but at last Mr. Clayton, who through it all had been trying to speak, succeeded in making himself heard above the din and shouting.

"Mr. Hillis is too late," he said with a smile, his hand on Vance's shoulder. "The Greenvale National Bank appreciates a man of honor, too. Our board of directors at a special meeting at five o'clock this afternoon elected a new cashier. His salary is to be $6,000 a year. And his name is Vance Carter."

That night before retiring, Vance took up his well-worn Bible. It had been his custom, since the days when as a little boy his mother had taught him the importance of reading his Bible every day, to read a few verses each night. As he opened the book, his eyes fell on a verse that had been heavily underscored some years before. It read, "Honor thy father and thy mother, that thy days may be long upon the land which the Lord thy God giveth thee."

Miss Lavinia's Call

Grace Livingston Hill

For years, Miss Lavinia had done servant's work in her brother's house—with no pay and no thanks. Then she received the letter.

Miss Lavinia was in her sister-in-law's kitchen, washing dishes, when the letter came.

For the last 25 years, she had spent most of her time in that same kitchen washing dishes; and it seemed to her that she would probably be there—washing dishes—when her call came to leave this earth. She sometimes wondered vaguely whether there would *be* a call for her; or whether, perchance, she might not be forgotten and go on washing dishes throughout eternity. Forgotten! That was what she felt herself to be.

Not that she had grown sour and hard over it; she was anything but that. There was always a gentle word upon her lips, always a

277

patient, ready acquiescence in any of the family plans that involved, as the family plans of the Wests always did, a shouldering of the heaviest part of the burden by Aunt Lavinia.

When times grew hard and her brother George decided to take his small capital and start in business for himself, it was his sister, Lavinia, who herself suggested that the kitchen maid be dismissed and that she could take the extra care upon herself while the children were little and demanded their mother's attention; then George could get on his feet and not be hampered by heavy household expenses. She had been sure that she could bring expenses down. And so effectually had she done it that there had never been a time in all those 25 years, with the children growing up and the expenses growing with them, when the family had felt they could afford to make a change in their domestic arrangements.

To be sure, she was entirely dependent upon her brother for support. That made some difference. She would think it over sometimes and remind herself that she ought to be most grateful that a home and work were provided for her. This was a new age in which women did strange things, and she was little fitted to cope with the business world in any way that could have supplied her a living. She ought to be exceedingly glad that she had her work, work that she could do, and could feel that she was making return for the respectable, comfortable home that she occupied.

She never murmured as the two girls grew up and found life too full for the help they had by tradition been expected to render when they were old enough. Harriet and Mabel were pretty and popular and bright. Of course she wanted them to go through high school and was proud when their father decided to send them to college. Without a thought, she kept on washing dishes that they might have good outfits for their four years' course of butterflying through an education, and she accepted without a murmur the cast-off gowns that they said weren't good enough to wear at college but would be plenty good enough for "Aunt Viny" to wear afternoons at home.

As if Aunt Viny ever had time to dress up "afternoons at home"! Miss Lavinia turned up the hems (she was smaller than either of the girls) and pieced down the sleeves—she couldn't bring herself to wear them elbow-length; it hadn't been seemly in her young girlhood, except for evening wear. She accepted gratefully the botched-up bonnets that her sister-in-law pieced for her out of the girls' cast-off finery. She wore Alice blue, grass green, gaudy tan and purple, and large black-and-white check uncom-plainingly, and she dyed the cerise poplin brown, meekly answering not a word when they jeered at her for the streaks it had acquired in the dyeing.

Without a murmur, she took the much-darned stockings of the family and "adapted" them for her use, setting in new feet, though the seams always hurt her tender flesh. She wore shoes that were too tight for her and gloves that were too large, and she scarcely ever had a new thing out of the store in all those 25 years.

When George Junior came into the kitchen while she was frying dough-nuts, she always gave him as many as he wanted and wiped up the mud tracks on her neat oilcloth pleasantly. She picked up after him and took his outrageous impudence patiently, acquiring a sweet air of protest like a frightened dove in his presence; yet she would have given her life at any moment to save his.

Maria, her sister-in-law, dealt in sarcasm; and it was to Miss Lavinia's gentle nature like vitriol in a cut. It grew to be the habit always to think that anything that went wrong in the family was Aunt Viny's fault; and she was perpetually anticipating blame and trying to prevent it by little nervous actions that only precipitated trouble.

Five years ago there had been a time when Miss Lavinia fully expected her brother to hire a servant and make things a little easier for her. Indeed, he spoke about it once or twice, for he was getting on well with his business. Then another brother out West died, and his orphaned boy, Donald, came to live with them, making what George Senior called "added heavy expenses." So Lavinia stayed in the kitchen and washed dishes.

Those five years had not made things any easier for Aunt Lavinia. The coming of Donald had not brought harmony. George Junior bullied him, and there was constant friction between them. When Donald had finished two years of high school, George Senior told him it was time for a boy in his position to go to work. He got him a clerkship in a freight office, and Donald swallowed his desire to be a boy a little longer and finish high school. He went to work, while George Junior loafed through three more years of high school and barely got through without disgrace.

Aunt Lavinia sighed a great deal in those days. She loved Donald. He had great frank brown eyes like her younger brother who was his father, and he always brought her a chair when she came in after the supper dishes were washed and she was free to sit down and read the morning paper a few minutes before going to bed. Sometimes when she crept into her narrow bed in the third-story back, the room that would naturally have been given to the servant, she lay a long time staring up at the dark ceiling and thinking how beautiful it would be if she could do something for Donald. But then of course she never could. She was nothing but a dependent. Donald was a dependent, too. It was hard to be dependent. She always wished at such times that she might go out into alien kitchens and earn a wage, that she might save it up and do what she wished with it, rather than be a dependent and have others order her life, no matter how kindly the ordering. But then of course that would hurt the family pride, and she mustn't think of it.

Thinking her meek, sad thoughts and sighing her deep, hopeless sighs, she gradually grew to have an expression of hopeless submission, eyebrows up high in the middle, down at the outside corners; mouth drooping; gentleness written over her whole face. The family thought she was happy. They blamed her, and berated her, and depended on her, and loved her in their way; but they never dreamed of her rebelling. She was theirs, and this was her life, what she was born for. Why should she not like it?

And then the letter came like a meteor dropped into the midst of the household!

Aunt Lavinia hadn't had any letters in years. The old schoolmate—a quiet girl who had married a missionary and gone to India and who used to write to her once a year—was gone to her reward. Nobody ever thought to write to her anymore. And when Harriet went to the door at the postman's ring and found that long, thick envelope addressed to "Miss Lavinia West," she stared at it in wonder and was about to open it as she sometimes did her mother's letters, thinking it an advertisement of some patent medicine, when her sister exclaimed, "Why, Harriet West! That letter belongs to Aunt Viny! Who on earth do you suppose she is getting a letter from? Aunt Viny! Oh Aunt Viny! You've got a letter!"

"Nothing but an 'ad,' of course," said Harriet disdainfully. "I'll put it on the mantel till you get your dishes done, Aunt Viny."

And Miss Lavinia meekly washed her dishes, pared the potatoes for dinner, and made a pudding before she washed her hands carefully at the sink and went to get her letter. Of course it couldn't be anything but an advertisement, as Harriet had said; but even that was something. There was a bright pink spot on each cheek. Did some fine instinct tell her that a crisis had arrived in her monotonous life?

"I'm going up to make the beds now," she explained to the curious girls, who by this time had discovered that the envelope bore the name of a famous firm of lawyers in the city. "I'll be down in time to put on the potatoes." And Miss Lavinia fled to her room.

"Isn't Aunt Viny strange?" said Harriet impatiently. "Just see how she acts about that letter, carrying it off by herself as if it were some great thing. I believe she's getting childish."

"I shouldn't wonder," assented Mabel, looking up from her perusal of the new fashion magazine, which had just arrived in the mail. "Look how unreasonable she was about going to that funeral the other day when we were going to have the Five Hundred Club here, and cake to bake, and sweeping to do, and all. Why, I believe she would have gone in spite of everything if I hadn't hid my old black coat, and it was the only decent thing in the house she could have worn to a funeral. Funny what a whim she took, and he was only an old schoolmate. You don't suppose she ever had a case [crush] on him, do you?"

"Not that I ever heard of," said Harriet. "Fancy anybody having a case on Aunt Viny!"

Up in her room, with trembling hands, Miss Lavinia was opening her letter.

It was only a few lines, but such amazing words were in them! Miss Lavinia could scarcely believe her senses. She had to get up and hunt for a clean handkerchief to wipe her glasses before she read them over again. Out of the stilted maze of legal phrases she gathered at last that a miracle had come to pass. Some money had been left to her! How much, or for what purpose, or from what source she did not stop to question. It might have dropped from heaven for aught she knew. With a strange, elated impression that the occasion demanded her utmost, she dropped upon her knees beside the neat bed that she had conscientiously "spread up" before opening the letter. No words came to her agitated mind or her trembling lips, but when she arose, there was a radiance upon her as if she had received a benediction; and when she went downstairs to put on the potatoes, there was a gentle dignity about her that kept the girls from questioning. Not for worlds would she speak of the matter until she was sure it was true. It seemed to her yet that there must be some mistake.

The letter had spoken of Mr. Stanley K. Washburn. Miss Lavinia's heart beat quicker and the pink grew softly in her cheeks as she thought about it. Why should Stanley Washburn leave her money? He had given her a rose once, standing by her father's gate in the dim twilight years ago, the night before he went back to college for his last semester before graduation. She had kept the rose carefully for years in her handkerchief box, until Mabel rummaging one day came upon it and crushed the withered leaves to powder, scattering the precious dust in the drawer. It had been so with most of the precious things in Miss Lavinia's life. She had only their memories in her heart.

Stanley Washburn had come back from his college commencement on a stretcher, the result of a railroad accident on his homeward trip. The years following had been filled with pain and a useless round of going from one physician to another in his own and foreign lands, until he had finally given up hope and settled down bedridden in the old home with his invalid sister—two invalids, the last of the family.

Meantime, Lavinia's father and mother had died, and she had gone to a distant part of the city to live with her married brother. The years had passed, and the two whose lives had almost touched went far apart with nothing but a crumbling rose to bind them. Lavinia had visited her old friends occasionally through the years—gentle, formal calls with sadness in their eyes and a show of cheerfulness on their faces. But gradually, as the cast-off garments that fell to her lot were less and less to her liking, she ceased to go; and at last his sister died. That had been three years ago. She had been only once since. Something Maria said once about her "traipsing off to see a *man*" had made her cheeks burn and kept her away. It hadn't even been possible for her to go to his funeral when he died. She had shed bitter tears about that in the secret of her bedroom in the night. It had been like all the other things in her life, something that had had to be given up.

But now he had left her some money, a sort of good-bye present, she supposed, if indeed it was really true and the lawyers hadn't made any mistake about it. It was beautiful of him. The tears filled her eyes at the thought. She held her head with more of an uplift than usual, and she managed to stay in the kitchen doing little things most of the time during the noonday meal. She wasn't hungry and dreaded lest the girls should speak again about her letter. Somehow she wanted to be by herself. It was so wonderful that someone had thought of her and left her a remembrance.

At half past two, Mabel and Harriet went off in their prettiest garments to the house of a friend, where they were going to "pour" at a reception.

At half past three, Miss Lavinia, having prepared the vegetables for the evening meal, made a lemon meringue pie, and washed up the lunch dishes, went quietly up to her room and prepared to go out.

She sighed as she put on the old brown poplin and wished she had something a little more respectable in which to go to see the lawyers. Out of respect to her old friend, she ought to look as well as she could. But she found Mabel's black cloak, which covered a multitude of discrepancies, mended a pair of black silk gloves, straightened out the bows on her rusty black hat, and then, dressed as neatly as her wardrobe allowed, she slipped down the stairs to the sitting-room door.

"I'm just going out for a little while, Maria," she said quietly, as if it were a common occurrence, and closed the door before Maria had a chance to take in what she was saying and object. She felt like a truant from school as she hastily shut the front door and hurried down the street to the corner, glancing furtively back, half expecting that Maria would call her back to question her.

Fortune favored her with a streetcar almost immediately; and she climbed in excitedly, scarcely able to believe that it was really she who was going secretly on this daring expedition. She paid her fare out of a worn, old pocketbook whose gaunt sides touched over a solitary dime and whose antiquated clasps were brassy with disuse.

The dime was all the money she had in the world. Her father had given it to her 40 years before, when at the age of five she had repeated for him perfectly the Twenty-third Psalm. She had hoarded it carefully all these years and had hoped to keep it all her life. She sighed as she laid it venturesomely in the conductor's hand. It seemed a sacrilege, but there had been nothing else to do. She could not ask any member of her family for car fare without explaining her errand, and that she would not do until she was sure there was no mistake. How they would jeer at her! Her cheeks grew crimson at the very thought. If there was nothing to it, her family need never know. Perhaps this was the time of need for which she had been keeping it. At least, there was no other way. It was too far to walk.

When she got her breath, she took out the letter and looked at it again to make sure of the street and number and to wonder again over its stately phrasing. It came to her to wonder for the first time how much the legacy might be. Probably $5 or $10. That would be a great deal for her to have of her own after all these years of absolute poverty.

But what if it should be as much as $50? Incredible thought! It almost took her breath away. She could buy Donald a brand-new suit of clothes so that he wouldn't have to wear George Junior's old ones that didn't fit him. She knew those baggy clothes were a great trial to Donald. Perhaps she could even pay for a term at night school for him. Donald had ambitions to be an electrical engineer someday, but the prospect looked rather dim. Night school would help him a great deal. Then, if there was enough left, she would buy a pair of nice new gray kid gloves for herself. It would not be selfish for her to do that much. Her old friend would be pleased if she did.

Then suddenly she reproached herself for such wild fancies, and her eyes filled with tears over the thought that anyone had cared enough for her to remember her in his will.

Tremulously at last she entered the lawyer's office, meekly murmured her name, and handed over the official-looking letter as her excuse for being there. But behold a miracle!

A gray-haired man of fine presence came forward deferentially, just as if she had been a queen, and conducted her to an inner office, where he placed her in a great leather chair. He could not have given her more honor and consideration if she had been the dead man's wife. The poor little woman was overwhelmed.

It appeared that the lawyer had been the lifelong friend and confidant of Mr. Washburn. The will, which left everything to Miss West, save a few small bequests to faithful servants, had been made some years ago; in fact, as soon as the sick man was told by his physicians that his case was hopeless and that he might pass away at any time. The lawyer added that the making of the will had been a great pleasure to his friend and that he had written a letter which was to be given to her after his death.

Miss Lavinia listened as in a dream to the wonderful story. She was endowed with what seemed to her a vast fortune. "Comfortably off," the lawyer expressed it. The property was well invested and bringing in an annual income of at least $3,500 in addition to the old Washburn homestead, which could be rented or sold as she chose. There was besides about $2,000 of ready money in the bank subject to her check. They gave her a bankbook and a checkbook, explaining their mysteries carefully, and even handed her a roll of bills, $50 in all!

Dear little Miss Lavinia in her dyed garments and her darned gloves grew white and pink as she looked at the lawyer and tried to understand. It was too marvelous, too wonderful, too incredible to happen to her. She looked at the money, and she looked at the lawyer. All that money in her hands at once! It simply could not be!

But when they put his letter in her trembling hand, and she saw the old familiar quirk to the L in Lavinia, the same he had written on the commencement-invitation envelope, a great light broke over her face. It was as if she had heard his voice speaking her name. Something seemed to rise within her, something that had long been crushed and forgotten. Was it her sweet self rising in wonder to a new life wherein someone really cared for her aside from what she might do for him?

She was overwhelmed no longer. She had his letter in her hand, and the mere touch of it enabled her to rise to the occasion. So quietly, so gently, with such well-bred dignity of thankfulness she received the news that the old lawyer thought within himself, as he escorted her to the elevator a few minutes later, what a pity she could not have been permitted to cheer the last lonely days of their friend! Surely here was a woman who would have been unselfish enough to give a few years of her life to an invalid.

In a kind of sweet daze, Miss Lavinia climbed into the homeward trolley and paid her fare out of a crisp new bill. At least she could now keep the other half of her precious dime as a reminder of her dear father. Her heart thrilled anew with gratitude to her old friend as she paid her fare and felt independent for the first time in her life.

It was not of the money she thought most as she rode home, but of the letter, the wonderful letter held close in her little darned glove. How wonderful after all these years to have a letter from Stanley Washburn! The years were bridged, and she stood once more beside the gate in the dusk, with a rose in the breast of her white gown.

When she reached home, she slipped quietly up to her room and changed her dress, buttoning the letter safely inside her blouse. Then she tucked her fat pocketbook away under a pile of clothes in her bureau drawer, giving it a loving pat, and went hurriedly down to the kitchen, for she could hear Maria rattling the range with indignant vigor.

"Well!" said Maria, straightening up from her self-imposed task. "So you've come back! Where in the world have you been? If I'd known you were going out, I wouldn't have begun to cut out Harriet's shirtwaists. One can't do everything at once. Look at the time of day! George will be here in half an hour, and this is his Building Society night, you know. He can't be late with supper."

"I guess I shan't be late," said Miss Lavinia serenely, glancing at the clock to make sure Maria had as usual exaggerated the time. Then she lifted the range lid capably, gave a glance at the fire, and pushed forward the kettle of hot water. In this brief time, the kitchen seemed to have assumed its normal complacency after the hurried onslaught of Maria.

"Go back to your shirtwaists, Maria. I'll manage alone," Lavinia said gently, and there was that in her tone that made Maria turn and stare curiously at her sister-in-law.

There had been times during the years when this sister showed a calm superiority that made Maria uncomfortable; but never before had she seen quite the look that Lavinia's face wore now, filled with a sort of soft glory that radiated from her eyes and seemed to set a halo above her prematurely silvering hair. It was almost as though she glimpsed for an instant the gentlewoman in this humble dependent of the family, their heretofore meek burden bearer. It was like a rebuke, as if Lavinia had been a great lady in disguise all these years. And yet she did not seem to have taken on any airs. Maria gave her a second puzzled glance and hurried out of the room. There had always been something about Lavinia she could not understand.

The dinner was only five minutes late after all, and Miss Lavinia did not hear the family jokes at her expense as she brought in the steaming dishes. She was thinking that it was only a little time now until she would be free to read her letter. She gave Donald a bewildering smile as she turned back to the kitchen, and he answered it with a grateful one. Donald was tired and discouraged that night. George Junior had been particularly trying with his lordly airs.

After dinner Donald slipped out to the kitchen and wiped the dishes for Aunt Lavinia. He often did it. It was their only chance to talk together alone, and it did the boy good to hear her kindly sympathy and brighten her monotony with tales of the office. Tonight, however, he was unusually silent. It seemed a long way ahead before he could hope to get where he could do anything worthwhile. Perhaps he would never get there.

Suddenly, however, his aunt looked up.

"Donald, I want you to write and find out what it costs to go to that college you were talking about the other day."

"What's the use?" said Donald dejectedly. "I couldn't ever go to college, no matter what it costs."

"Yes you could!" said Miss Lavinia decidedly. "There's going to be a way. I see a way now, and I want you to write the letter this very night and find out all about it."

"Aunt Lavinia!" Donald never called her "Aunt Viny," as the others did. It was one of the things about him that made him different from the rest. "What do you mean? You can't mean anything, of course. And, besides, I couldn't go to college; I've never finished high school."

"There are preparatory schools, aren't there? I want you to write and ask them what preparatory school they want you to go to."

"Aunt Lavinia!" Donald almost dropped the big yellow mixing bowl he was wiping.

"Never mind, child. You do as I tell you," said Aunt Lavinia alertly. "I'll tell you all about it tomorrow. Don't say anything," she added under her breath as George Junior banged into the kitchen, loudly demanding the hatchet.

It was late when Miss Lavinia finished and got up to her room at last. With trembling fingers she opened her letter, touching the page gently as if it were human and sensitive.

> *My dear Lavinia* [it read],
>
> *When we stood in the dusk by your father's gate that night so many years ago, I was happy in the thought that I would soon be in a position to ask you to be my wife. When I gave you a rose, I hoped you would understand that I loved you. How beautiful you looked to me with that rose tucked in your little white dress!*
>
> *You know what happened and will understand that the time never came when I, a hopeless invalid, could honorably ask you to share my broken life. But I have loved you all these years.*
>
> *I am not, however, going to burden you with the tale of my love*

and disappointment; for the years have gone by, and I no longer know whether my love would interest you. But it has been a great pleasure to me to think that I might at least, when I was gone, have the privilege of leaving to you my possessions and so providing for you as I would have loved to do if you had been my wife.

I have thought sometimes that I saw in your eyes an answer to my feeling for you, but then I have reproached myself, for how could any woman care for a broken man upon his bed?

And so, my good friend, if nothing more, as my friend I am leaving you all that I have in this world. Yet if, in the providence of God, you ever cared for me, then know that all a man's soul may give to a woman's my soul gave to yours; and whatever place in your heart and thoughts you choose to give me, I am content. It is enough for me now to think that I may leave you independent for the rest of your life.

I would suggest that you leave the money invested as it is. It has been my study and pleasure to place it safely where it will bring you a steady, continual income, and I commend to you my old lawyer friend, who will advise you wisely in all business matters. You will hardly care to live in this old house. The neighborhood has changed since the days when we all lived about here, but I should be glad if you can find time to look after and dispose of the things in the house—my sister's and my own. We were the last of the family. I have full confidence in your sweet judgment. I leave you unhampered and rejoice that I may have so much part in your dear life.

I bid you farewell.

Your friend or lover, as you choose,
Stanley K. Washburn

She crept into her bed at last and lay there, staring into the darkness of the room as if it were filled with glory-light. No thought of death or darkness or separation came to blight that first joy of her knowledge that she was beloved. It was enough that he loved her, had loved her through the years. She could live her days out joyfully now. She would make his money bring joy to others. She was happier than she had ever dreamed of being on this earth.

Once a great pang shot through her to think of his long years of suffering and wanting her, and she not knowing it or being able to minister to him. Then it came to her like a revelation that through it his greatness of soul had been born, and so she was content.

She told them the next morning at the breakfast table, quietly, as if it were quite a common occurrence.

"George," she said as she passed her brother his second cup of coffee, "I want to tell you that I've had a little money left me by an old friend, and I shan't be a burden on you any longer." As if she had ever been a burden in that house!

"Money!" screamed George Junior jubilantly. "Then you'll buy me that motorcycle I've wanted for so long, won't you, Aunt Viny?"

"Money?" said George Senior, putting another lump of sugar into his coffee. "That sounds good. Money's always welcome when it's coming our way. How much is it?" He spoke as if it were coming to the common coffer.

"It's enough to keep me quite comfortable," said Miss Lavinia in the self-effacing tone she had used during the years to put herself into the background.

Her brother laughed. "I guess you don't have much idea how much it does cost to keep you, Viny, do you? You never had much to do with money matters. You've always been well taken care of and not had to bother where your daily bread came from."

"Yes," sniffed Maria, "I guess you don't have much idea about what things cost, Viny." There was righteous implication in her tone that intended to convey the high cost of Miss Lavinia's living all these years.

Miss Lavinia's soft brown eyes told no tale of how distasteful this conversation was to her nerves, long accustomed to such as this. She only answered with dignity, "I shall have an income of about $3,500 a year."

"Great Scott!" George dropped his teaspoon into his cup with a clatter. "Thirty-five hundred a year! Why, Viny, you're crazy. You don't know what you're talking about. You mean $3,500 in all, don't you? Even that's a great deal for *you* to have left you."

"Aunt Viny doesn't realize what a big capital an income of $3,500 a year would mean," said Harriet patronizingly. Harriet had been a stenographer in a business office for six months after she left college and thought she knew a great deal about business matters.

"Well, I should like to know who on earth would leave Aunt Viny money, anyway," said Mabel saucily. "I guess you'll likely find there's some mistake, Aunt Viny. People don't leave big sums to strangers that way."

"Be still, Mabel," said her father sharply. "Let your aunt talk. Viny, who'd you say left this $3,500 to you?"

Donald's face was red with indignation, and his fists were clenched under the tablecloth; but Miss Lavinia answered with a sweet lifting of her radiant eyes and a gentle dignity that was both convincing and awe-inspiring.

"It was my old friend Stanley Washburn, George, who used to live near us on Chester Avenue when we were young. There's no mistake about it, for I went to see the lawyer yesterday. I shall have an income of at least $3,500 a year."

"You don't say!" said Mr. West, sitting up excitedly. "Stan Washburn! That poor fellow that got knocked up on the railroad? So he's dead at last! Well, I must say it was decent of him to leave you his money."

"Well, he's better off," sighed Maria piously. "I'm sure I shouldn't want to live a long life of suffering. I should think you'd be glad now, Viny, that you took my advice and didn't keep running out there. It can't be said of you that you were after his money."

"Is that the man whose funeral Aunt Viny was so crazy to go to?" broke in Mabel. "*Now* we see what *you* were up to, Aunt Viny."

But Miss Lavinia had fled to the kitchen, and no one but Donald had seen the tears in her eyes as she reached for the empty coffeepot.

"It's a pity this couldn't have come three years ago, when you were building the new store," suggested Maria in a low tone to her husband. "You could have managed the double building then and enlarged the business."

"Yes, it might have come in handy," said George reflectively, folding up his napkin and putting it into the ring. "Strange! Stan Washburn! I never knew he was stuck on Viny. Viny!" he called to his sister. "You say you went to see the lawyer yesterday. Well, you'll be wanting to get the business part settled up right away. It's always better. I'll arrange to get away from the store this afternoon and go down with you. I think I can fix it up to invest your money in the business."

But Miss Lavinia was standing in the kitchen door, her soft eyes bright with the recent tears, her cheeks red, and her soft lips set firmly.

"Thank you, George," she said gently. "But I shall not need you. Everything is all arranged. The money is well invested, and Mr. Washburn wished to have it remain where it is. I shall not need any help."

Then she turned and shut the kitchen door quietly after her.

"Well, upon my word! Such airs!" said Harriet. "Mother, how are you going to get along with an heiress in the kitchen? I'm sure I didn't suppose Aunt Viny would get her head turned like that by a little money. She seems to have forgotten all we've done for her."

"Done for *her!* What have you ever done for her?" muttered Donald under his breath. "What has *she* done for *you,* you'd better say!"

And Donald marched off into the kitchen, followed by George's sneering, "Well, there's a pair of you, I should say!"

Further conversation, however, was interrupted by the reappearance of Miss Lavinia.

"I've been thinking," she said; and the family, looking up, perceived about her a new air of confidence that commanded their attention. "I shall have a great deal to attend to the next few days and shall scarcely have time for my usual work. Mr. Washburn has asked me to look after some of his sister's and his things, and this must be attended to at once. If you're willing, Maria, I'll run over to Chloe Whitely's and get her to come for a week or two till you can look around and see whom you want to get permanently."

"Certainly, if you have the money to pay her," said Maria contemptuously. "Of course I suppose you'll run the house, now that you have a little money."

"Oh, why, Maria, I don't want to do anything you don't like, of course," said Lavinia, conscience-stricken, "but I'll be very glad to pay for some good help, anybody you'll select to take my place. I thought you'd like Chloe because she's washed for us so long, and knows all our ways, and how we cook. You see, I shall have to be away for several days; it may be longer. I can't tell how long it will take me, nor what plans I shall make."

"Oh, of course," said Maria, still offended. "I should have supposed you'd want some of your family to advise you, but you seem sufficient to yourself. Perhaps you'd like one of the girls to go with you."

"Thank you," said Lavinia dubiously, "but I think perhaps I ought to go alone—at first, anyway."

During the next few days, the West family suffered a physical and mental disturbance somewhat similar to a volcanic eruption; and when it was over, they found a decided change in the face of their landscape. Through it all Miss Lavinia went her serene way, untroubled and untrammeled. For in truth she was a new being. The sharp words, broad hints, and covert sneers that would have crushed her meek soul to earth in former days went unnoticed in the high altitude to which she had attained.

She went shopping for three whole days.

Donald appeared in a new suit at dinner the second night, to the discomfiture of his cousin George Junior, who'd expected to shed his own suit before it was half worn out, on the pretext that Donald needed it. However, he forgot his grievance the next morning upon the arrival of a shining new motorcycle.

All that day packages began to arrive and were stacked up on the hall hat rack, until they overflowed its ample limits.

"Gee!" said George Junior, coming home to lunch black and blue from his first ride. "But she can spend the money. Guess I'd better strike her for some more things before she gets away with it all."

"Yes," said his mother anxiously, "she needs a guardian. She'll just spend it all and be back on our hands to support again. I declare, George," she said, turning to her husband, "someone ought to stop her."

"Guess no one can stop her. The money's her own," said George Senior, drumming reflectively on the window seat.

But the third evening Miss Lavinia brought down a lot of those packages. There was a rich wonderful satiny silk of purple, with deep black and rich green shadows in it, such as Maria had coveted for many a day. There were two charming gold wristwatches for Harriet and Mabel, besides a lot of pretty things in jewelry and lingerie that the watchful aunt had long wished to buy for them all. Also, before she went up to her room, she handed her brother a check for $500, which she said she hoped would pay for someone to take her place for a while and also get him the big leather chair and desk he had coveted for his library.

Somehow the atmosphere of the family changed a good deal that evening. They weren't exactly overwhelmed by their gifts, munificent as they were; but they were mollified. After all, you wouldn't have expected them to bow down to her, meek, quiet little woman that she was, still in her handed-down, dyed, and made-over garments, her hair combed in the same plain way they had known it for years, her feet encased in an old pair of Harriet's shoes with the heels worn down at the side.

But the great surprise came the next morning.

It was strange enough not to have Aunt Viny down in the kitchen before anyone else was up; but to have her actually late to breakfast was a thing the family quite resented, even in spite of the gifts of the night before.

"Well, really! So you've come down at last!" said Maria in her sharp tone, forgetful for the moment of the luscious purple silk. And then the family dropped their knives and forks, sat back, and stared.

For there on the threshold stood not Aunt Viny in her faded poplin, rusty bonnet, darned gloves, and shabby shoes, but a lady! A stranger she seemed to be at first. She was attired in a simple, exquisitely tailored fine gray suit, a coat, and a skirt with a glimpse of a soft gray silk blouse beneath and a fine white lace collar. On her head was the sweetest little gray hat of fine straw, with gray and white wings that seemed to nestle like a dove about the fluffy silver hair that waved over her calm forehead. Her hands were encased in soft gray suede gloves; her shoes were trim, well-fitting, and new; over her arm was thrown a long, soft camel's hair coat of gray; and she carried a small handbag of gray leather and a larger traveling bag of black.

After observing these details, their eyes traveled back to her face. A beautiful one, sweet and gentle, with soft brown eyes that had in them something familiar. What was this beautiful stranger doing in their dining room? A feeling that the indignity was somehow due to Aunt Viny arose in their breasts; and then the lady spoke, and the voice was the voice of Aunt Viny!

"I'm sorry to be late," she said, "but I thought I'd better be all ready before I came down. Mr. Benson, the lawyer, is coming pretty soon to take me to the house; and it won't do for me to keep him waiting."

The family caught its breath as one man and one woman in sudden relief and indignation. Aunt Viny had no right to startle them all that way. But astonishing thought! *This* was Aunt Viny, and she was *beautiful!* How had she managed it just with clothes? Who knew she could look like that? The girls turned sick with envy and mortification. They hadn't taken in yet what she said; they had only taken in that it was Aunt Viny.

Calmly, as if her new belongings had been with her all her life, Miss Lavinia walked over to the dining-room couch, deposited her cloak and bags, and drew off her gloves, apologetically saying, "I put these on to be sure they would go on quickly the second time." Then she took her seat at the table.

Mechanically and in silence, they handed her a plate. Maria, disturbed as by the presence of a guest at table, rang for hot coffee, and she hoped the rolls

were not cold. When had she ever taken so much solicitude for Lavinia before? But a lady clothed in tailor-made trimness was somehow different from Viny in her kitchen gingham.

"I thought I'd better tell you all that I don't suppose I'll be coming back to stay; so you can fix up my room as you like," said Miss Lavinia. "I know the girls have been wanting a bay window in their room, and I left something up on their pincushion that will help build it. I shall be back and forth, of course, but not probably to stay overnight. I'm going to take Donald with me; so you can have his room for the extra guest room we've needed so long. I can't tell just how long it will take me to get the house ready to sell; but I may be there a month yet, anyway. Donald has to give his month's notice before leaving the office. Then we are going to hunt around and find a nice little home near the college he wants to go to and settle down for the next five or six years. We haven't got our plans made yet, but we hope you'll all come and see us often."

Had a bomb been thrown into the room and exploded, it could not have more completely knocked the senses out of the family. They simply sat and gasped, as the erstwhile meek burden bearer brought out one after another her calm, astonishing facts.

And then, before a single one could summon a word, the doorbell rang and the lawyer arrived.

It was quite obvious that nothing suitable to the occasion could be said with only a pair of thin portieres separating the imposing stranger from their voices. And in five minutes more Miss Lavinia was seated in the lawyer's great shining car, waving her pretty gray glove to them happily, with Donald in the front seat beside Mr. Benson.

The family stood on the front porch and watched them go, still speechless from astonishment.

"Who ever knew she was *beautiful?*" exclaimed Harriet as the car turned the corner and was lost to view.

"Anyone can look that way if they can buy such clothes," said Maria with a toss of her head.

"Wasn't that handbag a peach?" said Mabel. "It was lined with moiré silk, pale rose color, and mounted in gold."

"I mean to ask her to buy me a car next Christmas," said George Junior, mindful of his cousin Donald on that front seat.

"That's the way Mother used to look when I was a little kid," said George Senior. "Mother was beautiful like that. And she always wore soft gray things." Then with a sort of wistful sigh, he turned back to his house that seemed suddenly desolate. Was it possible that Aunt Viny had made so much difference?

Queen Esther's Petition

Dixie Wolcott

The family desperately needed a friend in high places, but they had none. So a substitute stepped in. But what could a seven-year-old child do to avert family disaster?

There was a deep scowl on the chief clerk's face as he ran his eye over the special delivery letter he held in his hand. He had the reputation, fairly won, of being the gruffest man in the department. Impatiently, he seized a pen and commenced a reply.

> Washington, D.C., July 10, 190–
>
> Dear Senator:
>   It will be impossible to reinstate your man Williams. I have already promised the place to Dawson. You know Dawson yourself, and there is not a better man in our party. I regret—

299

The door of the chief clerk's room was pushed gently open.

"Well?" he exclaimed, without raising his eyes.

"Please may I come in?" asked a sweet, childish voice.

He glanced up and, with a whistle of astonishment, laid down his pen. Standing on the threshold was a little girl with laughing blue eyes and sunny curls. A big straw hat was pushed back, and the eager face was flushed with the July sun.

"Well," he said gruffly, "aren't you already in?"

"Oh, yes," replied the child, dancing lightly across the room. "But your guard—"

"The messengers?"

"Yes," she assented, "the messengers. They said you mustn't be 'sturbed, but I 'splained that I am Queen Esther and had to see you on most 'portant business, so they let me by."

"Queen Esther?" he asked.

"Not truly, of course. My real name is Alice—Alice Williams—but I'm pittending I'm Queen Esther, and"—with a deep bow—"you are Ahasuerus!"

The chief clerk stared at her in amazement.

"And I've come to save my people," she went on. "Not a sure 'nough nation, you know, but just Mother. You haven't asked me to sit down," she added.

The red lips had a pretty trick of pouting, and with unwonted gentleness he stooped and lifted the child to his desk.

"Now, King Ahasuerus," she said, swinging her feet and twirling her hat by the blue ribbon, "we can talk more comfo'bly, but first, are you a Medunpersian?"

The chief clerk cleared his throat. "I think not," he answered slowly. "Why?"

"Oh, I'm glad," she replied, with a contented little sigh. " 'Cause as you aren't, you can change your mind about 'smissing my papa."

"Did he send you here?" he demanded.

"Oh, no, no!" said the child. "He wouldn't never have let me come; nor Mother most of all. I"—in a whisper—"I runned away! But won't you please, *please,* promise you won't never tell?" she asked beseechingly.

"Yes, I'll promise"—for the first time smiling down into the eager little face.

"Cross your heart?"

"Cross my heart."

"Father said you were the one to come to, but he'd rather starve than ask a favor of you. I couldn't let Mother starve, you know, so I thinked if you weren't drefful cross, I'd ask you myself, and so I just runned off, and"—approvingly—"I think you're very nice."

"Thanks, Queen Esther."

"Yes, right nice, though you don't smile very much, but p'raps you've your own troubles. You might tell me 'bout 'em if you have. I symperthize with my own beau'ful mother, you know."

"Is your mother very beautiful?" he asked, leaning forward.

"Oh, yes," replied the child. "So lovely, you can't think. But, you see, she's had nervous persuasion ever since Father lost his money, and the doctor says she mustn't never be worried, and"—shaking a tiny finger at him—"now you've gone and worried her!"

"I'm sorry," he murmured, as though matters were reversed and he were but seven and his accuser 35.

"You see," she said, growing confidential, "Father doesn't talk 'bout nothing but the fortune he lost, and all the time he just thinks gracious goodness if only he could live his life over again, and then sometimes he drinks to forget about it."

"Cowardly brute!" muttered the chief clerk under his breath.

"So, 'course, there's nobody to think about Mother but me, and yesterday—" The child flushed and hesitated.

"Well?"

"Father said the rent was only just paid till tomorrow, and—and we haven't any money at all, and there's no use for him to try, 'cause everybody's 'gainst him."

If it weren't for Dawson's former kindness to me . . . , the chief clerk thought to himself, but the child broke in on his thoughts.

"And then Mother cried, and you know she mustn't never do that 'cause it makes her worse; and if she gets worser all the time," continued the little philosopher, "she'll die, and I reckon if Mother died, nobody would want to live, would they?"

The blue eyes were full of tears, and he quickly interposed.

"Well then, Queen Esther, what is your petition?"

"Why, you just put Father back again! Won't you please?"

It is one of the best places in the office, and Dawson must have it, he repeated to himself as a sort of moral support, but the pleading voice went on.

"Please, Ahasuerus. I just want you to let him stay till I'm big enough to take care of Mother. It won't be so drefful long."

"As soon as you are big enough to do that," he answered, smiling, "you'll go off and marry some rich man—"

"No, no," she interrupted. "That's a orful thing to do! Once upon a time, Mother said, there was a little girl who had yellow curls just like me, and she used to be very happy, and there was a boy—I forget his name—"

"John?"

"Yes, John. How did you know? Well, he used to carry her books to school, and one day when the bridge was broken—"

"He carried her over the stream—"

"Yes, and they used to go nutting and sledding together, and he always brought her the first flowers, and they were happy and loved each other, and they said when they growed up they'd get married. But when she was big, a rich man came and asked her to marry him, and her mother told her to, and she did. But the rich man lost all his money and it served her right, but she wouldn't never have been happy anyhow, 'cause she just kep' on loving John, though she tried not to orful hard. I reckon she'd been in the habit of it so long, she couldn't stop. And I'm never, never to act like that, 'cause it's the wickedest thing there is, Mother says."

The chief clerk had bowed his head on the desk.

"I'm 'fraid you're drefful tired of me," she said softly, slipping down, "and I must be going now or Mother'll miss me."

"Good-bye, Queen Esther," he said. "I will think your petition over and grant it if I can—and thank you for coming."

"You are welcome," she replied sweetly. "But Mother must have been mistooken when she said you hated her. You're so kind, I reckon you couldn't hate anybody, could you?"

"At least not your mother," he answered, smiling down at her.

"Nobody couldn't do that. Remember, you mustn't never tell I came 'cause you crossed your heart, and that's more than a Medunpersian. Good-bye." And the rosy little mouth was put up to be kissed.

The chief clerk rose and, walking over to the window, stood gazing out for a long time. Then he turned and rang for his private secretary. To him he dictated a letter:

Washington, D.C., July 10, 190–

Dear Senator:

Your letter of the 10th has been received. I take pleasure in informing you that your man J. R. Williams has today been reinstated.

Very truly yours,
John E. Mitchell, Chief Clerk

"God Save Queen Esther!" he muttered as he rang for a messenger.

Teaching True

Dorothy Waldo

There are those with mere talent, large and small; and there are those who are undeniably virtuosos. Should the former dare to teach the latter?

When the letter came, the Morris family gathered at once for a conference. "Of course you can do it, Alice," said her mother. "You know everyone likes to hear you play."

Alice crumpled the envelope in her hand. "But, Mother, don't you understand that playing simple tunes for unmusical people in a little town is very different from teaching the violin in a very important private school near a big city? Everyone knows good music there."

"You have been well taught, Alice," said her father quietly from his wheelchair. "You might have gone far if—" He broke off abruptly with a downward glance at his body, so shrunken under the lap robe.

"Don't, Father dear! You know I have been very, very happy here in the high school, and probably I never could have succeeded as a fiddler. Besides—"

"Oh, come on!" interrupted the irreverent Jack. "You know you can make all the old ladies cry anytime. Besides, think of the salary! Just three times what the stingy Southbury school committee will pay you. Think what we all could do with that money!"

Think indeed! Alice smoothed the crumpled letter out on the table before her. To teach the violin and English at the famous Beechmont school! To have all that money each month! Father could have the massage that might restore his health; Mother might lose that tired wrinkle; Jack could stay on at his beloved school; even little three-year-old Teddy might profit by it. But—was it honest? It did not seem to her that she was capable of teaching the violin. She had so often met in New York struggling violinists with acquirements much greater than her own. She turned to her father.

"Daddy," she said, laying her hand on his, "is it honest?"

Her father smiled. "Women are often overly conscientious about business matters," he said. "Remember that, though you have not a great technique, what you *can* do, you do well. I should write to Mrs. Vose at Beechmont, telling her how you feel and let her decide whether she still wants your services."

To Alice's astonishment, the principal of Beechmont seemed undisturbed by her letter of confession, and it was settled that she should take the position in a month. As preparation, she worked over a few of the best pieces of music in her limited repertoire. She knew that at the school she must play and play often.

"Choose simple things and do them well," said her father. "Most violinists do big things badly."

How she blessed the work of that greatest of contemporary violinists, Jules Circeaux! It seemed almost as if he had known her problem and that out of all the world of music, he had chosen the loveliest things and arranged them expressly for her to play.

Her last night at home she played for them all as they sat round the crackling fire.

"I can announce my program in one word," she said with a laugh. "It's Circeaux. We have Bach, arranged by Circeaux; Paganini, simplified by Circeaux; et cetera, edited by Circeaux."

Then, watching the firelight flicker on their dear faces and wondering whether she could succeed for them, she began to play.

Presently, Jack stirred. "Now, Alice, play the 'Home Tune' before I go to bed, will you? Mother, you play the accompaniment for her."

Once more Alice drew her bow across the strings while her mother picked out the accompaniment from her father's manuscript. It was her own tune now, the one she had made for them around the fire and for which her father had written the accompaniment.

"Here we are, all sitting around the fire," she said, beginning with the first low G-string notes.

Jack interrupted. "Yes, and then Father and Mother begin to talk together; I can hear them."

Alice smiled. She did not need to interpret that music—they knew every note. In silence, she played to the very end, tenderly, with the consciousness that it was the last time.

"Those last notes mean the fire's out, and everyone's got to go to bed," said Jack.

The first weeks of her work at Beechmont went far more easily than Alice had dared to hope. Of her ability to teach English, there had never been any question. Her violin pupils proved to be beginners, and she soon realized that her sound, if limited, knowledge was helping them. As the busy, happy weeks slipped by, she began to be thankful that she had had the courage to try the work.

Not until the end of the second month did anything happen to arouse her sleeping doubts of herself. A new pupil came: a little, eager girl, tingling with the love of music and the desire to begin to study the violin. She was different from those other uninspired pupils. She listened absorbed, where others waited only for the hour of teaching to end. Alice realized grimly that within two years this child would test all of her powers. She determined that all she could teach her should be taught true.

Then a chance remark by a pupil to whom she was holding up Adele as an example made her heart sink.

"Of course Adele ought to do better than I!" said the sulky child. "Look at her uncle!"

"What has Adele's uncle to do with her playing?" asked Alice patiently.

"Don't you know?" asked the child. "Why, her uncle is Circeaux, and of course she ought to do well. His wife is Adele's very own aunt."

Alice heard no more of the child's grumbling. Adele the niece of Jules Circeaux! And she, impostor, was teaching her the violin!

It did not astonish her very much, somehow, when she met Miss Vose in the hall that very day, to find her beaming with pride and importance over some news that had just arrived.

"My dear, I have such a treat for you!" said the principal. "The great Jules Circeaux comes here tonight with his wife. Of course, they and little Adele will dine with me. In the evening I have asked several people in to meet them, and I want you to come and play for us. Some of those little things you play so well."

"Oh, no!" gasped Alice. "I couldn't, Miss Vose—I couldn't!"

Miss Vose frowned a little. She was not used to being opposed. "But certainly, my child. Everyone praises your work here at Beechmont. You are certainly qualified to play as I ask you to."

The unmusical lady moved majestically away, and Alice shut herself in her room, sick at heart. To stand before him whom she so reverenced—to reveal

to him that in that great art which must be real to be beautiful she was a
mere pretender—seemed more than she could bear. Those others did not
know enough of music to realize it; he would see the truth the moment she
first drew her bow across the strings.

In keen distress, she paced up and down her room. It did not help that
there was a jubilant letter from home, acknowledging a check from her.

Father's paralysis seemed less complete, and Jack was at the head of his class. Well, she had given them a little time of help, at any rate. She would have that to think of, after the great Circeaux had told them all and had put a real violinist in her place.

At last the hour came when she could delay no longer. Deliberately, she dressed and, with her violin under her arm, started down the long hall to Miss Vose's apartment. As she approached the door, a man crossed in front of her from a side corridor. She recognized him at once: Jules Circeaux, the great, the dreaded. Quick decision came to her. Those twittering people on the other side of that door would never understand, but he should know that she knew.

"Monsieur," she said.

The figure turned courteously. "Mam'selle? Ah, a violinist!"

Alice spoke rapidly: "Yes, I teach the violin here. I teach Adele. I want to tell you myself what you will realize if I am forced to play. I know I am not a good violinist. I ought not to be holding this position. I have to, though, and I can honestly say that what I know I do teach true."

The great violinist was smiling kindly down at her. "The little lady is greatly distressed," he said. "Perhaps there is no need. If she can teach true, the greatest can do no more."

He opened the door, and Alice, cold with dread, entered the brilliantly lighted room. It seemed only a second before the principal was blandly insisting that she play for the master, only a second before she found herself facing a politely expectant group of parents and instructors.

"Play one of those little things we all like," urged Miss Vose. "I want Monsieur Circeaux to hear them."

Then, in a flash, the monstrosity of it dawned upon Alice. "Those little things" were all Monsieur Circeaux's. There was scarcely a piece of music in her repertoire that he had not arranged and played himself at his great concerts. She could not stand up there and ruin them for him. For a minute, she felt her hand grow clammy on the neck of her violin. Then out of her desperation grew determination, and she spoke quite calmly.

"I think I will play you something else if I may. It is a very simple melody called the 'Home Tune.' At first, the mother and father are supposed to be sitting by the fire, talking quietly. Then the boy interrupts with some of his school news, and the three-year-old asks for a story about what the fire fairies are doing. After it is told, the family sit quietly and dream into the embers."

Then she began to play. As the familiar double stops formed under her fingers, the dear, dim picture grew in her mind. Gradually, the staring, rustling group in front of her faded, and she was playing for the loved audience for whom she had composed the music. In memory she saw the smile on her mother's gentle face, she heard Jack's pleased voice say, "Now I come in," and Teddy's clear, high little "An' now the fairies dance-an'-sing." Even as she played, she smiled at the way Teddy pronounced "dance and sing" as one word.

The last note ended, and there was a hushed silence. Then a parent wiped away a furtive tear, and the principal said in a crisp, satisfied tone, "That is very sweet. Now, play one of those—"

But Jules Circeaux had walked over to Alice.

"Did you write that music?" he asked quietly.

"Why, yes," said she, startled. "But how did you—"

"Is there an accompaniment? Who wrote that?"

"My father; it is in my room."

"Will you get it and let me play it for you? I should like to hear the music again."

So the bewildered girl found herself playing the "Home Tune" again, playing as if in a dream, with the great Circeaux for an accompanist. When the music ended for the second time, the master turned his back upon the audience.

"I want to talk to you," he said. "You were right in what you said: You are not a fine violinist. Why are you teaching here?"

Quietly, she told him.

"This 'Home Tune' was for your family?"

She nodded.

"Then listen. You told me that you tried to teach true. I know that is so, for I have this afternoon heard Adele play. The fundamentals of her work are right. Your technique is not far advanced, but its principles are excellent. You are much better fitted to teach here than many with a more showy accomplishment."

At that Alice gave a little gasp of unbelief, but he paid no attention to it and hurried on: "But this music—this is different. I spend my lifetime trying to find music for the hearts of the people. I find it pretty and brilliant and sentimental, but oh, so rarely—real. You said you tried to teach true. I believe you, because your music plays true."

"Thank you—but I—" stammered Alice.

Again he hushed her. "Listen only a minute," he said. "I want this music. I want to play it to my audiences, to make them see the firelight and hear the little boy's fire fairies. I will give you $1,000 for the privilege of playing it, and a royalty on every copy that is sold with my accompaniment. Is it enough?"

For an instant, Alice felt the quiver of her lips getting beyond her control. Then, under that kindly, eager smile of Jules Circeaux, she pulled herself together.

"It would be too much if it were not for them," she said. "Do you really want it? And do you mean that you really want me to stay here—and teach Adele?"

The master smiled again. "Dear child," he said, "when Adele is grown, she will count herself blessed to have worked with a little lady who has a three-fold care: to teach true, to play true, and to live true."

Home for Thanksgiving

L. D. Stearns

Spending Thanksgiving at home once meant everything to Rosalie Coleman. But that was before Aunt Dele with her millions came into her life, the millions that would be Rosie's when the adoption papers were signed—after one last Thanksgiving at home.

Rosalie Coleman stood in the center of the big, somewhat shabby living room and glanced confusedly about. The greetings were over—the hugs, the kisses, the happy cries. She turned shining eyes from her mother to her father, then to the group of younger Colemans. Ted and Terry, the 15-year-old twins; Netty, aged eight, and Faith, just turned five. Her coat, a beautiful fur, lay on the floor, where she had flung it upon rushing in, a full hour earlier than expected. Her small, fashionable hat was tilted rakishly over one ear. With a tremulous laugh, she tossed it on top of the coat. She had traveled 1,000 miles to eat Thanksgiving dinner at home.

That, she told herself in swift thought, *was what money could do.*

"I don't know whether I'm really here or still thundering along the road," she said a bit shakily.

"We know, eh, Mother?" Mr. Coleman chuckled.

"You've grown to be a real picture, Rosie, the prettiest thing I have ever seen." Pride thrilled her mother's voice. She picked up the hat, touching it almost reverently, and put it on the table. "You shouldn't be careless with such lovely things, daughter, and I never saw such fur shine the way it does in this coat. Do you see, Father?"

"That coat cost a pile of money," declared Mr. Coleman.

"I suppose it did. I don't know how much. I admired it one day when Aunt Dele and I were looking for a neck piece. The next day I found it in my room." She wrinkled her brow into faint lines. "I feel like Rip Van Winkle," she asserted. "I can't make these youngsters look real."

"I'll go fix a lunch," Mrs. Coleman announced. "I don't suppose you've had a thing to eat since you started."

"Indeed, I have. I don't want a thing until mealtime. But I do want to clean up. My trunk's on the way. If it comes before I'm down again, make them carry it upstairs, Dad." She opened an unbelievably beautiful bag and extracted a plump purse. "I guess there's money enough in that to pay the bill." She tossed it on the table, and the next moment, with a burst of song, she was running upstairs and into her own room.

It was faintly chilly. She looked at the thermometer. "Seventy ought to be warm enough. I used to get along on 65 and think I was lucky to have the chill taken off. I guess I've been getting soft."

She slipped off her dress, went into the bathroom, and turned on the water. She heard the outer door open and shut, a heavy tread up the stairs, a thump.

"That trunk's heavy," a gruff voice complained.

I guess it is, thought Rosalie. Next moment she sobered. Was it possible it was three years since she had been in that room? She recalled, as vividly as if it were but yesterday, how she had shivered the last morning, how she had descended, still shivering, to breakfast.

"There's no justice," she had stormed with the sharp certainty of youth, "in one half of the world freezing while the other half has all the heat and the fun."

She seemed once again to see the tenderness in her mother's eyes. "Yet, after all, dear, there is always another side, a side we do not know. We, at least, know we have our home and each other."

"Oh, I know, but I'd like a little more."

Then the doorbell had rung; and when her mother opened the door, there stood Aunt Dele, whom Rosalie had never seen, but had never expected to see. When a child, she had thought of her as living in a house of gold and eating from dishes of gold. For Aunt Dele was the possessor of more millions than any of the family dared even surmise. Yet seen on that November morning, she had appeared a very ordinary person, after all.

She had slipped unceremoniously into a place at the breakfast table, eaten with relish, and explained that she had recently returned from a year in Paris; that she was now about to start on a tour of the United States; that she planned, in a year or two, to go on a trip that would encircle the world. She had suddenly remembered that Rosalie was of about the age to enjoy traveling. Also, she would enjoy Rosalie. She had no daughter. If, after finishing the tour of the United States, Rosalie and her parents agreed, she and Jim, her husband, would legally adopt the child, who would then have all that money could give.

That afternoon, on a late train, Rosalie had gone forth with Aunt Dele into a new world. This was her first visit home. In the intervening years, every state in the Union had opened its treasure-houses for her inspection. She had forgotten, almost, how it felt to shiver after a bath in a none-too-warm room.

She had at first sent home a large share of her allowance, but it had been returned with a letter from her father in which tender appreciation stood hand-in-hand with firm determination. They were happy and comfortable, he had written, needing only what his own efforts could provide. So she had restricted herself, thereafter, to simple gifts. Now, as soon as the adoption papers were completed, she would start on that trip around the world. No girl in her right senses, she had decided, would throw away such a chance.

Opening her trunk, she took out a brown velvet frock. There would be company, and she might as well be ready. Dan, at least, would be sure to come. But when she looked at herself in the glass [mirror], she frowned. It did not seem quite the thing. It set her off too definitely from the others. She took it off and shook out the other dresses she had brought. None appeared suitable. They had seemed all right when she had packed. In fact, she had thought little about it—just brought ones she liked. She had forgotten she was turning the knob of a door opening upon a different kind of life. There was not a thing her mother would let her wipe dishes in.

She ended her inspection by putting on the simplest. She fluffed her hair into place, started to leave the room, stopped, and glanced thoughtfully about. What good times she had had in this room! Returning to her trunk, she took out various parcels. Gathering them into her arms, she ran downstairs.

Throwing back the living-room door, she poised lightly in the opening. "Catch!" she cried, aiming one of the parcels at her father and another one at her mother. She dropped a glorious doll into Faith's arms and a second one into Netty's, tossed a fur cap and gloves to Ted, and a neck piece to Terry. Her eyes sparkled as her father exclaimed over an assortment of hose, handkerchiefs, and ties, and her mother over shimmering silk for a gown. Then she curled into the great chair before the blazing fire.

"Gas logs can't compete with honest-to-goodness wood and flame."

"But you wouldn't want to change just the same." Terry stopped caressing her neck piece, her eyes suddenly blazing. A tense silence, like some alien spirit, wove a cool, dim cloud of unease among them.

"When one walks through a garden of loveliness," said Mrs. Coleman, "with power to choose the best bloom among them all, one does not select merely the largest, or the sweetest, or the brightest, but the all-around best."

"Aunt Dele," responded Rosalie a little nervously, "thought that if I started back directly after Thanksgiving, we could go on to Florida at once; and then about the first of April we'll sail on our world trip, if you folks say so."

Something caught in her throat. She had not quite realized before what it really meant to exchange homes—parents; that after the final papers were passed, it would not be "Aunt Dele" and "Uncle Jim" but "Father" and "Mother." For a second her sight dimmed. The glow of her cheeks turned to white.

Again Terry bridged the silence. "I knew you meant to do it. I told Mums dear yesterday that home was home, all right, but millions were millions. But after all, you know, all the adoption papers in the world aren't going to change anything real. Mums dear and Dad aren't going to stop being the father and mother God gave you to, just because you choose to play you have changed 'em for others."

"That's enough, honey." Mrs. Coleman shook her head at the culprit.

"She's right, of course," said Rosalie. "It doesn't really change things, except to sort of give me an extra father and mother. You'll always be Mums and Dad. And I'll gain all the education of travel and all the delights of it as well."

"You won't have to work, either, no dishes to wash. Just sort of grow, like flowers," Ted championed his twin.

"Suppose we plan our Thanksgiving feast," proposed Mr. Coleman.

"We thought that we would have a real banquet. With all the leaves in, the table will seat 20. You make up a list, Rosie, and I'll do the rest. Ask whomever you like," announced Mrs. Coleman.

Rosalie's face sparkled. "How jolly! Aunt Dele told me I could spend—"

"You'll be my girl, unshared, until the day after Thanksgiving," her father's voice crossed hers. "What I can't pay for, we'll do without."

"All right, Dad." Making her way to the telephone, she looked up a number and gave it to central. Next moment her eyes appeared to deepen a little. "Dan! It's me, myself! Rosalie! Have you forgotten how to argue? Come on over, and we'll renew our youth. And say, Danny, we're planning a jubilee for Thanksgiving because I'll be going back next day, and I don't know when I'll be here again—not for three or four years, anyhow. Aunt Dele and I are going to circle the globe, and we'll most likely take our time about it. We want you and Margery for dinner, of course. . . . What? Oh, you didn't let me finish. I was going to include your father and mother. They're a special contribution to Mums and Dad. Oh Dan, do come! Go on, now, and find out. . . . Good! I knew they would. You'll be over tonight, Danny? Fine!" She hung up. "Dan thought his mother wouldn't give up the home dinner. I knew he and Margery wouldn't come unless I asked them all. He said, under the circumstances, they'd come." She wrinkled her white brow and returned to the telephone.

Mrs. Coleman and the twins went to the kitchen. The smaller children went with Mr. Coleman on a trip to the store. After a few moments, Rosalie left the phone and followed her mother and the twins to the kitchen.

"Whatever do you think? Nobody I want will come. They won't leave their own homes. They all say they are sorry, and all that, and will be around to see me, of course, but want to be home for Thanksgiving."

"Good for them!" exclaimed Terry. "That's what I thought they'd say. Even Dan wouldn't have come if you hadn't baited your hook with the rest of his family."

"Terry!"

"Thanksgiving is a home day, dear." Her mother's voice was conciliatory. "Never mind, we'll have a gala day, anyhow."

When Dan and Margery Ellis burst in a few minutes later, declaring they had smelled johnnycake and run over for a share, Rosalie's eyes flamed into quick delight, then were dimmed almost directly by a faint shadow. Soon she and Dan were arguing as heatedly as in the old days.

"Four years at college and starting here at the very foot, Dan, when you might start almost, if not quite, at the top with your uncle Ben! Why, it's absurd."

"There you are, all off ballast, as usual." Dan's tone was impatient. Something a little hurt, or disappointed, perhaps lurked in his fine eyes, which could not seem to leave Rosalie's face. "One can't start at the top, Rosie. How in the world is one to get to the top unless he climbs there?"

"Do you mean to say your uncle Ben—"

"Oh, of course, if one wants merely to be carried to the top and dumped there, to be left until he falls down because he hasn't learned to stand on that sort of footing, that's another matter. I don't happen to want that kind of thing." He laughed. "I've a notion it's going to be fun to hew my own path and write my own name on a peak of my own choosing. I want to experience in some small degree the kind of thrill even God must have felt when He said, 'Let there be light,' and light appeared."

Almost before supper was over, the doorbell began to ring as one after another of neighbors and friends came in. Every instant of the evening was packed with greetings, jollity, and friendliness.

The days flew by as if on wings. What a dear Faith was! Rosalie found herself wondering more than once whether there was ever another one so sweet. Netty followed her about like a small shadow. Ted and Terry, a little aloof, watched her with clear, thoughtful eyes. Dan usually dropped in late in the afternoon and remained for supper. Then, tucked about with fur robes, they would go flying merrily over the hills or along ghostly country roads.

"If you're going into another part of the world, young woman, you ought to carry a clear picture of this one along, too. Look at those stars now. You want to remember when you're on the other side of the world, Rosie, that the same stars watch over us all. If things ever happen to go wrong, don't forget that God gave you two feet to stand on and two hands to work with.

I don't suppose anything will go wrong; but just in case things seem to, remember that a certain keynote will always bring them out right."

It was the night before Thanksgiving, and there was a dreary little feeling in Rosalie's heart. "Do you know, " she said, looking thoughtfully about, "it seems as if everything—the trees, the bare bushes, even the rocks—are all whispering, 'Good-bye, good-bye.' "

"I used to think," Dan responded slowly, "that someday you and I together would build the most beautiful home in all the world."

Rosalie moved restlessly. A little of her bright color faded. "You don't know, Dan, how wonderful it is to have money, all you want of it," she said. "I wish Dad would let me do more for the family. I could send home so much, and no one would ever miss it. All I have to do, absolutely, is to ask, and all I want is mine."

Dan's eyes held hers. "They don't need it, Rosalie. Your dad provides all they need. He couldn't take your aunt's money. He prefers to make his own. I don't blame him."

Rosalie woke the next morning with the odor of pumpkin pies in her nostrils. It was a gorgeous day. As she stood by her window, it seemed to her that an almost perfect peace rested over the vast countryside. But strangely it had no place in her heart. Blankly, her gaze traveled about the familiar yard; her mouth changed from a rosy curve to a straight, hard line. Turning, she went slowly from the room.

The morning passed swiftly. When the table was all set, the last touches given, she returned to her room and slipped into the brown velvet dress she had discarded on the evening of her arrival. Absently, she smoothed her hair into place, her gaze on the far line of the horizon. When would she stand here again like this, dressing for Thanksgiving? Her mouth, in spite of her efforts, drooped a little. Her eyes were shadowed. Her hands were cold.

From the hall, Terry's cool young voice drifted in almost insolently. "Millions! What are millions, Ted? I'm sure that Governor Bradford got

more honest-to-goodness fun and thrill out of watching corn and wheat grow than Rosie'll ever get out of all Aunt Dele's servants and money."

By the soft rustling sound that followed, Rosalie knew the twins were sliding down the banister.

She gave a last critical look into the glass, went slowly from the room, and started down the stairs. Halfway down, she paused and returned to her room. Crossing to her bed, she dropped swiftly to her knees. Prayer somehow had not seemed to have a place at Aunt Dele's. She had not taken it up since returning home. But she had often knelt by this bedside in former days.

Suddenly, it had seemed to her that she should like the memory of prayer just in that one spot, to accompany her about the world. When she entered the dining room, they were all seated at the table, waiting.

Rosalie glanced about the table and met Dan's eyes with a crooked little smile. Next moment her eyes widened; a sort of quick, bright knowledge seemed suddenly to add new depth, new beauty, to them. A deeper color crept into her cheeks.

"I forgot something. I went back for it, and while I was getting it, I laid the first little foundation stone of the—most beautiful house in the world. You won't need to bother with those papers tomorrow, Dad." Her voice sang. She was not conscious of the joy in it. Her face was transfigured by a glow that all Aunt Dele's millions had been unable to bring into it. "I'm going to stay home until—maybe—Dan and I'll make the trip together. I'm going to learn to stand on my own feet."

For a moment there was not the slightest sound. Into Mrs. Coleman's eyes there flashed a dazzling light. Dan pushed back his chair and crossed to the window. He could not face anyone just then. Reaching out, her father's hand met Rosalie's. Next moment his head was bowed.

"I knew," came Terry's triumphant whisper, "that Rosie was real gold inside."

Then the words she had missed for three years fell like a bit of music on Rosalie's soul: "For all Thy mercies, Lord, we give Thee praise."

The Littlest Orphan and the Christ Baby

Margaret E. Sangster, Jr.

My mother loved this story and read it to me countless times while I was growing up. When she heard I was preparing this second story collection, she had one request: "Please include 'The Littlest Orphan.' "

The Littlest Orphan gazed up into the face of the Christ Baby, who hung, gilt-framed and smiling, above the mantel shelf. The mantel was dark, made of a black, mottled marble that suggested tombstones; and the long room—despite its rows of neat, white beds—gave an impression of darkness, too. But the picture above the mantel sparkled and scintillated and threw off an aura of sheer happiness. Even the neat "In Memoriam" card tacked to the wall directly under it could not detract from its joy. All of rosy babyhood, all of unspoiled laughter, all of the beginnings of life, were in that picture! And the Littlest Orphan sensed it, even though he did not quite understand.

The Matron was coming down the room, with many wreaths, perhaps a dozen of them, braceleting her thin arm. The wreaths were just a trifle dusty; their imitation holly leaves spoke plaintively of successive years of hard usage. But it was only two days before Christmas, and the wreaths would not show up so badly under artificial light. The board of trustees, coming for the entertainment on Christmas Eve, never arrived until the early winter dusk had settled down. And the wreaths could be laid away, as soon as the holiday was past, for another 12 months.

The Littlest Orphan, staring up at the picture, did not hear the Matron's approaching footsteps. True, the Matron wore rubber heels—but any other orphan in the whole asylum would have heard her. Only the Littlest Orphan, with his thin, sensitive face and his curious fits of absorption, could have ignored her coming. He started painfully as her sharp voice cut into the silence.

"John," she said, and the frost that made such pretty lacework upon the windowpane wrought havoc with her voice. *"John, what are you doing here?"*

The Littlest Orphan answered after the manner of all small boys. "Nothin'!" he said.

Standing before him, the Matron—who was a large woman—seemed to tower. "You are not telling the truth, John," she said. "You have no right to be in the dormitory at this hour. Report to Miss Mace at once"—Miss Mace was the primary teacher—"and tell her that I said you were to write five extra pages in your copybook. *At once!*"

With hanging head, the Littlest Orphan turned away. It seemed terribly unfair, although it was against the rules to spend any but sleeping hours in the dormitory. He was just learning to write, and five pages meant a whole afternoon of cramped fingers and tired eyes. But how could he explain to this grim woman that the Christ Baby fascinated him, charmed him, and comforted him? How could he explain that the Christ Baby's wide eyes had a way of glancing down, almost with understanding, into his own? How could he tell, with the few weak words of his vocabulary, that he loved the Christ Baby whose smile was so tenderly sweet, and that he spent much of his time standing, as he stood now, in the shadow of that smile? He trudged away with never a word, down the length of the room, his clumsy shoes making a feeble clatter on the bare boards of the floor. When he was almost at the door, the Matron called after him.

"Don't drag your feet, John!" she commanded.

And so he walked the rest of the way on tiptoe. And closed the door very softly after him.

The halls had already been decorated with long streamers of red and green crepe paper that looped along, in a halfhearted fashion, from picture to picture. The stair railing was wound with more of the paper, and the school-room—where Miss Mace sat stiffly behind a broad desk—was vaguely brightened by red cloth poinsettias set here and there at random. But the color of them was not reflected in the Littlest Orphan's heart as he delivered his message and received in return a battered copybook.

As he sat at his desk, writing laboriously about the cat who ate the rat and the dog who ran after the cat, he could hear the other orphans playing outside in the courtyard. Always they played from four o'clock—when school was over—until five-thirty, which was suppertime. It was a rule to play from four until five-thirty. They were running and shouting together, but in a stilted way. The Littlest Orphan did not envy them much. They were all older and stronger than he, and their games were sometimes hard to enjoy. He had been the last baby taken before a new ruling, making six years the minimum entrance age, had gone through. And he was only five years old now. Perhaps it was his very littleness that made the Matron more intolerant of him—he presented to her a problem that could not be met in a mass way. His clothing had to be several sizes smaller than the other cloth-ing; his lessons less advanced. And so on.

Drearily he wrote—and listened, between sentences, to the scratching pen of Miss Mace. . . . The dog had caught the cat. And now the man beat the dog. And then it was time to start all over again, back at the place where the cat ate the rat. Two pages, three pages, four pages . . . Surreptitiously, the Littlest Orphan moved his fingers, one by one, and wondered that he was still able to move them. Then, working slowly, he finished the last page and handed the copybook back to the teacher. As she studied it, her face softened slightly.

"Why did the Matron punish you, John?" she asked, as if on impulse, as she made a correction in a sentence.

The Littlest Orphan hesitated for a second. And then: "I shouldn't have been in th' dormitory," he said slowly. "An' I was!"

Again Miss Mace asked a question. "But what," she queried, "were you doing there? Why weren't you out playing with the other children?"

She didn't comment upon the fault, but the Littlest Orphan knew that she also thought the punishment rather severe. Only it isn't policy to criticize a superior's method of discipline. He answered her second question gravely.

"I was lookin' at th' Christ Baby over the mantel," he said.

As if to herself, Miss Mace spoke. "You mean the picture Mrs. Benchly gave in memory of her son," she murmured. "The pastel." And then, "Why were you looking at it—" She hesitated, and the Littlest Orphan didn't know that she had almost said "dear."

Shyly the child spoke, and wistfulness lay across his thin, small face—an unrealized wistfulness. "He looks so—nice," said the Littlest Orphan gently, "like he had a mother, maybe."

Supper that night was brief, and after supper there were carols to practice in the assembly room. The Littlest Orphan, seated at the extreme end of the line, enjoyed the singing. The redheaded boy, who fought so often in the courtyard, had a high, thrilling soprano. Listening to him as he sang the solo parts made the Littlest Orphan forget a certain black eye—and a nose that had once been swollen and bleeding. Made him forget lonely hours when he had lain uncomforted in his bed—as a punishment for quarreling.

The redheaded boy was singing something about "gold and frank-kin-sense and myrrh." The Littlest Orphan told himself that they must be very beautiful things. Gold—the Christ Baby's frame was of gold—but frank-kin-sense and myrrh were unguessed names. Maybe they were flowers—real flowers that smelled pretty, not red cloth ones. He shut his eyes, singing automatically, and imagined what these flowers looked like—the color and shape of their petals, and whether they grew on tall lily stalks or on short pansy stems. And then the singing was over, and he opened his eyes with a start and realized that the Matron was speaking.

"Before you go to bed," she was saying, "I want you to understand that you must be on your good behavior until after the trustees leave tomorrow evening. You must not make any disorder in the corridors or in the dormitories—they have been especially cleaned and dusted. You must pay strict attention to the singing; the trustees like to hear you sing! They will all be here—even Mrs. Benchly, who has not visited us since her son died. And if one of you misbehaves—"

She stopped abruptly, but her silence was crowded with meaning, and many a child squirmed uncomfortably in his place. It was only after a moment that she spoke again.

"Good night!" she said abruptly.

And the orphans chorused back, "Good night."

Undressing carefully and swiftly, for the dormitory was cold and the lights were dim, the Littlest Orphan wondered about the trustees—and in particular about the Mrs. Benchly who had lost her son. All trustees were ogres to asylum children, but the Littlest Orphan couldn't help feeling that Mrs. Benchly was the least ogrelike of them all. Somehow she was a part of the Christ Baby's picture, and it was a part of her. If she were responsible for it, she could not be all bad! So ruminating,

the Littlest Orphan said his brief prayers—any child who forgot his prayers was punished severely—and slid between the sheets into his bed.

Some of the orphans made a big lump under their bedcovers. The redheaded boy was stocky, and so were others. Some of them were almost fat. But the Littlest Orphan made hardly any lump at all. The sheet, the cotton blanket, and the spread went over him with scarcely a ripple. Often the Littlest Orphan had wished that there might be another small boy who could share his bed—he took up such a tiny section of it. Another small boy would have made the bed seem warmer somehow, and less lonely. Once two orphans had come to the asylum, and they were brothers. They had shared things—beds and desks and books. Maybe brothers were unusual gifts from a surprisingly blind providence, gifts that were granted only once in 100 years. More rare, even, than mothers!

Mothers—the sound of the word had a strange effect upon the Littlest Orphan, even when he said it silently in his soul. It meant so much that he did not comprehend—so much for which he vaguely hungered. Mothers stood for warm arms, and kisses, and soft words. Mothers meant punishments, too, but gentle punishment that did not really come from deep inside.

Often the Littlest Orphan had heard the rest talking stealthily about mothers. Some of them could actually remember having owned one! But the Littlest Orphan could not remember. He had arrived at the asylum as a baby—delicate and frail and too young for memories that would later come to bless him and to cause a strange, sharp sort of hurt. When the rest spoke of bedtime stories, and lullabies, and sugar cookies, he listened—wide-eyed and half-incredulous—to their halting sentences.

It was growing very cold in the dormitory, and it was dark. Even the faint flicker of light had been taken away. The Littlest Orphan wiggled his toes under the cotton blanket and wished that sleep would come. Some nights it came quickly, but this night . . . Perhaps he was overtired, and it was so cold!

As a matter of habit, his eyes searched through the dark for the place where the Christ Baby hung. He could not distinguish even the dim outlines of the gilt frame, but he knew that the Christ Baby was rosy and chubby and smiling—that his eyes were deeply blue and filled with cheer. Involuntarily, the Littlest Orphan stretched out his thin hands and dropped them back again against the spread. All about him the darkness lay like a smothering coat, and the Christ Baby, even though he smiled, was invisible. The other children were sleeping. All up and down the long room sounded their regular breathing, but the Littlest Orphan could not sleep. He wanted something that he was unable to define—wanted it with such a burning intensity that the tears crowded into his eyes. He sat up abruptly in his bed—a small, shivering figure with quivering lips and a baby ache in his soul that had never really known babyhood.

Loneliness. It swept about him—more disheartening than the cold, more enveloping than the darkness. There was no fear in him of the shadows in the corner, of the creaking shutters and the narrow stairs. Such fears are discouraged early in children who live by rule and routine. No—it was a feeling more poignant than fear, a feeling that clutched at him and squeezed his small body until it was dry and shaking and void of expression.

Of all the sleeping dormitory, the Littlest Orphan was the only child who knew the ache of such loneliness. Even the ones who had been torn away from family ties had, each one of them, something beautiful to keep preciously close. But the Littlest Orphan had nothing—nothing. . . . The loneliness filled him with a strange impulse, an impulse that sent him sliding over the edge of his bed with small arms outflung.

All at once he was crossing the floor on bare, mouse-quiet feet. Past the placidly sleeping children, past the row of lockers, past the table with its neat cloth and black-bound, impressive guest book. Past everything until he stood, a white spot in the blackness, directly under the mantel. The Christ Baby hung above him. And though the Littlest Orphan could not see, he felt that the blue eyes were looking down tenderly. All at once he wanted to touch the Christ Baby, to hold him tight, to feel the sweetness and warmth of him. Tensely, still moved by the curious impulse, he tiptoed back to where the table stood. Carefully, he laid the guest book on the floor; carefully, he removed the white cloth. And then staggering under the—to him—great weight, he carried the table noiselessly back with him. Though it was really a small, light table, the Littlest Orphan breathed hard as he set it down. He had to rest, panting, for a moment, before he could climb up on it.

All over the room lay silence, broken only by the sleepy sounds of the children. The Littlest Orphan listened almost prayerfully as he clambered upon the table top and drew himself to an erect position. His small hands groped along the mantel shelf and touched the lower edge of the gilt frame. But the Christ Baby was still out of reach.

Feverishly, obsessed with one idea, the Littlest Orphan raised himself on tiptoe. His hands gripped the chill marble of the mantel. Tugging, twisting—all with the utmost quiet—he pulled himself up until he was kneeling upon the mantel shelf. Quivering with nervousness as well as the now-intense cold, he finally stood erect. And then—only then—he was able to feel the wire and nail that held the Christ Baby's frame against the wall. His numb fingers loosened the wire carefully. And then at last the picture was in his arms.

It was heavy, the picture, and hard—not soft and warm as he had somehow expected it to be. But it was the Christ Baby nevertheless. Holding it close, the Littlest Orphan fell to speculating upon the ways of getting down, now that both of his hands were occupied. It would be hard to slide from the mantel to the table, and from the table to the floor, with neither sound nor mishap.

His eyes troubled, his mouth a wavering line in his pinched face, the Littlest Orphan crowded back against the wall. The darkness held now the vague menace of depth. Destruction lurked in a single misstep. It had been a long way up. It would be even longer going down. And he now had the Christ Baby, as well as himself, to care for.

Gingerly, he advanced one foot over the edge of the mantel and drew it back—sharply. He almost screamed in sudden terror. It was as if the dark had reached out long, bony fingers to pull him from his place of safety. He wanted to raise his hands to his face, but he could not release his hold upon the gilt frame. All at once he realized that his hands were growing numb with the cold and that his feet were numb, too.

The minutes dragged by. Somewhere a clock struck—many times. The Littlest Orphan had never heard the clock strike so many times, at night, before. He cowered back until it seemed to his scared, small mind that he would sink into the wall. And then, as the clock ceased striking, he heard another sound—a sound that brought dread to his heart. It was a step in the hall, a heavy, firm step that, despite rubber heels, was now clearly recognizable.

It would be the Matron, making her rounds of the building before she went to bed. As the steps came nearer along the hall, a light, soft and yellow, seemed to grow in the place. It would be the lamp that she carried in her hand.

The Matron reached the door and peered in. And then, with lamp held high, she entered the room. And her swift glance swept the row of white beds—each, but one, with its sleeping occupant.

The Littlest Orphan, on the mantel, clutched the Christ Baby closer in his arms—and waited. It seemed to him that his shivering must shake the room. He gritted his teeth convulsively as the Matron's eyes found his tumbled, empty bed.

Hastily, forgetting to be quiet, the woman crossed the room. She pulled back the spread, the blanket. And then, as if drawn by a magnet, her eyes lifted, traveled across the room—and found the small white figure that pressed back into the narrow space. Her voice was sharper even than her eyes when she spoke.

"John," she called abruptly, and her anger made her forget to be quiet, *"what are you doing up there?"*

Across the top of the Christ Baby's gilt frame, the eyes of the Littlest Orphan stared into the eyes of the Matron with something of the fascination that one sees in the eyes of a bird charmed by a cat or a snake. In narrow white beds all over the room, children were stirring, pulling themselves erect, staring. One child snickered behind a sheltering hand. But the Littlest Orphan was conscious only of the Matron. He waited for her to speak again. In a moment she did.

"John," she said, and her voice was burning, yet chill, with rage, "you are a bad boy. *Come down at once!*"

His eyes blank with sheer fright, his arms clasping the picture close, the Littlest Orphan answered the tone of that voice. With quivering lips, he advanced one foot, then the other. And stepped into the space that was the room below. He was conscious that some child screamed—he himself did not utter a sound—and that the Matron started forward. And then he struck the table and rolled with it and the Christ Baby's splintering picture into the darkness.

The Littlest Orphan spent the next day in bed, with an aching head and a wounded heart. The pain of his bruises did not make a great difference; neither did the threats of the Matron penetrate his consciousness. Only the bare space over the mantel mattered—only the blur of blue and yellow and red upon the hearth, where the pastel had struck; only the knowledge that the Christ Baby—the meaning of all light and happiness—was no more, troubled him.

There was a pleasant stir about the asylum. An excited child, creeping into the dormitory, told the Littlest Orphan that one of the trustees had sent a tree. And that another was donating ice cream. And that there were going to be presents. But the Littlest Orphan did not even smile. His wan face was set and drawn. Dire punishment awaited him after his hurts were healed. And there would be no Christ Baby to go to for comfort and cheer when the punishment was over.

The morning dragged on. Miss Mace brought his luncheon of bread and milk and was as kind to him as she dared to be—your Miss Maces have been made timorous by a too-forceful world. Once, during the early afternoon, the Matron came in to examine his bruised head, and once a maid came to rub the colored stains from the hearth. The Littlest Orphan caught his breath as he watched her. And then it began to grow dark, and the children were brought upstairs to be washed and dressed in clean blouses for the entertainment. They had been warned not to talk with him, and they obeyed—for there were folk watching and listening. But even so, flickers of conversation—excited, small-boy conversation—drifted to the Littlest Orphan's waiting ears. Someone had said there was to be a Santa Claus in a red suit and a white beard. Perhaps it was true. The Littlest Orphan slid down under the covers and pulled the sheet high over his aching head. He didn't want the rest to know that he was crying.

The face-washing was accomplished swiftly. Just as swiftly were the blouses adjusted to the last tie, string, and button. And then the children filed downstairs, and the Littlest Orphan was left alone again. He pulled himself up gingerly until he sat erect, and he buried his face in his hands.

Suddenly, from downstairs, came the sound of music. First, the tiny piano, and then the voices of the children as they sang. Automatically, the Littlest Orphan joined in, his voice quavering weakly through the empty place. He didn't want to sing—there was neither rhythm nor melody in his heart. But he had been taught to sing those songs and sing them he must.

First there was "O Little Town of Bethlehem." And then a carol. And then the one about "gold and frank-kin-sense and myrrh." Strange that the words did not mean flowers tonight! And then there was a hush—perhaps it was a prayer. And then a burst of clapping and a jumble of glad cries. Perhaps that was the Santa Claus in his trappings of white and scarlet. The Littlest Orphan's tears came like hot rain to his tired eyes.

There was a sound in the hall. A rubber-heeled step upon the bare floor. The Littlest Orphan slid down again under the covers, until only the bandage on the brow was at all visible. When the Matron stooped over him, she could not even glimpse his eyes. With a vigorous hand, she jerked aside the covers.

"Sick or not," she told him, "you've got to come downstairs. Mrs. Benchly wants to see the boy who broke her son's memorial picture. I'll help you with your clothes."

Trembling violently, the Littlest Orphan allowed himself to be wedged into undies and a blouse and a pair of coarse, dark trousers. He laced his shoes with fingers that shook with mingled fear and weakness. And then he followed the Matron out of the dormitory and through the long halls, with their mocking festoons of red and green crepe paper, and into the assembly room, where the lights were blinding and the Christmas tree was a blaze of glory.

The trustees sat at one end of the room, the far end. They were a mass of dark colors, blacks and browns and somber grays. Following in the wake of the Matron, the Littlest Orphan stumbled toward them. Mrs. Benchly— would she beat him in front of all the rest? Would she leap at him accusingly from that dark mass? He felt smaller than he had ever felt before, and more inadequate.

The children were beginning to sing again. But despite their singing, the Matron spoke. Not loudly, as she did to the children, but with a curious deference.

"This is John, Mrs. Benchly," she said, "the child who broke the picture."

Biting his lips so that he would not cry out, the Littlest Orphan stood in the vast shadow of the Matron. He shut his eyes. Perhaps if this Mrs. Benchly meant to strike him, it would be best to have his eyes shut. And then suddenly a voice came, a voice so soft that somehow he could almost feel the velvet texture of it.

"Poor child," said the voice, "he's frightened. And ill, too. Come here, John. I won't hurt you, dear."

Opening his eyes incredulously, the Littlest Orphan stared past the Matron into the sort of face small children dream about. Violet-eyed and tender. Lined, perhaps, and sad about the mouth, and wistful. But so sweet! Graying hair, with a bit of a wave in it, brushed back from a broad, white brow. And slim, white, reaching hands. The Littlest Orphan went forward without hesitation. Something about this lady was reminiscent of the Christ Baby. As her white hand touched his and tightened on it, he looked up into her face with the ghost of a smile.

The children had crowded almost informally to the other end of the room, toward the tree. The dark mass of the trustees was dissolving, break- ing up into fragments, that followed the children. One of the trustees laughed aloud. Not at all like an ogre. A sudden sense of gladness began—for no understandable reason—to steal across the Littlest Orphan's consciousness. Rudely, the voice of the Matron broke in upon it.

"I had warned the children," she said, "not to disturb anything. Last evening, before they retired, John deliberately disobeyed. And the picture is ruined in consequence. What do you think we had better do about it, Mrs. Benchly?"

For a moment, the lady with the dream face did not speak. She was drawing the Littlest Orphan nearer, until he touched the satin folds of her black gown. And despite the Matron's voice, he was not afraid. When at last she answered the Matron, he did not flinch.

"I think," she said gently, "that I'll ask you to leave us. I would like to talk with John—alone."

And as the Matron walked stiffly away, down the length of the room, she lifted the Littlest Orphan into her lap.

"I know," she said, and her voice was even gentler than it had been, "that you didn't mean to break the picture. Did you, dear?"

Eagerly, the Littlest Orphan answered, "Oh, no—ma'am!" he told her. "I didn't mean t' break th' Christ Baby."

The woman's arms were about him. They tightened suddenly. "You're so young," she said. "You're such a mite of a thing. I doubt if you could understand why I had the picture made. Why I gave it to the home here, to be hung in the dormitory. . . . My little son was all I had after my husband died. And his nursery—it was such a pretty room—had a Christ Child picture on the wall. And my boy always loved the picture. . . . And so when he—left . . . " Her voice faltered. " . . . I had an artist copy it. I—I couldn't part with the original. And I sent it to a place where there would be many small boys who could enjoy it as my son had always—" Her voice broke.

The Littlest Orphan stared in surprise at the lady's face. Her violet eyes were misted like April blossoms with the dew upon them. Her lips quivered.

Could it be that she, too, was lonesome and afraid? His hand crept up until it touched her soft cheek.

"I *loved* th' Christ Baby," he said simply.

The lady looked at him. With an effort, she downed the quaver in her voice. "I can't believe," she said at last, "that you destroyed the picture purposely. No matter what she"—her glance rested upon the Matron's stiff figure, half a room away—"may think! John dear, did you mean to spoil the gift I gave—in my small boy's name? Oh—I'm sure you didn't."

All day long the Littlest Orphan had lived in fear and agony of soul. All day long he had known pain—physical pain and the pain of suspense. Suddenly, he buried his face in the lady's neck—he had never known before that there was a place in ladies' necks just made for tiny heads—and the tears came. Choked by sobs, he spoke.

"No'm," he sobbed, "I didn't mean to. . . . It was only because I was cold. And lonesome. An' th' bed was—big. An' all th' rest was asleep. An' the Christ Baby always looked so pink . . . an' glad . . . an' warm. An' I wanted t' take him inter my bed. An' cuddle close!" He burrowed his head deeper into the neck. "So that I wouldn't be cold anymore. Or lonesome—anymore."

The lady's arms tightened about the Littlest Orphan's body until the pressure almost hurt—but it was a nice sort of hurt. It shocked her, somehow, to feel the thinness of that body. And her tears fell quite unrestrained upon the Littlest Orphan's bandaged head. And then all at once she bent over, and her lips pressed ever so tenderly upon his cheek.

"Not to be cold," she whispered, more to herself than to the Littlest Orphan, "or lonesome anymore! To have the nursery opened again—and the sound of tiny feet in the empty rooms. To have the Christ Child smiling down upon a sleeping little boy. To kiss bruises away again. Not to be lonesome anymore, or cold—"

Suddenly, she tilted back the Littlest Orphan's head and looked deep, deep into his bewildered eyes.

"John," she said, and his name sounded so different when she said it, "how would you like to come away from here and live in my house with me? How would you like to be my boy?"

A silence had crept over the other end of the room. One of the trustees, who wore a clerical collar, had mounted the platform. He was reading from the Bible that visiting ministers read from on Sundays. His voice rang—resonant and rich as an organ tone—through the room.

" 'For unto us a child is born,' " he read, " 'unto us a son is given.' "

The Littlest Orphan, with a sigh of utter happiness, crowded closer into the arms that held him.

And it was Christmas Eve!

The Third Rose

Joseph Leininger Wheeler

This is the story of two men and the woman they loved—many years ago . . . once upon a wartime Christmas.

The surf was up at Point Arago on the Oregon coast. The surf was up all over the world. It was December 17, 1941. Only 10 days before, the Japanese had bombed Pearl Harbor. No American—child or adult— living then will ever forget the static-plagued radio and the breaking voice of Edward R. Murrow; the broadcast sounds of antiaircraft guns, bombs, and explosions; sirens wailing up and down the auditory register like roller coasters on an eternal circular track; the heart-stopping whine of dive bombers plummeting full-throttle at sitting-duck targets below; and the pain-wracked voice of Franklin Roosevelt announcing to millions clustered around radios that this was a date "which will live in infamy" and that the United States was now at war.

Forever after, these searing sounds, coupled with newsreel footage and newspaper and magazine illustrations depicting the carnage and sinking battleships, would separate the world that existed before from the world that came after.

It was a somber Christmas that year.

John first realized he loved Margaret one balmy November day in 1941 while they were walking barefoot on Bandon Beach in Oregon. Taking Margaret by the hand, John led her away from the sea's edge to their favorite sand dune and enthroned her there. Self-consciously, he opened a well-worn book and turned to a certain page. Then, his face aglow with more than he knew, he recited, without once looking at the page, Yeats' haunting "When You Are Old" (1893). It seemed to Margaret both bizarre and oddly touching, in the morning of her beauty, to be the recipient of such lines as these:

> When you are old and gray and full of sleep,
> And nodding by the fire, take down this book,
> And slowly read, and dream of the soft look
> Your eyes had once, and of their shadows deep;
>
> How many loved your moments of glad grace,
> And loved your beauty with love false or true,
> But one man loved the pilgrim soul in you
> And loved the sorrows of your changing face;
>
> And bending down beside the glowing bars,
> Murmur, a little sadly, how Love fled
> And paced upon the mountains overhead
> And hid his face among a crowd of stars.

As John reached the seventh and eighth lines, a wave of scarlet flooded his face. Both young people instinctively knew, in that moment, that something had come to an end and something had begun. Nothing would ever be the same. "Pilgrim" was ever after John's pet name for Margaret—and the sea-framed image of her long, dark tresses blowing westward in the wind were etched for all time on his heart.

Gazing into John's eyes, Margaret knew, without a shadow of a doubt, that sometime this Christmas he would ask that crucial question that determines earthly destiny more than any other—and her love-lit sea-blue eyes telegraphed what her answer would be.

But how could she have known the waves her sister had set in motion by an old bale mill?

In September, Margaret's sister Beatrice had written to her about Walter, a young man who had just transferred to the parochial college she attended in northern California. He was a senior theology major and so irresistible that most of the girls on campus melted at the sight of him. Apparently, he had every talent and gift the good Lord could give: His wit was rapier-sharp, his mind was second to none, and his smile would cause a nun to repent her vows; he could also sing like Sankey and preach like Moody—when he finished a sermon, dry eyes were a vanished species. For good measure, Walter had a wickedly irresistible sense of humor and the kind of looks and physique Michelangelo would have traveled far to capture in marble.

But so far, rhapsodized Beatrice in her letter to Margaret, *this paragon has not succumbed to the open invitations in the admiring eyes of so many campus beauties. The question everyone is asking is, "Who in the world is he* waiting *for?"*

Then, in October, while on a picnic at the Old Mill in Napa Valley, Walter made the mistake of wandering over to where Beatrice sat enshrined in a stone cleft by the towering water wheel. To the music of the water cascading listlessly into the amber pond, they got to know each other better. Thus Beatrice—already signed, sealed, and delivered to Anthony, Walter's best friend—became personally acquainted with the "Campus Dreamboat" (so designated by no less than the campus newspaper). An incurable match-maker, she couldn't pass up an opportunity like this. So on the spur of the moment, she entered another candidate into the lists: her sister Margaret. Why she did such a thing, she was never afterward able to explain, for she dearly loved John and had, for some time, accepted him as her brother-in-law-to-be.

Whatever the reason for her mischief, once started, she fired every cannon on her ship. She described her sister's beauty, vivacious personality, lovely smile, pixieish sense of humor, attractive figure, bookwormishness, poise, wanderlust, and—for good measure—her close walk with the Lord.

When she had fired her last shell, Walter laughed as he hadn't in months, causing everyone within hearing range to wonder what in the world had happened to him. "What a setup!" he finally managed to say. "No woman could be *that* perfect!" Nevertheless, the damage was done: He now *had* to find out for himself, harassing the not-overly reluctant Beatrice until she finally broke down and invited him home with Anthony and her for Christmas. He accepted, on condition that he provide the transportation.

Along the way, in his sporty new Buick, he pumped the couple for addi-tional tidbits of information. Anthony, having had second and third thoughts by this time, was beginning to regret the whole thing as he concep-tualized what effect bringing "Dreamboat" home with them was likely to have on the all-but-engaged Margaret and John. To him, bringing Walter home was tantamount to giving a lion free rein in a henhouse.

By now even Beatrice was realizing the fuller implications of what she had done, the forces she was setting in motion. If she could have recaptured her words at the Old Mill, she would have—but it was too late. This particular lion had never in his life taken no for an answer if he really wanted some-thing. Perhaps . . . oh, pray God, perhaps he wouldn't be any more impressed with Margaret than he was with the coeds back on campus.

Anthony, knowing even before he opened his mouth that his warnings would have no more effect than a garden hose against a volcano, told Walter that his sister-in-law was as good as engaged to a young man the whole family loved.

At last they crossed the state line into Oregon, chugged up and over the Siskiyou Pass, and began their long descent to the coast. Even though the nation had entered what would later be known as World War II, towns they passed through had a festive air about them. It would be, after all, a Christmas to remember when the boys were gone—many, never to return.

Reaching the coastal road at last, the three friends turned north toward Coos Bay; finally, they could see, up on the hill, the large two-story house that dominated everything between the forest and the highway: Home. Walter turned onto a long gravel road, circled up and around to the back of the house, and then cut the engine.

Anthony and Beatrice went in first and were promptly engulfed by the family. Belatedly, they remembered their driver, still waiting in the ante-room, and went after him.

Walter was escorted into the homey living room in a state of intense expectancy. Never before had his anticipations been so high. Four of Beatrice's five sisters were in the room, waiting for them. Mama, the only other person who knew what was afoot, had sent Margaret off for a walk—knowing John would follow—as soon as her eagle eye had spied Walter's car turning into the long driveway. She, too, loved John—almost as much as Papa did.

Walter, not in on Mama's diversionary tactics, kept searching for the sister who would answer to Beatrice's description. As each sister was introduced—Daphne, Christina, Melissa, and Jasmine—each attractive in her own way, his spirits rose and fell.

Thirty of the longest minutes in Walter's lifetime later, Margaret and John slipped back into the house. Beatrice, having reached the long-delayed moment of truth, stumblingly went through the introductions, hoping against hope that Walter would be a good boy and let her off the hook. Instead, there occurred what she had most feared: an explosion of awareness between the two.

All Margaret did was smile. But that five-letter word hardly did justice to a weapon that had already bewitched the entire male population of the county. Papa—who certainly ought to know, since it had been used with such unfailing success on him—had summed it up best: "That deadly smile of hers is both impish and demure. How in God's green earth can mortal man resist a combination like that?" Walter broke no records in that respect: He was poleaxed, not even having the saving grace to hide his condition. The rest of that eventful evening passed in a roseate haze for the principals. They spoke occasionally to each other in mere words, but almost continually with their eyes. John, so attuned to Margaret's every vibration and nuance, sensed the difference immediately. Already he felt a withdrawing of her inner spirit—his Pilgrim—and he was deeply troubled.

Later that night, John trudged up the creaking stairs to the attic aerie, where he always slept when visiting Margaret. As he wearily lay down on the cot by the window, he felt he had somehow been battered black and blue during the evening. He looked out the window, as he always did at night, down to the coastal highway where ghostly headlights in the fog searched for passage to somewhere. Always before, this bed had represented home, because once he had come to know Margaret more than six years before, it had been inconceivable that home could be anywhere except with her. But now he had a chilling sense that he might be evicted: that he was in danger of being thrown out onto that foggy highway himself . . . to begin another search for he knew not what. Certainly, he could not even imagine loving another woman.

As for Walter, he had gone to bed almost in a state of shock. Well he knew how unutterably dear Margaret was to John. In fact, "dear" was the ultimate understatement: She was John's whole world, and every time he looked at her, his undiluted love was unmistakable. But Walter knew that were John the dearest male friend he had ever known, he could not possibly have surrendered the field short of the altar.

Margaret, too, found sleep elusive. Her sisters had given her a hard time, for they loved John like the brother they had lost so many years before. Heretofore they had assumed the certainty of his brother-in-law-hood. Nevertheless, they knew their sister well enough to realize that this complete stranger, in one short evening, had pulverized her almost-impregnable defense system. Margaret, loving John deeply, was furious with herself for her patent inability to hold Walter at bay; she was equally angry with Walter for wrecking what should have been the happiest Christmas of her lifetime.

The standoff continued day after day, with most of the rounds seemingly won by John, for Margaret respected his right to be first in her company. But the victory was somewhat hollow, for John felt himself now only partly in possession of her love. When they were alone, he felt he had two-thirds of her; but when Walter was in the room, it was an entirely different story. He could feel the aerial shock waves as the inner spirits of Walter and Margaret challenged each other, communed with each other, longed for each other.

On the twenty-fourth of December, the denouement finally came. Long into the previous night Walter had tossed and turned, unable to find sleep. He candidly took stock of the situation and concluded that things didn't look very good for him; here he was, nearing the time when he'd have to return to college, and he was getting nowhere. Should he leave without a decision in his favor, he felt confident that the combined forces of family preference and John's residence in that part of the state would eventually break down the last of Margaret's resistance. Only with a bold stroke did he have a fighting chance. But all his life, he would be known for such risk-taking; it was his willingness to seize the moment and take control that would make him a millionaire before he was 30.

At breakfast, John, sitting next to Margaret as usual, began to feel that the tide was at last beginning to shift in his favor. Somehow, Margaret's smile promised more than it had yesterday. Perhaps all was not lost after all.

Across the table, Walter was reaching the same conclusion. There was not a moment to lose. As they got up from the table, his voice cut through the babble of voices and moving chairs: "Margaret, could I speak with you for a moment?"

All action and speech froze in midair.

Walter led Margaret into the front parlor and within two minutes pulled off what proved to be the greatest selling job of his long and illustrious career: He persuaded her that she owed him a few minutes alone with her. Since they both loved the sea, and since it was such an absolutely perfect morning, and since he was leaving soon (as he had hoped, her face blanched as he spoke these words), surely she would grant him one small favor: take a short ride to the beach with him. Smiling, she allowed that perhaps it might be arranged.

Walter went out to spruce up the car and warm the engine. Inside, he overheard loud voices: Papa was apparently most unhappy about something. More time passed. More voices. This time it was Mama, apparently trying to mediate. Almost he felt he had lost . . . then Margaret came flying out of the house, her face flushed, and signs of recent tears confirming his suspicion that her exit had not been an easy one. The car was already rolling as she lightly slipped aboard.

When Margaret had informed John that she would be gone a short while with Walter—wasn't it sweet of him to take her for a ride to the beach in his shiny new Buick?—John was under no illusions as to the mettle of his antagonist. If Walter could pull off what he had in two minutes, give him sole possession for a few hours—especially with this particular woman, and at the beach, for good measure—short of a miracle, the game was lost. And, worst of all, he wasn't even being permitted to be on the scene; all he could do was worry and fear the worst.

The hours inched their way across that fateful day. Everything in the sprawling two-story house stalled to a virtual halt; family members tried to avoid meeting each other's eyes—especially John's, which were brimming with misery. The morning hours passed and afternoon came. Papa kept looking at his watch and muttering things. Mama kept out of range whenever possible.

Late in the afternoon, as evening shadows fell, the one-two slam of car doors ricocheted through the silent house. Faces froze during the interminable period it took Margaret and Walter to climb the long set of outside steps, open the front door, and walk through the outer parlor into the inner one. Every eye was riveted on the couple—every eye but John's. Heaven and hell were no further away than one glance at Margaret, so he preferred to remain suspended between. Then he heard her speak, and her voice had bells in it—bells of joy that no cloud of mere words could ever counter; bells that tolled the death of all his dreams—for what was the use of anything without Margaret there to share it with him?

Across the room, Papa's face had hardened into gray stone. In his heart, he had long ago adopted John as the son he had always longed for, since his own had died an untimely death. And Mama's face ignited with waves of burning pain, for she too had long loved John with all the intensity of a sonless mother. The five sisters just sat there, and for the first time in living memory, they were silent. Walter, in the egocentricity of youth, thought only of his own rapture, scarcely giving a second thought to the one he had displaced.

As Margaret registered the full impact of her decision in the faces of those around her, the bells ceased to ring in her voice. Well she knew how John must be feeling; she could read it in the anguish etched in his face, the abject slump of his body, and the unspoken thoughts that had always arced between them. She knew all this but could do nothing about it, for her standards of evaluation were those of the young, who worship power, success, charisma, physical prowess, good looks, and passion. Walter had them all.

John, on the other hand, was unfortunate enough to embody traits women often don't appreciate until the traumas of the years reshuffle their priorities. His were the gifts of tenderness, empathy, understanding, introspection, sensitivity, serenity, and imagination.

Through swollen eyelids on that never-to-be-forgotten Christmas Eve, John watched paradise recede from him. Margaret still went through the motions, still attempted to include him, but they both knew it was a sham. The heart, that unpredictable instrument,

had shifted its center of gravity 180 degrees. One moment, John represented the perceived future; another moment, he did not. There were no ragged edges; it was a clean break.

On Margaret's face was that inward glow that illuminates a woman during that ever-so-short blooming period we label, for want of a better phrase, "falling in love."

As for John, it was the last night he would ever spend in that house.

In the morning, Margaret found on her bureau a single long-stemmed red rose and, leaning against the stem, an envelope. It was the first thing she saw when she awoke from a troubled sleep. She slipped quickly out of bed, a radiant smile on her sleepy face; then she stopped in dismay, her hands flying to her ghostly cheeks. The writing was John's, not Walter's.

Even before she opened the envelope, she knew it was the end of something that only days before had embodied her fondest dreams. The note was short—the shortest John had ever written her.

Dec. 25, 1941

> *My dearest Margaret,*
> *It is clearly over. Yet, if you should change your mind, just send*
> *me a red rose, signing the card "Pilgrim," and I shall come to*
> *you, if it be in my power to do so. I shall always love you.*
>
> > *John*

Margaret's sisters awoke to the sound of weeping, the most tempestuous sobbing they had ever heard from their sunny sister. When asked what it was all about, she could only point mutely to the note and rose. Each read it . . . looked at her pensively . . . and quietly left the room. This was *her* battle, *her* decision, and she would have to live with the consequences for the rest of her life.

Margaret and Walter were married the first day of May. Through the years, they were about as happy as husband and wife can be on this troubled planet. Margaret soon discovered that living with Walter was a perpetual adventure. He loved fast cars, fast boats, and fast planes, and he was ever on the move, making deals that were ever more lucrative than those that went before. During the war, he made a fortune; after the war, he merely augmented it. He tried numerous vocations: preacher, teacher, auctioneer, real estate salesman, politician, entrepreneur, and all-around tycoon—filling each role with incredible energy, joie de vivre, and robust laughter.

Margaret was his Guinevere, the mistress of his splendid homes, villas, and mountain resorts. With Walter she was able to satisfy her yearning for travel—and that always in first-class luxury. She bore him two children, but only one survived. So excruciating was the second delivery for Margaret that Walter swore never to inflict another pregnancy upon her.

During their many years together, Walter and Margaret never heard whether or not John had survived the war. But John *did* make it through. Rather perversely, fate brought him safely through battles in which he hoped to die. Gradually, however, he rediscovered his love of life, and just before the Battle of Guadalcanal, he invited God back into his heart.

After the war was over, John took stock of his options and determined that he would not permit the loss of Margaret to destroy him. Taking advantage of the GI Bill, he went to college and earned a degree in architecture. Increasingly lonely, he began to search for someone to spend his life with. Several years later, he found her, and she was everything he had hoped she would be. Life was good.

It seemed impossible that anything could slow the juggernaut of Walter's life and his far-flung involvements and enterprises—but it happened, nevertheless. Three days after their forty-third wedding anniversary, he was diagnosed as having cancer—both terminal and fast-spreading.

Five weeks later, one spring afternoon, he asked Margaret to push his bed over to the large picture window that overlooked San Francisco Bay and the Golden Gate Bridge. The sun was setting, gilding the blue into bronze. A sleek ocean liner (one they had traveled on several times) had just cleared the bridge and was heading out to sea. He sighed audibly . . . and she knew what he was thinking.

Life is such an overconscientious accountant, mused Margaret to herself. *When one is given the world on a silver platter, the reckoning tends to come earlier. Here is Walter, at the very height of his powers, and suddenly it's all over. Why, oh why, God?*

She sensed that he had turned and was looking at her. The look in his dear hazel eyes was more than she could handle: the look that told her that, after all the long years, she was still *everything.*

He took her hands in his. She could feel him trembling—from deep inside. "Don't cry, dear," he said in his now rather ragged voice as he searched for the tissue box. "Don't cry. . . . We've had it all. I've been lucky—far luckier than most—in that most all of my dreams have come true. There isn't much I wanted to do that I haven't. . . . Don't let them give me one of those idiotic sentimental funerals when I go. . . . Dear . . . promise me there'll be no funeral. Just cremate what little there is left of me"—he looked down ruefully at his emaciated body, comparing it with what it had been—"and have the ashes carried out to sea, way out beyond the Golden Gate, and dropped overboard. So when you wish to think of me, just walk down to the shore, as you so love to do . . . and listen to the waves coming in."

He paused so long she thought he had dropped off to sleep. But no, he had only been thinking—about *her.* There was that tender look again in his eyes, which remained in full strength even while his body was ravaged by wave after wave of pain. "Any regrets, dear?" he asked. "Any regrets at all?"

"None!" she responded instantly. "Oh, Walter, if I had it to do all over again . . . " Her eyes—her still impish eyes—twinkled wickedly through tears. She could see his face visibly relax, and a smile struggled against the only force he had ever been unable to outwit.

Those were his last words. He died with that smile on his face.

And she was alone.

Several long years passed, and life began to regain its savor. To take her mind off her loss, Margaret resumed her volunteer stints at the local hospital. She also resumed her traveling to the far corners of the earth. Often she would book passage with her sister Melissa, just to have someone with her to keep the loneliness in check.

Then it happened. . . . At a family celebration in a distant California city,

Margaret happened to sit behind a man who looked vaguely familiar. Then he turned and spoke to the woman at his side—and she knew! Her stupefied "John!" escaped her before she could check it, causing him to turn around and look at her. He knew her instantly. He introduced his wife, Phyllis; and Margaret introduced her daughter, Diana. They spoke only briefly, Margaret finding herself strangely tongue-tied. Then John turned around and faced the front again. The program went on without her—for all she could see in her blurred vision was that dear face now turned from her. For the first time in 47 years she knew he was alive. Alive!

As long as Walter had been alive, so dominant was he that the force field of energy he generated blotted out thoughts of all who were not part of his personal galaxy. Hence, during all those rushing years rarely had the pace of life slowed down enough for much introspection. But now, with that dynamo quiet, memories, cold and silent, flooded back upon Margaret, compounded with 47 years of interest: as if a towering dam had buckled under irresistible pressure and unleashed with a vengeance the no longer placid waters imprisoned behind. In such torrents did they engulf her that she stood to her feet, dazed, and left the family celebration without being able to explain her untimely exit to anyone, even her astonished daughter. The only rational thought that filtered through this deluge brought her anything but peace: *After all these years the fire still burns!*

Margaret returned to her life, only now she was lonelier than ever. She was hungry again, but not for Walter. That part of her life had come and gone, like a gigantic meteor, utterly all-consuming, igniting the sky with its radiance. When such a shooting star burns out, no one who has lived with it for long could possibly desire a second ride. Flesh and blood can handle such an experience only once in life.

Margaret was reminded of Elijah: After the whirlwind came the still, small, quiet voice. So it was that, after all those sonic years, she yearned, she longed, for John. But it was too late. Too late.

Now Margaret used travel, not as the joy it had always been before, but as an escape—an escape from memories of John. Now she rarely came home but could be found instead in Nepal, in Bali, in the Australian Outback, in Patagonia, in Dubrovnik on the Dalmatian Coast, in the foggy Aleutians, in the Bay Islands . . . always moving on, in a vain effort to forget.

One humid afternoon, as she fanned herself on the hotel balcony in Papeetè, Tahiti, the maître d' brought her a letter on a tray. It was from her daughter.

Nov. 12, 1991

> *Dear Mother,*
>   *Your grandchildren are growing up without you. Wouldn't you like to be there for them before it's too late?*
>   *By the way, just heard that the wife of your old sweetheart died of cancer. A year ago, I believe.*
>
>   *Much love,*
>   *Diana*

Two days later, Margaret was home. Now it was even worse, for there was no longer any human barrier separating her from John. But would he, after all these years, still be interested in her? Would he so resent her rejection of him that he'd refuse to have anything more to do with her? After almost half a century, could he possibly still care for her in the old way? If he *did* still care, why hadn't he written her?

The weeks passed, and Margaret's composure continued to unravel strand by strand: She was rapidly degenerating into a nervous wreck. True, she had, by some diligent sleuthing, managed to secure John's address; but she was of the old school, not the new one. Thus she did not dare take the initiative herself. She called her daughter and asked for advice. Instead, she was invited to come visit that weekend.

Standing by the window in Diana's living room, listening to carols on the radio and admiring the Christmas lights decorating neighboring houses, Margaret thought about that wonderful/terrible Christmas of 1941. Suddenly, Diana's voice broke into her reveries.

"Mother, I've been wracking my brain, trying to think of some way you could contact your John without appearing too forward. When he left, was it a clean break, or did he leave an opening—" She stopped as her mother's hands flew to her face. "Mother, what is it?"

"Oh, how could I have forgotten! He left a rose the morning he left, Christmas morning. I cried as I never had before, or have since. A rose . . . and . . . a note."

"What did the note say?"

Margaret recited softly, " 'My dearest Margaret—' " Her eyes filled with tears, and for a moment she didn't say anything. Then, "I had just jilted him, and he . . . he still called me 'dearest.' "

Diana smiled.

" 'My dearest Margaret,' " her mother continued. " 'It is clearly over.' " She paused, a stricken look in her eyes. "Oh it was, it *was,*" she wailed, "but it's not, oh pray God, it's *not!*"

Regaining her composure, she continued: " 'Yet if you should change your mind, just send me a . . . a red rose, signing the card 'Pilgrim' . . . " She looked up at her daughter and explained, "That was his pet name for me. It's from a poem by Yeats. We both memorized it."

"Can you remember any of the lines?"

"Let's see." Margaret paused, wrinkling her forehead. Finally, in exasperation, she sighed: "I do remember that Yeats begins by telling his beloved that when she is old—oh, I am old now, aren't I! . . . When she is old and thinking back to when she wasn't, when she was still . . . "

"Beautiful?"

"Yes. Beautiful. . . . Wait! I do remember that one middle stanza. The one that expressed his love for me.

"How many loved your moments of glad grace,
And loved your beauty with love false or true,
But one man loved the pilgrim soul in you
And loved the sorrows of your changing face."

As she came to the last words of the stanza, Margaret collapsed, her tears falling unchecked like silver rain.

Diana sat there quietly, a pensive look on her face. This was a mother she had never known before. Where had she been all these years? When her mother had regained her composure, Diana asked, "Did the note say anything else?"

"Yes . . . 'just send me a red rose, signing the card 'Pilgrim' . . . and I shall return to you if it be . . . ' " Here Margaret paused for control. " ' . . . if it be in my power to do so.' "

"Was that all?"

"No. A thousand times no! He ended with these six words: 'I shall always love you. John.' "

"Do you think he really meant that?"

"Yes! Back then, anyway. But the big question is . . . is . . . "

"Whether or not he still does today?"

"Yes," her mother whispered.

It was the twenty-first day of December.

John stood in the front room of his modest split-level home in the Oregon highlands, gazing absentmindedly out at the falling snow and snow-covered pines. Christmas alone. . . . He didn't know how he was going to handle it again. The children had invited him home to be with their families, but somehow he just couldn't seem to get in the mood.

But it was more than that.

These days he seemed to be living more and more in the past. Phyllis was part of that past now, never to return. "No more to build on there." In fact, he asked himself, was there anything or anyone to build on at all? Was his life over?

The raucous ring of the doorbell jerked him out of his dream world. Who could be calling on a day like this? He certainly wasn't in the mood for company, he thought as he pulled open the door.

A florist deliveryman was standing there, the snow already frosting his blond head. John closed the door and opened the slim package. Nestled in green tissue paper was one of the loveliest red roses he had ever seen. He lifted it out of the box and inhaled its fragrance. Then, wondering who it could be from, he poked around in the paper until he found a small white envelope. His eyes widened in disbelief as he read the message on the card. It consisted of but one word: *Pilgrim.* On the back of the card there was no name, but there was an address and phone number.

I t was the twenty-third day of December.

Margaret's heart was racing like a cold engine on a frosty morning. Two entire days had passed, and she hadn't heard anything. Had she been foolish to imagine that John would still be interested in her? After all, she was an old woman now, with precious few good years left.

She leaned against her bedroom window and gazed idly out at a sight she never tired of: the booming surf off Point Lobos. One of Walter's last gifts to her had been this little hideaway overlooking one of the grandest views on the planet.

Always she had maintained a childlike faith in God. And her prayers were rarely formal things; rather, they were as casual as if she were chatting with a friend. This one was true to form:

Oh, God, have I done it again? Did I move too quickly . . . before I had Your blessing? But oh, Lord, I am so lonely . . . and John was so good to me all those years ago when I was young. But that's what worries me, Lord. Will he think I'm still pretty? Will he . . . will he still love me?

Looking out the window, she noticed that the fog was coming in—and the gulls were protesting. Suddenly, the phone rang, shattering the stillness. It was the gateman.

"Sorry to disturb you, ma'am, but a package just came for you. The man who delivered it declared it urgent; said it *had* to get to you today. Shall I bring it up?"

Within minutes, the gateman was at her door with a long box engraved with the imprint of her favorite Carmel florist. After thanking him and hastily closing the door, Margaret opened the box with trembling fingers. There she beheld three perfect red roses. She refused to pick them up, however, until she found out who had sent them and what the message was. She opened the small envelope gingerly, as though afraid it would explode in her hands.

On the small sheet of stationery were these words:

> *Dearest Pilgrim,*
> *Second Rose received; am returning. First Rose long since dead; am sending replacement. Third Rose to present my case— and Emily:*
>
> > *Where Roses would not dare to go,*
> > *What Heart would risk the way—*
> > *And so I send my Crimson Scouts*
> > *To sound the Enemy.*
> > *—"Where Roses Would Not Dare to Go" (1883)*
>
> *If they are persuasive enough, I'll see you at Bandon Beach, Dec. 25, 9:00 A.M., in vicinity of Yeats Sand Dune.*
> > *Until then,*
> > *Your John*

It was Christmas morning on Bandon Beach.

At exactly nine o'clock, a tall, graceful woman descended the steps leading down to the beach. The roses of youth were in her cheeks, and pinned to her breast was a corsage of three crimson roses.

At the bottom of the steps, she kicked off her shoes. Rounding a huge rock, she saw him, standing by a sand dune that looked vaguely familiar. When she got close enough to read his eyes and see his open arms, she broke into a run.

Pilgrim had come home.

> Long years apart—can make no
> Breach a second cannot fill—
> The absence of the Witch does not
> Invalidate the spell. . . .
>
> The embers of a Thousand Years
> Uncovered by the Hand
> That fondled them when they were Fire
> Will stir and understand.
>
> —Emily Dickinson, "Long Years Apart" (1876)

Note to Reader: Text was revised July 1, 1998.

About the Contributors

Ida Alexander wrote for family and Christian magazines during the first two decades of the twentieth century. Today, virtually nothing is known about her.

Ewart A. Autry. After an exhaustive search, I was unable to find any information on this author.

(Irene) Temple Bailey (188?–1953) was born in Petersburg, Virginia, and became one of the most popular, and highest paid, authors in the world during the first three decades of the twentieth century. Besides writing hundreds of stories that were published by the top family magazines of her day, she also wrote books, including *Judy* (1907), *The Trumpeter Swan* (1920), *The Dim Lantern* (1923), *Peacock Feathers* (1924), *The Holly Hedge* (1925), *The Blue Window* (1926), and *Wild Wind* (1930).

Lynnette Baughman is a contemporary freelance writer.

Pearl S. Buck (1892–1973) towers over twentieth-century American literature, being one of those rare few who were awarded both the Pulitzer prize and the Nobel prize for literature. Born in Hillsboro, West Virginia, she spent much of her early life in China. Her best-sellers include *The Good Earth* (1931), *Dragon Seed* (1942), *Peony* (1948), and *Imperial Woman* (1956).

Grace Ethelyn Cody. After an exhaustive search, I was unable to find any information on this author.

Bob (Robert Bernard) Considine (1906–1975), a Washington, D.C., columnist, journalist, and author, wrote one of the most widely carried columns in the nation. He also collaborated with Babe Ruth on *The Babe Ruth Story* (1948); with Ted W. Lawson on *Thirty Seconds Over Tokyo* (1943); and with Jonathan M. Wainright on *General Wainright's Story* (1946). He is the sole author of such books as *MacArthur the Magnificent* (1942), *Innocents at Home* (1950), and *Ripley: The Modern Marco Polo* (1961).

Kathleen Read Coontz. After an exhaustive search, I was unable to find any information on this author.

Annie Hamilton Donnell (1862–?), early in the twentieth century, was one of the most beloved family writers in America. Besides writing prolifically for family and inspirational magazines, she also wrote books, such as *Meeting Cousin Agatha* (1898), *Rebecca Mary* (1905), *The Very Small Person* (1906), *Glory and the Other Girl* (1907), and *Miss Theodosia's Heartstrings* (1916).

Ella A. Duncan. After an exhaustive search, I was unable to find any information on this author.

Ruth Garren, freelance writer and publicist, today writes from eastern Tennessee.

Arthur Gordon (1912–) still lives and writes on his natal seacoast near Savannah, Georgia. During his long and memorable career, he edited such renowned magazines as *Good Housekeeping, Cosmopolitan,* and *Guideposts*. He is the author of several books, including *Reprisal* (1950), *Norman Vincent Peale: Minister to Millions* (1958), *A Touch of Wonder* (1974), *Through Many Windows* (1983), and *Return to Wonder* (1996), as well as several hundred short stories.

Frances Greenman. After an exhaustive search, I was unable to find any information on this author.

Grace Livingston Hill (1865–1947) was born in Wellsville, New York, and lived most of her life in Swarthmore, Pennsylvania. A prolific columnist, short-story writer, and novelist, she is significant for another reason: Her books have not only stayed in print but have also gained in popularity during the half-century since her death. Her books include *Cloudy Jewel* (1920), *The Beloved Stranger* (1933), *Rainbow Cottage* (1934), *White Orchids* (1935), *April Gold* and *The Substitute Guest* (1936), and *Brentwood* (1937).

Edith Hoffman James. After an exhaustive search, I was unable to find any information on this author.

Ira Rich Kent (1876–1945), born in Calais, Vermont, was an editor of *Youth's Companion* (1900–1925) before serving as editor at Houghton Mifflin for the rest of his career.

Frederic Loomis lived for a time in Alaska, then obtained a medical degree and settled down as an obstetrician in northern California early in the twentieth century. In the two books he had published by Knopf, *The Bond Between Us* and *Consultation Room*, Loomis grappled with the true meaning of life and human relationships.

William T. McElroy (1867–1933), during his long ministerial career with the Congregational Church, somehow found time to write a number of stories for family and inspirational magazines.

Mabel McKee, early in the twentieth century, was responsible for some of the most memorable inspirational literature in print. Sadly, little is known about her today.

Arthur A. Milward, printer and freelance writer, lived in England and California before retiring in Pennsylvania.

(Charles) Fulton Oursler (1893–1952), a Baltimore-born writer, journalist, screenwriter, author, and editor, cast a giant shadow over his time. Besides writing screenplays such as *Behold This Dreamer* (1927) and *All the King's Men* (1929), he is the author of books such as *The Great Jasper* (1930), *The Greatest Story Ever Told* (1940), and *Modern Parables* (1950). He also edited *Metropolitan, Liberty,* and *Cosmopolitan* magazines and served as senior editor of *Reader's Digest.*

Jesse (James Cleveland) Owens (1913–1980) was born in Danville, Alabama, and grew up in Cleveland, Ohio. After winning four gold medals at the 1936 Olympics in Berlin, he was elevated to worldwide superstardom.

Grace S. Richmond (1866–1959) was born in Pawtucket, Rhode Island, and lived most of her life in Fredonia, New York. Not only were her many short stories and serializations published in the top women's magazines of her time, but she also was one of the most popular and highest paid novelists of the first half of the twentieth century. Among her best-selling books are *The Indifference of Juliet* (1905), *The Second Violin* (1906), *Red Pepper Burns* (1910), *The Twenty-Fourth of June* (1914), *Foursquare* (1922), *The Listening Post* (1929), and *Bachelor's Bounty* (1932).

Margaret E. Sangster, Jr. (1894 –1981), granddaughter of the equally illustrious Margaret E. Sangster (1838–1912), was born in Brooklyn, New York. Editor, scriptwriter, journalist, short-story writer, and novelist, she was one of the best-known writers of the early part of the twentieth century. Along the way, she served as correspondent and columnist for *Christian Herald Magazine*, as well as writing books such as *Cross Roads* (1919), *The Island of Faith* (1921), *The Stars Come Close* (1936), and *Singing on the Road* (1936).

L. D. Stearns. After an exhaustive search, I was unable to find any information on this author.

Josephine DeFord Terrill wrote prolifically for Christian and family magazines early in the twentieth century. Today, virtually nothing is known about her.

Dorothy Waldo. After an exhaustive search, I was unable to find any information on this author.

Phil Walker still lives, writes, and broadcasts in his native Fort Collins, Colorado. He has been recognized many times by the Colorado Broadcasters Association for his *Visions* series. On radio station KCOL, his morning program has been running for so long he is considered the Voice of Northern Colorado. In 1995, his book *Visions Along the Poudre Valley* was published.

Dixie Wolcott. After an exhaustive search, I was unable to find any information on this author.

Wallace Dunbar Vincent. After an exhaustive search, I was unable to find any information on this author.

Acknowledgments

"Revolutions," by Ida Alexander. Published in *The Youth's Instructor,* January 23, 1923. Reprinted by permission of Review and Herald® Publishing Association, Hagerstown, Maryland.

"In a Chinese Garden," by Frederic Loomis. Included in Loomis, *The Bond Between Us* (Berkeley: Loomis Publishing Company, 1946). If anyone can provide knowledge of the whereabouts of surviving Loomis family members, please relay the information to Joe Wheeler, c/o Focus on the Family.

"The Golden Moment." Author unknown. Published in *The Youth's Instructor,* June 11, 1918, and in Review and Herald's *Their Word of Honor and Other Stories,* 1940. Reprinted by permission of Review and Herald® Publishing Association, Hagerstown, Maryland.

"'Sing for Me,'" by Arthur A. Milward. Published in the July 1979 *Reader's Digest.* Copyright 1979 © by The Reader's Digest Association and Arthur A. Milward. Reprinted by permission.

"When Lincoln Passed," by Mabel McKee. Published in *The Youth's Instructor,* February 4, 1930. Reprinted by permission of Fleming H. Revell, a division of Baker Book House.

"A Boy Who Loved Lincoln," by Kathleen Read Coontz. Published in *St. Nicholas Magazine,* February 1927. Copyright not renewed.

"The Spirit of Valley Forge," by Wallace Dunbar Vincent. Published in *The Youth's Instructor,* February 23, 1926. Reprinted by permission of Review and Herald® Publishing Association, Hagerstown, Maryland.

"For Better or Worse," by Lynnette Baughman. Published in the December 1996 *Reader's Digest.* Copyright © 1996 by The Reader's Digest Association, Inc. Reprinted by permission.

"Bobbie Shaftoe." Author unknown. Published in *The Youth's Instructor,* September 4, 1928. Reprinted by permission of Review and Herald® Publishing Association, Hagerstown, Maryland.

"When Tulips Die in the Spring," by Ruth Garren. Published in *Insight's Most Unforgettable Stories* (Hagerstown, Md.: Review and Herald® Publishing Association, 1990). Reprinted by permission of the publisher and the author.

"The Story of a Stepmothering," by Annie Hamilton Donnell. Story originally appeared in *The Christian Endeavor World* and then in *The Youth's Instructor,* March 4, 1913. Reprinted by permission of Review and Herald® Publishing Association, Hagerstown, Maryland.

"Interview with an Immortal," by Arthur Gordon. Included in Gordon, *Touch of Wonder* (Old Tappan, N.J.: Fleming H. Revell, 1974). Reprinted by permission of the author.

"The Canopy Bed," by Temple Bailey. Included in Bailey, *The Gay Cockade* (Philadelphia: Penn Publishing Company, 1921).

"Father," by Edith Hoffman James. Published in *The Youth's Instructor,* April 24, 1923. Reprinted by permission of Review and Herald® Publishing Association, Hagerstown, Maryland.

"At the Close of His Career," by Grace S. Richmond. Published in *The Youth's Companion,* December 1900.

"Ready for Heaven," by Ewart A. Autry. If anyone can provide knowledge of the earliest publication and date of this story, please relay this information to Joe Wheeler, c/o Focus on the Family.

"Annie, the Railroad Dog," by Phil Walker. Included in Walker, *Visions Along the Poudre Valley* (Fort Collins, Colo.: Phil Walker Communications, 1995). Reprinted by permission of the author.

"A Matter of Honor," by William T. McElroy. Published in *The Youth's Instructor,* July 23, 1929. Reprinted by permission of Review and Herald® Publishing Association, Hagerstown, Maryland.

"Miss Lavinia's Call," by Grace Livingston Hill. Included in Hill, *Miss Lavinia's Call and Other Stories* (Philadelphia and New York: J. B. Lippincott Company, 1949). Reprinted by permission of R. L. Munce Publishing, Inc.

"Queen Esther's Petition," by Dixie Wolcott. Published in *Munsie's Magazine*, September 1902.

"Teaching True," by Dorothy Waldo. Published in *The Companion for All the Family*, January 30, 1919.

"Home for Thanksgiving," by L. D. Stearns. Published in *The Youth's Instructor*, November 18, 1930. Reprinted by permission of Review and Herald® Publishing Association, Hagerstown, Maryland.

"The Littlest Orphan and the Christ Baby," by Margaret E. Sangster, Jr. Included in Sangster, *The Littlest Orphan and Other Christmas Stories* (New York: Round Table Press, 1929).

"The Third Rose," by Joseph Leininger Wheeler. Copyright © 1991. Reprinted, with revisions, by permission of the author.

About the Editor

Joseph Leininger Wheeler's earliest memories have to do with books and stories—more specifically, of listening to his mother read aloud both in public and to him at home. Wheeler recalls that, as soon as he was able to read, he followed his mother around the house, relentlessly reading his storybooks to her.

Shortly after Wheeler turned eight, his parents moved from California to Latin America as missionaries. From the third through the tenth grade, he was home-schooled by his mother. Of those years, he says today, "I was incredibly lucky and blessed. My mother, a trained teacher and elocutionist, was a voracious reader of books worth reading and had memorized thousands of pages of readings, poetry, and stories. All of that she poured into me. Wherever we went, she encouraged me to devour entire libraries."

At 16, Wheeler returned to California to complete his high school years at Monterey Bay Academy near Santa Cruz. Because of his inherited love of the printed word, Wheeler majored in history at Pacific Union College in the Napa Valley, completing both bachelor's and master's degrees there. After completing a master's in English at California State University in Sacramento, Wheeler attended Vanderbilt University, where he obtained a Ph.D. in English.

Today, after 34 years of teaching at the adult education, college, high school, and junior high levels, Wheeler is Professor Emeritus at Columbia Union College in Takoma Park, Maryland. The world's foremost authority on frontier writer Zane Grey, Wheeler is also the founder and executive director of Zane Grey's West Society and Senior Fellow for Cultural Studies at the Center for the New West in Denver, Colorado. He is editor/compiler of the popular *Christmas in My Heart* series (Review & Herald; Doubleday, Dell, Bantam); editor/compiler of the story anthologies *Dad in My Heart* and *Mom in My Heart* (Tyndale House); and editor/compiler of the *Great Stories Remembered* and Classic Collection series for Focus on the Family (Tyndale House). Along the way, Wheeler has established nine libraries in schools and colleges, as well as building up his own collection (as large as some college libraries).

Joe Wheeler and his wife, Connie, are the parents of two grown children, Greg and Michelle, and now make their home in Conifer, Colorado.

Photo by Joel Springer
(chief photographer for Review & Herald)

There's Nothing Like a Great Story!
Other Outstanding Offerings by Joe L. Wheeler, Ph.D.

Great Stories Remembered II

You've just read the book. Now listen to your favorite tales on audiocassette! Condensed from the hardcover collection and read by master storyteller/editor Joe Wheeler, this book-on-cassette is ideal entertainment for road trips, bedtimes, family get-togethers . . . anytime! Two-audiocassette package.

Great Stories Remembered

The original best-seller, this volume is filled with touching accounts, warm narrations, and exciting adventures written during the 1900s but misplaced through the years. Treat your family to another collection of such tales compiled by editor Joe Wheeler. Highlighting the virtues we hold dear, it's a keepsake your loved ones will cherish! Hardcover and audiocassette.

Focus on the Family's "Classic Collection"

Great literature is timeless—it upholds traditional values and transcends the years as few things do. And unlike any other series on the market, the "Classic Collection" is truly unique! Selected for the quality of its content and the value in its message, every classic tale features:

- the Christian content other editions often omit
- the complete text, updated for easier reading
- student-tested discussion questions that help readers get the most out of each inspiring novel
- woodcut illustrations from the book's original printing
- and an in-depth introduction by Joe Wheeler, Ph.D., detailing the people, places, and historical events that influenced the author and surround the story

Featuring such great works as *Little Women, Ben-Hur, A Christmas Carol,* and *Robinson Crusoe,* it's a collection like no other.

• • •

For more information or to request any of these resources, simply write to Focus on the Family, Colorado Springs, CO 80995, or call 1-800-A-FAMILY (1-800-232-6459). Friends in Canada may write to Focus on the Family, P.O. Box 9800, Stn. Terminal, Vancouver, B.C. V6B 4G3, or call 1-800-661-9800. Visit our Web site—www.family.org—to learn more about the ministry or to find out if there is a Focus on the Family office in your country.

Welcome to the Family!

Whether you received this book as a gift, borrowed it from a friend, or purchased it yourself, we're glad you read it! It's just one of the many helpful, insightful, and encouraging resources produced by Focus on the Family.

In fact, that's what Focus on the Family is all about—providing inspiration, information, and biblically based advice to people in all stages of life.

It began in 1977 with the vision of one man, Dr. James Dobson, a licensed psychologist and author of 16 best-selling books on marriage, parenting, and family. Alarmed by the societal, political, and economic pressures that were threatening the existence of the American family, Dr. Dobson founded Focus on the Family with one employee—an assistant—and a once-a-week radio broadcast, aired on only 36 stations.

Now an international organization, Focus on the Family is dedicated to preserving Judeo-Christian values and strengthening the family through more than 70 different ministries, including eight separate daily radio broadcasts; television public service announcements; 11 publications; and a steady series of books and award-winning films and videos for people of all ages and interests.

Recognizing the needs of, as well as the sacrifices and important contribution made by, such diverse groups as educators, physicians, attorneys, crisis pregnancy center staff, and single parents, Focus on the Family offers specific outreaches to uphold and minister to these individuals, too. And it's all done for one purpose, and one purpose only: to encourage and strengthen individuals and families through the life-changing message of Jesus Christ.

• • •

For more information about the ministry, or if we can be of help to your family, simply write to Focus on the Family, Colorado Springs, CO 80995, or call 1-800-A-FAMILY (1-800-232-6459). Friends in Canada may write Focus on the Family, P.O. Box 9800, Stn. Terminal, Vancouver, B.C. V6B 4G3, or call 1-800-661-9800. Visit our Web site—www.family.org—to learn more about the ministry or to find out if there is a Focus on the Family office in your country.

We'd love to hear from you!